# THREE
# TICKETS
# TO PEORIA

# THE COMPANY OF GOOD WOMEN

*Almost Sisters* (2006)

THE COMPANY OF GOOD WOMEN

# THREE
# TICKETS
# TO PEORIA

*a novel by*

NANCY ANDERSON • LAEL LITTKE
CARROLL HOFELING MORRIS

DESERET
BOOK
SALT LAKE CITY, UTAH

**Library of Congress Cataloging-in-Publication Data**

Anderson, Nancy.
   Three tickets to Peoria / Nancy Anderson, Lael Littke, Carroll Hofeling Morris.
      p. cm. — (The company of good women ; 2)
   Sequel to: Almost sisters.
   ISBN 978-1-59038-720-7 (pbk.)
   1. Female friendship—Fiction. 2. Mormon women—Religious life—Fiction.
3. Domestic fiction. I. Littke, Lael. II. Morris, Carroll Hofeling. III. Title.
   PS3601.N5444T47 2007
      813'.6—dc22                                                                    2006100469

Printed in the United States of America
Publishers Printing, Salt Lake City, UT

10   9   8   7   6   5   4   3   2   1

*To the company of very good women*
*who have enriched our lives with their presence:*
*our mothers, daughters, sisters, teachers, and friends.*
*And to those women whose examples, seen from afar,*
*made a difference.*

## Acknowledgments

Our heartfelt thanks go to all those who shared knowledge and experiences that helped us make our characters and story come to life: Barbara Higinbotham and Ginger Franz, for insight into clinical depression; Tricia Cox of Rocky Mountain Search Dog and her K-9 companion, Chloe, for teaching us how to find Fred; Leland Hofeling and Nicholas Anderson, who guided us through gun handling and self-defense; Cindy Heigl, figure-skating coach, and Diane Erickson and Jan Michaletz, both mothers of skaters, for information on the world of young figure skaters; Roger Allen, for insights he gained as a bishop and a family counselor into issues faced by Mormons with same-gender attraction and their families; Douglas Silfen, for advice on Jewish traditions. And a special thanks to John Morris, for help in last-minute document formatting and management.

# Prologue
## 2004

It was obvious to the observers in the pizza parlor that the three women in matching appliquéd denim jackets were enjoying themselves. It wasn't that they were being loud or noisy. They spoke in normal voices, occasionally chuckling and once in a while even giggling, but their animated faces and the way they sometimes reached out to clasp hands attracted attention.

"We've almost made it," the red-haired one said. "Just one more year to go."

"One more to go in The Pact to meet in twenty-five years. That's the easy part. Deciding if we've made it to COBhood is harder." The blonde looked at the others. "What about that? Do you feel like a COB? Either of you?"

The redhead smiled ruefully. "I still think that's a title reserved for Gabby. The original Crusty Old Broad."

"Dear Gabby. I miss her," said the blonde. "But I feel her influence all the time."

The one with dark curly hair smiled. "Me, too. Striving for COBhood has been like North on our compasses all these years. It's got us through some tough times. Like that horrible week in St. George in 1987."

"How did we get past that?" the redhead asked. "It was a real free-for-all."

"We changed," said the blonde. "And our relationship changed, too. We found ourselves headed in a different direction."

"Yes," the curly-haired one said, "but with detours along the way."

They all nodded. The redhead touched the blonde's arm. "Remember, Juneau, when you lost Max? You said it was as if you'd packed for a vacation in Hawaii and then landed in Peoria instead."

"Yes," said the blonde. "And I discovered you can learn a whole lot in Peoria."

# Chapter 1

## 1987

JUNEAU

"Relationships change," Juneau said.

Without looking up from his computer, Greg said, "What relationship are you referring to?"

Juneau was surprised that her husband had responded to her statement. They'd shared the small workroom he'd built in the garage for some time now, and she'd figured he was so used to her mutterings that he wouldn't pay any attention.

"My friendship with Willadene and Erin," she replied. "We haven't quite got back on a firm footing after our blowup in St. George."

Greg nodded. "Too bad. After all those years of being joined at the hip."

"Joined at the hip? We scarcely ever see one another. We've been together only three or four times since we met at BYU Education Week back in 1980." That was when Juneau, Deenie, and Erin had boarded with Gabby Farnsworth, self-proclaimed Crusty Old Broad—COB. After several days with her, they'd decided they wanted to grow into being COBs, too. Later, they'd made The Pact to get together in twenty-five years to see how they'd fared in their quest.

Greg leaned back in his chair to gaze at her. "What about all the letters? And phone calls?"

"We do stay in touch, but we don't seem to connect the way we did before. Our relationship used to be easy. Fun."

"Maybe you've gone past easy, Juney. Maybe your problems are bigger now than they were before."

There was no question about that. Willadene was facing a difficult late pregnancy, complete with a newly discovered heart murmur. Erin was wearing herself out trying to be perfect, and she was still letting old feelings about her absent father color her relationship with her husband, Cory.

And herself? Among other things, she was facing the dubious honor of being the first of the three to have an unmarried, pregnant teenage daughter.

"Maybe I'm not ready to be a grandmother," she murmured. And immediately regretted it. Greg's face closed down, a scowl replacing the pleasant look he'd worn before. "You won't be a grandmother," he said. "Misty is not keeping the baby."

Juneau felt her neck get hot. "Well, I'll still be a grandmother, regardless of whether she keeps it. And you'll be a grandfather. Greg, this baby will be flesh of our flesh, blood of our blood, no matter how he was conceived."

Greg looked up sharply. "So you've decided it's a boy."

"I feel it is."

"And are you going to name him Max?"

His question was a slap in the face that opened old wounds, but Juneau kept a grip on her emotions. "Misty will name him."

"His adoptive parents will name him," Greg said firmly. He turned to his computer, indicating the conversation was over.

Maybe it was—for the moment. Juneau wasn't ready to tell him that she wanted this baby. Not just for Misty but for herself. She hadn't been able to have another baby after miscarrying Max, and she felt incomplete, as if she needed to raise another child or at least take part in raising one. But maybe that was just her old nemesis, Guilt, still hanging around.

She'd never told Greg the anguish she'd felt when she thought she'd wished Max away. That was the biggest thing on the list of Guilty Secrets she'd kept from him over the years.

As Juneau stood there glaring at Greg's back, Misty came into the little room. Her normally pencil-thin sixteen-year-old body was beginning to bulge in the middle. She looked waxen against the dead-black color she was dyeing her hair these days.

"Any chance I might use your computer for a while?" she asked Greg. "I have to do a book report."

"You may use my typewriter." Juneau pointed at it. "I was thinking of going for a walk anyway."

"Typewriter?" Misty said with an exaggerated sneer. "Mom, I'm a girl of the '80s. Almost '90s."

Greg stood, gesturing toward the computer. "Be my guest, girl of the whatevers. I'm joining your mother. We've both been glued to our machines too long today."

"Thanks, Dad." Misty settled into the computer chair.

"What book are you reporting on?" Juneau asked.

"Yours, Mom. *The Third Bird*. You're my favorite author."

Juneau grinned at her. "I'd like to read the report when it's finished." She touched Misty's shoulder as she headed for the kitchen to pick up Philip Atwater's leash. The big dog turned into a flurry of wags and excited whinings when he heard the leash being removed from its hook in the broom closet.

"Go ahead, Juney," Greg called. "I want to get something from my briefcase."

He carried a sheaf of papers as he came striding up the hill to catch her and Philip Atwater. Her mind slipped into writer's mode, constructing a Regina-and-Reginald scene, as she, Willadene, and Erin often did in their letters.

*"I picked up the divorce papers," Reginald said. "I've brought them along for you to sign. You see, I've fallen in love with this cute little coed from Cucamonga."*

Greg held out the papers as he reached Juneau's side. "I called LDS Social Services for the paperwork for Misty's baby's adoption," Greg said. "It came yesterday. I want you to help me talk her into signing."

She stopped, staring at him. "After what I said a little while ago, why would you ever think I'd agree to that?"

"Juney, please. Start using your head instead of your heart for a change. Right from the first you've regarded this baby as a blessing rather than the disaster it is."

"This baby *is* a blessing! What Misty did was a disaster, but the baby isn't." She paused, choosing her words carefully. "Greg, this is a vitally important matter that involves our whole family—you, me, Misty, and Nicole. We all have a voice in it."

"I agree. Especially Misty." His voice rose in exasperation. "But we're the parents, the adults. It's up to us to guide her in the right direction."

"We haven't done such a good job so far, have we?"

Juneau saw her jab hit home, but Greg remained firm. "Maybe not, but we don't have to let the situation go from bad to worse. We need to present a united front when we talk to the girls."

"United behind what you think is best, you mean."

"That's not fair. When we talked to the bishop, he said the same thing, remember? Church guidelines recommend that a child born out of wedlock be adopted by parents it can be sealed to in the temple. It's the best course of action, if you put the child's welfare ahead of your own feelings."

Juneau sighed. She couldn't deny what he was saying. She recalled Bishop Marlow's listing the dangers of a teenage girl rearing an out-of-wedlock child. "There's always the problem of economics," he'd said, "and the mother's trying to keep up with school. If the baby is left with grandparents, there's confusion about who Mom is." He'd given other good reasons for allowing the baby to be adopted, in addition to the most important—becoming part of an eternal family. But Juneau couldn't bear the thought of letting her grandchild go to another family. "Maybe Misty will shape up and . . ." She didn't even finish the sentence. Much as she wanted to hope, the likelihood of Misty changing her ways was remote.

"So you'll support me in this family council?" Greg asked.

She inclined her head, letting him interpret the gesture as he would.


Greg got right to it when they were all gathered in the family room with Philip Atwater sprawled in the middle of the floor. "We're here to talk about the baby."

Nicole's eyes lit up, and she raised a hand. "I'll set up the crib, if you'll get it down from the top of the garage, Dad."

"Forget it, Nicole," Misty said. "Dad said way last month that the baby's not coming home."

"Well, I didn't think he meant it. Do you want to give it up?"

"No," Misty said. "But Dad *said.*"

Nicole cast a glance at Greg. "Dad? If it's not coming home, where's it going?"

Greg looked uncomfortable. "To a good home where it will have a mother *and* a father. A family."

"This baby has a family. Misty and me and Mom and you. And Philip Atwater. And Beto and the rest of the Sanchezes. And all the people in the ward. How much family does it need?"

"You're right, Nicole," Greg said in a soothing tone. "But it needs a Forever Family. A mother and a father it can be sealed to in the temple. That's the counsel of Church leaders, and I think we should follow it. Now, I have the papers Misty needs to sign. The baby will go to LDS Social Services, who will find a family to love it and take care of it."

"No!" Nicole stood and faced her father. Misty stood, too, putting a hand over her mouth. "I don't feel so good," she said.

Juneau hurried to help Misty to the bathroom. "Greg," she said sharply, "that's enough for tonight."

When Misty finished retching, Juneau questioned her thoroughly to make sure she wasn't having pains such as those that had heralded her own miscarriage of Max years before. Then she sent Misty off to bed and returned to the family room. Greg was still standing there, but Nicole had gone.

"That didn't go so well, did it?" he said.

"No. But you did state your case." She paused. "Greg, I don't think Misty is up to making a decision about the baby right now. Maybe we ought to wait until it's born. See it first. Get acquainted with it."

Greg shook his head. "That will just make it harder." He narrowed his eyes. "Are you trying to make this harder, Juney? You know that if she holds the baby, something's going to kick in and she won't want to let it go."

"Would that be so bad?"

"Do I need to go over it all again?"

"But you can't just snatch it away before any of us see it, Greg. Misty can't sign the papers until after she's held her child in her arms. That would be too cruel."

Greg was silent for a moment. Then he said, "Okay, Juneau, but don't

expect *me* to get acquainted with the baby. I don't intend even to see it."
His shoulders slumping, he left the room.

She watched him go, thinking it had been a long time since he'd
called her Juneau.

## ERIN

October 7, 1987
Dear Juneau and Deenie, dear friends,

I am so glad I can still call you that. There were moments in St.
George when I wasn't sure we would hold it together, especially
when we got into that brawl.

It was easier to be friends with the one-dimensional Juneau and
Deenie, because I could be one-dimensional, too. But I'm willing to take on the challenge of loving the complicated Juneau
and Deenie, the ones who aren't always happy, who have
secrets, and can really let go when provoked! Why? Because
you know the good and the bad about me—and you still love
me.

Juneau, I have no idea what's going to happen with Misty's
baby, but I know in my bones he will be a blessing. To whoever
raises him. If you were really serious about getting some COBish
input, here's mine: Receive that little person with love . . . or,
if it's necessary, let him go with love.

Deenie, if The Great What If rears his ugly head, sic the COBs,
both senior and aspiring, on him.

Love,
Erin

P.S. We all need to call Gabby every so often. She needs our
support, even though she won't ask for it. I can't imagine what
it must be like having a grandson who's in trouble with the law.

## WILLADENE

"Easy boy," Deenie said softly as she slipped a pair of thinning scissors between Rauf's tender hide and the knot of cockleburs she was
working out of his chin hairs. The old dog whimpered but stayed still.
"What a good dog." She clipped off the offending clump and ruffled his

hair to signal she was finished. Rauf licked her hands as he awkwardly stood up.

Deenie slowly stood up, a little awkwardly herself. "Walkies?" she asked Rauf. Ignoring the offer, he lumbered into the family room and onto the cushion she had covered with squares of her boys' outgrown flannel shirts, circled three times, and flopped down. In an instant he was snoring loudly.

"Poor old fellow," Deenie said as she rubbed the ache in her lower back. "I guess we're both starting to feel our age."

At only five months along, she was already experiencing the pelvic floor pressure and low back pain that had troubled her in the last months of her pregnancy with Beth. She'd managed the discomfort then, but she'd been twenty-six and bubbling with health and anticipation. Now she was thirty-five and already feeling used up.

Despite her weariness, she decided to make fresh cinnamon rolls, a favorite family treat she hadn't produced since becoming pregnant. She was knuckle deep in kneaded dough when the doorbell rang. "Door's open," she called. "I'm in the kitchen."

"It's Aunt Stell, Deenie. I've come for a visit."

"Be with you in a sec," she answered cheerily and then muttered, "Oh, great. A morning with the queen of the midwives!" Stella Stowell Jensen was the older sister of Deenie's father, John Stowell. She was a Cache Valley midwife of vaunted reputation who laid claim to the Stowell Sight, a deeply spiritual intuition that manifested itself in the ability, among other things, to sense problem pregnancies. She was a force to be reckoned with and not easily avoided. Sighing, Deenie plopped the glossy dough into a greased bowl, set it to rise, and went to face Aunt Stell.

"What a pleasant surprise," she said as she walked into the living room.

"I doubt if it's a surprise, and whether or not it's pleasant pretty much depends on you," Stella responded in her usual curt manner. "I've come to talk to you about this pregnancy."

Deenie bristled. "If you've had an intuition, I don't want to hear it. I decided ten years ago that the Stowell Sight is nothing but an active imagination mixed with a little knowledge and a desire to do good. If it were anything more, I'd be a Stowell midwife, and Sunny wouldn't be suffering the way she is today."

"Oh, for Pete's sake," Stella said. "It's been almost twenty-five years since your sister was born and all our lives changed. You weren't the only one hurt. Get over it!"

Deenie was shocked to hear the same words she had flung at her friend Erin only a month ago. Were her old complaints about the circumstances of Sunny's birth as exhausting as Erin's complaints about her unknown father? Was she, like Erin, clinging to old hurts and misgivings? She didn't know how to defend herself against Stella's attack, so she attacked back. "Been dreaming dreams, have you?" she asked nastily.

"Yes. Dreams of you, pregnant and drowning within reach but refusing to take my hand! What do you have to say about that?"

Deenie instinctively put her hands over her belly in a protective gesture. "Aunt Stell, that's horrible."

"So, are you going to tell me what's going on, or do I have to figure it out myself?"

Deenie didn't answer. Too many months of keeping things to herself sealed her lips.

"Okay, have it your way." Stella looked Deenie over critically. "You're over five months, and you haven't gained any weight. But you're retaining water in your face, hands, and feet. It's only 10:30 in the morning, and you look totally exhausted. In fact, I'd say you look a lot like Sunny when she's having an episode with her heart."

Stella's eyes narrowed. She leaned forward and studied Deenie more closely. "That's it, isn't it? You're having trouble with your heart."

"Heart murmur," Deenie conceded. "Dr. Slater says she thinks it's probably the kind that shows up with pregnancy, but it could be related to the rheumatic fever I had after Sunny was born. In any case, you don't have to worry. She's keeping an eagle eye on me."

"That explains part of my nightmares, but it doesn't explain why no one in the family knows you could be in serious trouble."

Deenie hated having to justify her reasons or choices, but she knew Stella wouldn't give up until she answered the question. "We've had some pretty rough times over the last few years, Aunt Stell. I wanted the family to be excited and joyful about this baby—without any What Ifs waiting in the wings. Can you understand that?"

Stella smiled softly. "Yes, I can." She offered Deenie her hands. "Let me help you, dear. Let me work with Dr. Slater. Trust me the way you used to. Please."

Deenie wanted to say yes. She was tired of bearing the burden of her health concerns all alone. Even though she had told the COBs all about it, it wasn't the same as having a shoulder nearby to lean on.

*What if I do accept Aunt Stell's offer?* she wondered. *Will I have to accept that the Stowell Sight and the other gifts of healing she lays claim to are real? The way I did back when I thought I had The Sight like all the other Stowell women? When I had a knowing about Max and didn't tell Juneau?*

Her thoughts jumped between the past and the present, between her rejection of The Sight and her need now for the kind of support Aunt Stell could give her. In the end her need for comfort overrode all other considerations. She took the hands Stella offered. "I'll try," she said. And at that moment, she meant it.

*Chapter 2*

WILLADENE

With Dr. Slater's enthusiastic support, Deenie began following Aunt Stell's recommendation of partial bed rest and occasional lazy strolls with Rauf. Since the poor old pooch now preferred the indoors and sleep to outdoors and play, Deenie spent most of her day sitting on the living room couch. Twice a week Stella came to take her blood pressure, listen to her heart, check her urine, and monitor her food intake.

When Deenie sat down one afternoon to write to the COBs, she hesitated, remembering the promise the three of them had shared in St. George. "No more fiction and sanitized truth for us," Juneau had declared. Deenie had agreed at the time, but how could she tell the others how troubled and disconnected she felt?

September 19, 1987
Dear COBs,

What's one step closer to COBhood? COBettes? COBeens? Whatever it is, I think we moved in the right direction in St. George. Gabby, you would have been proud of the way we resolved our personal and communal tantrums.

The Griff—The Great What If—still lives here, but he's in a carbohydrate-induced stasis. Everyone I know is on a "Let's Get Deenie Fat" campaign. With their help I'm beginning to look like a balloon with arms and legs. I hope I get the same support for taking it off after the baby is born.

Roger is working on polishing his dissertation. He will present and defend his research during the month of March. We are all cheering him on.

Carl is a sophomore in high school this year, and it looks like he's going to make the sophomore football team. He's thrilled, even though the team rules are very strict. Paul has started middle school (grades 7–9) and is taking it all in stride. Beth is burning an energetic swath through fourth grade, Primary, and Girl Scouts. Her main focus at the moment is talking Roger and me into letting her move into the guest room so she can have a bathroom of her own.

And here is an announcement of special importance and delight to all of us: Our sweet Sunny has reached one of her life goals—she's received her GED! She had the help of a devoted tutor and the support of the family, especially Roger's sister, Bert. Plus the school officials, who were willing to administer the test one section at a time.

Sunny's been limited by some brain damage at birth and even more by her frail physical health, but she's never given up wanting to graduate, like Roger and Bert. She's absolutely sure in her faith that her Heavenly Father will help her learn the things He wants her to know, no matter how long it takes. Her delight in her achievement is wonderful to see.

Juneau, anything new on the to-keep-or-not-to-keep front? I am praying for you and Misty. Erin, I am eager to hear more news about the redheaded Catholic boy.

> Love to all,
> Deenie

It wasn't the letter Deenie needed to write. She hadn't lied, though. She'd only left out things. Like admitting The Sight was a true gift and confessing that she'd received a premonition about Max that summer in Provo. *Could Juneau's baby have been saved if I'd only spoken up?* she wondered yet again. She'd worn out that question and still had no answer.

With a shake of the head, she folded the three copies of the letter, stuffed and stamped three envelopes, clipped them to the house-mounted mailbox with a clothespin, and hoped for rapid replies.

JUNEAU

September 22, 1987
Dear Gabby, Erin, and Deenie,

I could sure use your collective wisdom at the moment. Greg and I had a real dustup about whether or not Misty will keep her baby. Greg says no, that we can't fit it into our lives. And he cites the Church position that babies need to be sealed to a family, which is hard to argue with. But I felt there was something more. After the girls went to bed, I asked him what the real reason was. He said, "Juney, can't you remember what it did to us to lose Max? And we never even saw him. I don't want to get attached to someone we'd lose again when Misty decides to move on."

He looked so sad that I slid over on the sofa and hugged him. That surprised him, because I'm normally not very demonstrative. He gave me one of those big smiles that I love (he has great teeth), and the earlier discord faded away. But he's pretty well stuck to his position. Well, my dear friends, I know you can't solve my problem, but I needed to tell someone. I can just hear you, Gabby, saying, "Trust God for the outcome." And that's what I'll try to do.

Not much other news—except that I resigned my calling as Spiritual Living teacher in Relief Society. I decided I couldn't stand up there in front of those women when I feel that some of Misty's predicament is due to my having failed her somewhere along the line. So right now I'm supervising the visiting teaching squad. Can I call it that? I always feel that we're a team of some kind, rah! rah! rah!

> Love,
> Juneau

## WILLADENE

Thanksgiving dinner at the Rasmussen house would have been perfect if the dog hadn't died.

The aromas of every good thing the matriarchs on both sides of the family knew how to make were rich and inviting. The food looked and tasted as good as it smelled, and during dinner the family visited with as much gusto as they ate.

"Say, Carl." Roger's sister, Roberta, known to the family as Bert, called loudly enough to be heard from the other end of the tables. "I heard you made first string on the sophomore football team. How are you liking that?"

"Just fine. I heard you're taking Grandma NeVae and Grandpa Will back to California with you for a visit. And to check out that guy you've been going with. How are you going to like that?"

Bert answered with raised eyebrows and a wide grin.

Over the conversations and requests for a basket of this or a bowl of that, Deenie heard her mother ask, "Sunny, what are you doing?" Margaret was pointing to a pile of select turkey bits Sunny was accumulating on the edge of her plate.

"For Rauf," Sunny said.

A moment later, Sunny leaned over and whispered in Deenie's ear, "I'm going to feed Rauf before Mom makes me help clear the table." Then she quietly slipped away.

Deenie pushed back from the table with a replete sigh. She rubbed her belly with regret when she realized she had no belt to loosen. The only way she was going to feel less stuffed was to gain another set of stretch marks or give birth.

When Sunny returned some time later, she touched Deenie's shoulder to get her attention. "Rauf won't wake up. I think he's gone to doggie heaven."

Within moments the entire family gathered around faithful old Rauf, who lay curled up on his favorite cushion in his favorite spot, sleeping eternal sleep. "Poor old fellow," Roger said, putting one arm around Deenie and the other around Paul.

"But, Daddy," Beth cried, wedging herself between them. "He can't be dead. He's our dog."

Grandpa Rasmussen squatted down in front of her. "Snowdrop," he said, gently cupping her cheek with his work-roughened hand. "Rauf was a very old dog. He lived this long, I think, because you loved him so much and he loved you. But no matter how much he loved you, he couldn't stay forever. He was tired and worn out and ready to go to heaven. That's the way Heavenly Father planned it for all living creatures."

Beth launched herself into her Grandfather Rasmussen's arms. Deenie watched as he gave Beth one of his special hugs. He'd always been able to comfort her children when they were hurt; she hoped now that the comfort would also reach Carl, her oldest. He stood apart from the others, looking down at the remains of his faithful pet. Deenie knew he wouldn't let himself cry, but his face revealed his grief. "We need to bury him," he said, pulling off his sweater and draping it over Rauf.

It was Deenie's father, John Stowell, who stepped next to Carl and put his arm around the boy. "I'd like to help you do that." The gesture surprised Deenie; her father was seldom physically affectionate with his grandsons.

From that moment, burying Rauf became a family affair. Bert helped Sunny and Beth plan a funeral service while Paul used his wood-burning set to style a marker for the grave. And all of them made suggestions as to how to bury Rauf in the solidly frozen ground.

It was Grandma NeVae who came up with the solution. "Remember that old freezer your Uncle Marty buried in the back of the orchard to use as a root cellar when he had this house? How about that as a crypt?"

It took two pickaxes and a lot of muscle for the men to locate the crypt-to-be beneath the dirt and snow. Then Grandpa Will and Roger removed the fittings, thoroughly cleaned out the freezer, and carefully lined the interior with sheets. When they were finished, Roger gathered leftover stones from the garden wall to finish off the gravesite.

Grandpa Stowell and Carl took time to groom old Rauf as best they could, brushing his hair smoothly down his back. Then everyone fell in behind Carl and Paul as they solemnly carried their beloved dog to his final resting place. Beth filled the corners of the crypt with Rauf's favorite toys and chews. Sunny placed her well-loved smiley-face quilt over Rauf and his canine treasures so they wouldn't be so cold in the ground. When the last loving task was finished, Roger closed the lid and turned the key for Rauf's peaceful rest and the safety of the children.

Beth and Sunny presented the brief service they had prepared. Beth's remarks were short but revealing. "Rauf was the nicest one in our family," she said in her most grown-up, eight-year-old voice. "He came when I called him. He was always glad to see me. I hope he's happy in heaven. And I hope he doesn't decide to belong to another forever family before we get there. Amen."

Sunny joined Beth, and they sang "Families Can Be Together Forever." Roger blessed the gravesite and the family, thanking the Lord for such a fine and faithful friend. The service concluded when Paul pounded the stake of his grave marker into the frozen ground and read the inscription:

Here Lies Rauf Rasmussen
The Best Dog Anybody Ever Had
Part of Our Family, 1976–1987

It wasn't until all the guests had departed and Deenie and Roger were cleaning the kitchen that Deenie discovered at the back of the counter a heavy envelope addressed to her. "Where did this come from?" she asked Roger.

He shrugged. "Don't know. Someone must have slipped it in the house while we were burying Rauf."

Deenie opened the envelope, which contained a set of keys and a note. "It's from Pat Crafton." She read the contents quickly. "Oh no," she whispered, reaching out one hand toward Roger for support. "I can't believe it."

Roger was by her side in an instant. "What is it?"

Speechless, she handed him the note.

"Dear Deenie," he read out loud. "My son Stan was killed in a training accident at boot camp yesterday morning. Mom and I are leaving immediately for Chicago with Reece and Ryan to help in arranging the funeral. I don't know when we'll be back. Here are the keys to the house. Could you pick up the mail and paper for us and keep an eye on things while we are gone? Pray for us. Pat Crafton."

Roger dropped the note next to the keys on the counter and drew Deenie into his arms. "It makes the loss of one faithful old pooch pale by comparison, doesn't it?"

She nodded. "It shouldn't be this way. Mothers shouldn't have to bury their children."

"No, they shouldn't."

"It could just as easily have been one of our children taken suddenly in an accident."

"Yes, it could have. There are no guarantees, Deenie. That's why God gave us faith."

"But I want guarantees. I *need* guarantees."

Roger hugged her tighter, and she leaned her forehead against his shoulder. "Should we tell the kids now?"

"Let's let it go until the morning. They've had enough sadness for today."

ERIN

Erin set aside the second Saturday in December to make Christmas cookies with her kids and The Women, which was what she called her mother, Joanna, and her grandmother, otherwise known as Grams or Ruth. She intended that the process would take place in the large, well-outfitted kitchen of her Edina, Minnesota, home, but her daughter, Kayla, had other ideas. "I want to make them at Grams's. It's more fun there."

Erin's eyebrows rose. Growing up in that house had been anything but fun; she had no memories of happy holiday baking. "Why do you say that?"

"It's little, like a playhouse. And I like the funny-colored cupboards in the kitchen."

Erin laughed aloud. She'd been trying to talk Grams into getting rid of the hideous mustard-colored cabinets for years.

Cookie Day dawned bright and cold. Just as Erin was getting the kids bundled up for the trek to the Minneapolis neighborhood she'd grown up in, her husband, Cory, returned from playing basketball at the church. It was one of the ways he kept the athletic build that, along with his Scandinavian good looks, had attracted her to him when they'd first met. Still did.

"Are you sure you don't want to come with us?" she asked.

"No, thanks. I'll leave it to you ladies. And my little buddy here." He bent to give two-year-old Mark a high five. Mark raised his pudgy hand to meet his father's with a slap and a giggle. Mark was blond and easy-going like his father. Kayla, a month shy of five, had Erin's red hair and intense temperament.

When Erin turned up the street to her childhood home, she was surprised to see Jake Ingram's maroon van parked in front. *Now that's interesting,* she thought. Ever since she'd met Jake, who owned the antiques store Finishing Touches, she'd hoped he and her mother would get together.

Jake bounded out the door as she pulled up to the house. Tall, large, and given to wearing plaid shirts and suspenders, he always made Erin think of Paul Bunyan. "Jakieee!" Kayla cried when he opened the back door of the minivan. Mark echoed her, reaching out his arms to be released from his car seat.

"I didn't expect to see you here," Erin said.

"Grams invited me. I think she has a crush on me." He grinned, running a hand over his bald pate. "Must be my good looks."

Watching the happy mess-making that followed, Erin decided Jake was right about Grams. She was in a lighthearted mood that Erin could ascribe only to his presence. So were Joanna and the kids, for that matter. *What's his secret?* she wondered.

In short order they made dough for several kinds of cookies. Mark and Kayla were the picture of concentration as they cut misshapen slices of cooled ginger cookie dough and cut slits in diamond-shaped fattigmand cookies, a Norwegian holiday favorite.

With her tongue caught between her teeth, Kayla pulled one end of a fattigmand through the slit to make a twist and then placed it on the baking sheet. "Did you make these when you were little, Grams?"

"Um-humm. My mother taught me how to make all the traditional goodies."

"Did Santa bring you lots of presents?" Mark asked.

"When I was little, he only brought one present for each of us. He brought me a pair of ice skates when I was six. My brothers taught me how to skate on the river near our house."

Kayla's eyes gleamed. "Could you do twirls like the skaters on TV?"

"With my brothers as teachers?" Grams's arched eyebrows rose, and her large, blue eyes gleamed. "I skated like a hockey player."

"I'm going to be a twirly skater when I grow up. I like the pretty dresses."

"Really?" It was the first Erin had heard of it.

"How was it growing up in a houseful of boys, Ruth?" Jake asked. "Did they torment you?"

"Heavens no. They treated me like a princess, but they sure were hard on Alfred when he was courting me. They weren't going to let just any man marry their little sister."

"He must have been quite the fellow to get your brothers' approval."

"No way he could, poor man. But he got the approval of the one who counted." Grams touched her chest. "Me."

By the end of the afternoon, racks of cooling cookies lined the counters. Jake and Joanna were finishing up the last dishes, and Grams was heating water for instant coffee. "Would you like Postum or hot chocolate?" she asked Erin.

Erin glanced into the living room to check on the children. Mark was asleep on the couch, blond hair damp against his forehead. Kayla lay in front of the TV, holding one of Ruth's afghans against her cheek. They wouldn't mind staying a little longer. "Postum, please."

"What a day," Jake said, settling into the largest of the kitchen chairs, the one Erin's grandfather had used when he was still with them. "Thanks for inviting me, Ruth." He turned to Erin. "I bet you liked baking cookies with your grandmother when you were little."

Erin glanced at Grams and then back to Jake. "We didn't do it often. That's why this has been so much fun for me."

Jake grimaced. "Sorry. I forgot that Christmas hasn't always been the best time of year for your family. Your grandfather . . ."

Out of habit, Erin held her breath, bracing herself for the usual outburst. To her surprise, Ruth said simply, "He died December 18th. I should have been prepared, given his first heart attack, but I somehow thought if I ignored the possibility, it wouldn't happen."

Erin and Joanna exchanged surprised looks—they'd never heard Ruth say that before. "What are you talking about, Mom?" Joanna asked.

"Larson family history, dear. Alfred's father died in his late fifties, and several uncles and cousins around sixty. All of them from heart attacks."

"You never told me that!"

Ruth paused, Jake's coffee mug in her hand. "The doctor said Alfred was getting better. He even gave him permission to go back to work for a few hours a day after New Year's." A succession of emotions crossed her face. "I really thought he'd turned the corner. I wouldn't have gone shopping otherwise. I wouldn't have left him alone . . ."

"You left him with me," Joanna said.

*And we went to the park,* Erin thought with the familiar sinking feeling. *To meet That Catholic Boy.* The father who'd never married her mother.

"I know it might have turned out the same even if I had stayed home, but I blame myself." Ruth's voice trembled and the coffee mug wavered. "Every Christmas, no matter how hard I try not to, I see him lying here on the rug, all alone. . . ."

The words took Erin totally by surprise. For the first time ever, Grams was talking about her husband's death without blaming Erin and Joanna for not being with him. Joanna took the mug from Grams and gently guided her to a chair. "I left him alone," Grams repeated more to herself than to the others.

Jake reached for her hand. "Ruth, would you be willing to do a guided imagery I used when I was a school counselor? It's a way of talking to people who have passed over, a chance to say the things we wish we had said earlier or could say now. I think it might help."

Ruth looked briefly at Joanna and Erin. Then she nodded, a slight motion.

"Great. You two can follow along if you'd like."

In his deep voice, Jake directed Ruth to close her eyes and focus on her breath as she inhaled and exhaled. Erin watched as her grandmother's breathing slowed. After several minutes, Jake said, "Now, Ruth, I know you believe in heaven. Visualize your idea of heaven and see who is in it."

Without any conscious decision to do so, Erin closed her eyes and followed Jake's instructions. She saw who was in her heaven—family members, both those living and those gone before, friends, the Savior.

"Now see your Alfred and tell him what you've wished you could say to him." An image popped into Erin's mind of her grandfather as he'd looked when she was small. She told him how much she missed him and how she wished he could have known his great-grandchildren.

After a long silence, Jake said, "Now, let Alfred speak. The Alfred as he now is, knowing much more about the meaning of life than he did when he was here on earth."

Erin sighed as she imagined her grandfather putting her four-year-old self onto his lap. She actually heard him say that if he could do it over, he would make sure she and Joanna felt safe, loved, and accepted. "I wouldn't care a whit what the neighbors thought about Joanna being pregnant and not married! It was none of their business."

Erin wasn't sure when she and her mother had joined hands, but as Joanna squeezed hers tight, she knew her mother had also followed Jake's directions. A few minutes later the imagery came to an end. The first thing Erin noticed when she opened her eyes was how light and free she felt. The second was how peaceful the faces of The Women were.

"Was that real?" Ruth asked Jake. "It felt real."

"Who's to say? If it changed something for the better, declare it real."

Grams sat a moment longer, then stood and gathered the cups. "Jake? If you haven't been invited anywhere else for Christmas Day, you spend it with us."

"I wouldn't want to barge in on a family gathering."

Grams glanced sideways at Erin, acknowledging that she had just invited Jake to Erin and Cory's on Christmas Day. Erin flashed her a reassuring smile and then turned to Jake. "Please come. We already think of you as family."

# Chapter 3

ERIN

January 11, 1988
Hi, Juneau, Deenie, and Gabby,

Thank you all for your Christmas cards! Deenie, that fabulous chocolate hazelnut torte from Pat Crafton's bakery was the absolute highlight of Christmas dinner.

Juneau, I'm on pins and needles wondering what you guys are going to decide about the baby. I realized when I read your card that Misty is due in February, same as Deenie. I'm sending off packages this weekend with baby things.

I can't believe Christmas has come and gone. Another year, another holiday photo of the family posed on our beautiful staircase. We'll be taking a lot of Johnson family photos on that staircase over the years. Pictures of Kayla (just turned five) and Mark (a couple of months past two) and their dates on prom night. Both of them in cap and gown for graduation. Mark holding his mission call. Kayla in her wedding dress. Oops. Why not Kayla with her mission call in hand?!

Did you notice Kayla's scar in the photo? It's behind the curl on her right cheek—the one she glued down! My friend Colleen Harrington and I were running the numbers after the Big Barn Sale last fall when Kayla tripped and fell on a half-buried piece of metal in the yard. The plastic surgeon did a great job, but even so, the scar is visible, and Kayla's very self-conscious about it. Cory and I are doing our best to help her feel lovely and loved, dear girl.

I think the Lord sent Jake, the gentle giant who owns Finishing Touches, as a special gift for our family. He brings out the best in Grams. The day we made Christmas cookies at Grams's he got her to talk about her childhood, which she hardly ever does. When she told how her brothers taught her to skate on a river near their house, Kayla announced that she was going to be a figure skater and get a medal for doing twirls. So of course, Grams gave her skates for Christmas, and Mom made her a little skating dress for her birthday. Cory's been teaching her the basics at a nearby arena. She wears her dress whenever they go.

That same day, Jake and Mom finally admitted that they've been dating for some time! I can't tell you how glad that makes me, especially since Jake and Grams are such buddies. She doesn't have to worry about being left behind if that relationship blossoms.

> Much love to you both,
> Erin

P.S. My half-sister Caitlin (I still can't get used to having a sister!), gave me a book of McGee family photos for Christmas. I got all teary when I saw the photo array of my father, Andrew, his parents, Sean and Margaret McGee, and their parents. All those people I'd never seen before, and so many of them with my eyes, my chin, my hair.

## WILLADENE

The second Sunday of January, Deenie watched her family leave for church without her. "Remember," Roger said as he ushered them out the door, "bathroom breaks only. Bed rest means bed rest!" Deenie pulled the worst face she could manage, making them all laugh. She smiled and waved as Roger closed the door behind them.

The minute the latch clicked, Deenie sagged into the pillows that supported her back, elevated her swollen feet, and propped up her belly on one side. She picked up the clipboard loaded with layers of paper and carbon and wrote, Dear Ladies, This is me.

In the space below, Deenie sketched a stick figure self-portrait of a hugely pregnant woman with clown-sized hands and feet, hair spiraling away from her head, crossed eyes, and a zigzag mouth. She added a capital letter G across the chest and continued writing.

> The G is a multipurpose label. It can stand for Gratitude, Guilt, or The Griff at any given time. For example, I am so grateful for the family's support since Dr. Slater put me on complete bed rest. The kids are doing as they're asked without complaint.

Roger has put off the polishing of his dissertation until the baby is born, and Aunt Stell is always on the scene. I don't know why that makes Mom uncomfortable, but it does.

The G flashes red for Guilt when I think about Pat Crafton. We haven't talked since she returned from Chicago, except for me expressing sympathy about Stan when she picked up her house key. I feel terrible about that—and worse when I think how grateful I am it wasn't one of *my* kids who died. In the middle of it all, I'm struggling with the same kinds of questions about Stan's death as I've had about Sunny's birth. Is there purpose in such tragedy? And if there isn't, how do we make sense of life?

To top it all off, I'm a perfect target for The Griff when Reece and Ryan are around. Acting out their anger and sorrow at this age could be a lot more serious than when they were nine and rolled up one pant leg, wore bandannas, and pretended they belonged to a gang. I hope for all our sakes that Carl is upwind from the fallout when they do.

Sorry this letter is so grim, but if we're going for reality instead of Regina, that's the way it is.

On the lighter and happier side, there may be romance in the wind, from what my mother says. Dave Fenton, our county sheriff, has been stopping by the bakery several times a week and ends up having a pastry and talking to Pat. Mom says it looks like "true like." Wouldn't that be something?

Getting bigger but not necessarily any better, although the doctor assures me that the old ticker is holding its own.

Deenie and Co.

P.S. Erin, thank you for the antique apothecary jars you sent. Dad made a railed shelf for them to go over the changing table in the nursery. They look grand!

## JUNEAU

On a bright day in late January, Juneau invited her friend and neighbor Marisol Sanchez to lunch at Charleyville, a pleasant buffet restaurant in downtown Pasadena with tall windows and classical music. She needed to get away from her typewriter, but that wasn't the only reason. She'd noticed that Marisol, normally so bright and cheerful, had seemed down for a while.

"I'm glad you suggested this," Marisol said. "These days, it seems I need a good excuse to get out of my grubbies and comb my hair." She smiled, a little ruefully, Juneau thought.

"I don't exactly dress up at home," Juneau said. "Philip Atwater is the only one who sees me most of the day, and he isn't critical."

"My kids don't care, either," Marisol said, "and . . ." She waved a hand as if dismissing whatever she'd been going to say. Looking up at the menu posted on the wall, she said, "Let's have something sinful today."

They settled on three-layer club sandwiches, pink lemonade, and a generous slice of chocolate cake to share. Vivaldi's *Four Seasons* played softly in the background as they enjoyed their food and talked about their daughters. Juneau gave an update on Misty, who was ready to give birth and a little scared of what was to come. Marisol reported that Isobel, who would be graduating from college the next June, had changed her career plans. "She's going into matrimony. So much for her idea of going to the Far East as a multilingual interpreter." She described her prospective son-in-law as they finished their sandwiches. Then she said. "By the way, what do you think of Nicole's new ambition?"

"What do you mean? As far as I know, she's still planning to be a champion baton twirler and enter the Miss America contest."

"Oh." Marisol shifted uncomfortably. "I guess I shouldn't have mentioned it."

"You have to tell, now."

"Well, my friend, Nicole says she'd like to be a nun."

Juneau sat back. "A nun? A Catholic nun?"

"I don't think you Mormons have nuns."

"She can't do that!"

Marisol's eyes narrowed. "You seemed to think it was all right when Beto thought he might like to be a Mormon missionary."

"But that's just for two years. Being a nun is for life."

"You do know she's been taking catechism classes with Beto."

"Yes." Juneau and Greg had given their permission because Marisol's son Beto had attended Primary with Nicole. Since they both turned twelve, he'd been going to Young Men and Young Women activity nights. "But . . ."

"But you don't want her turning Catholic." Marisol's voice was chilly. "Would it be all that bad, Juneau?"

"I'd be lying if I said no. My religion means so much to me."

"Mine means so much to me, too."

Juneau could feel tears sting at the back of her eyes. Marisol had always been as faithful in attending Mass, kids all spit-and-polish, as she herself had been in going to her Mormon meetings. She reached out to take her friend's hand. "Sorry, pal. You know well enough that I suffer from flapping of the tongue. Forgive me?"

"Maybe I should make you genuflect and kiss my ring." Marisol grinned as she spoke, and her spirits seemed to lighten. "You know what I think influenced Nicole to change her career plans? That movie, *The Nun's Story*, starring Audrey Hepburn. She and Beto have watched the video together several times."

Juneau nodded thoughtfully, remembering how much she'd liked the movie herself. "She wouldn't be the only one influenced by seeing Hepburn play Sister Luke."

"Who knows? It may be just a passing fancy," Marisol said lightly. She divided the chocolate cake, sliding a plate with one half toward Juneau.

"Maybe," Juneau said. She thought about Nicole's previous ambitions to dig for mummies and then to be a baton twirler. She was now in the twirling squad of the Pasadena High School marching band. "Perhaps she can be the first baton-twirling nun to become Miss America."

They laughed together and dug into the cake.

ERIN

February 1, 1988
Dear Juneau and Willadene,

You won't believe what's happened. I've met my father, face to face! Caitlin and I were having dinner at the St. Paul Grill the night before she was scheduled to leave for Hawaii. We were just starting on our entrees when Andrew J showed up with a client in tow. He was as surprised to see us as we were to see him.

He covered it well, though. He greeted us as if it were the most normal thing in the world to see both his girls together, and he gave me the same kiss on the cheek that he gave Caitlin. We chatted for a few minutes, and then the hostess whisked him and his client away.

I didn't realize how tense I was until Caitlin told me to breathe. She said Andrew was nervous, too, because she noticed that the tops of his ears turned neon, a sure sign of stress! I'll be interested to see what happens now that we've passed that hurdle. Coincidence brought us this far, but now I think it's up to us.

There were more surprises yet to come that night. Caitlin and I were talking about Andrew's wife, Charlotte, who's suffering from a flare-up of her MS. When I asked Caitlin if MS is inherited, she said it didn't matter either way, because Charlotte isn't really her mother!

Caitlin's mother is Andrew's first wife, Brenda. She lives in Hawaii (that's why Caitlin flies over every year) and is married to her third or fourth husband. You could have knocked me over with a feather when I heard that. Caitlin just smiled and said, "See, you and I are more alike than you ever imagined. You had an absent father, and I've had an absent mother."

So the McGee Family Soap Opera continues! Stay tuned for the next installment.

Love,
Erin

## JUNEAU

Juneau was undecided about whether to bring up the subject of Nicole's new ambition with her family. She thought about it until the following Monday, which was their monthly What's the Beef Night. They'd called it Gripe Night until Wendy's started airing their Where's the Beef? commercial on TV. Inspired, Nicole had suggested they change the name, so What's the Beef Night it became.

The rule was that they couldn't air gripes until after the meal, so they chatted while they ate, talking about the happenings of the past week. Juneau mentioned that she'd had lunch with Marisol on Friday.

"Oh," Nicole said, "then she probably told you about my wanting to be a nun."

Greg choked on his food. "You what?"

"I like the catechism classes I've taken with Beto," Nicole said cheerfully. "I've decided I want to convert and become a nun so I can go to Africa and be a nurse."

Juneau chuckled as she watched Greg process that bit of information. Nicole's pronouncement must have sounded ludicrous to him because he took it as a joke. He grinned at Juneau and then turned to Misty—and his grin faded. Juneau turned to look at Misty, too.

The girl sat stiff and straight, a startled expression on her face.

"Misty," Juneau said, "is something wrong?"

Misty looked embarrassed. Leaning closer to her mother, she whispered, "I'm all wet, but I didn't have to go or anything."

Juneau's heart thumped. Keeping her voice calm, she said, "I guess your water broke. Remember the film we saw? Sometimes it's the first sign that the baby's coming."

Misty rose shakily to her feet. "You mean tonight? Now?"

"Maybe. Greg, call Dr. Hart and tell him things have started."

Nicole jumped up. "I'll pack her suitcase. Where are the diapers, Mom? And the little nighties and stuff?"

"Forget them," Greg said gruffly. "We're not bringing it home."

Nicole whirled on her father. "Well, it still needs clothes! Are you going to send it off naked?"

Grumbling, Greg got up and headed for the telephone. A few minutes later he announced, "The doctor says to bring her in. I'll go start the car."

Misty's labor was long and hard. Juneau held Misty's hand and listened to her squeal and grunt and pant, the age-old sounds of childbirth. She'd chosen to do it naturally, without anesthetics. So like Misty. But even with her focus on her daughter, Juneau couldn't help thinking about Greg and that folder of adoption papers.

The baby was a boy. "His name is Gideon," Misty said as the nurse laid him beside her on the gurney. Her right arm curled around him. "From the Bible. The guy who fought the Midianites." She flashed a brief grin at Juneau. "See, I did pay attention in Sunday School."

Juneau moved closer to look at the baby lying at Misty's side as Dr. Hart did what was necessary on the other side of the draped sheet. Gideon was a sturdy little fellow, close to eight pounds of him, and twenty-one inches long, the nurse announced. He wailed briefly, and then Juneau could have sworn he rolled his eyes upward to look at Misty. His mama. He stopped crying.

"I love him, Mom," Misty whispered. Her face was sweaty, and she looked bedraggled, but her eyes shone with wonder and discovery.

"So do I," Juneau whispered back.

"What are we going to do about Dad?"

What indeed?

Greg was sitting impassively reading an old *Newsweek* magazine when Juneau went to tell him and Nicole about Gideon. He looked up, one hand tightening on the folder of adoption papers.

"It's a boy," Juneau announced. "His name is Gideon."

"Oh, wow." Nicole sprang to her feet. "I'm an aunt! Can we see him?"

Juneau nodded. "Dr. Hart said we can go to Misty's room as soon as they move her there."

"I don't want to see him," Greg said. "You can take the papers for Misty to sign." He held out the folder.

"Not a chance. That's something you're going to have to do yourself, Greg."

When they were allowed to go to Misty's room, Juneau was glad to see that her face had been washed and her hair combed. The baby was in a little plastic bassinet on wheels beside her bed. A young nurse lifted Gideon, all swaddled in a blue blanket now, with a tiny blue cap on his head. "Who gets to hold him first?" she asked.

Misty wore a tired smile as they passed him around, first to Nicole, who snuggled him and whispered something in his small pink ear, then to Juneau, who kissed his fuzzy little head. Nicole took the adoption folder from Greg's hand, and Juneau placed the baby in his arms.

Greg stood stiffly. He glanced briefly down at the baby and then at Misty and cleared his throat as if he were going to make a pronouncement. Just then somebody dropped something out in the corridor, making a loud, rattly noise. Greg's arms tightened protectively around the baby. He gazed again at the small face, and his breath caught. Slowly he lowered his head to the blue blanket, and his shoulders shook.

"Hello, Gideon," he whispered softly. "Hello, little grandson."

Nicole silently slipped the folder of adoption papers into the wastebasket.

February 4, 1988
Dear Gabby, Willadene, and Erin,

I'm a grandma! Can you believe it? Gideon Gregory Caldwell. A perfect name for a future president, don't you think?

Marisol is giving a baby shower, bless her. Everyone seems to be joyfully accepting Gideon into the world. And Greg is the most doting grandfather you ever saw! He's quite pleased about supplying the "Gregory Caldwell" part of Gideon's name.

Love,
Juneau

ERIN
February 17, 1988
Dear Gabby, Juneau, and Deenie,

I'm so thrilled that Misty is keeping the baby! It touched my heart to hear how Greg fell in love the minute he held the little sweetie. I couldn't help thinking about his absent daddy, though. I hope he doesn't have to wait as long to meet his father as I did to meet Andrew J.

Big hugs and kisses to all,
Your Erin

*Chapter 4*

WILLADENE

Evangeline Rose Rasmussen was delivered kicking and screaming, three weeks early but perfectly healthy, at 1:00 P.M. February 6, the same afternoon Carl Rasmussen fell down the stairs at Crafton Catering, broke his right leg in two places, and landed face first at the feet of the county sheriff, Dave Fenton. He was followed down the stairs by a six-pack of beer cans, which exploded on impact, drenching them both in the yeasty brew. But even that stench did little to hide the scent of the sticky sweet smoke curling down the stairs from the landing where Reece and Ryan Crafton stood, looking shocked and dismayed. One of them gripped a smoldering joint of marijuana in his hand. In the confusion Fenton couldn't tell which one, so he called an ambulance for Carl and then cuffed both the Crafton twins and hauled them along with him to the hospital.

At least that's the story the emergency room nurse told the admitting nurse, who told the neonatal nurse, who told the obstetric nurse, who told Deenie before either Roger or Sheriff Fenton could break the news.

The fact that the boys were neither drunk nor stoned did little to defray the gossip that swept the valley. Everyone seemed focused on the juicy tidbit that it was Sheriff Fenton, a law officer with a decided partiality for Pat Crafton, who had apprehended the three minors. Then there was the bizarre coincidence that while Willadene Rasmussen was being rolled into recovery after having had another baby (whatever was she thinking?), Carl was being wheeled into emergency surgery to repair the compound fracture of his right leg.

Deenie heard bits of a dozen versions of the events on the phone and in the hallways of the hospital. The What If she had been worrying about for the last three months had become a very real and very ugly What Is. When Roger came to take her home two days later, she left with the gossip, actual and imagined, racing through her mind and the howls of seven-pound Evvy ringing in her ears. Carl, who was released from the hospital the same day, scrunched his silent, lanky self into the back of the van. His right leg, in a cast up to his hip, was propped between the two middle seats on a blanket covering his gym bag. His crutches were wedged between his leg and the safety seat that held a howling baby. No one spoke. No one could, over Evvy's unabated shriek.

Deenie couldn't nurse, and she was devastated.

"Bottle feeding may not be what you would prefer," Dr. Slater said sympathetically, "but it isn't the end of the world. I'm more concerned that the heart murmur is still there. I'd like to have you follow up with a cardiologist just to be certain everything is okay."

When word got out that Evvy Rasmussen would be a bottle baby, Deenie was inundated with advice. No matter how the comments were couched, it all boiled down to the same thing in the end—Evvy would be fine, so buck up and get on with it. No one asked Deenie if *she* would be all right with bottle-feeding Evvy. Breast-feeding her babies was one of the miracles of motherhood she cherished. She was grieving and guilty and truly not herself, but no one noticed except Evvy, who turned frantic the minute Deenie picked her up.

Deenie wondered why she bothered to get dressed, since the pair of sweats she slept in looked exactly like the pair she spent the day in. Not changing would make one less thing she would have to do when doing anything at all took too much effort.

"Don't forget your mom's coming this morning to pick up Beth for a weekend with Sunny," Roger hollered from the nursery. "I'll get Evvy dressed and meet you downstairs."

When the doorbell rang, Deenie was still sitting on the edge of the bed, staring at her feet. "Shower!" she commanded herself. Even that energy-draining process was more appealing to her than going downstairs and listening to her mother rhapsodize over the "family baby." *That's who she is,* Deenie thought. *Not my baby. The family's baby.*

She stood numbly under the water until it started to cool and then dressed without looking in the mirror. As she walked toward the top of the stairs, she could hear Roger and her mother together in the family room.

"Deenie seems to be struggling," Margaret said.

Deenie could hear the worry in her mother's voice, and she could imagine Roger's expression when he replied, "She had a hard time after Beth was born, too. She was better by her six-week checkup, though I don't remember her being this twitchy. I keep an eye on her, for everyone's sake."

*Twitchy? Keep an eye on me?* Deenie felt The Griff's laughter clear down to her toes as he escaped from the box where she had locked him in the back of her mind.

That afternoon a package from Juneau arrived. It was a mother's journal with pages embellished with humorous stickers and some of Juneau's favorite quotations. Deenie took to mindlessly doodling in it, scrolling an endless design from one sheet onto another while Evvy slept. A few days later she started adding words. Not out of desire to record her thoughts but out of guilt and remorse for the ruined treasure.

> *Evvy's blessing is scheduled for the first Sunday in March. I think it's too soon to take her out, and I know for sure it's too soon for me, but Roger says it's time. When Roger and Mom were making plans, I said, "Why don't you bless her to be quiet once in a while?"*

> *Roger gave me one of his extremely disappointed looks as if to say, "Who are you and what have you done with my wife?" I wish I knew the answer.*

> *February 27: Carl, the beer, and the broken leg are a mystery I am letting Roger solve. He says the booze and pot were a posthumous gift from Stan dropped off by a military buddy, who'd promised to make the delivery, if and when it was needed, so the boys could hoist a brew and take a toke to remember Stan. Some kind of a military male bonding thing.*

> *Roger, Pat, and Dave Fenton are working with the boys and juvenile court to settle the question of possession. Roger says he'll let me know*

*what the judge says when it's final. If Pat and Dave are having a romance, it is the only nice thing that's happening around here.*

*March 1: Evvy's blessing has been postponed.*

Evvy turned one month old, and Deenie still hadn't been back to church. On fast Sunday in March, seeing how much Roger and Beth wanted to take the baby with them to church to show her off to the entire ward, Deenie tried to pull herself together and get ready. She made it as far as the slip and hair stage before faintness and tingling in her hands forced her back into a bathrobe. When the family left without her, bundled in jackets and radiating good cheer, no one remembered to kiss her good-bye.

ERIN

February 17, 1988
Dear Gabby and Juneau,

Do you have the same feeling that I do—that something's wrong in Wellsville? When I talked to Deenie after Evvy came, her voice didn't sound right. I've called several times since then, and I always get the same response: Deenie's asleep; Deenie can't come to the phone; she'll call you later. I asked Roger once what was going on, and he said, "Just a case of garden-variety baby blues."

Gabby, what can you tell us? Please call. I don't want to wait for a letter.

Your Erin

JUNEAU

February 25, 1988
Dear Erin,

I've tried calling, too. Sounds to me like more than "garden-variety baby blues." I wonder if Roger has ever heard of down-and-dirty outright depression?

Worried,
Juneau

## ERIN

March 3, 1988
Dear Deenie,

Gabby told Juneau and me that you're having a tough go of it. Whatever that means, you're in my prayers, my dear friend. Remember, the COBs stick together!

*Regina hurried down the empty street, attempting to flee the sound of The Griff's heavy footsteps behind her. She tried to call for help, but her throat was so dry, no sound came out. Suddenly, three burly men stepped in front of her. She shrieked, but the bruiser wearing a hat said, "Cool it, lady. You're not the one we're after."*

*He motioned, and she turned to see The Griff slow down and then stop.*

*"Go on home now, lady," the man with the hat said. "We'll take care of him. Boss's orders."*

So if The Griff shows up, remember I've sent a special squad of angel thugs who are bigger than he is!

Love,<br>Erin

## WILLADENE

In the month after Evvy's birth, Deenie started living in her head. She had to. With numb lips and tingling hands and the sensation that someone was always standing behind her, her body no longer felt like her own. She took minimal care of herself and her baby and began living out What If scenarios in her imagination.

*March 17, 1988: Evvy doesn't feel safe when I hold her. That's why she fusses when she's with me. I dread being alone with her. Too often, I put her in her crib, crawl in my own bed, pull the covers over my head so I can't hear her cries, and try to escape into sleep.*

Sleep. *All I want to do is sleep!*

Deenie wrote on. She described how the hot breath of The Griff burned the back of her neck while he followed her through the house. She wrote about the days when her legs and arms felt so heavy that getting dressed in the morning was impossible, about the days when her heart raced so fast she thought it would burst. What if it did? Would the family be happier? Would Roger remarry and live happily ever after, grateful that he had been spared more time with someone so flawed?

As she wrote, Deenie felt a great darkness opening up. It expanded with each word until it filled the universe inside her. More frightened than she had even been, she dropped to her knees to pray. No words came. She knew not even God could help her now. Someone had stolen her soul.

"Evvy's out of clean sleepers." Roger, already late for work, handed the baby over to Deenie. "I'll be home at 10:30 to take you to see Dr. Slater. Aunt Stell's coming at 10:00 to watch the baby while you get ready."

"What about Dr. Slater?" Deenie asked brightly, pretending to be Deenie the Competent again so that no one would notice she wasn't Deenie at all anymore.

"It's your checkup," Roger said, clearly concerned.

"But that's not until March twenty-third."

"Today is the twenty-third." Roger put down his briefcase and started taking off his coat. "I'll call in and take the whole day off."

Deenie felt a sudden surge of anger. "Don't be silly. You, Aunt Stell, the doctor. I've got it. You don't have to treat me like Sunny just because I got the dates mixed up."

The shock on Roger's face made Deenie even angrier, but as he left the house, she noticed he was walking as if the weight of the world were on his shoulders. As suddenly as she had been overpowered by anger, she was now flooded with guilt and shame. Her heart pounded loudly in her chest. The familiar tingling began in her legs and lips. She hurried toward the nursery to put Evvy in her crib while she was still in control. The need to flee, to run, to hide, was all consuming.

"*Deenie, Deenie, Deenie,*" The Griff whispered to her as she rushed down the hall. "*When are you going to listen to me? They'll all be better off without you.*"

Five minutes later, Evvy woke up crying for no discernible reason. Roger had fed, burped, and changed her just before leaving. Frantically, Deenie tried every comfort technique that had worked with the other children, to no avail. She gave up and put Evvy back in the crib. Leaving the nursery door open, she hurried to the kitchen, turned the radio on full blast, and began folding the wash piled on the table. The harder Evvy cried, the faster Deenie folded. She sighed with relief when the crying ceased.

"I bet she's dead," The Griff said with satisfaction. "I bet she choked on her own spit while you were listening to music, you nasty, selfish thing."

"Shut up!" Deenie yelled as she dashed for the stairs. "Get out of my head. Get out of my head!"

Evvy started howling again the minute Deenie picked her up. Her back was wet and stinky from top to bottom. She needed a bath and a full change of clothes. How am I going to get her clean? Deenie fretted. She hadn't dared bathe the baby alone since coming home from the hospital. What if the water was too hot? What if the room was too cold? What if Evvy slipped out of her hands and crushed her skull on the tile floor?

At least she'd be quiet then. In horror at her ugly thought, Deenie nearly dropped Evvy. She steadied herself for a moment. Then with deliberate intent, she placed Evvy at the dry end of the crib and backed away. She shut out the sound of her daughter's screams as she took one step backwards after the other, the familiar heaviness slowing down time until a single movement took forever. She kept backing away until she hit the wall and slid down into the corner by the door.

"Ahhh," The Griff whispered. "Time to come inside and rest." Deenie fought the seduction in his voice, biting her lip until it bled. "Don't do that! Come deeper, Deenie, where it's darker. You can sleep for as long as you want, and then if you like, we can play hide and seek. You won't ever have to worry again."

Weary beyond measure, Deenie turned her back to the room, curled up as tiny as could be, and gave in.

"Deenie. Deenie! Wake up!" a voice insisted from far away. On some level Deenie knew it was intended for her, but it didn't mean anything.

"What is it, Aunt Stell?" another voice intruded.

Deenie curled up tighter . . .

"Roger, call 911."

and dug deeper . . .

"We need an ambulance."

. . . into the darkness inside.

## JUNEAU

March 22, 1988
Dear Deenie,

Gabby called to say Roger told her you're in the hospital. Dear girl, let us know if you're all right and that sweet new baby, too. What can we do to help? Should we come riding to the rescue?

I'm doing fine as a grandma. I love wee Gideon as if he were my own—which he is, in a way.

> With much love and concern,
> Juneau

## ERIN

March 25, 1988
Dear Gabby, Dear Juneau,

I simply can't come to grips with Deenie being in the hospital because she's "having difficulties." Until St. George, I had this image of her that was part Molly Mormon, part Superwoman, ready for everything (remember her purse, full of items for every emergency?), and strong enough to take on any challenge. I still believe that's who she is at the core and that she'll come back to her family and to us stronger than ever. I'm joining my prayers to yours.

> Love,
> Erin

## WILLADENE

When Deenie first became aware of herself, she had the sensation of floating in a sea of nothingness. She thought she had opened her eyes, but there was no way to tell for certain. The world around was a dense blankness that no light penetrated.

*Am I dead, then?* she wondered. She was filled with both fear and anticipation. She twisted against the darkness, straining to discover the tiniest shaft of light. *Where's the family? All the dead ones? Where's Rauf?* A resurrected bark or even a ghostly tail-wag of welcome was the least she expected. If she expected anything at all.

*Not dead? Then what?* Deenie drifted on, too tired to care how long. *If you want me, you'll have to come and get me,* she thought to her kindred dead.

Something cold and hard pressed down on Deenie's chest, jarring her to her ragged senses.

"It's all right, Mrs. Rasmussen," a disembodied voice told her. "You're safe here." A warm hand rested on Deenie's shoulder as if to reassure her.

"Where am I?" Deenie croaked. The nurse held out a hospital mug of ice water. Deenie drank gratefully.

"You're in the hospital." The nurse put the mug within Deenie's reach.

"Am I dying?"

"No, dear."

"Did I have a heart attack?"

"No, but it certainly could have seemed like it," the nurse replied.

"Then what?"

"You'll have to discuss that with Dr. Greenwood. She'll be making rounds in about an hour."

"Dr. Slater's my doctor," Deenie protested.

"Not in this hospital," the nurse answered and hurried out the door.

In the days that followed, Deenie learned that Dr. Sally Greenwood, the head of her department and specialist in anxiety disorders and post-partum psychosis, was indeed her doctor in this hospital, University Hospital in Salt Lake City. In this wing, 5 West—the psychiatric wing—where Roger had left her, alone and vulnerable, in the care of strangers.

Deenie cried through her first week on 5 West, refusing to participate in group therapy or take any of Roger's phone calls until Dr. Greenwood confronted her. "This isn't a hideout, hotel, or spa, Deenie," she said.

"This is a place where people come to face their emotions and learn to deal with them. If you don't want to be here, you can leave."

"I can't go home like this!" Deenie snapped in shock. "I have a brand-new baby and children who need my care."

"Then stop feeling sorry for yourself, find out what you need to do to get better, and start doing it," Dr. Greenwood said.

Right then and there Deenie determined she would get better. It was a task, and Deenie knew she was good at tasks. So she engaged, learning the vocabulary of mental illness. She put *dissociation* at the top of her list of words she didn't like but needed to know and understand. She listed mental health techniques she needed to learn: red flagging flawed responses, reassigning meaning, and staying present. She slogged her way through group and private sessions with Dr. Greenwood, her notebook and pencil in hand, determined to find and log all the ingredients to her very own recipe for mental health.

There were two moments of blinding insight for Deenie in that difficult time. The first came during a grueling hour with Dr. Greenwood when Deenie told the truth about The Griff.

"Deenie, the best antidote for a distorted What If is a deep awareness of and appreciation for What Is. Look around you and recognize here and now. Be fully present with all your senses. What Is is where we live, Deenie. What If is a tool that can help us predict the possible consequences of our actions to keep us safe and on the right track. The Griff is a natural part of you that has gotten out of control. Rein him in with a good dose of What Is."

"You mean like count my blessings?"

"It's as good a place as any to start," Dr. Greenwood said, smiling.

That evening Deenie wrote ten copies of a note to herself and posted them around her room. They read, "When What If gets out of control, slap him upside the head with WHAT IS!"

The second insight came when she confided to Gabby on the phone that she didn't know which of the many versions of herself she'd confronted in the hospital was the real Deenie. Gabby responded, "While you are finding out who you are, my dear, don't forget to whom you belong. You have a Heavenly Father who loves you."

That night Deenie taped up a second set of ten notes reading "I belong to my Father in Heaven, and He loves me."

With her emotions balanced by medication and new insight, Deenie made great strides toward finding herself during her last week at University Hospital. The one thing she couldn't get past was her anger at Roger. Intellectually, she accepted that he'd had no choice other than to admit her, but she'd felt so abandoned when she'd first awakened in her hospital room, terrified she was dying with no one who loved her there for comfort.

Nevertheless, a morning came when she awoke longing to see her family and hold her dear abandoned baby in her arms. She was ready to go home.

# Chapter 5

WILLADENE
April 11, 1988
Dear Friends,

Roger tells me you've all sent notes and made phone calls while I've been ill. I'm sorry I wasn't in any condition to acknowledge them.

In case you've been wondering (of course you have!), I've been in 5 West of University Hospital in Salt Lake City. The psychiatric wing. I packed my bags for perfect motherhood and ended up a danger to both my baby and myself. But with the help of an excellent doctor and some equally excellent medications, I am on my way to recovery or, more accurately, discovery of where I've been and how I got there.

I am becoming comfortable with the boogie words of my mental illness: postpartum psychosis, clinical depression, and generalized anxiety disorder. Street phrases are easier: Nuts. Loony Bin. Around the bend. They may not be medically accurate, but they are spot on when it comes to describing the situation.

The loony bin, by the way, is a much nicer place than you would imagine. Most of the patients I met openly acknowledged why they were admitted. They were dealing with their problems and helping others do the same. From their point of view, it's the folks outside who are nuts—and don't know it—that are really scary. Food for thought.

Speaking of food, we have a culinary fairy in our neighborhood. Meals magically appear in the kitchen or on the doorstep with no visible human transport. The only people who bring food *and* stay to chat are NeVae, Aunt Stell, Pat, and Pat's mother, who is Grandma Streeter to all of us. Sunny, too. She's just glad to see me again, bless her. And my sweet Evvy at last accepts me as another person in the house to love her. That's progress.

The other children do their best, but it's been hard on them. Roger's parents, NeVae and Will, are back from their stay in Bert's apartment near UCLA. (NeVae loved the warmth. Will took an instant deep dislike to Bert's then-boyfriend.) They check in every day in the most matter-of-fact way, bringing encouragement and hope. But my mother and dad seem genuinely frightened to be around me, and Roger and I are distant strangers, even though we are going to therapy with Dr. Sally Greenwood once a week.

The day came and went when he was to have defended his dissertation. I know he must have postponed it, because he was home all day. He didn't mention it, and neither did I. He still sequesters himself in his study—not wanting to bother me, he says.

I have moved Evvy into my room so that she's near me all the time. Being able to look at her without fear of harming her is tremendously fine.

Juneau, I often think of how you described your feelings after losing Max, as though you had packed your bags for Hawaii and ended up in Peoria. I know how that feels firsthand now and wonder how many trips there will be to that destination for each of us.

I'm praying for a level section in this roller-coaster ride. Pray with me, please.

Deenie

ERIN

April 25, 1988
Dear Deenie,

What a brave woman you are, Deenie. Brave and strong and courageous. I hope you know that if we aspiring COBs lived in Wellsville, we'd be among those who walk through your door—and stay to visit. Whatever you've gone through, you are our Dear Deenie, and we love you.

Your Erin

## JUNEAU

April 27, 1988
Dear Deenie,

I knew you'd come through all right! After all, you're a COB (on the road to becoming, at least)!

Love,
Juneau

## JUNEAU

Juneau was proud of the way her sixteen-year-old daughter took over being a mom to Gideon. For the first three months, Misty made her way uncomplainingly through endless diapers and even pulled some all-nighters when he had colic. She stuck with nursing him despite swollen, tender breasts and sore nipples. She came home straight from school to take over from Juneau, his bassinet by her side as she did her homework. Often she sang the old lullabies Juneau had sung to her and Nicole when they were tiny.

But it didn't last. One day Juneau discovered her huddled in Greg's recliner with Gideon in her arms, her face buried in his blankets. She was sobbing.

Juneau hurried over to stroke her hair. "What's the matter, honey?"

Misty raised her head, tears dripping off her chin. "You don't want to know, Mom," she said.

"Maybe I can help," Juneau offered. "Maybe it's just a case of baby blues."

Misty shook her head, gulping back sobs. "It's a case of baby regrets. I wish I'd never had Gideon."

Juneau's shock must have shown, because Misty broke into fresh sobs. "I love him, Mom, I do. But my life is over. All I do any more is go to school and tend Gideon."

Juneau had a moment of wishing wisdom could come to young girls before a baby was involved. While she was formulating some kind of advice, Misty went on. "Mom," she said, "what would you think of my offering him for adoption now? Dad gave me really good advice before Gideon was born, but I didn't want to listen then."

The thought of giving up Gideon made Juneau's throat close. She could barely breathe, much less talk. Greg had been right. Losing him would be like losing Max all over again. No, much worse. Max had never been a reality.

She took a couple of deep breaths and then said, "Have you thought this through, Misty?"

"As much as I ever think things through. I know I'm flaky. I flap around doing my own thing and never think of the consequences. Gideon would be better off without me. He needs a family."

"He has a family," Juneau said. "Remember what Nicole said?"

Misty paused. Her next words caught Juneau completely off guard. "I want to go away, Mom. Maybe go live with Grandpa and Grandma for a while. They've invited me, you know. Gideon, too. But their motor home would be too crowded with Gideon. That's why I was thinking of adopting him out."

*Oh yes,* thought Juneau with a surge of fury. Traveling with the Peripatetic Paulsens while they worked on the latest installment of their popular mystery series would suit restless Misty just fine. She forced herself to speak calmly. "I think we need to have a family council about this. Make the decision together. We all love Gideon, you know."

Misty sighed and jiggled the baby, who had awakened and was beginning to fuss. "I know." She looked up at Juneau. "Maybe you should be the ones to adopt him."

Juneau nodded. "Maybe we should."

May 7, 1988
Dear COBs, both senior and aspiring,

Presto, change-o! One minute I'm a grandmother, and now I'm a mother. Well, not quite officially. There is some sort of hang-up because Misty won't name the father—either possibility. Whoever he is, he needs to sign off, too, before we can adopt Gideon and then have him sealed to us. For now, Greg and I are the baby's legal guardians.

I can't say becoming Giddy's guardians was a painless transition, but Misty didn't hesitate when it came to the final signing. Now she's off to join my parents in Oregon. She wouldn't consider staying even until the end of the school term.

I'm left with Guilt for company. Is it my fault Misty's life has taken the course that it has? Or can I run it back a couple of generations and blame it on Disappearing Letitia, my great-grandmother, who skipped out on her own grave?

With Giddy dependent on my care, that old bugaboo of writing vs. mothering has reappeared. My writing suffers, but no way can I give it up. The man named Clyde in Mrs. Jarvis's ongoing writing class told me I have a case of "divine discontent," which he says is what drives people to create. Maybe he's right.

Right now I have to go be Mama. Giddy wants his bottle.

Love,
Juneau

P.S. I'm typing this on Greg's computer. He predicted I would eventually capitulate and give it a try. And that I'd like it. He was right on both counts.

## ERIN

In late May, Caitlin surprised Erin with an invitation to the McGee house to meet Charlotte. Erin hesitated to accept because Andrew had specifically asked her not to go there. Caitlin waved away Erin's concerns. "That was then; this is now. Bring the kids."

"How do I explain who they're going to meet?"

Caitlin grinned. "Just tell them they're going to meet my mother."

Erin was nervous when she drove up to the McGee house, and Kayla and Mark were full of a wild, expectant energy. An expression, Erin thought, of the feelings she was trying to hide.

Caitlin came out to greet them as Erin pulled her car under the porte cochere. She hugged the kids and then led the way through a room full of beautiful antiques, up a wide, curving staircase, and into what she called the family room. There was a mini home theater and upholstered seating at one end of the room, a jukebox, a refreshment center, and a billiard table at the other. The floor was a checkerboard of black and white granite.

As they entered, a plump woman dressed in navy sweats rose with the help of a cane. She looked completely ordinary, quite out of place in the amazing room, Erin thought. Her black hair was pulled back in a ponytail, her cheeks were flushed either by nature or illness, and her dark eyes glinted with good humor.

Caitlin introduced Erin to Charlotte, who gave her a warm hug and said, "Call me Lottie." Then Caitlin presented the children. "Kayla, Mark, this is my mother, Mrs. McGee."

Kayla took Charlotte's hand with a perplexed frown. "You don't look like Caitlin," she said. "You don't have red hair."

Charlotte chuckled. "No, dear. Caitlin got her red hair from her daddy."

"Caitlin looks like my mommy. She's my 'nother mother."

"She does, indeed."

"This is my little brother, Mark." Again Kayla paused, frowning slightly. "He looks like my daddy. I look like my mommy."

"Yes, you do." Charlotte smoothed Kayla's red curls. "You are a very grown-up little girl, Miss Kayla. Would you like to sit here and talk with us ladies or check out the toys over there with Mark?" She pointed to a play area set up on a brightly colored rug.

"Over there."

Erin watched the kids get settled and then sat down beside Charlotte on the leather couch. It didn't take long for her to see why Caitlin loved her stepmother. Charlotte was down to earth, easy to talk to. They were chatting away like old friends when a young Hispanic woman entered the room with a tray of hors d'oeuvres for the ladies and crustless PB and J sandwiches cut into shapes for the kids.

"This is Theresa Morales. She's the one who keeps the household going. I don't know what I'd do without her." Charlotte patted Theresa's back and smiled fondly.

Theresa put the food on the coffee table where they could serve themselves and set out an assortment of beverages. Then she turned to Charlotte. "By the way, Andrew called. He's going to stop by before he drives out to the site in Prior Lake."

Erin made an exasperated sound. "Sorry, but that's too much of a coincidence. First I bump into Andrew at the St. Paul Grill, and now he just happens to come home when the kids and I are here? I'm being set up."

"My fault, dear," Lottie said with a guilty grin. "I knew how badly he wanted to meet Kayla and Mark."

Erin barely had time to compose herself before Andrew came into the room like a gust of wind. He bent to kiss Lottie and then said, "Hi, girls. Are you having a nice lunch?"

Erin started to answer, but Andrew's attention had already shifted to the kids, who were still playing in the toy corner. His expression was similar to those Erin had seen on the faces of clients holding some item they'd wanted for years. *He's hungry for grandchildren!* she thought.

Lottie touched Andrew's arm to get his attention. "Do you have time for a sandwich?"

"I should probably get going."

"Oh, sit down," Charlotte said with an indulgent smile. "You have time. Kayla, Mark, come meet Caitlin's daddy, Mr. McGee."

Kayla stared unabashedly at Andrew as she approached. "Your hair is funny colored."

"Yes," he said, laughing. "It used to look like your mommy's and Caitlin's, but I'm older than they are, and it's getting white."

Kayla continued her study. "Caitlin looks like you. My mommy looks like you, too."

Erin felt a shiver run up her spine. It had been a mistake to come, but she'd thought Andrew wouldn't be here.

Andrew didn't seem disturbed at all. "Yes, she does, doesn't she?"

"I look like Mommy and Caitlin," Kayla said.

Fearing what Kayla might say next, Erin introduced Mark. "Andrew, this little guy is my son, Mark. He's two and a half. Mark, this is Caitlin's daddy."

"Put 'er there," Mark said, holding up his little hand up for a high five.

Andrew obliged, grinning. Then he said, "What's that in your ear?"

Mark frowned and tugged his earlobe.

"Come here, and let me get it out for you." Andrew touched Mark's ear. When he pulled back his hand with a flourish, it held a quarter. "My goodness! How do you think this got there?"

He handed the quarter to a puzzled but delighted Mark.

"Do that to me!" Kayla demanded, and Andrew complied.

Watching them, Erin remembered that her mother had said he'd done a coin trick to amuse her when they'd first met, standing in line at a concession stand on Harriet Island.

The old trick was still a reliable icebreaker, because now both Mark and Kayla chattered easily with Andrew as they ate their sandwiches. But Erin's relief was short-lived. When Kayla finished her sandwich and soda, she turned back to the earlier subject. "Mark doesn't look like us. He looks like daddy," she said.

"Your daddy must be a handsome man," Andrew replied.

"He has blond hair like Mark. My mommy's daddy has hair like yours. He's a red-headed Catholic boy."

Erin gasped, and Andrew's jaw dropped. "Where did you hear that?" Erin demanded. "From Grams?"

"Nooooo. You said it. You were talking to Daddy in the bedroom."

Erin covered her eyes, wishing she could drop through the floor and down into the earth. Clear to China, if possible.

"What's a Catholic?" Erin heard Kayla ask, her child's voice full of innocence.

"That's a question I can answer," Andrew said with a slight grin. "There are many different churches in the world, Kayla. The Mormon church is one of them. The Catholic church is another. You and your family belong to the Mormon church. Caitlin and Charlotte and I belong to the Catholic church."

Kayla thought for a moment and broke out into a delighted giggle. "Then you're a red-headed Catholic boy!" She paused, considering, and then asked solemnly, "Are you my mommy's daddy?"

In the same second that Erin comprehended Kayla's words, Andrew J McGee said, "Yes. As a matter of fact, I am."

JUNEAU

Juneau had a major Guilt attack the first night she went to Bob's Big

Boy with the man named Clyde after Mrs. Jarvis's writing class. She'd been eager to talk to him ever since he teased her about having "divine discontent" the night before Misty left for Oregon. They hadn't been able to discuss it at the time, and she'd been mulling it over the whole week.

"I've been thinking about 'divine discontent,'" she said after they'd placed their orders. "Where does the expression come from?"

"Charles Kingsley," Clyde said. "You probably encountered him somewhere along the line in your studies as an English major."

She nodded. "I recall he was a British novelist and sometime poet. But that's about all."

"The full quotation is 'To be discontented with the divine discontent, and to be ashamed with the noble shame, is the very germ and first upgrowth of all virtue.'"

"Nice," Juneau commented. "So he was writing about the creative arts?"

"Haven't a clue." Clyde grinned. "That's my own application. I figure anything that pushes anybody to produce something is a gift from God—and thus the 'divine discontent.'"

Juneau would never have guessed Clyde was a religious man. Some of his comments in class had been decidedly cynical, and she'd thought he was an atheist or an agnostic at best. It was interesting to see this new side of him.

The waitress brought their orders, and after she left, Clyde said, "Tell me about your new role as mother of your grandson."

"I just happen to have pictures." She grinned as she took them from her purse.

By the time they left the cafe, it was 11:15 P.M. Juneau was aghast. How had the time gone so quickly? They had gotten into a literary discussion as Clyde slowly consumed his hamburger, and even into quotes from Gilbert and Sullivan operettas, which they discovered they both had a passion for. Clyde knew all the words to "I've Got a Little List," among others, and Juneau quoted "Things Are Seldom What They Seem." They'd laughed a lot. And then it was 11:15. Juneau rehearsed excuses all the way home. She found Greg in the computer room, lost in some kind of intricate program. He looked up when she greeted him, saying, "A little late, aren't you?"

"Yeah, a little."

"I'm glad you're home safe." He returned to his work, and after a moment she left, her evening with Clyde filed away with the rest of her Guilty Secrets.

# Chapter 6

WILLADENE

Deenie paused, clothespin in hand, to turn her face to the sun. Being home was as wonderful and as terrible as Dr. Greenwood had warned her it might be. There were troubling days like last Sunday, when Roger came home to tell her she had been released from her position as Spiritual Living teacher without prior notice. But there were also days like today, when doing something as simple as taking the wash off the line filled her with deep contentment.

"Deenie," Roger called from the back step, "your mom and Aunt Stell are here to visit. I'm running out to the farm. I'll take Evvy with me."

Mother and Aunt Stell, together? Deenie's eyes narrowed with suspicion. Something was up. She finished taking the clothes off the line and carried the basket into the house. At the door of the family room, she heard Stella say to her mother, "Tell her the truth. You have to."

"What truth, Mama?" she asked as she joined them, dumping the clothes on the table for sorting.

Margaret glared at Stella. She grabbed a receiving blanket from the table and began to fold it. "Your Aunt Stella thinks talking over the day Sunny was born might be of some benefit."

Deenie froze, T-shirt in hand. "I don't see how," she said carefully.

"There are things we need to get out in the open," Stella insisted. "Starting with how you remember it, Deenie."

Deenie looked from her mother to her Aunt Stell. "You really want to know? It was the day I did something wrong that caused Sunny to be born mentally retarded. It was the day you stopped loving me."

"Oh, Deenie!" Margaret dropped the blanket she was folding, her face aghast.

"Told you," Stella said. She turned from Margaret to Deenie. "Start at the beginning, and tell us everything."

Deenie had never talked about that day. She wouldn't have then, either, except for the huge debt she owed Stella for recent loving care. She began in a flat tone. "I remember being excited at first. Mom was counting contractions, and I was feeding her ice chips and putting cool cloths on her forehead. I felt so grown up, so much a part of something important. Like my being there really mattered. Then things went wrong." She looked at Stell. "You said it was taking too long. Then you left, and I was alone with Mom doing the long-stroke massage like I'd been taught . . ."

Deenie gripped the T-shirt in her hands. "Then Mom made this terrible sound. I pulled back the drape over her knees, and there was blood everywhere. I remember thinking I'd done something wrong, but I didn't know what. After that everything went so fast. The ambulance came and took her away, and I waited for someone to tell me what was happening, but no one did." She glanced up. "And then everyone started disappearing."

"Disappearing?" Margaret flashed a startled look at Stella and then back to Deenie.

"You were gone," Deenie said simply. "Dad came home to say I had a sister, but she'd been taken away. To Primary Children's Hospital. The next morning the boys left to stay with friends, and I was sent to Aunt Stell's. But then Grandma Stowell picked me up after school one day and told me I had to stay with her because Aunt Stell had to help with Sunny until you were ready to come home.

"I waited for you at the window every day. When you did finally come home, everything had changed. Aunt Stella wasn't your best friend anymore, and I wasn't your best girl. That's when I decided the only thing I could do was be the best big sister any little girl could ever have. So I did."

She picked up a pair of jeans to fold. "That brings us up to date. Personally, I don't feel any better," she said acidly. "Do you?"

"That's not all that happened," Margaret objected. "You tell her the rest, Stella. You remember parts that I never will."

"If that's what you want, Maggie. But Deenie already knows more than she thinks she does." Stella turned to Deenie. "You said it yourself.

I went to Salt Lake City because your mother was wearing herself out going back and forth from a relative's house to the neonatal unit. Even with me there to spell her, it was too much. The strain of not knowing whether Sunny was going to live or die, of not getting enough sleep and not eating properly on top of that difficult birth took a huge toll on your mother's physical—and mental—health.

"By the time Sunny was well enough to come home, things had gotten so bad for your mother that she had to be admitted to LDS Hospital. After a while she improved physically, but it was clear she was lost in some dark place emotionally. Finally they transferred her to the psychiatric unit—"

"Mom!" Deenie saw the truth in her mother's face, in the tears shimmering in her eyes.

"—where she was treated with electroconvulsive therapy for deep depression. It worked, and she came home."

"Shock therapy? Mama!" Deenie grabbed her mother's hands.

"You said everything had changed when I got home," Margaret said slowly. "The truth is, I'd changed. The . . . treatment . . . helped, but it left gaps in my memory. I didn't know where the bread pans were stored or how to write out a check at the grocery store."

"Or where you and I always sat at story time," Deenie said with sudden understanding. "Or how to double-braid my hair . . ." Her voice trailed off.

"I remembered I had a daughter I loved, but I didn't remember the details that made our relationship precious." Margaret paused. "Stella kept pushing me to tell you the truth, but then Sunny had a crisis—"

"And I got sick and had to stay at Grandma Hunter's."

Margaret took Deenie's face in her hands and met her eyes directly. "You didn't do anything wrong that day, Deenie. I have never blamed you for what happened to Sunny. Not ever. I loved you then, and I love you now."

"But, Mama," Deenie said, pulling back, "if you didn't blame me, why have you been so . . . so . . ." Deenie couldn't find the words to say what she meant.

"Hard on you?" Stella filled in.

Deenie nodded.

"I didn't want you to ever go through something like that. I thought if I could make you strong enough . . ." Margaret's voice trailed off.

"Didn't work, did it?" Deenie stood and began pacing. "What about you and Aunt Stell? Why did you two stop being friends? Was it because of Sunny?"

"No! The doctors said that even if I had been in the hospital earlier, it probably wouldn't have made a difference for Sunny."

"Then why?"

"Yes, Margaret." Stella's voice was intense. "Why did we quit being friends?"

"Because you were there!" Margaret burst out. "You saw it all. You were the one who wiped the spit off my chin, who took care of me when I couldn't take care of my most basic needs. Every time I see you, I remember every horrible, humiliating, painful moment of it."

"But that's not what I see when I look at you. I see my sister-in-law, my friend, a remarkable woman I would do anything for. No matter what."

"Regardless, I feel *less* whenever we're together."

Stella gave her hallmark snort of disgust. "Well. Get over it!"

Margaret started to say something but hiccupped hugely instead. Deenie and Stella burst into laughter and after a moment, Margaret joined them. The sounds cleansed the room and opened their hearts to one another in a way they hadn't experienced for years.

ERIN

June 7, 1988

Dear Gabby, Deenie, and Juneau,

Remember that old TV program, "Kids Say the Darndest Things"? Well, you should have been flies on the wall the day I took the kids to meet Caitlin's stepmother, Charlotte (Lottie). Things went well until Andrew showed up. Right away, Kayla noticed that he looks like Caitlin, who looks like me. She kept asking questions, and Andrew kept answering them. Before I could blink, Andrew had announced he was my father and Kayla had claimed him as her Grandpa Andy!

I knew Kayla and Mark would blurt it all out the next time they saw The Women, so I made an end run and told Mom first. She thought it was funny! Maybe having Jake in her life has changed her perspective. Grams reacted totally out of character, too. She's seventy-seven and doesn't have the energy or will to be angry at him anymore.

Now Kayla is pushing for a family get-together with "Grandpa Andrew," "Grandma Lottie," and all the other Grands. Mark, who follows her lead in everything, has joined the chorus. I don't know whether to laugh or cry.

One final thing. I found out that Caitlin can't have children. She didn't say why, but it makes me wonder if that's part of the reason she doesn't settle down in a relationship. She dates a lot, but no one special.

So that's the news from Lake Wobegon. Hopefully, there won't be any new shocks or revelations for quite some time. And no, I have no intention of planning a big family gathering.

Your Erin

## JUNEAU

Gideon was a joy. And a challenge. By the time he was seven months old he was scooting himself around the house, examining at close hand every object in his world. He unloaded kitchen cabinets and bureau drawers. He pulled books from shelves within his reach and giggled with pleasure at the nice sound the pages made when he tore them out. He sampled Philip Atwater's dog food.

When Juneau had been a new mother with Misty, she'd been too nervous to enjoy her baby. Then, with Nicole coming along two years later, she'd been overwhelmed. Mothering Gideon was completely different. She could relax and let herself enjoy his baby company and the wonder of seeing the world through his brand-new eyes. She loved his giggle and the way a dimple flirted in his left cheek. She let herself imagine a future with him always in it.

Then one day a young man came to her door. He was as tall and skinny as a broomstick. At first, Juneau thought he was a will-work-for-food candidate, going door to door for handouts. He wore knees-out jeans and the remains of a blue shirt. His long blond hair was pulled back into a ponytail held in place by a red bandanna, and his beard was unkempt. Juneau remembered her dad describing someone in one of his books as looking like "ten miles of bad road." That description certainly applied to this young man.

"Mrs. Caldwell?" he asked politely.

"Yes." The one nice thing about him was his eyes, blue with heavy dark lashes. She decided not to be alarmed by his presence.

"I'm Trace," he said. "Trace Cassatt."

She waited.

He waited.

"Am I supposed to know you?" she asked.

He shifted his feet. "I thought Misty might have mentioned me."

"You know Misty?"

"I used to." He gazed steadily at her. "I think I'm Gideon's father."

Juneau stared, wishing she'd never opened the door. Wishing Philip Atwater would chase the stranger off her step. But the dog merely wagged his tail. She opened the door a little wider. "Maybe you'd better come in. Would you like a glass of water? Or orange juice?"

"I just want to see Gideon," Trace said. "Then I'll go."

"He's napping," Juneau said shortly. "Who told you his name?"

"Misty. She wrote to me that she had a baby."

"So what makes you think you're the father?"

Trace hesitated. "Do you really want me to tell you, ma'am?"

She shook her head and then waved at the sofa. "Maybe we should take time to get acquainted before Gideon wakes."

"I'd like that, ma'am," he said, sitting down.

She took the armchair across from him. "I must say you're something of a surprise, Trace. Misty wouldn't give us a clue as to who . . ." She'd been going to finish with "the two possibilities are," but maybe he didn't know there'd been another besides himself. She left her sentence dangling.

"I'm sorry," he said. "I shouldn't have sprung myself on you. But I want to do right by Gideon."

Juneau considered that. "How old are you, Trace?"

"Nineteen, ma'am."

"What do you do for a living?"

"Not much of anything," he admitted. "I've painted a few houses. Dug ditches. Mixed cement. That kind of stuff."

"So how do you intend to contribute to Gideon's keep?"

"I'll get a job," he said. "Permanent."

She wondered if he had any decent clothes for interviews, but that wasn't something she could ask him yet. "You said your last name is Cassatt? Like the painter?"

He nodded. "Mary Cassatt. No relation, but I like her paintings, especially the ones with children in them."

Despite herself, Juneau found she liked this raggedy young man who sat stiffly, that traitor Philip Atwater curled up at his feet. She was about to ask him where he'd met Misty when a cry came from Gideon's room.

Trace stood up immediately. "He's awake."

"I'll get him," Juneau said. "It'll take a few minutes. He probably needs changing."

Gideon's cheeks were rosy from his nap, and his blond hair slightly damp, sticking up in spikes. His dimple danced as he crowed at her. She picked him up, burying her nose in his neck, breathing in the dampness, the scent of baby powder with a slight overlay of wet diaper.

How dare that ratty kid out there say Gideon was his? There was no resemblance between the two of them. He was hers, and hers alone.

Quickly she changed his diaper and then pulled on a tiny pair of striped denim overalls, one of the gifts Misty had received at the shower Marisol gave for her. "Here he is," Juneau announced, carrying him into the living room.

Trace's face lit up. His eyes were tender. "Hi, guy," he said softly.

Gideon regarded him solemnly for almost a minute. Then he giggled and reached out. Trace took him, his arms curving as if he were used to holding babies. "Hello, Gideon," he said. "Hello, son."

"How can you know?" Juneau's voice was resentful.

"I just know." Trace let Gideon lean back a little so the two of them could survey each other. Then he began to sing.

Little boy, little boy,
Does the sun rise for you?
Little boy, little boy,
Is the moon for you, too?
The stars in the skies
Are just for your eyes
The whole world is yours,
Little boy, little boy.

"I'm not familiar with that song," Juneau said. "It's nice."

"Thank you, ma'am," Trace said. "It's one of mine."

Gideon, visibly enchanted by the melody, reached out a pudgy hand to touch Trace's cheek. The gesture, simple and sweet, made Juneau want to weep.

# *Chapter 7*

JUNEAU

June 29, 1988

Dear Ladies,

You'll never guess what's happened! Gideon's father showed up, Trace by name. I called Misty, and she confessed that he really is the father. She said she told us there were "two possibilities" because she didn't want us going after him. She likes him, she says, and she knew that he'd want to help out. Why that wasn't all right with her, she didn't say. Misty the Mysterious. Misty the Obtuse.

One thing I know: Trace is Gideon's father. He has a dimple just like Giddy's in his cheek. I didn't notice it at first, because he was sporting a shaggy beard. But it was unmistakable after he shaved. He's stated his intention to be part of Giddy's life and help with his support—on what he makes as a fry cook at McDonald's!

When Greg heard that, he huffed and puffed. On first meeting Trace, he said he'd like to kick his backside from here to Las Vegas. But the gentle guy grows on you, and Greg rather surprisingly asked if he'd like to apply for a job that was open in the media room at the university! I have the feeling that's the moment when Trace became part of our family.

Misty seems happy with my parents. They say she's going to school regularly and keeping up with her homework. She even goes to church with them. Greg has made noises about putting through adoption proceedings now that Gideon's father has shown up. But Misty says she doesn't want to do it just yet. Do you think she might be aiming to get together with Trace? I admit to having mixed feelings about that.

As for Nicole, she and Beto have decided they are both going to medical school so they can really contribute something to the people of Africa when they go there as a nun and a priest. What can I say?

One more thing. My niece Rhiannan, my brother Flint's daughter, called to say she'd love to visit in early August before she leaves for a BYU semester abroad in London. She's such a darling girl, and I'm really looking forward to having her here.

You just never know what's around the corner, do you?

Love,
Juneau

WILLADENE
June 1, 1988
Dear COBs,

*Can she bake a cherry pie, Billy boy, Billy boy?*

Yes, I can bake a cherry pie! But I can't make Roger feel loved enough to move back into our room.

I can build a campfire from scratch, too, but I can't make Beth feel like we're still a family or convince Evvy I'm the mommy. Some days I think it would be easier to cross the plains than get my life into order. Putting things right with my mother has helped, but it's no magic bullet where the rest of my life is concerned. I can't force myself to go back to church, either. I'd rather ford the Sweetwater or pluck a chicken than face the questions and censure.

Right now, life seems darn hard! And no, Juneau, you never know what's around the corner or over the horizon.

Deenie

When Deenie repeated the same litany in her next joint session with Roger and Dr. Greenwood, she was faced with crisp counsel rather than pity. Dr. Greenwood sent her and Roger home with therapy journals to keep and share and another assignment—to do whatever it took so that Roger felt comfortable sleeping in his own bed.

Gabby was equally unsympathetic when Deenie reiterated her fear of going back to church. "There is power in obedience, Deenie," she said.

"Get your back to the bench, no matter how you feel about it, and keep doing it until it starts to feel right again." Deenie did.

The next step was starting family counseling. The first session including the kids didn't go well, but they kept at it. Deenie decided that getting your heart right with your family and with God was indeed like crossing the plains. Once you got headed in the right direction, you had to keep putting one foot in front of the other, no matter what obstacles rose up on the horizon.

## ERIN

June 25, 1988
Dear Friends,

I couldn't resist sending you a photo of my little figure skater! See that huge smile? That's the way Kayla always looks at the rink, unless she's concentrating. Or picking herself up off the ice!

Part of the reason she has so much fun in class is her great teacher. Whitney has an unending supply of tricks and techniques to help her kiddies have fun and feel confident while learning. By the way, the first thing these little skaters learn is how to fall and how to get back up—their biggest concern! To my surprise, they learn to jump right off the bat, starting with bunny hops, which Kayla loves. She insists on wearing to class the dress Mom made her, even though she wears a jacket over it.

Mark's got the bug, too. He's never happier than when Cory takes him and Kayla to Family Skate. Cory holds Mark in front of him and pushes him along so he feels like he's really skating. I tried getting on the ice once, and once was enough—I'm happy being the cheering section. Cory doesn't need three novice skaters to take care of!

Your Erin

## JUNEAU

Rhiannan arrived in late August, as fresh and full of promise as a rainbow after a storm. She had long, glossy black hair and sparkling dark eyes, inherited no doubt from her mother Valerie's one-fourth Cherokee lineage, and her lips curved naturally upward in a smile. Juneau gathered her happily into their extended family and watched Trace, whom she'd invited to dinner, slide into infatuation.

"You have to tell us what you want to see while you're here," Juneau said over dinner.

"I'm looking at what I came to see," Rhiannan said, gazing around the table.

"That can get dull pretty fast," Nicole said. "I was looking forward to going to our favorite theme park. We never get to go unless somebody comes and we take them."

"Well, I certainly wouldn't want to deprive you," Rhiannan said with a grin. "When do we leave?"


They went to everybody's favorite theme park on Saturday. Trace manned Gideon's stroller, and Rhiannan walked alongside, returning the smiles they got from friendly people who obviously assumed they were a happy little family. They all went first to the rides Gideon could enjoy before he got tired and fell asleep. He chortled with delight at the bright lights and music and bouncy little cars in which they rode. Later, when he finally nodded off, slumping down in the cushions of his stroller, Greg and Juneau took him over and let the young people go off by themselves to enjoy the magic of the park.

They bought cones and found seats in the welcome coolness of an ice-cream parlor. Greg sat down with a sigh. "Isn't it funny how things have worked out? I'm happier now than I've ever been. With our family, I mean. I wish Misty would be more a part of it, but I love being around all these young people. Rhiannan included." He paused for a lick of ice cream. "Would you say she's awakened Sleeping Handsome?"

"You mean Trace?" Juneau had been watching with interest Rhiannan's effect on the young man. When Rhiannan learned he played the guitar, she'd insisted on a family sing-along. They'd stayed up until the wee hours of the morning, singing and laughing. Since then, Trace had brightened, had begun to laugh and have fun. He had even bought a new shirt.

"I worry a little," Juneau said, "because Rhiannan has some of the qualities of Misty and Nicole—Misty to pick up lonely people and Nicole to do good. I think she's attracted to him, but I want it to be for the right reasons."

Greg bit the bottom out of his cone and, like a little kid, sucked out the melted ice cream. "She could do worse. Trace is a fine young man," he said. "A hard worker. They really like him in the media room. They've already put him over all the electronic equipment." He paused, looking at her. "I'd like to get him enrolled in classes. I know he can't hack the expenses yet, so I'd like to help him out."

"Like investing in something likely to bring major returns? It's fine with me."

"Thanks, Juney. I think it will be a great investment. " He grinned meaningfully. "Especially if there's a possibility Rhiannan might make him a real member of the family someday."

"I think you're jumping the gun, dear. Even if you're not, Rhiannan's leaving in a couple of weeks for her semester in London."

"But she'll be back in six months."

Before Rhiannan went home, the family had a chance to reprise their sing-along, this time for the whole ward at the annual "I Didn't Know You Could Do That" party. When Rhiannan saw the announcement about the party in the church bulletin, she suggested they work up a number. "Trace can do some guitar stuff—"

"And Rhiannan can do some piano," Trace said immediately. "She plays, you know."

That's how the Caldwez Family Players came into being. Rhiannan led them all—the Caldwells and the Sanchezes—in some playful numbers such as "The Old Family Toothbrush" and "On Top of Spaghetti," which were a hit with the audience. Then Trace did a totally insane song about Farmer Potter's pig, which involved grunts and snorts as well as thumps on the body of the guitar, which Gideon loved. He finished with "Little Boy," his own composition that he'd sung when he first visited Juneau and Greg's house.

They were the favorites of the evening, judging by the applause that followed. Trace and Rhiannan held hands as they took their bows, and Juneau noticed the look that passed between them. *Oh, boy*, she thought.

All too soon, they were at the airport saying their good-byes to the young woman they'd all grown to love. When her flight was called, Rhiannan hugged the family and then took off a colorful blue and silver scarf and wound it around Trace's neck. "Back in medieval times," she said, "a knight wore his lady's colors as he rode off into battle." In front of all of them, she gave him a long hug and a fervent kiss and then sprinted down the jetway to her plane.

Afterward, life in the Caldwell family seemed flat and dull. There was a lot of talk about "next time Rhiannan comes . . ." Trace, especially, seemed diminished. He was also afflicted with doubts.

"Juneau," he said one night after he'd been to dinner and was helping with the cleanup, "do you think I'm good enough for Rhiannan?"

"Whatever would make you think you wouldn't be?" she asked.

"She has so much to offer." His expression was troubled and earnest. "She's so pretty and smart and talented and all. The only thing I have is a guitar and a really thrashed car."

"Trace," Juneau said with feeling, "you have so much potential. I just know you're going to do really good things with your life."

Obviously moved, Trace replied in a ragged voice, "Thank you. You don't know how much that means to me."

"Well, you mean a lot to us," Juneau said, her own voice husky.

As if to prove what she said, Greg told Trace later that night that he and Juneau wanted to pay his college expenses for the coming year. "Just to get you started." Trace protested, wavered, and then accepted. Juneau caught a look in his eye that told her he was already making plans for the future.

After he'd left for his small rented room, Nicole hugged Juneau and Greg and said, "That's the very best thing you've ever done."

ERIN
> September 22, 1988
> Dear Gabby and Deenie, Dear Juneau,

> We've celebrated two milestones this month. First, Colleen's EJ

(named Erin Joy after me, you might remember) was baptized. Then Kayla Marie started kindergarten. Having both those things happen in the same month really made me realize how fast time is passing.

When Steve baptized EJ, I had a moment when I could see Cory baptizing Kayla and Mark. I think Cory was also looking ahead, because he squeezed my hand and smiled. The kids, five and a half and almost three, were most impressed by the way "Uncle Steve" put EJ under the water.

Kayla has been looking forward to kindergarten for months. The night before school started, we had a special family supper with The Women, Cory's folks, and Jake. After supper, Cory and his father, Skip, gave Kayla a blessing. A little later, Kayla got a call from her Grandpa Andrew, who wished her luck. She was so excited, it took forever for her to go to sleep.

After meeting Andrew at The Grill, I had this silly idea that he and I would spend time together, getting to know each other after all these years. Well, he's skipped right over me. The person he's interested in is Kayla. I admit to some resentment about that.

Anyway, when Kayla got on the bus the next morning, she looked so small and eager that I got all emotional. Mark tugged on my hand and said, "It's okay, Mommy. I'm still here!" Bless him. I was really glad that I'd managed my clients so I could spend time with him that day. While I was watching him climb on the wooden boat in our neighborhood park, I found myself wondering if it wasn't time for Cory and me to have another baby.

I haven't said anything to Cory about it yet. I'm waiting for the right time. His company, Behind the Scenes, is swamped, which means he is, too. He gives the Reagan presidency the credit for that—all those fancy parties the Reagans host have inspired the moneyed set to do the same.

I can't complain too much about his workload, because I'm pretty busy myself. I didn't start out to create a real business— I just wanted to earn some money of my own. I use what's left over after taxes and tithing to pay for skating lessons and such.

Juneau, here's a Guilty Secret for you: I have a savings account I haven't told Cory about. I started it when I got my first job at fourteen, so it's pretty substantial by now. I suppose I ought to tell him before we go to the temple in a couple of weeks. We're driving down to Chicago with Steve and Colleen for stake temple day.

Or maybe not.

Your Erin

P.S. Have you been reading the headlines about poor Princess Di and her floundering marriage? I'm fascinated by them—also a Guilty Secret, but not in the same category as my savings account.

October 26, 1988
Dear Friends,

Here's another Guilty Secret, worse than the other two I confessed to in my last letter: I'm a bad mother. Before you say that's hogwash, let me tell you what happened.

We had the Big Barn sale a couple of weekends ago. It was a roaring success. For the first time, Colleen and I agreed that it's reached its limits—we couldn't have handled one more customer or one more car. Paula Craig (my friend and business mentor) said that was good news. It meant we were at the point of needing to take the next step—having a spring Big Barn Sale. She repeated her offer to be our business coach, and we took her up on it.

To celebrate, Cory and I invited the Harringtons for a boat ride on the St. Croix the following Saturday. It was a gorgeous day, and the colors along the river were spectacular. We dropped anchor at a little island where we ate lunch and let the kids play on the beach. I was more relaxed than I'd been in weeks, and I honestly didn't realize that Kayla had lost her hat, leaving her scar unprotected. Worse still, I didn't think to keep reapplying that icky zinc-based sunscreen to it.

By the time we pulled into the marina, her scar was flaming red and she was in pain. I felt horrible about it but not as bad as when I took her to her doctor on Monday. He examined her scar and said, "Your mommy doesn't take very good care of you, does she?"

Talk about getting a whack up the side of the head! Cory says it's not all my fault, but I feel like I'm doing well as a business-woman and terrible as a mother. How do I get out of this funk?

Your Erin

WILLADENE
November 7, 1988
Dear Friends and Family,

Erin, that doctor should have his mouth stuffed with a dirty sock! As far as the funk goes, I think it's time for a reality check. Give yourself credit for all you're doing right. Make adjustments where you need to. And for Pete's sake, enjoy your wonderful life!

Did you notice the return address with Roger Rasmussen, Ph.D., on it? Yes, he's finally earned the right to use those initials after his name! We are all so proud of his academic accomplishment. We had a massive celebration that included everyone Roger has ever known, worked with, or taught.

Utah State University rewarded him with the offer of a full-time position on staff. He has decided to accept the job, but what he really wants is to find a position in educational administration. He has lots of ideas on how a school should be run, and he wants a chance to try them out.

Seeing how happy Roger is in having reached this goal makes me remember how mean I acted when he first made the plans for it. All I could see was my own side of the story. I never allowed myself to understand how important it was to him.

The kids have reached some milestones, too. Carl has his dri-ver's license and parental permission to start dating Ashley White, a girl from school. His favorite song is "Don't Worry, Be Happy," which he plays multiple times on hectic days. Do you suppose he's trying to tell us something?

Paul has completed his hunter safety course and has been rewarded with a handsome .22-caliber rifle from Grandpa Will.

When Beth declared that she expects a New Year's Day on the Rasmussen range with a rifle of her own when she turns twelve, Will looked as if he'd swallowed a frog. My dad stepped into the breach and invited Beth to go with us to the gun club in Logan. I think he was hinting that he'd like me to start going with him again. Mom says that if I get someone to take her place baby-sitting Evvy, she'll come with us.

Evvy's "doing a Giddy"—getting into every cupboard she shouldn't. Sunny calls her Itty Bitty Baby Crawly Bug. The boys have shortened it to Buglet, and she answers to that name. She's a joy.

I've done the most growing up in the family this year. Houdini never mastered a trick trickier than fitting the New Deenie into the old Deenie's life!

I've learned that mental illness is not a character flaw and that being grown up means accepting the responsibility for my own emotions, successes, and failures. I've learned that the light at the end of the tunnel is not an on-coming train and that there are angels among us, doing the work of our Heavenly Father in caring for His children.

Our family angel, Aunt Stella, is retiring from midwifery to work in hospice. How's that for courage? As she says, "I've helped a lot of people into the world. Now I'm helping them out." Makes sense, in a way.

The Rasmussen family wishes you a "perfect brightness of hope" for the future.

> Sincerely and dearly yours,
> Deenie

ERIN

November 11, 1988
Dear Gabby, Juneau, and Deenie,

Congrats to Roger and everyone else in your family for steps forward, large and small.

I think we've made a huge step forward ourselves. Remember how I said I wasn't going to entertain the McGees? I couldn't avoid it after Kayla and Mark invited Caitlin to Sunday dinner when she came to pick me up for an antiques run. Kayla begged her to bring Andrew and Lottie along, too. What could I do but say I'd love to have them?

Later, I caught Kayla on the phone inviting The Women, too. I grabbed the phone to tell Mom it was a mistake, but she said she'd be glad to come! Grams sniffed at the idea of being in the same room as That Catholic Boy, but she said she'd come if Jake did.

I was really nervous the day of the dinner, but Cory said not to worry. "Have some faith in your parents, Erin. They're both very fine people." Still, I had a bad moment when Mom and Andrew came face to face after so many years. They just looked at each other for the longest time, and then Lottie said, "Well, go ahead, hug her!" He did, but he was wise enough to only shake Grams's hand.

Lottie and Grams hit it off from the first, and Andrew delighted the kids with more magic tricks. Kayla chattered away with everyone—she was the magnet that brought us all together. You should have seen Mom and Andrew smiling at each other. It was like they agreed that if Miss Kayla Marie Johnson was the result of their fling and the years of drama afterward, it couldn't have been all bad.

I was really proud of how Grams handled a tough situation. She's used to sharing Kayla with Cory's parents, but seeing her great-granddaughter so taken with That Catholic Boy and Lottie was pretty hard on her. A couple of times, I saw Jake pat her hand to calm her down, but all in all, she conducted herself like a real lady.

When I was little, I used to dream of having big family celebrations with my mother and my father and all sorts of relatives. I guess dreams can come true! Or is it that miracles can happen?

Your Erin

## JUNEAU

Trace and Rhiannan had kept the mailman busy ever since she'd left for London in August, transatlantic phone calls being too expensive for both of them. Juneau could always tell when Trace had received a letter. He glowed. He shone.

Sometimes he read passages telling about Rhiannan's adventures in the big city and what theater productions she'd gone to. "I saw Agatha Christie's *Mousetrap*," she wrote in November. "I kept pinching myself and asking if this could really be me sitting in a theater in London, England, watching the longest-running show ever."

"She's flying home for Christmas," Trace reported happily one evening when he came to dinner. "She'll go to Texas first and then fly out here for the New Year's Day Rose Parade."

"That's great, Trace," Juneau said. "We'll all love to see her."

"Yeah," Trace said, almost shyly. "I was thinking maybe I could fly to Texas to greet her at the airport."

Juneau smiled at his eagerness but said, "Give her a few days with her family. Then you can greet her at LAX when she comes here."

Trace nodded. "I guess I'll have to be satisfied with that."

But he didn't get to do it. On December 21, 1988, someone blew up Pan Am Flight 103 over Lockerbie, Scotland. Rhiannan was one of the 259 passengers and crew members who went down with the plane.

# Chapter 8

ERIN

January 1, 1989

Dear Friends,

What a year 1988 was—so much that was good mixed with so much that was difficult. Gideon and Evvy, despite the circumstances of their births, are such miracles. The sudden passing of Rhiannan is so sad. Again, my deepest sympathy to you and your family, Juneau. Trace, too. Maybe it would help ease the pain if you created a place of remembrance for her, like you did Max.

On the good side, we had a surprise at Christmas this year, the very best kind. Mom and Jake are engaged! Jake gave this sweet little speech about how much he loved Mom and wanted to spend the rest of his life with her. He said he wanted to create a home for Grams, too. She started to cry then, poor dear. I think she was afraid of being left alone.

That's not the only change. Skipp's parents, Trina and Harold, are in their late eighties now and need to be near family. They'll be moving soon into a senior residence near our church in Bloomington. So next year there will be quite the gathering at our place.

I'm looking forward to sitting down with Cory to talk about what we want to accomplish in the coming year and create a plan for getting there. We've been doing this on New Year's Day for a few years now, and I love the time we spend together, dreaming about our future.

Wishing you love, peace, and the comfort of the Spirit this New Year.

Love,
Erin

JUNEAU

January 9, 1989
Dear Gabby, Deenie, and Erin,

I'm sorry I haven't been in touch since I called all of you about my niece Rhiannan's death in the Lockerbie crash. But there are no words. Not even anger at the hideous wretches who blew that airplane out of the sky can make a dent in our sorrow. Our beautiful, vital, joyful Rhiannan is gone. The only thing that enables us to go on is our belief that we will see her again.

We all went to the memorial service for her in Texas, except Gideon, who stayed with Marisol. Misty and my parents flew directly from Oregon to Texas, and the rest of us drove—Greg, Nicole, Trace, and I.

Trace is devastated. He says it's like the rest of his life has been. Just when things begin to look really good for him, the sky falls—only never as bad as this. I wish there were a class I could take in Mothering 401 because that's what he needs right now. That's what all of my family needs. What can I do to comfort them? How can I gather my children together as a hen gathers her brood under her wings, as it says in the scriptures?

Seeking solace,
Juneau

Juneau had never considered herself matriarch material, but with the death of Rhiannan in December, the role was thrust upon her. She remembered Gabby saying at one time that in a crisis, take care of yourself first so that you will be able to care for others. Like on an airplane, she reflected, where the flight attendant tells you that if the oxygen masks fall from overhead, you should first put on your own before attempting to assist others.

It was on the trip to Texas that Juneau realized her extended family was looking to her in this terrible crisis. She had pulled one person close to her, then another and another. She had wrapped her arms around them, held their hands, patted their backs. But where does the one who provided comfort look for consolation? She found herself returning again and again to the words from Handel's *Messiah,* parts of which the ward choir (that occasionally she was a part of) had rehearsed to sing at the

Christmas service. "He shall feed His flock, like a shepherd," she heard in her mind, the rich contralto of her friend Sharma coloring it with comfort as she sustained the legato of that passage. "And He shall gather the lambs with His arm, and carry them in His bosom."

Like the flock, she needed to be fed by the Savior's love so she could be the earthly bosom in which the young lambs would be carried.

Juneau also kept thinking of one of the Spiritual Living lessons she'd taught. The theme, that we gain experience and growth through adversity, had been supported by a quotation from Doctrine and Covenants 58:3–4: "Ye cannot behold with your natural eyes, for the present time, the design of your God concerning those things which shall come hereafter. . . . For after much tribulation come the blessings."

But what blessings could come from sweet Rhiannan's death? In the lonely reaches of her soul, Juneau cried out that it simply made no sense.

She'd been able to remain strong during the time in Texas. She'd had to. Flint had been too flattened by grief to comfort others. And though their parents were there, they perched on the periphery as always, flitting in to provide genuine succor and support—for a moment or two. And then they were gone.

The memorial service for Rhiannan was sweet. Her friends, celebrating what life she'd had, told funny and endearing stories of things she'd done. And touching stories of how she'd inspired them. Afterward the Relief Society fed them at the church; then they'd all gone home. There had been nothing to bury.

Back home, Juneau tried one day to express to Greg what she was feeling. "I'm trying to see a reason in all this," she said, "and find the blessings that are supposed to come after the tribulation."

He was sympathetic as he reached for her and drew her into his arms. "Juney, honey," he said, "you'll drive yourself crazy trying to make sense of it right now. Give it time." He kissed her cheek softly and released her. He'd meant to comfort her, but it didn't work. *Why does he always shut me down right when I need to talk?* Juneau thought.

Clyde didn't. In fact, he encouraged her to talk. "Mrs. Jarvis told us about your niece," he said as they found their way to their usual table in a corner of Bob's Big Boy after their Thursday night class. "I'm so sorry,

Juneau." He pulled out a chair for her to sit on. "We always think these terrible things happen to somebody else. It makes us aware of our mortality when it happens close to home."

"Yes," she said. "I guess we just have to accept it."

"No!" His voice attracted the attention of others, and he lowered it as he said, "Remember Dylan Thomas? 'Do not go gentle into that good night.'"

She looked up at him. "He was talking about one's own death, wasn't he?"

"Actually, about his father's impending death. But why not anybody's death?"

"But Rhiannan's already gone. What do I rage against now? How do I find a reason for her death?"

He sat down and leaned across the table. "Don't look for a reason for her death. Look for a reason for her life. What did she do to make a difference?" He reached out and took her hand. "You're a writer, Juneau. What can you say to those young people you write for about her life? How can you use it for good?"

Images of the time she'd spent with Rhiannan and the tributes given at her funeral flashed through her mind. "I don't know if I can do her justice. I'm not a good enough writer."

"You are, Juneau," Clyde said. "Or you can become one. If she inspired people, then use that inspiration."

For the first time since the terrible message had come, Juneau felt her spirits lift. She began to see beyond the tribulation. Maybe she could rise to the task.

When Clyde walked her to her car, she allowed him to pull her close in a warm hug, where she lingered a moment longer than was necessary.

## WILLADENE
January 10, 1989
Dear Friends,

Juneau, we were so sorry to hear about the loss of your dear niece. I feel for Trace, too. That dear young man. Sunny remembers about Max and worries that since Rhiannan's death you have "too much sad" in your life. I told her you had Gideon to help cheer you up and that made her glad.

Erin, I keep thinking about what the doctor said after Kayla's scar got sunburned on the boat trip. What could he have been thinking, to tell a child that her mother doesn't take good care of her? That kind of offhand comment can cause an ugly misperception that can fester and perhaps even turn into a tragedy.

Mom and I know that all too well. After so many years of being somewhat estranged, we're now developing a wonderful new closeness. The air has finally been cleared between Mom and Aunt Stell, too. The three of us are beginning to rediscover what was lost when Sunny was born. I've got more COBs in my life than I realized!

My brother, Nathan, took time this past Christmas to remind me that after the trials come the blessings. I told him that personally I'd take the blessings without the trials! But I am grateful for all the good that has come out of what we've been through this past year.

I told the whole family about the heart murmur, which recent tests confirm is still there. They were upset until I explained that as long as I take precautions against getting colds, the flu, or infections, I should be fine.

Roger and I have renewed our commitment to each other and to our marriage. We've been spending our Saturday mornings in the Logan temple. I can't tell you what it means to sit in the tranquillity of the celestial room with my husband next to me. We want nothing more than to have that same sweet spirit within the four walls of our home. Some days I think we're getting close.

Erin, give my congratulations to Jake and Joanna. I've always thought they belonged together. There's a wedding in the offing here, too. Pat has accepted a marriage proposal from the good sheriff! She and Dave will be sealed in the Logan temple on May 12 this year. They are insisting on a small dinner for family and friends after they get married. Who do they think they're kidding? The whole community is going to be in on it!

I've run out of news to tell, so I'll sign off.

Love to all,
Deenie

P.S. Erin, I've decided to let my hair grow longer. What do you think?

JUNEAU

January 15, 1989
Dear Friends,

Thank you for your sweet words of consolation. Deenie, tell Sunny that I do indeed have "too much sad" in my life but that Gideon does help me get over it. And Erin, I'm so grateful for your suggestion to create a place of remembrance for Rhiannan. I told the family what you said, and when we were all together for family home evening last Monday, we had a lovely ceremony and buried the scarf she gave to Trace right next to the little grave where Max's Christmas stocking is. It made us all feel better.

So life goes on, but I couldn't survive without you guys. Go, COBs! Which reminds me how awkward it is to address you as Senior and Aspiring. You know how they say if you want to be something, think of yourself that way. We'll know when we've really arrived and can dub ourselves officially then, but in the meantime, Deenie and Erin, let's just call ourselves COBs. Okay?

Much love,
Juneau

ERIN

January 27, 1989
Dear COBS!

Thanks for giving us permission to call ourselves COBs, Juneau. I feel more COBish already!

Deenie, what you wrote about your "new and improved" relationships was inspiring—and the part about going to the temple with Roger was very sweet. Makes me wish we had a temple in the Twin Cities so we could go more often. It's a long haul from here to Chicago, so we only go a couple of times a year.

About your hair. (How's that for going from the sublime to the ridiculous?) What do you mean by "long"? Long as in chin-length? Shoulder length? Down the middle of your back? All one length or layered? Bangs or no bangs?

My advice is that you shuck out the bucks to go to a very good stylist. Why? Because long hair not well cut looks just . . . long. Think shoulder length so you can wear it in a ponytail, with some layering to frame your face and give volume.

Mom and I are having fun talking wedding plans. She and Jake want just family for the ceremony itself and then an open house afterward. Mom thought it would be nice to have Bishop Harding officiate—she met him when Mark was blessed. Here's a surprise: Andrew and Lottie and Caitlin are coming!

At first, it seemed way too strange for Andrew to be at Mom's wedding, but I don't think there would even be a wedding if he and Mom hadn't spent time together, talking about everything that had happened between them. Who'd a thunk it?

Juneau, I've still been thinking about Rhiannan. My head is full of *Whys*. Why didn't the still small voice tell her not to board the plane? Why couldn't the plane have been grounded because of mechanical difficulties? And one big *What*. If there's a purpose to everything, what is God's purpose in this?

Is it awful that I'm feeling enormously grateful for the health and safety of my children? They're so full of energy and curiosity. They believe that there'll be a tomorrow—and that it'll be good. Kayla watched the women's Olympic figure-skating competition last year wearing her skates and the dress Mom made her. When Debi Thomas won her bronze medal, she said, "I'm going to get one of those." And she still believes it.

Mark is a chubby version of his daddy, who has already turned him into a football fan. Cory invited Steve to bring his family over this Super Bowl Sunday. You should have seen the guys and their boys sitting together on the big couch watching the game. Mark hoots and hollers just like Cory, and little Ricky even got into the spirit, waving his arms and legs like crazy and making excited sounds.

That dear Ricky. He's so lucky to have the parents he does. Ever since Ricky was born, Steve and Colleen have been doing the exercises suggested by the early childhood specialist they are working with. They've had to teach him how to do everything that other kids learn to do naturally—even how to turn his head to the source of a noise! They celebrate every step forward, no matter how small.

Colleen asked again the questions she'd asked me when Ricky was only a few months old. "Do you think they'll be friends when the grow up?" All I could say was, "I hope so." None of us knows what's just around the bend.

Love,<br>Erin

P.S. SOS to Juneau. The bishop called me to teach the Beehives in Young Women. I've never gotten along with teenagers, even when I was one. Help!

# Chapter 9

WILLADENE

The second Friday of April, Beth came home from what Deenie had thought was a tea party at the house of her new best friend, Danielle (Danny) Donovan, with alcohol-soaked threads hanging through both her newly-pierced ears.

"It was easy, Mommy," Beth said, primping in the mirror over the fireplace. "You freeze your ears with ice cubes and then poke them with a needle and thread. Now all I need is some little studs to keep the holes open until they heal. Totally wicked!"

Her unusual use of slang was followed by a request for pink lipstick to go with her shirt and permission to skip church on Sunday so she could spend the day with Danielle's family sledding on the last snow in the canyon.

"Our family goes to church on Sundays," Deenie said.

"I know, but it's just this once, and I really, really want to go. Pleeeease?"

"Doing what Heavenly Father wants us to do instead of what we want to do is part of growing up," Deenie replied firmly. "If you're grown-up enough for earrings and lipstick and making your own choices, you have to be responsible for those choices—not just to us but to God. We will be going to church on Sunday—and you will be going with us."

"Danielle said you wouldn't let me go," Beth yelled and ran for her room.

Deenie hadn't bothered to follow. There was no point in trying to talk to Beth in such a mood. Her daughter was rapidly becoming the "Bratty Beth" Paul had nicknamed her. *Okay,* Deenie thought, *so there aren't any guarantees. Can't there at least be a regular payoff for all this work?*

What Ifs and the resulting scenarios kept Deenie awake all night, so Roger kissed her cheek and told her to sleep in the next morning. He would go to the temple on his own. She was still struggling with her frustration over Beth when one of Evvy's distress howls propelled her out of bed.

She rescued her daughter from the crib and went downstairs. In the family room she found Beth curled up on the couch with ice packs on flaming, puffy ears, staring cross-eyed at her very first prepubescent pimple blossoming on the side of her nose.

"That is so gross," Paul said to Beth as he turned up the TV volume to drown out Evvy's howls. "But now your ears and nose match."

Just as Beth screeched a reply, and Carl yelled at them both to be quiet, Roger arrived home from the temple. He took in the scene, turned off the TV, and whistled to get everyone's attention. "We're going to start this day over, beginning with family prayer. Then I'll make the french toast. Carl, get some of Mom's homemade jam from the pantry. Paul, you have juice duty, and Beth can set the table."

"But my ears," Beth protested.

"They'll still be there when you get finished," Roger responded unsympathetically. "Hop to it."

It wasn't easily accomplished, but the children eventually obeyed. "Thanks," Deenie murmured to Roger as they sat down to eat.

After breakfast Deenie was trying to figure out how to separate Beth from the threads hanging out of her red and oozing ears without causing too much pain or another major scene when the doorbell rang. It was Roger's mother.

"Look what I found in my garden galoshes." NeVae held out a peculiarly noisy cardboard box as she stepped inside.

Immediately the whole family gathered to peer at the smelly, mewling ball of rough and wiry, tawny fur in the box. "He's another Dumped Dog, just like Rauf was, isn't he, Mother?" Roger asked.

NeVae nodded. "I thought you might be interested."

"You bet," Roger said. He picked up the puppy and displayed him to the family. "Look at his funny, stubby tail. And the size of his feet. He's going to be big!"

"How big?" Deenie asked suspiciously.

NeVae raised her eyebrows. "Let's just say if he were a horse he'd grow up to be a Clydesdale."

"Awesome!" said Carl.

"Totally!" Paul agreed, as Evvy screeched and strained toward the puppy from the high chair.

"Whoa," Deenie protested. "Clydesdales are fine in a barn, but I don't want one as a house pet!"

"You can't say no, Mom" Paul picked up the puppy and studied him face to face. "He's our dog. I know it."

Deenie gave him a long look and then sighed. "I guess we have a dog."

"All right, Mom," Carl whooped. Paul put the puppy on the floor, and the boys began trying out names again.

"Why, he's just a big old Pooh Bear," Beth said, watching the puppy's waddle from the hind end.

NeVae clapped with delight. "That's it, then. He's Winnie the Pooh Bear. And he's all yours. I knew you wouldn't be able to resist him." As she left, she called over her shoulder a cheerful invitation for dinner on Sunday.

The puppy began earning his keep immediately—Beth held him for comfort while Deenie removed the pus-logged threads from her ears and applied medicine to the wounds. Then Beth kissed him on the head and put him down on the family room carpet where he promptly piddled.

"Paul," Deenie hollered, "you claimed him. Now you can train him. Outside!"

When Paul returned with the tired puppy, Deenie asked, "Why did you say you knew he was our dog?"

"Actually, your dog, Mom," Paul replied. "I just knew."

"But how?"

Paul tilted his head to one side. "The same way I knew that Carl hadn't done anything that bad when he got arrested. The same way I knew Evvy would be a girl before she was born. The same way I knew you would be all right when you got sick. I just knew."

"Why haven't you told me any of this before?" Deenie questioned, wondering if The Sight had appeared in any of the Stowell men before now.

"You wouldn't have listened, Mom," Paul said. At the door he turned and said quietly, "You won't tell Aunt Stella about this, will you? I just can't see myself as a midwife."

## JUNEAU

Juneau didn't know how she would have survived without her writing. Her mood, no matter how she tried to change it, was somber, dark, downbeat. She needed to learn to laugh again. And she did, on the day she went to visit teach Sister Kittridge.

The poor little lady was in bed with a bad cold, so Juneau made a large chicken and noodle casserole for dinner and then scooped some of it into a pretty ovenproof bowl. She took it with her when she went to see Sister K, after depositing Gideon with Marisol.

"Come in," Sister K called from her bedroom when Juneau knocked. "The door's not locked."

"I brought dinner," Juneau called back. "I'll leave it here in the kitchen."

"You sweet thing." Sister Kittridge coughed before she could go on. "I was lying here thinking I didn't have energy to fix anything."

Because it was almost 5:30 P.M., Juneau turned on the oven to preheat. Setting the casserole on the counter, she went into Sister K's bedroom. "How are you feeling?" she asked.

Sister Kittridge, so small and wispy that she barely showed beneath the cheerful patchwork quilt, offered a wavering smile. "Like I've been trampled by a herd of porcupines."

Juneau smiled. "That's a colorful description."

"Sit down, Juneau." Sister K gestured toward a bedside chair. "I'm real happy for company. How's the writing coming along?"

Juneau told her about wanting to write something to honor Rhiannan and how hard it was in her present mood.

Sister Kittridge clucked sympathetically. "It was such a shame that lovely girl had to die. Sometimes life is a nasty old mule that kicks you right in the heart."

"That's a nice metaphor," Juneau said. "I think you should have been a writer, Sister K."

Sister K gave her shy grin. "To tell the truth, I did want to write when

I was young. But I got so busy raising my six kids that I never got around to it." She gazed reflectively out of the window. "I guess my children are my books, and pretty interesting ones at that."

A hot smell came from the kitchen. Probably the casserole warming up. Juneau went on chatting until the stench of something scorching filled the room. Sister K didn't say anything, but of course, the cold had stuffed her nose. Suddenly, Juneau remembered she hadn't even put the casserole in the oven! With a hasty "Excuse me," she dashed for the kitchen, where smoke seeped out around the edges of the oven door. She flung it open and was horrified to see stacks of paper, all of them scorched around the edges and some definitely smoldering.

"Oh, boy," she said. "What have I done?"

Turning off the oven, she snatched a stack of papers and saw they were family group sheets, pedigree charts, old letters. She looked with dismay at Sister K, who'd gotten out of bed and propped her frail body against the door frame. "I've burned up your family genealogy," Juneau gasped.

Sister K took the news in good humor. "I'd say it's a comment on my ancestry, full of horse thieves and other rogues. Their souls are probably all a trifle singed, like the papers." She chuckled as she stirred through the scorched family group sheets Juneau had put on the table.

"Look at old Benjamin Hartwell here. Spent his life as a pirate. And Belle Forrest. I won't even mention how she earned her living before she married my great-grandfather and eventually became a sweet little old petunia like me." She burst into such laughter that it brought on a coughing spell. Unable to help herself, Juneau began to giggle, too, and then to laugh outright.

"I'm really sorry," Juneau gasped when she could. "I didn't even think to check the oven before . . ."

"No reason you should check it," Sister K said. "Not many people use an oven for a filing cabinet. But I never bake anymore, so I put my family in there. I didn't expect them to be roasted!"

They laughed so hard they had to sit down. "I'd better go," Juneau said, "before I put you in the hospital."

Wiping her eyes, Sister K said, "Haven't you heard that laughter cures what ails you? I feel good enough now to go mix a batch of cement for my new back steps."

Juneau felt better, too. And she had an idea for the first line of her Rhiannan book. She would write not about Rhiannan but about a girl who loses her best friend. It would start out, "My best friend, Renata, is no more substantial than a wisp of smoke. She's a ghost."

When Juneau told her family how the burning of Sister Kittridge's papers had pulled her up out of the pits, she saw a look in Trace's eyes that hadn't been there for a long time. "How about I take what's left of Sister Kittridge's genealogy and put all the information on the computer for her?" he said, his voice full of new purpose.

And Sister Kittridge, who'd told Juneau she'd outlived her usefulness, reported that she and her scorched genealogy papers were in demand for display at every family history fair in the area.

## WILLADENE
April 21, 1989
Dear COBs,

Joanna and Jake getting married and Andrew among the guests. Who'd a thunk it? And Juneau, I've heard of cooking the books, but I never thought it meant genealogy! I bet we see Sister Kittridge in one of your stories.

I have a Who'da of my own. My dad, mom, and I are shooting together at the gun club. Dad bragged so much that Nathan and Jerry drove up to challenge Mom and me. To my surprise and great satisfaction, my target scores were the highest. My dad dubbed me Dead-Eye Deenie.

Then Beth asked me to be part of her school project on what makes parents unique. I was worried that she was going to present me as the mommy who went nuts. It was almost as unnerving to be presented as Dead-Eye Deenie, Mommy with a Gun. Bet she gets an A.

We have a strange kind of love-hate relationship going on. She seems proud of the gun business, but when the mental health issues come up, she makes mean, angry remarks. Dr. Greenwood says that's to be expected. Beth trusted me to be her mommy, and all of a sudden I wasn't. Now I want to be again. Sounds familiar, doesn't it?

Roger and I still see Dr. Greenwood once a month. We're moving in the right direction, even though there are plenty of "rocks in the stream."

I have been asked to be a visiting teacher and am looking forward to it.

> Love,
> Deenie

## ERIN

James Ingram and Joanna Larson were married on a lovely May afternoon in the living room of the Johnson house in Edina.

At the appointed time, Bishop Harding took his place on the staircase, Bible in hand. Jake and his son, Tim, stood at the foot of the stairs, waiting for the bride. Jake was impressive in his dark blue suit and gray and lavender tie. Erin smiled, knowing that under the jacket were suspenders especially ordered with a design of hearts and wedding bells.

Erin signaled the string quartet from Wayzata High School to begin the processional. Then she nodded to Kayla, who wore a pink chiffon dress and held a basket of flowers. But Kayla balked before entering the dining room. "My scar," she whispered urgently to Erin. "Is it covered?"

Erin tweaked a curl over part of the scar. "Nobody will notice it," she said, giving her daughter a little push. With that assurance, Kayla entered through the dining room, casting rose petals before her. Mark followed with rings on a satin pillow. His little face was solemn as he concentrated on doing his job right.

Erin watched Mark until he had reached his position, and then she turned to The Women. Joanna looked radiant in the blue-gray wedding suit she had sewn herself. Grams, who was giving Joanna away, wore a dress of lavender crepe. The similarity in their looks was striking at that moment—high foreheads, arched eyebrows, large, pale blue eyes, and movie star cheekbones.

"I love you both so much." Erin kissed them and then stood back as they walked the short distance to where Jake waited.

The ceremony was simple, with Bishop Harding speaking on the blessings of marriage, Jake and Joanna saying vows they had written themselves, the traditional "I dos" ending with "I now pronounce you man and wife."

When Jake kissed his bride, Erin didn't even try to wipe away the tears rolling down her cheeks. Congratulations and hugs were given, and the photographer set up his equipment to take photos of the bridal pair and the family. At Kayla's insistence, Erin had the photographer take some shots that included Andrew, Charlotte, and Caitlin and one of herself with her father and half-sister.

"How are you going to explain these in your genealogy?" Caitlin asked with a grin.

"Easy," Erin said. "You're family."

Guests began arriving for the open house at two and continued in a steady stream for three hours. Erin was touched by the number who came to celebrate with Jake and her mother. People stayed, with many still lingering even after the quartet left and the caterers began cleaning up and loading their van.

Finally, Joanna and Jake changed into casual clothing and took their leave, heading for the downtown hotel from which they would depart for New York the next morning. Erin waved good-bye with a great sense of satisfaction. She stood on the steps, her arm around Cory, thinking this was one of the most wonderful days of her life. It had been full of everything she had hoped for—love, music, friendship, and promise.

Then she looked up at Cory, and her smile faded. Everything she had thought was so right about this day was all wrong, because something was terribly wrong with Cory.

The fleeting expression Erin had caught on her husband's face spoke of inner turmoil and deep grief. It was disconcertingly similar to the expression she'd seen on the drive to Nauvoo the summer before Mark was born. He didn't know she'd seen his distress that day, and she'd never found out what had caused it; she was too afraid to ask. Now, she'd seen another glimpse of the same distress, whatever it was, and she felt it like a stone weighing against her heart.

He gave one last wave as the limo disappeared from sight and then looked down at her, catching her in a frown. "Hey, there. There's nothing to be sad about. You're not losing a mother. You're gaining a stepfather."

*But am I losing a husband?* she wondered.

## JUNEAU

As Juneau's Thursday night rendezvous with Clyde became regular occurrences, they also became Juneau's biggest Guilty Secret. When she recognized how much they meant to her, she mentioned them to the COBs.

Gabby was first to call. "What do you two talk about?" she asked. "The same things you talk about with Greg?"

"No," Juneau admitted. "It's like a whole different language."

"Explain, please?"

"Well." Juneau thought it over. "We talk books and music and poetry. Greg likes murder mysteries and car crash movies. Clyde shares my interest in old films, like *Casablanca* and *Citizen Kane*." But it was more than that. She and Clyde talked about motivating factors and consequences of decisions and nuances. Greg wouldn't be caught dead with a nuance.

There was a short silence. Then Gabby said, "You asked in your letter if this relationship is dangerous. I think it could be, which probably makes it even more attractive to you, dear. Think carefully about what you want before you decide what you're going to do about it."

*Lot of help that is,* Juneau thought. "Maybe I should buy a CTR ring," she said.

"Great idea," Gabby said. "Choose The Right."

Willadene's response was much the same as Gabby's, except stronger. "Whoa, girl," Willadene said. "You're not just exchanging an occasional idea with the man; you're going out with him on a regular basis, spending late hours alone with him, sharing your deepest thoughts. That's called dating when you're single. When you're married, it's called betraying your spouse. A short trip farther along that road, and it's called adultery."

Juneau recognized the truth in what Willadene said. Still, she had several male friends with whom she shared interests and conversations. Dr. Tim Hart, for instance. On nights when the stake activities committee met, they often spoke together of their mutual interest in dramatics and the stage. There wasn't anything wrong with that.

On the other hand, she didn't go out for snacks with him.

The next Thursday night Juneau told Clyde she couldn't stay after class. "Next week, perhaps?" he said.

"Perhaps." She hurried away.

At home she found the Guy's Club in the little garage room, grouped around Greg's computer. That's what Greg had started calling them— himself, Trace, and Gideon. And Philip Atwater. Trace was seated at the computer, and Greg sat next to him. Gideon was in his high chair, watching. Philip Atwater sat on the floor, also watching as if he understood what was going on.

When she greeted them, Greg glanced over his shoulder. "I'm teaching Trace how to write music on the computer," he said.

Trace and Gideon turned to greet Juneau with smiles. Philip Atwater's tail thumped the floor as he looked up at her. Then, as if the four heads operated on one neck, they all turned back to the computer.

*I might as well have gone to Bob's Big Boy with Clyde,* she thought, disgusted. The next week she did.

ERIN

May 17, 1989

Dear Gabby, Juneau, and Deenie,

My mom is now Mrs. Jake Ingram, of Hopkins, Minnesota. The wedding was very touching, and they were both radiant with joy.

Now The Jays (Jake and Joanna, who else?) are living in his 1940s brick house on a tree-lined street in Hopkins, a suburb with an old town center not that far away from us. Grams is happily settled in her new mother-in-law apartment at the back, which she's filled with new furniture in mauve, blue, and cream. Wouldn't be my choice, but she's thrilled.

I think Grams was more than ready to leave the old house and the old neighborhood—I can certainly relate to that! It's amazing to see how easily she's made the transition. She's already gotten acquainted with her eighty-five-year-old neighbor, Marcella, and her cat, Shakespeare. Marcella actually talked Grams into going with her on the shuttle to the senior center to do crafts and play cards! Grams was feeling her age (seventy-nine) after the move, but Mom says she's perked right up lately.

I'm glad she's busy and happy. For so long, she was the light of Kayla's life, but that's changing. Kayla's made a lot of friends in kindergarten, and she's busy with play dates, summer day care, and skating lessons, so she doesn't ask to visit Grams as often as she did when she was younger.

Now that the wedding's over, I feel there's an empty space in my life that should be filled with activity. The only thing on our schedule (other than the usual) is our Saturday afternoon swing class.

We've met an interesting African-American couple there, Doug and Lucky Brown. (Juneau, should I say black or colored? I'm so out of touch with what's politically correct.) They run an after-fire cleanup business, helping people sift through the mess to see what can be saved. Did you know there was such a thing?

Doug is skinny and hyperactive. He compulsively snaps his fingers but in a way that's almost silent. Lucky has curves on top of curves. She always wears kente cloth as a muumuu or wound around her head or her hips, and she alternates between a rich jive way of talking and straight-up Midwestern diction.

Every so often, she and Doug fall into something she says is "call and response." It's like when Martin Luther King would say something in one of his speeches and the audience would respond with "Yes, Lord! Amen, brother." In comparison to her, I feel very flat and colorless.

Cory enjoys the Browns' company as much as I do. They are so energetic and lively! Guess we need some of that. Cory's been in a strange mood lately, I don't know why. I could write it off to Behind the Scenes being busy, but that would be too easy.

Your Erin

JUNEAU

One day in late May Misty called. She'd been a fairly faithful correspondent, writing about her life with Juneau's parents and making wry
comments about school. And asking about Gideon's progress.

"Guess what, Mom?" she said. "I'm coming home."

Juneau felt a frisson of anxiety, but she merely said, "That's good
news, honey. What changed your mind about living with the Peripatetic
Paulsens?"

"Well," Misty said, "for one thing they're not going to be so peripatetic any more. They've found a cabin in the woods they really like. It's
just right for them, with an upstairs writing room that has a window looking out at Mt. Hood. They think they're going to buy it."

In a way Juneau was relieved. Her parents were in their mid-sixties
now. "So when are they planning to settle down in this little house in the
big woods?"

Misty giggled. "That sounds like Laura Ingalls Wilder, Mom. They're
arranging to buy it right now. But it's too far out in the trees for me.
Besides, I'll be graduating next month, so I need to move on."

Before Juneau could say anything, she added hastily, "Don't come up.
I'm not staying for the commencement ceremony."

Juneau started to protest but then just said, "Have you applied to col-
leges?"

"I've decided to go to Pasadena City College. That will give me a
chance to be there and get to know Gideon better. Trace, too, now that
he's hanging around."

Trace hanging around? Juneau had told Misty in letters how he was
making a really good life for himself, how he was backup sitter for Gideon
whenever needed, how he and Greg got along so well. Hanging around
was not an apt description for Trace's presence in their lives. She had the
thought that Misty's returning home would not be in the best interest of
either Gideon or Trace.

But how could she say that to her child? "So when are you coming,
honey?"

"As soon as school's over," Misty said.

"Let us know when to pick you up at the airport."

"Don't worry about picking me up, Mom. I'm hitching a ride with a guy I know." She hung up before Juneau could respond.

Juneau stared at the buzzing phone receiver in her hand. Another guy?

"Sometimes I think she's changed, and then I realize she hasn't," Juneau told Clyde on Thursday evening at Bob's Big Boy. "So what am I going to do?"

Clyde smiled. "Remember what Robert Frost wrote? 'Home is the place where, when you have to go there / They have to take you in.' You'll take her in, and you'll love her, no matter what."

"But will I?" Juneau was very serious. "Can I still love her if she barges in and upsets what's working very well at the moment?"

"She's graduating from high school, Juneau. That's a plus."

"She's always been smart," Juneau said. "At least academically. That's what bothers me so much, I guess. She has so much potential, if she'd just use it in the right direction."

"I don't think that's what's really bothering you."

*He knows me too well,* Juneau thought. When she spoke it was almost a whisper. "I'm afraid she may be thinking of getting together with Trace and taking Gideon away from me."

"There's the rub," Clyde said. "Are you thinking what's best for her or what's best for you?"

"I don't know," she admitted. She hated having to look at her own motives, but it felt so good talk to someone about her deepest fear. Someone who really listened. All Greg had said was, "Things will work out, Juney. Wait and see." Then he'd turned back to his computer.

ERIN

June 29, 1989
Dear Friends,

Have you been as haunted as I was by the news coverage of Tiananmen Square? I'll never forget that extraordinary photo of the young man bringing a row of tanks to a standstill. It

reminded me of how blessed we are to live in a free land and
how petty most of my frustrations and challenges are. That
young man faced the tanks—all I have to face are my own
fears, real or imagined. (Yes, I know. I've stolen FDR's line.)

Thinking of all my blessings,
Erin

# Chapter 10

WILLADENE

July 18, 1989

Dear Juneau and Erin,

Reece and Ryan graduated last month with class rankings to make a mother and a new stepfather proud. The boys grinned like Cheshire cats the whole day. When I asked them what they were up to, they said I'd have to wait and see. I hope Carl does as well this coming year.

My foray into obedience school with Bear has been great. He can come, sit, stay, heel, and leave it with the best of them. I wish the training techniques that work so well on Bear would work on Beth. She's been out of control!

We nearly had a tragedy on our hands at the Fourth of July picnic. Beth took Danny for a ride on Grandpa Will's tractor mower without bothering to learn how to use the brakes. If it hadn't been for one of the cousins being close enough to stop the thing when Beth started screaming, she would have piled them both into a cement wall. And I thought I was protecting Beth from Danny's influence all this time. Who was I kidding?

The boys are doing fine. They put together a weight set in the garage. Carl wants to bulk up for football his senior year, and Paul wants to be like Carl.

As for me, I have good days and bad days, but the good now outnumber the bad. And the bad really count as good when compared to the bad days a few months ago. The Griff has been reduced to the size of a Spanish peanut—but he's still around.

Later: I was just interrupted by the strangest phone call from Gabby's gentleman friend, Jonas. He's quite concerned about Gabby, who, he says, is wearing herself out with worry now that her grandson Kenny's out on parole. Kenny's parents, Cecelia and H. G. Junior, want him to live at home. His sister, Sophie, says if he does, she's moving to Gabby's. And his brother, Bryan, says if Kenny moves home, he's giving up his apartment in town and moving back home himself. Guess he thinks he needs to watch out for his folks, who are pushovers when it comes to Kenny. Junior blames Gabby for it all.

The minute Jonas hung up, I called Gabby to ask if we could meet for lunch, and she put me off, saying she was too tied up with Pioneer Day activities and to call her in August. I will, and I will let you know immediately if the cavalry needs to ride to the rescue.

> Love to all,
> Deenie

The uncomfortable phone call from Jonas made Deenie pause to consider what she knew about Gabby's family. She knew Gabby's husband, Hyrum Golden Farnsworth Senior had owned several car dealerships, which Junior had taken over on his father's death. She knew that Gabby and H. G., as Gabby called him, had been estranged for years before his death, living separate lives under the same roof.

Deenie also knew that Gabby held something against Junior and his wife, Cecelia. Whatever it was, it had caused an ugly rift: Junior, Cecelia, and their oldest son, Kenny, were on one side; their younger children, Bryan and Sophie, on the other. She didn't really know Junior and Cecelia, hadn't really wanted to, her feelings about them having been colored by Gabby's obvious disapproval.

*That's not fair*, she thought, as she stood musing in her kitchen. From her recent experience with her own mother, she was acutely aware that things were seldom what they seemed. It made her wonder what truth lay behind Gabby's current distress.

## ERIN

Erin tugged at a clump of quack grass that had invaded the hosta garden flourishing in the shade of the big oak tree on the east side of the backyard. Then she wiped the dirt from her hands and walked over to where Cory was adjusting the soakers in the raised bed planted with vegetables. "Did I tell you last night that Angie Dunmeyer called? She's invited us to come out on the Fourth for potluck and fireworks watching. She and Norm have that great view across the bay from their front yard, remember?"

"Yeah, but we're supposed to be at Pete's big party on the Fourth."

"Oh, darn. I forgot. Do we have to go?"

He shot her a sideways glance. "Behind the Scenes gets a lot of client goodwill from this event. We didn't go last year, because you didn't want to. Pete expects me to show up this year, whether you and the kids come or not."

She signed loudly. "I'd really like to go to Angie's. What if we took two cars and the kids and I left after a couple of hours? Then you could meet us later at Angie and Norm's."

"That might work, as long as you don't skip out too early."

"Skip out? You make it sound like I'm not supporting you."

"Well, I have gone to a lot of parties alone."

"If that's true, it was because the kids needed me or I had a deadline." She bristled. "I do work, too."

"I know. There always is a reason."

"Wait a minute, what—"

At that moment, Mark called from the sandbox, wanting Cory and Erin to see the roadway he was building for his trucks. Erin was glad for the distraction. Ever since she'd joined Cory in the pretense that the moment after The Jays' wedding hadn't happened, she'd been reluctant to engage him in any real communication. She was afraid of what she might have to hear.

As she got ready for bed that night, she realized she had to talk to him. Really talk. The way she and Juneau and Deenie had talked in St. George. She waited until he was finished with his shower and walked into the bedroom. Screwing up her courage, she said, "Cory, I got the idea when we were talking this morning that you think I'm letting you down."

He ran his fingers through his damp hair, his gaze wary. "I don't think you realize how often you stay home when my friends or family have invited us over. You never go to watch me when I play on the ward softball team. I think I'm the only guy there without a cheering section."

"Oh, come on. I can't believe all the other wives are always there."

"How would you know? You haven't been once since Colleen and Steve moved out of the ward. Guess you only went then to talk to her."

"Do you really think I'm that self-centered and selfish?"

He waved the question away. "Any answer to that is going to get me in a world of trouble."

"You brought up the subject. Answer the question."

Cory sat down on the window seat across from her, but he didn't look her way. "You are a wonderful woman. What you do on a daily basis is amazing. You take great care of the kids and the house, and the relationship you've created with your mom and Grams is nothing short of a miracle."

"I hear a *but* coming."

"What do you do that is just for me? That includes me in more than a peripheral way? For no reason except that you love me?"

"Everything I do is for us," she said indignantly. "We're a family."

"You didn't answer my question. As far as what you do for the family—you do a lot of things so you can feel good about yourself."

His words hit so close to home, she couldn't think of a single thing to say in her defense. After a moment, he shrugged, turned off the overhead light, and climbed into bed.

She climbed in on her side and lay wide awake, sickened by the recognition that he was right. Yes, she made sure he always had clean, pressed dress shirts in his closet, when it would be easier to send them out. She kept the house immaculate—with the help of a housecleaner who came bimonthly—so he could bring home company any time he wished. She entertained his coworkers and clients.

*So what?* asked her inner voice. *You don't do those things for him. You do them so you can feel like you're a good woman. A good Mormon woman.*

The next morning she caught him as he was about to walk out the door. "Cory? You were right last night. I haven't been thinking of you. I'll go to Pete's party, and the kids and I'll be at the rest of the softball games."

"Forget it, okay?" he said. "I was feeling sorry for myself. I'll talk to Pete today and see if it's okay for us to take the early shift. We can probably make it to Angie's in time for the fireworks."

As she stood on the front steps watching him drive away, she wondered how long he'd been feeling sorry for himself and why.

Cars were already parked along the street in front of Pete's elegant brick Federal style house on Prior Lake when Erin and Cory arrived. Following the beat of a '50s song and the flags that lined a pathway, they walked around the house to a party in full swing. The sweep of lawn down to the lake was dotted with kiosks offering food and drink and canopy-shaded tables and chairs where clusters of people were seated. Teams were playing volleyball at a net on one side of the lawn, and children were swarming over the play area on the other.

Cory took her hand as they joined the crowd. "Thank you for coming, Erin. This means a lot to me." That was obvious. He beamed as clients, coworkers, and Pete complimented him in her presence. "You're lucky having this guy," Pete said. "Keep him happy."

"I will," she said, meaning it. It was sad to see how Cory soaked up her attention like a bone-dry sponge—he looked happier that day than she'd seen him in a long time. She was glad she'd made arrangements for the kids to spend the afternoon with his parents, who had also agreed to take them out to Angie's for the party.

Erin and Cory arrived at the one-time vacation cottage built by Angie Dunmeyer's grandfather with still more than two hours to spare before the scheduled Excelsior fireworks. They were greeted with waves and hugs, a smile from Kayla, and a near-tackle from Mark. Norm cooked their hamburgers to order, and Angie brought them drinks after seating them at a card table under a huge oak tree.

After they ate, Cory went to play ball with the kids, and Angie sat down beside Erin. "It's nice to see your mom and Jake so happy," she said, gesturing to where Joanna, Jake, Grams, and Cory's folks were sitting. "I always thought they belonged together, right from that Christmas party when they first met."

"That's right, you and Norm were at that party, weren't you?"

Angie nodded. "I'm glad Cory's parents brought the kids. They're very nice people."

"They are, aren't they? I'm lucky to have them for in-laws."

"How long have they been married?"

"They'll celebrate their thirty-fifth anniversary this year. Amazing."

"Norm and I celebrate twenty-eight years together in September. We're taking all the kids and grandkids on a vacation to Yellowstone."

Remembering something she'd heard Angie say years before, she asked, "Do you still call Norm 'Mr. Allnut'?" Mr. Allnut was the Humphrey Bogart character in *The African Queen.*

"Yes, and I'll always be his 'Old Girl.'" A pensive look crossed Angie's face. "I'd like to be his Old Girl forever."

"You're not having troubles, are you?" Erin asked, alarmed.

"Heavens, no! It's just that I've been intrigued by the idea of Forever Families that you Mormons have. I'd like Norm and me to have a bond like that."

Erin's attention was momentarily diverted by the sight of Cory on hands and knees giving piggyback rides. "It's love that creates that kind of bond between two people," she said, more to herself than to Angie. "Even between two who have been married in the temple."

"I believe that. I'd just like to think I had a little extra insurance."

"What do you mean?"

Angie met her gaze. "I think I'd like Cory and that friend of his I met way back—Steve, is it?—to teach me about your church."

*Chapter 11*

JUNEAU
July 20, 1989
Dear Gabby, Deenie, and Erin,

Remember me? I'm sorry I'm such a poor correspondent this year. Perhaps I could blame it on being a creaky old granny trying to keep up with a toddler, but it's a whole lot more than that. Isn't it funny how the traffic of life jams up every now and then?

Where shall I begin? Since the last time I called, Misty arrived home safely—with another stray guy, Ira, average height, a little stocky. He wears his dark hair in a buzz cut and has a nice car, but he dresses just like Trace did when he arrived—threadbare, out-at-the-knee jeans, and a ratty T-shirt. Seems to be the uniform of young people these days!

He and Misty walked in and dropped another bomb on us. On their trip south they detoured to Las Vegas and got married at one of those little wedding chapels on the Strip!!! How could they do such a thing? Misty turned eighteen a couple months ago, so I guess it's a done deal.

I love my daughter. She has so many good qualities! I hope they come to her rescue someday. In the meantime, I can only cross my fingers and say my prayers.

I'll admit this only to my fellow COBs, but I'm vastly relieved that Misty won't be disrupting Trace's life and also that she and Ira haven't said a thing about taking Gideon away from Greg and me. More Guilty Secrets to add to my lengthy list.

Misty and Ira went to church with us on Sunday. Ira had to borrow a tie from Greg. He said he hadn't worn a tie since his bar mitzvah. We hadn't known he's Jewish, although with a name like Ira Greene we might have guessed. He adds another colorful tile in the mosaic that is my family.

So that's the news, dear ladies. You know, I was wondering the other day what has happened to Regina and Reginald. I haven't thought of them for a while. Do you think they ever got married? And are raising a family?

*Regina smiled wistfully as she sat by Reginald's side in the purple twilight. "Do you remember our wedding, Reggie?" she asked.*

*"How could I forget?" His eyes were tender as he gazed at her. "You were a vision in white, my darling. And I thought I could never be happier."*

*"Are you still that happy, my fuzzy bear?"*

*"Oh, much more," he sighed, "what with our incredible little family. What about you, my little bunny?"*

*"I love our sweet family, too," she said. "All of them: the twins, Denzel and Daphne; the triplets, Hazel, Filbert, and Wally; the quads, Daisy, Maizie, Margie, and George." She sighed. "But I have to admit I'll be glad when some of them are old enough to go to kindergarten."*

Till next time.

Love,
Juneau

## ERIN

August 3, 1989
Dear Juneau,

Congratulations! I think. I find the saga of Misty as fascinating as the saga of your Great-Grandmother Letitia, she of the empty grave. But I know that living a drama isn't anywhere near as entertaining as reading one—or writing one. So keep breathing, dear. Give Giddy a hug for me.

Your Erin

## JUNEAU

That year Juneau often pondered the ironies of life. After Max was gone, she had prayed for a son. Now she had three—Gideon, Trace, and Ira—who could qualify for the title. All courtesy of Misty. Life was unpredictable, quirky, capricious. She was reminded of the old saying that you should be careful what you pray for, because you just might get it. Sometimes she worried about what quirk or twist the future might bring next.

Twists from the past worried her, too. Erin's reference to her great-grandmother reminded her that sometimes you never did find out the reasons for some of the twists. She'd been trying since 1980 to find out why Letitia wasn't buried under the headstone that bore her name. Sometimes she wished Aunt Hattie had never given her the picture of what she now referred to as "The Empty Grave."

But at the moment, life was good. Much to Juneau's surprise, it seemed as if Misty and Ira might really make a go of their hasty marriage. They found a scrubby little apartment in Alhambra, and both of them got entry-level jobs. They both gained admittance to Pasadena City College. Not only that but they melded easily into the assortment of people that Greg and Juneau had accumulated as family. Ira and Trace, oddly enough, became good friends. Gideon and Ira became buddies. Nicole, Beto, and Ira became a triumvirate of religious seekers, sometimes talking far into the night about Mormonism versus Catholicism versus Judaism.

And Ira encouraged Nicole and Beto in their latest plan, which was to go with the rest of the Sanchezes to a big family reunion in their ancestral village in the mountains of Mexico, possibly in the spring. Marisol had an old *abuela*, a grandmother, there who would be celebrating her ninetieth birthday. There were also uncles and aunts and cousins by the dozens. Juneau hadn't been happy when Nicole asked if she could go, but Marisol assured her that chaperones were a big thing in her family and Nicole would be perfectly all right, so Greg and Juneau had given their permission.

Sometimes Juneau had to stand back a few feet and marvel at how the jigsaw puzzle of her life could fit together as well as it did. Ira told her one day that it was because she and Greg were accepting of things as they were. "You don't have a preconceived notion of what a person or a family has to be," he said. "You take us all as we come."

The funny thing was, she did have preconceived notions. But the mental picture of what she and Greg and Misty and Nicole should be as a family had blurred somewhere along the way. To tell the truth, she loved her family as it was.

She had a chance to talk at some length with Ira one day when she'd invited the whole troop for dinner. Ira, as always, helped her in the kitchen while the rest of the family and Philip Atwater sprawled in front of the TV, watching a Dodgers' game. Ira was showing her how to make kugel, a tasty noodle dish he said was a traditional part of his family's feasts. "Are you sure you don't mind missing the game?" Juneau asked.

"My dad always watched ball games," he told her. "So I didn't."

"Hmmm. So how else did you rebel?"

He gave her an admiring look. "You understand rebellion."

"Not really," she said. "But I've known enough Jewish boys to think you're not typical."

He nodded. "They're smart. High achievers. Driven to excel. Go into high-paying professions."

She grinned. "So when are you going to medical school?"

"If my parents had their way, I'd be there now," he said. "But since that's what they expect, that's what I don't do. They had Harvard in mind. So I went to a trade school, became a carpenter."

"Like another Jewish boy a few centuries ago."

Ira nodded. "It drove my parents crazy."

"Ah-hah." Juneau popped the casserole dish of kugel into the oven. "You really do have issues."

"Where do you suppose that comes from? My parents are great. But they pushed me every day of my life, until I left home. I wanted to see what else the world offered."

"So what has it offered?"

"Misty," he said simply.

"That's sweet."

"Yeah." He started scrubbing a bunch of carrots. "Sorry we threw you a curve when we just went off and got married."

"Another rebellion?"

He considered that. "I guess you could say so. I knew it would offend my parents for me to marry a shiksa."

"Meaning a non-Jewish girl," Juneau said. "Not much of a foundation for marriage, is it?"

"That's not the foundation." He paused. "I love Misty. She's exciting. Unpredictable. And smart. Very much her own person. She tries not to show it, but she has a loving heart." He looked at Juneau. "I don't think she's going to stay with me for very long."

Juneau put an arm around his shoulders, her eyes stinging. "You really understand her, don't you?"

He nodded. "Thanks for listening. I'm glad you're my mother-in-law. For a while."

"I'm glad you're part of my family," Juneau responded. "For as long as you want to be."

## ERIN

August 16, 1989
Dear Friends,

I'm writing this letter on my new computer! The Jays gave it and a printer to us as a thank-you for hosting the wedding. How cool that once I've written the letter, all I have to do is print out multiple copies! I'm saving the letters as a sort of journal.

The news from Lake Wobegon: First, I lived through girls' camp! Second, the local missionaries, along with Cory and Steve, are giving the discussions to my buddy Angie. She requested that Colleen and I come, too. We had our first meeting a few days ago, and it really went well. She's started reading the Book of Mormon, but it's a little slow going. Norm plagues her by quoting Mark Twain, who called it "chloroform in print."

It strikes me as odd that Angie should want Cory to teach her now, at a time when he's in such an odd place. There's nothing I can put my finger on, but it's clear something is bothering him. When I brought up the subject, he made a joke about going through an early mid-life crisis (he's only thirty-four). I told him, "Buy a red sports car, and get over it!" I half expect him to drive up in a red convertible one of these days. If he does, he'll say I gave him permission to buy it.

Any other time, I would have put his restlessness down to dissatisfaction with work, but he's happy at Behind the Scenes, especially since the company has been hired to do some work for the Timberwolves, our new basketball team. You know how he loves the sport.

I got Cory to agree to making Friday night our date night, hoping that it would help us get closer. We've enjoyed being together, but there's still this odd rift I can't bridge. Maybe it's that "seven-year itch" I recently read about in an article on Princess Di and Prince Charles's marriage troubles. (They were married just three months before Cory and I were, remember?)

Do couples actually go through some crisis or another after being married that long? I guess I'd like to think that this bumpy stretch is nothing unusual.

Love,
Erin

P.S. Kayla and Mark keep us hopping. Kayla's enthusiasm for skating, which was ratcheted up a notch by her being in the spring show, got Mark wanting to skate, too. Now he's in the class that gets kids ready for Tot Hockey. Kayla will start first grade this year, and Mark will be in a Montessori preschool. They're striking out on their own, discovering what they have an interest for. I don't know why that makes me sad—it's what kids are supposed to do.

## WILLADENE

In early August, Deenie ignored Gabby's insistence that she didn't need checking up on and drove down to Provo. "I'm coming to take you to lunch," she said. The minute she saw Gabby, her worries were confirmed. Gabby's face, usually radiant with health and enthusiasm, was pale, and her eyes were devoid of feeling.

Deenie did her best to cheer Gabby up, but she felt as if she'd failed when she hugged her friend good-bye. On the drive home, she tried to think of how she would describe the situation to Dr. Greenwood. What was the word she used so often? *Affect*. Gabby's personal affect was as flat as if a steamroller had squished her. *A steamroller named Kenny,* Deenie thought.

The first thing she did on arriving home was call Dr. Greenwood, whose advice was simple—Don't play therapist. Stay close and let her tell you what's wrong when she's ready. *So we'd better get close,* Deenie thought. The moment she hung up, she called Juneau and Erin. One hour later, plans for a Labor Day weekend getaway in Park City were underway with Erin, Juneau, and a subdued but pleased Gabby on board. The way things fell into place was miraculous—even one of the charming cottages on Park Street was available. *This is meant to be,* Deenie thought, and she began making lists for the trip.

"Are you sure you're up to this, Deenie girl?" Roger handed her a casserole for the cooler.

"No, but I'm going to go anyway. I owe this trip to Gabby."

Deenie closed the cooler, now chock full of offerings from friends and family, including six dozen oatmeal cookies made by Sunny and Margaret. And the COBs were going to be in Park City only three nights!

"Going by all this food, you have a lot of people who love you," Roger said.

"Either that or I have a lot of people who are afraid I'll crack up again." Deenie's voice was devoid of humor.

Roger looked at her with concern. "Where's that coming from?"

"I guess I'm afraid of slipping, myself. It takes so much work to keep the good thoughts in and the bad thoughts out. I'm on alert every minute. Checking my thinking, waving the red flag, altering my behavior if necessary. It's exhausting to think myself through every day."

He pulled her into his arms, stroking her back as he murmured words of comfort and encouragement. "I didn't realize you felt that way. I've been amazed at the progress you've made, Deenie. Everyone else, too. I'm sorry I haven't told you that before."

Deenie softened in his embrace. She lifted her face for his kiss just as Beth walked into the room, her friend Danny Donovan following.

"Gag me with a spoon!" Beth pantomimed the action, making Danny laugh.

"My folks neck on the glider on the deck all the time." Grinning, Danny handed a beribboned gift bag to Deenie. "Beth told us about the COBs and the romance novels. Mom thought you and your friends might like these."

Deenie opened the bag. It was filled with novels by Emily Loring and Grace Livingston Hill and a note, which Deenie read aloud. "Hope these are sweet enough. Lark Donovan."

"Tell your mom thanks for me," Deenie said to Danny. She watched the girls leave the room and then said, "That was nice of her, especially since we've never met."

"Danny's father, Shawn, is a professor in the engineering department," Roger said. "Whenever I see him on campus, he always takes time to say hello. Maybe we should have them over."

"Good idea. I'll call her right before I leave," Deenie promised.

Roger grabbed her hand. "I've got something to show you." Grinning hugely, he led her through the garage to the alley behind their lot. Parked close to the rock wall at the back of her garden was Will Rasmussen's extended-cab pickup truck. At least it looked like Will's truck, Deenie thought, but it was painted a brilliant red with racing stripes in orange and yellow. In the back a huge transport kennel was bolted to the floor of the truck bed.

Roger dangled a set of keys in front of her. "For you, from my dad."

Smiling at her dropped-jaw surprise, he continued. "Dad never uses this truck anymore. He decided that anyone with a nickname like Dead-Eye Deenie and a dog like Bear needed wheels to live up to them." He tossed the key ring at Deenie; she caught it easily. "Unlock this baby and rev up the engine."

Deenie did exactly that. As she adjusted the rearview mirror, she discovered a little brass charm hanging from a thin golden chain. It was a tiny representation of the Book of Mormon compass, the Liahona.

"From me," Roger said. "To remind you to stay on the path that always comes home to us."

Blinking back tears, Deenie climbed out of the truck, straight into Roger's arms. "There's no place I'd rather be."

After she'd made the call to Lark, Deenie and Roger loaded the truck. Then they called the family together for the travel prayer. When she was buckled in and ready to go, Roger gave her a quick but firm kiss. "We all love you, Deenie. Remember that. You are so worth loving." Then he stepped back and slapped the front fender in a good-bye gesture.

*What does that mean—to be worth loving?* she wondered as she drove out to the freeway. *What do you have to do to be worthy of love?* When Deenie had asked Dr. Greenwood a similar question recently, she said, "I believe all you have to do to be worthy of unconditional love in this life is to be born." *Was that what Roger meant? Or did he mean all the changes I have been working on make me worthy?*

"Here I go," she muttered. "Deenie to the rescue, but this time I have more questions than I have answers."

# Chapter 12

JUNEAU

"Are we close?" Juneau peered through the windshield of the rental car she and Erin had picked up at the Salt Lake airport. It was hard to see the numbers on the refurbished miners' cottages along Park Street in the old town of Park City.

"It's right there," Erin said, pointing to a green cottage with a covered front porch perched in a row of other small clapboard houses.

Juneau had barely parked the car when the door of the cottage was flung open, and Deenie leaped down the steps, arms open wide. "You're here!" She grabbed Erin in a fierce hug and then Juneau.

"Whoa!" Juneau said, pulling back. Whatever she had expected, this slim, vibrant, in-charge woman dressed in a bright T-shirt, tailored jeans, and boots wasn't it. "Look at you, girl!"

Then Gabby walked out on the porch. She looked shorter and thinner, and her hair was now completely white. She was smiling, but it wasn't the easy smile Juneau remembered.

"Guess what I've brought," Gabby asked after hugging Erin, too. "Cowboy cookies!"

"The four of us and cowboy cookies. Now I know our Crusty Old Broads convention has begun," Erin said.

They sat at the little painted table in the corner of the living room with a big plate of cowboy cookies and glasses of cold milk all around. Not that much later, they enjoyed the fried chicken and potato salad Gabby had brought for their evening meal. "Backwards supper," Juneau said, grinning. "Nicole and Misty used to love it when we ate dessert first."

"Do you realize that it's been nine years since we first met?" Gabby asked, looking around the table at the three women.

Erin nodded. "A lot of water's gone under the bridge since then."

Juneau added, "Some of it over those stones in the stream you talked about, Gabby. Thanks for giving us that bit of wisdom. It's helped me get perspective on things when I needed it."

"Don't know that it's helped me all that much lately," Gabby said shortly.

Deenie touched her arm. "I guess you're talking about Kenny."

"Yes, but I'd rather not get into that tonight. Right now, I want to know about you dear women, my COBs in the making."

"I want to know how you got so slim," Juneau said to Deenie. "You're looking really fine."

"Thanks. Getting healthy is part of my learning how to live in a new way—a way that's better for all of us."

"Can you tell us one thing that's made a difference?" asked Erin.

"No," Deenie said.

Juneau raised her eyebrows at the abrupt reply.

"I wasn't being rude," Deenie said. "That's my advice. After years of saying yes to everything, I'm learning to use the New Deenie No. It's not a Knee Jerk No. It's a Considered No."

"I'm familiar with that Knee Jerk No," Juneau said. "It's attached to everything Gideon does. It's also the first word he ever said, so we make a nice duet, the two of us."

"The No-No Two-Step," Gabby said, smiling. "I remember doing that."

Erin looked sober. "I think I do the Knee Jerk No too often, but I also say yes too often. Maybe both at the wrong times."

"Saying yes too often was a big theme in the television special KSL did on depression a few years back," Gabby said. "I think it must be something every woman has to struggle with. Including me. I brought the tape with me, by the way. Jonas saw the special when it was aired, and he sent to KSL for a copy. We watched it several times together over the years. After about the fourth time, I looked at him and said, 'I think I'm depressed.' And he said, 'That's why I got the tape. I thought you needed the chance to figure it out for yourself.'"

"What have you figured out?" Juneau asked.

"Pretending that everything is okay only works for so long. And things kept secret begin to stink."

"Do you want to tell us about it?" Deenie asked.

Gabby shook her head. "Not tonight."

"Then how about a little primal scream therapy," Deenie suggested. "We could all stand in the backyard and howl at the moon. I promise, we'll all feel better if we do!"

Juneau laughed. "I wonder what the police will say when they come and find four ladies of indeterminate age baying at the heavens?"

The next day they strolled the streets, stopping in specialty shops and galleries before eating lunch at a restaurant with outdoor seating. They thoroughly enjoyed their outing and the naps that followed. As the sun went down behind the mountain, they ate supper, cleaned the kitchen, and retired to the living room, where Deenie had built a fire in the wood-burning stove.

"What a great day," Juneau said, stretching her feet out in front of her. "I really needed this break."

"Me, too," Deenie said. "I'm glad Jonas suggested it."

"Jonas suggested it?" Gabby's eyes narrowed at the mention of her gentleman friend. But then she smiled. "That meddling old goat. He worries about me. First the tape and now group therapy."

"He loves you," Juneau said. She and the others had the pleasure of seeing Gabby blush as she made a slapping motion and snorted, "You watch too many soap operas, Juneau."

"What I'd really like to watch is that tape on depression," Erin said. "Would it be all right to do it now?"

The content of the tape left them in a reflective mood. "To think that I believed I was the only one who ever felt like that," Erin said. "I could have used this tape and maybe some meds after Mark was born."

"You all know about my descent into the maelstrom," Juneau said. "I didn't get past it until we buried Max's Christmas stocking in the back-yard. And had that wonderful week at your house, Deenie. Bearing one another's burdens really does make them light."

"You into the maelstrom and me into the looney bin," Deenie said.

"I'm not discounting what you went through. But, my friends, you were depressed. I was mentally ill."

Juneau clasped her hands tightly as she listened to Deenie describe her slide into that dark space and her battle to get out of it. "I had to rethink everything I ever believed about myself," Deenie said. "The world I lived in, and the people I loved. It was like sitting in front of an empty loom with all the threads that had been my life unraveled on the floor. I've had to sort them out and choose the ones that will allow me to weave my new life in the old frame. And add some new threads, too."

"Maybe that's what Grams has been doing," Erin said. "Reweaving her life with some old and new threads. Mom, too." She smiled. "Jake is a nice fat woolly thread that strengthens and brightens everything."

"Some of my threads were so hidden I could hardly see them," Deenie said.

"Guilty Secrets, I bet," Juneau offered, and they all laughed.

Except Deenie. "I found out what happened after Sunny was born." She told them about her mother's hospital stay and the aftereffects of her mother's shock treatments, adding, "I thought all these years that she'd changed toward me because I was bad or not wanted." She looked around the room. "Isn't it funny how we can create a whole world around what we think has happened, when it isn't true?"

"Sounds like me and Grams," Erin said. "I thought Grams hated me because Mom and I weren't home when Gramps died. Truth was, she hated herself for not being there. Grief and Guilt again."

Juneau noticed a grim look in Gabby's eyes. "Sometimes guilt is not a misperception," Gabby said.

"Surely you don't have anything to feel guilty about," Erin said.

"Of course I do!" Gabby's voice was sharp. "You don't get to be my age without having sins of both omission and commission—it's part of being human."

"Kenny?" Deenie ventured.

"I'm sure I have something to answer for with Kenny, but that's not who I was thinking of." She leaned back in her chair and sighed. "I had two sons. Junior and a boy named Caleb. Caleb was the sun in my sky. I loved him . . . more than I should have, maybe."

She paused, and Juneau could see that she was looking into the past. "When he was twelve and Junior was fifteen, we went camping near Provo River. It was running dangerously high and fast at the time, and we told the boys they couldn't go down to the river without us."

There was a stillness of held breath as Gabby spoke.

"I had too much on my mind that day. H. G. and I . . ." She paused, and then as if she'd decided she didn't want to go that direction, she said, "I wasn't watching the boys the way I should have. One minute Caleb was there, the next . . ." She held her hands palms up, a helpless gesture. "We never did find him. If I'd only been with him instead of . . ."

Deenie reached for Gabby, but Gabby waved her off. "It's my fault that Caleb went missing. I grieve over him every moment of every day. Sometimes I can't bear to look at Junior because he reminds me that I don't have Caleb."

Juneau wasn't sure she should say what was in her heart, but she did, couching her words carefully. "It must be hard for him to know he isn't loved."

Gabby turned away from her. "Junior and Kenny aren't easy to love. They're too much like H. G."

"I've had lots of opportunities lately to discover there's more to people than I think," Juneau said. "When I've given them the chance, they show unexpected sides. Maybe there are parts of Junior you have no idea of. Maybe even parts you could grow to love."

"Perhaps." Gabby folded her napkin and put it down on her unfinished salad. "I guess it's no secret now that I'm not the fount of wisdom you thought I was when you came for Education Week."

"You still are, as far as I'm concerned," Juneau said. "I've gleaned a lot of common sense and guidance from you over the last nine years. I call them Gabbyisms."

"Gabbyisms?" The older woman smiled.

Erin nodded. "A kind word never broke anyone's mouth."

"Put your back to the bench," Deenie said. "That meant a lot to me."

"For me, it was the Tennyson quote," Juneau said. "'Tho' much is taken, much abides.'" Noticing the emotion glistening in Gabby's eyes, she added, "You know, when we're in a tough spot, we often ask our-selves, 'What would Gabby do?'"

"Hah!" Gabby shook her head. "After what you've heard this time, I bet you won't be asking yourselves that anymore!"

"Sure we will," Erin countered. "More than ever, now that we know you earned COBhood the hard way."

Juneau saw how the remark pleased Gabby, who straightened her back and smiled, a COB once more.

Later that morning when Sophie arrived to take Gabby back to Provo, they stood on the sidewalk, reluctant to part. "Don't let so much time pass between visits," Gabby said.

"We won't," Erin and Juneau said at the same time.

"That's one promise you'd better keep," Gabby said. "I don't know how much longer my old bones will still have meat on them."

Sophie helped Gabby into her car. Then Juneau, Deenie, and Erin waved them down the street and out of view. They stood on the sidewalk, each lost in her own thoughts. As they turned to go back into the cot-tage, Juneau said, "I wonder if she'll ever tell us what really happened with H. G. and Caleb."

ERIN

> September 6, 1989
> Dear Deenie,
>
> Wasn't Park City great? Loved your new look. Watch for some-thing in the mail. I saw it and thought of you and Roger!
>
> Erin

WILLADENE

> September 15, 1989
> Dear Gabby, Erin, and Juneau,
>
> I've thought about our time together in Park City every day since I got home. If I could bottle what happens when we're all together, I'd make my fortune. Not only that, I cut back on the visits with Dr. Greenwood as a result of our talks. How's that for group therapy!

The vet told me a while back that Bear's personality and strength make him a good candidate to be a search-and-rescue dog. (The instructor at obedience school said the same thing.) I wasn't interested, because for Bear to be a search-and-rescue dog, I would have to be a search-and-rescue person!

But I changed my mind after you told us about Caleb, Gabby. I want to do anything I can to help prevent another mother from suffering in the same way you have. As a result, Bear and I will begin the long trek toward qualifying as an SAR team at the start of the year.

In the meantime, I'll recertify with the Red Cross in first aid and CPR and start a class in canine first aid. So once again, being with the COBs has set me going in a new direction. And the decision to do so feels so right. COBs rule!

Gabby, Jonas tells us that Kenny has found a place of his own and a job as a motorcycle repairman. He seems to be getting on with his life remarkably well for someone so recently released from prison. Makes me think he has the help and support of a mentor. Has Jonas taken on Kenny the way he took on Bryan years ago?

Erin, the mood plate arrived, and it's hilarious! Roger wants his indicator glued to "in the mood."

Love,
Deenie

JUNEAU

September 16, 1989
Dear Gabby, Willadene, and Erin,

Gabby, I need you. The young people in my family seem to regard me as the Delphic Oracle these days, coming to seek advice. What do I know?

Yesterday it was Ira who came. He said Misty's starting to get restless again, after just these few months of marriage. Poor boy, he wanted to know what he could do to settle her down. As if I had any idea! The best I could do was tell him about the Letitia Syndrome, about how my great-grandmother was so restless that she set out to see the world, leaving behind her family and even her grave! Or at least that's what I think from the little I know. It makes a good story, but I really wonder if we can blame the family wanderlust completely on her.

I like Ira. He's a very pleasant young man, although he has a thing about rebelling against his family. He says they would call him a nebbish for studying literature and poetry rather than medicine or law. I wonder . . .

He came over once just as I finished a phone call with Flint. I guess he noticed I looked kind of down because he asked, "Bad news?"

"Ongoing," I said. "That was my brother. He's still so broken up over his daughter's death that he can barely speak."

Ira nodded sympathetically and said, "The Talmud tells us, 'The deeper the sorrow, the less tongue it hath.'"

So true. He quotes from the Talmud a lot. I think I can learn more from him than he from me. I wish I could help him with Misty.

Take care of your dear selves.

Love,
Juneau

That night after class, Clyde had a bit of advice to offer Juneau after she'd told him about Misty's restlessness and confessed to a bit of her own. "You and Misty need to go to Idaho and find out if there actually is a Letitia Syndrome," he said as they sat at their usual table at Bob's Big Boy. "There must be somebody who remembers what happened to her."

"My mother knows, but she won't tell."

Clyde nodded. "Then that's where you start. Take her to Idaho with you."

"Fat chance of that. Even if she said yes, I know her. She'd find one reason after another to postpone going."

"You won't know until you ask."

"I suppose it's worth a try." She put a hand out to clasp his in thanks. He held it until she finally pulled it away.

WILLADENE

November 14, 1989
Dear COBs,

Beth has turned twelve and is now officially a member of the Young Women program and reveling in the fact she gets to do things with the big girls. We celebrated with an English high tea à la Jane Austen, which was exactly what she wanted. She got the presents she wanted, too: perfume, lip gloss, nail polish, a subscription to a teen fan magazine, and four pairs of pierced earrings—arrrrgh!—to go with her healed ears.

After the guests left, Beth informed me that she is going to spend her birthday money on a bra (she thinks she is ready for one) and some big girl panties—and she didn't want me to go with her. I'm having visions of something with French cut legs and inserted lace.

> Arrrgh again,
> Deenie

P.S. Bear and I start search-and-rescue training in January, including weather prediction and wilderness survival. Can you imagine? Me neither.

ERIN

November 19, 1989
Hello, Dear Friends!

Juneau, I was glad you asked Gabby for advice regarding Misty, because I have no idea what I would do—or what one should do—in such a situation. Actually, I don't think there's anything *to* do, since it's her choice. She does seem to move out of your circle and then return. Maybe the most important thing is to let her know that you love her.

There! I gave advice after all.

Deenie, I agree with what you said when you wrote after our visit at Park City. When I look back at our get-togethers over the past years, it seems to me they get better all the time, because our sharing gets richer and deeper.

But Gabby wasn't the only one whose willingness to share made a difference. You made a difference, too, by being open and honest about your hospitalization. I have to say that the New Deenie is quite the gal!

What you said about the New Deenie No has been on my mind a lot. I think I say no too often to Cory and not often enough to Kayla. In fact, I think I spend way too much time dealing with these two high-energy, high-maintenance people and not near enough with little Markie, who bobs along in their wake.

Your Erin

P.S. Were you glued to your TV like I was when the Berlin Wall came down? The images of the young people taking possession of the wall and Germans from both sides streaming through the Brandenburg Gate gave me the shivers. Who would have thought that such a monumental change could happen so quickly?

# *Chapter 13*

JUNEAU

Juneau didn't know what had possessed her to invite an army to Thanksgiving dinner. It all started when she decided to invite Bert, Willadene's sister-in-law, who was doing her doctoral work in anthropology at UCLA, and her parents, Wilford and NeVae Rasmussen, who were spending their winter in California to get away from the cold. Bert had come to dinner once before, and she had been delightful company. Then, since Beto would surely be coming, Juneau figured she might as well invite Marisol and the rest of her family, except her husband, Manny, who was in Mexico on an extended buying trip. So that would be . . . how many? Juneau counted. Fourteen, with all her family.

When she mentioned her plan to Greg, his face brightened. "Oh, hey," he said, "I've been wondering if we might invite Hal Udall. He's pretty lonely these days. You know Hal—teaches in the math department?"

Juneau remembered having met him over a year before, just after he'd lost his young wife to cancer. "Sure," she said. "What's one more?"

"Three," Greg said. "He has two kids. And as long as we're inviting a crowd, could we include the missionaries assigned to our ward?"

It wasn't until she'd invited all of them—and they'd all accepted—that she actually counted up and realized that would be nineteen people to seat. And feed. Then her mother called. "Juney," Pamela Paulsen said brightly, "Daddy and I will be in your area doing research in two weeks. Any chance we could share Thanksgiving with you?"

"Mom, need you ask?" Juneau said.

It was then she panicked. She could manage the food, but how could she sardine twenty-one people into her small house? Her small, *messy* house. What with spending so much time on her writing and with Gideon, cleaning was always at the bottom of her priority list. Old mail spilled from untidy stacks on the telephone desk. Clothes and toys and towels were everywhere. Philip Atwater's paw prints were on the kitchen floor, and Gideon's handprints, some mixed with drool, were on the walls.

As Juneau's old feelings of inadequacy returned to haunt her, she called Gabby and explained the whole situation. "It's like expecting Moses and the children of Israel to show up at my house for dinner. How am I going to get everything in order before they arrive?"

"So your house is messy," Gabby said. "Is anybody bleeding? Are little children dying because of it?"

"No. But you know the old guilt syndrome. Mormon women are supposed to have spotless houses and shining windows."

"And a smile on our lips and a song in our hearts," Gabby said.

"Well . . . yes," Juneau said, grinning.

"You want advice? Stop worrying about the mess. Make a lovely dinner and enjoy your guests."

At the end of the first week of November Flint called. "Good news, sis," he said. "My transfer has gone through, so Valerie and I and the boys will be at Camp Pendleton in less than two weeks."

"Just in time for Thanksgiving," Juneau said. "I hope you'll all come up to dinner. Mom and Dad will be here, too."

"Super," Flint said, sounding almost like his old self. "It will be like old times." His voice fell away, and Juneau knew he was thinking of Rhiannan. "Almost."

"Can't wait to see you," Juneau said, mentally adding to the guest list. Twenty-five guests for Thanksgiving dinner!

She tried to put a fun face on it when she told her immediate family about it at family home evening on Monday. "We'll eat in shifts," she said. "We'll use paper plates."

Ira's eyebrows rose. "Why?"

"What do you mean, why?" Juneau gestured to include the crowded table in the small dining room. "There's scarcely enough room here for the seven of us and Gideon's highchair."

"Who says we have to eat inside?" Ira asked. "Your patio is going to waste. November is a warm and wonderful month here."

The Mexican tile patio stretched all the way across the back of the house, but Juneau hadn't even considered eating there. The tiles were dirty. The shrubs needed pruning. The flowerbeds grew weeds. But would anybody bleed because of that? Would little children die?

"It might do," she said, still a bit doubtful.

Ira nodded. "You're talking to the observer of hundreds of weekly family gatherings. Uncle Schlomo used to direct traffic with a bullhorn, and I was his righthand man. Until I skipped." He grinned. "I'll do the tables and setup."

"I'll do the turkey and dressing," Trace volunteered. "My grandma's secret recipe." It was the first time he'd ever mentioned his family.

"Mom!" Nicole raised her hand as if in school. "Beto and I will decorate the tables. His mom has lots of stuff from Mexico that we can use."

"And my mom makes salsa to die for," Beto offered and then frowned. "Do you think the Pilgrims had chips and salsa?"

"If they didn't, they missed a good thing," Greg said, adding, "I could try my hand at pies. My mom always made hers with fresh squash. She showed me how the Thanksgiving before I went on my mission."

"Now you tell me," Juneau teased.

The only one who didn't join in on the planning was Misty. She sat somewhat removed from the others, staring through the French doors, off toward the mountains. Juneau again felt a pang of worry. It was Misty's "wandering" look.

As guests began to fill the little house on Thanksgiving Day, Juneau had another moment of panic. Then she saw Ira in action, and she relaxed. Taking on the role of majordomo, he escorted people out onto the patio where he'd moved some easy chairs as well as every regular chair in the house. It was he who put Bert, looking pretty and a little exotic in a black pantsuit with brown embroidered animals all over it, with Hal Udall after Gideon towed his two daughters off to play. Juneau watched them chatting and laughing and thought, *Now, there's a pair!*

Marisol came with her children Vincent and Isobel, as well as Isobel's boyfriend, Hector. *What's one more at this point?* Juneau thought, accepting the tubs of salsa and chips they offered. When she saw how quickly they were emptied, she hoped everyone would have room for the turkey Trace was presiding over.

There was a bad moment when Flint and Valerie and their boys arrived. Flint came in with a big smile on his face, but it crumbled and slid off when he saw Juneau. They fell into a hug. Trace came over, and Flint gathered him in, too. They all wept together, producing enough tears to float if not a battleship, at least a raft, as Flint said later.

By the time the Peripatetic Paulsens arrived, Juneau and Flint were ready to greet them with cries of real joy. "I'm so glad you could be here," Juneau said and meant it. She was a little appalled at how old they were looking and wondered if living in a nonmobile house in the Oregon woods was wearing them down. But they were cheerful and enthusiastic about their new book.

Then the missionaries arrived, sweaty after having pumped their bikes all the way up the hill. The house and yard were filled with the sounds of people laughing and talking, enjoying each other's company. Only Misty held herself apart.

The meal, if not perfection, was close enough to it that nobody noticed. "Wipe out," one of the missionaries declared as he finished his last bite of Greg's fresh squash pie and rubbed his stomach.

"Nap time," Pamela said.

"Ha!" Greg scoffed. "Who can nap when the football games are on?"

The Guys Club, including Flint and his sons, retired to the family room to watch the Detroit Lions take on the Cleveland Browns. The missionaries helped with the cleanup before going to an appointment.

When the evening began turning cool, Ira brought all the chairs back inside, and everybody found a place to sit. Ira started telling stories of his Jewish family get-togethers, complete with Uncle Schlomo's jokes. The Peripatetic Paulsens entertained with snippets from the plot of their new mystery book. Then Trace got his guitar, and they finished the evening singing, all of them together, including some lively Mexican folks songs performed by Marisol and her family and Nicole.

After that, Gideon lay down on the floor by Philip Atwater, who was snoring like a buzz saw, and went to sleep. The day was almost over, but Juneau couldn't bear to see it end. To prolong it just a bit, she asked Trace to sing some of his own compositions, ending with the plaintive ballad he'd written to commemorate Rhiannan. It was met with silence. Not sad, just a remembering.

That's the way it was that unplanned day when Juneau invited too many people to Thanksgiving dinner and even more showed up. It was one of those days from which she knew everyone present would count time, saying, "That was before (or after) the great Thanksgiving we had at Greg and Juneau's house." They would remember it, talk about it, wish to recapture the magic of those few hours when such an unlikely crew all worked together to bring off something good and great and wonderful.

But Juneau would also remember it as the day she saw once again that faraway look in Misty's eyes.

WILLADENE
December 5, 1989
Dear COBs,

Juneau, what is going on out there? When I called NeVae at Bert's, she answered in her happy voice. She said they're having a wonderful time. She wanted to know why I didn't tell her you were such a wonderful cook and such a good friend to Bert. Then she asked how I felt about interracial families. When I asked Bert what was up, she just laughed.

We are trying for less Claus and more Christ in our celebration. We had a family home evening about it, suggesting the kids secretly give gifts of service in the neighborhood, then write how that made them feel, and tie the notes up with red ribbon on the tree as presents for Roger and me. Beth said she'd way rather buy a present instead.

Wishing you all a Spirit-filled holiday season.

Love,
Deenie

P.S. Gabby, we will be delighted to join you and Jonas for New Year's Eve, weather permitting. Shall we dress up for the occasion? I would love to get Roger into a tux.

# Chapter 14

## 1990

JUNEAU

January 1, 1990
Dear Grand COB and Wannabes—actually, COBs all:

Today Gideon and I are home alone, and he's still asleep, so I'm indulging in some computer time. Yes! I did say computer (or compooter, as Gideon says). I'm totally converted. It's a miracle machine.

I sent the rest of the family off to the Rose Parade, laden down with ladders and a board to stretch between them to sit on. They left about 4:30 A.M. to get a decent spot on the parade route, so I have time to write letters before Giddy wakes up. I have a big pot of chili, made from scratch, simmering on the stove, so my house smells like Willadene's—fragrant and inviting. We'll have an early lunch when my family gets back about 11:00. Then it's nap time for me (the Guys Club will be glued to the football game).

So that's how my year has started. Happy days, my dearies.

Love,
Juneau

P.S. Guess what! Our stake is doing a production of *Music Man* this July, and I've been given the part of Eulalie McKecknie Shinn, the mayor's wife. Tim Hart, the doctor who delivered Gideon, is Mayor Shinn. He says I should learn both parts in case he's called away to a delivery. Rehearsals don't start until April. I can hardly wait!

WILLADENE

January 5, 1990
Dear COBs,

I'm starting the New Year with big plans. I invited my favorite people to a mother-daughter slumber party! Lark and Danny,

Mom and Sunny, Grandma Streeter and Pat, and Aunt Stella are all coming. Lark's offered to cook something rare in the West, she says—a Good Philly Cheese Steak. I think it will be lots of fun.

I hope the big sleepover will help strengthen my relationship with Beth. Sometimes talking to her is like trying to plug in a lamp when you can't see the socket. If you're off just a smidgen, there's no connection.

NeVae won't be here because she and Will haven't returned from California. Apparently Bert has been dating Hal Udall, the gentleman she met at Juneau's house on Thanksgiving. They often include NeVae and Will and Hal's two daughters, Ami and Atsu, in their plans. NeVae won't willingly give up being a part of that.

We're curious about Ami, ten, and Atsu, eleven. NeVae's been worried about how to "be" around the girls, whose mother was from Ghana. She's never known any African-Americans personally and asks for any advice any of you can give.

Other news at home: Carl and his girlfriend, Ashley, have started making insane plans for the senior prom: renting a limo, dinner at the most expensive place in Logan, and an elaborate party afterwards. I asked when they were planning to dance. Carl shrugged and said it didn't matter as long as they got their pictures taken! It costs a lot, and it's coming out of his savings/mission fund. He never says he isn't going on a mission, but I think his actions tell it all.

Reece and Ryan blessed the sacrament on Sunday. It wasn't the first time they've done it, but it was the first time I noticed how they had the look of being grown men with a purpose. That's a look I'd like to see on Carl's face.

Juneau, I've finished reading *The Chosen*, by Chaim Potok. You're right. There are parallels to consider. My mother kept distance between us to protect what she considered a personal and shameful secret. But she didn't think in terms of consequences as Reb Saunders does when he chooses to raise Danny in silence to teach him compassion.

Nevertheless, I learned about compassion like he did, looking from the outside in at my family life. I don't think I would have as much understanding and compassion for the human condition if Mom had given me the unqualified love I so needed. (She does now, thank heaven!) On the other hand, I spent too many years believing she couldn't love me because I was guilty, flawed, and unworthy, and now I have to unlearn that part of the unintended lesson. It makes me wonder what unintended lessons my children learned while I was ill.

On that same topic, dear Gabby, here is a question out of love and from the heart. What do you think your keeping Junior at a distance means in his life? Could he feel "less" for it, as I did with my mother? And because of that feeling, is he indeed less than he could be? Grandma Streeter says as parents we do the best we can with what we've got when we're young, but when we know better we do better, and we never quit parenting. Is there still a chance for you to be a mother to your boy? I hope so.

Love,<br>Deenie

## ERIN

January 30, 1990
Dear Gabby, Juneau, and Deenie,

Thanks for the calls, dear COBs. I'm sorry that you worried when you didn't get a Christmas card from us. The passing of Cory's grandmother Trina right before Christmas put sending cards at the bottom of our list.

It doesn't seem fair that last year at this time we were mourning Rhiannan and this year, Trina. What is it about Christmas, I ask you? Although Jake did propose to my mom last year, so I guess that goes on the other side of the scale.

Kayla (she's seven now) insisted on going to the viewing. She very solemnly touched Trina's cheek and said, "She's in heaven, right? This is just the leftovers?" Then she hugged me and said she was glad her daddy and I were all here! I pray we'll be "all here" for a very long time.

Trina's death so close to Christmas was hard on Harold. Grams understood what he was going through in a way the rest of us couldn't. When we were at The Jays' for Christmas dinner, she and Harold spent a lot of time sharing experiences and comforting each other. It was very sweet.

Cory's been in an extremely odd place since Trina's death. He spent New Year's Day in front of the TV. When I asked when he wanted to do our yearly review and planning, he said if I needed a plan, I could pull out the one for 1989, change the date to 1990, and call it good.

He went through a hard time when his mom's parents passed away. Maybe this is the same thing. I have to hope that he will come back to us, the same way he did then.

It was good for all of us when the Browns invited us to bring the kids to the Roller Garden in St. Louis Park during the holidays so Mark and Kayla could meet their daughter Shakeela. Shakeela's learning to do roller figure skating, so she and Kayla made quite the pair!

I told Lucky and Doug about NeVae's concern over Ami and Atsu. They got a real kick out of imagining two older-generation white folk from rural Utah acquiring half-black grandchildren. Lucky's advice was, "You tell that NeVae not to make too much out of their blackness but not to pretend she doesn't see it. If she has a question, she should ask. When they talk, she should listen. They'll give her an education. That's the real truth." Doug said, "Amen!"

> Hope that helps!
> Your Erin

P.S. They also said to tell NeVae that she doesn't need to become an expert on Ghana because "those girls are Californians!"

As January slid on a huge ice storm into February, Erin began watching Cory, reading something into every word he said, every time he was morose or silent, and every time he was late coming home. The old explanation of needing to work with clients—even in cases when she had reason to know it was true—was no longer sufficient for her. And his silence alternating with nonstop talking jags made her wonder if he was on something.

What disturbed her most was his uncharacteristic shortness with the children. His love for them was the deepest, truest part of him, yet he often snapped at them when they demanded his attention, startling them into tears. When she pointed out how his lack of patience was affecting them, he apologized and promised to do better. "I've just got a lot on my mind."

*I wonder what—or who—that is,* she thought.

He seemed to wake up the Saturday he berated Mark, who had come inside crying after being bombarded in a neighborhood snowball fight, telling him to grow up and stop being a sissy. "You're mean!" Mark stormed. "I wish Uncle Steve was my daddy. He never yells at Ricky, and Ricky can't do anything!"

"What did you say?"

Erin saw shock on Cory's face as he waited for Mark to answer.

"Ricky can't do anything." Mark squirmed to get out of Cory's grasp. "He's stupid."

"Mark!" Erin said. "You know Ricky isn't stupid. He's doing the best he can."

"I am tooooo." Blubbering, Mark looked up at his father. "Why aren't you nice to me like Uncle Steve is to Ricky?"

Cory picked him up. "Hey, buddy, I'm sorry I yelled at you. You're my best man, right?" But Mark only cried harder. Cory cancelled a game of racquetball and spent the afternoon with Mark and Kayla. Erin ordered in pizza for supper, and they played games on the family room floor until the kids' bedtime. After such a wretched beginning, the day ended with hugs and kisses all around when Erin and Cory put the kids in their beds.

Later, after they had straightened the house and watched the nightly news, Erin turned off the TV and kissed his cheek. "I'm going up to bed. How about you?"

"I've got a few things to do first," he said. "You go on. I'll come up in a little while."

"You've said that a lot lately. I wish you'd come now."

"Just give me a few minutes, okay?"

With a sigh, Erin climbed the stairs, still hoping he might change his mind. When he finally did come to bed much later, it seemed to her that a strangeness hung about him like an unfamiliar scent.

## JUNEAU

When the phone rang one afternoon in early December, Juneau thought it was Greg calling to say hello in the middle of the day as he often did. Instead, a full-volume voice said, "Mrs. Caldwell?" Juneau detected a strong New York accent, recognizable from the days when the Peripatetic Paulsens had lived for a while on Long Island.

"Yes," she said.

"Solomon Greene here. Ira's dad," the voice boomed. "I hear you've taken in my wandering boy."

"Oh," Juneau said. "Ira. Yes."

"My sympathies." Solomon Greene chuckled. "Does he give you a bad time?"

"Not at all. We love having him around, Mr. Greene."

"Call me Solomon, Mrs. Caldwell."

Juneau began to relax. "I will, if you'll call me Juneau."

"You got it, Juneau. Ira's told us a lot about your family. Doesn't write often, but he tells us how your family does things. Probably to show how dysfunctional ours is." His laugh blasted in Juneau's ear.

"Solomon," she said, "any family that could produce a nice young man like Ira can't be all that dysfunctional."

"It makes him happy to think we are. Then he can rebel. He thinks we don't understand, and that inspires him to go against everything we say. If we'd told him we wanted him to go off and find himself, he'd have bee-lined straight to Harvard. So we encouraged him to go to medical school. He thought we'd be disappointed when he took off to Oregon instead."

Juneau chuckled.

"Reverse psychology. Works like a charm." Solomon paused. "My boy sure does love your daughter, Juneau."

"He told us you'd be upset about his marrying a shiksa."

"Figured he'd say that. Fact is, we're happy that his life is so good right now. Don't tell him I said that."

"All right, if that's the way you want it."

"Best way right now. Maybe things will change. Well, just wanted to get acquainted. My wife, Thelma, sends her best. Wants to thank you for taking care of Ira."

"It's a pleasure, Solomon. He fits right into our family."

"Bless you, Juneau." The booming voice wobbled just a bit. "We do love that boy, you know. But don't tell him I said so."

As Juneau punched in Greg's number to tell him about the phone call, she wondered What If? What if she did tell Ira that there need not be a rift in his relationship with his parents?

She wouldn't, though. Nor would she tell Ira's parents that Misty might soon be leaving their son.

# Chapter 15

WILLADENE

"Lark's sandwiches smell divine." Pat Fenton stretched out on Deenie's family room couch, propped her feet on the matching hassock, and took a deep swallow from a cool glass. "Someone else in the kitchen, someone else cleaning up for company. What more could any woman want?" She held up her stockinged feet, wiggled her toes, and looked hopefully at Danny and Beth. "Maybe someone to give me a foot rub. How about it, girls?"

"Get in line," Grandma Streeter said. "In the case of foot rubs, it is definitely age before beauty and . . ."

"I know, Beauty was a horse." Pat filled in the nonsense good-naturedly.

"So, don't be a nag." Groans and laughter followed Grandma Streeter's awful pun.

"Grub's up!" Lark Donovan entered, carrying a tray of fragrant, juicy sandwiches. "Authentic Philly Cheese Steak. Get 'em while they're hot."

Everyone in the room grabbed a napkin, a plate, and a share of the oozing goodness. Deenie watched it all with glee. Everything was turning out just the way she wanted: good company, good cheer, good food, and the men spending the night at the farm. The expansive, easy feeling she was enjoying was hugely different from the anxiety she used to feel when entertaining.

Deenie grabbed a sandwich of her own. She bit down on the oven-fresh roll, savoring the juices from paper-thin slices of prime rib browned to perfection, provolone cheese, caramelized onions, green peppers, and mushrooms. "Oh, my," she said, and took another bite. Bear sidled up to her side for a taste.

"Leave it," she commanded. The big dog backed away quickly.

"That's impressive," Lark said. "How's the SAR training going?"

"Bear's going to be a star," Deenie said between bites. "But our trainer is one tough cookie."

"What's the secret in the sandwich, Lark?" Pat asked through a mouthful of food. "We're all dying to know."

Lark grinned. "First, you need a really nice butcher . . ."

As Lark went on, Deenie took another giant bite of her sandwich, relaxed, and let the pleasure of the moment sink in. It was close to two years to the day that Evvy had been born, Carl had been arrested, and she had begun her descent into hell. She never could have imagined this gathering or anything like it then. *Good women,* she thought. *God bless them.*

"Anybody for dessert?" Pat asked, interrupting Deenie's musings. "I brought filled cookies from the bakery. Raspberry. Date. Raisin."

"I want to taste them all," Sunny announced.

Deenie smiled at her, thinking how beautiful she looked. She wore a soft sweater in clear blue to match her startling eyes. Her blonde hair was cut in an attractive bob, and her pixy face was made up in spring colors. With surprise Deenie realized that except for Sunny's thinness and the fine veins visible on her face and hands, she looked like any other young woman enjoying herself.

The phone rang, and Beth ran to answer it. Deenie could hear her talking softly, and then she squealed. "Really?" she gasped. "Are you trying to psych me out, Grandma?" Then, "Ohhhh!"

Beth hung up the phone and came dancing into the room. "I've got a secret, I've got a secret! I'll give you a clue. It has six Ds."

"Does it have anything to do with Valentine's?" Lark asked the obvious. Beth nodded.

"Does it have anything to do with love?" Margaret asked. Beth nodded again.

"Is it about Bert?" Grandma Streeter asked. Beth was so excited now that she hopped on one foot and then the other with her hands over her mouth.

"Easy peasy," Pat said. "If it's about Bert and Valentine's and love and something that starts with a D, it can only be a diamond."

"She's engaged, she's engaged. And she's getting married in August." Beth trumpeted. "But that's only one D. Guess again."

No one could figure out what the other Ds stood for. When the game grew thin, Beth finally gave in. "One D is for Bert's two new Daughters. They're all coming here, this summer! The other Ds are for Bert getting a Date set to Defend her Doctoral Dissertation. Grandma says she bets you can't say that fast five times."

As the evening went on, the group shifted and changed. Smaller conversation circles formed and then reshaped. Aunt Stella pulled a bottle of massage lotion out of her tote and corralled Beth and Danny into learning how to do the requested foot rubs.

Lark revealed her career as a graphic artist by sitting next to Sunny and telling her stories while drawing illustrations on the back of napkins. Deenie moved from group to group, not wanting to miss a single sentence of the conversations.

At one point Beth stopped the foot rub she was giving to pick up a fussy Evvy, calm her, and then rub noses with her. As she passed Deenie, they bumped hips and exchanged a high five.

It was part of the emotional shorthand Deenie had once shared with her daughter, and she had missed it since the pierced-ear debacle. Its reappearance now reassured her that the bond she had with Beth had only been stretched by their conflicts, not broken.

But What If? Deenie stopped what she was doing and sat down on the floor with her back to the couch to sort out her thoughts. *This isn't a Griff kind of What If,* she told herself. *It's the kind Dr. Greenwood said could lead to more understanding. What if I'd lost the memories of those sweet gestures when I was in the hospital? Where would Beth and I be if I'd forgotten our nose rub after bedside prayers, or doing nails on girls' night, or peanut butter and banana sandwiches, or high fives when things are good?*

As Deenie contemplated the possibilities, a greater compassion for the loss and confusion her mother had experienced after Sunny's birth blossomed in her heart. It was like Nathan had said in his Christmas letter: Truth and understanding come to us when we're ready to accept them.

"Can I get anyone more of anything?" Deenie asked as she began to rise.

"No!" came the universal answer.

"Stay where you are," Margaret said. She sat down behind Deenie on the couch and began to take out Deenie's ponytail.

"Mom, what are you doing?"

"Darling girl," Margaret said in the same sweet voice she had used years ago, "Mother's going to double braid your hair."

## ERIN

Erin hustled the children through the March downpour up the sidewalk to Jake's house. Joanna opened the door as they reached it, saying, "Quick, quick! Come in!" She and Erin got the wet slickers off the kids, and then Joanna sent them back to the kitchen where Jake and Grams were putting milk and cookies on the table.

"You said you needed privacy to talk to Cory this afternoon." Joanna's eyes were full of worry. "Is something wrong?"

"Oh, Mom, Cory's left me." Seeing the shock on Joanna's face, she hastened to add, "Not literally, but it seems to me lately that he's . . . gone. He doesn't look at me when I try to talk to him. And when I gave him that onyx ring when he was made vice president of Behind the Scenes, he gave me a church hug and kissed my cheek." She swallowed hard, but a sob escaped her lips.

Joanna drew her into a hug, patting her back and murmuring that everything would be all right.

"No, it won't. I think he's having an affair."

"Not Cory!"

Hiding her face in her mother's shoulder, Erin said, "We haven't been intimate for months now. Whenever I try to interest him, he always has something he needs to do. I know I'm not the most exciting person in bed, but I ache to love him. And to have him love me."

"Oh, sweetie! I had no idea. What are you going to do?"

Erin took a step back and straightened her shoulders. "Make him talk to me. Make him tell me what's wrong."

Cory was watching basketball in the great room when Erin returned home. She walked in front of him, blocking his view. "Turn off the TV."

He gave her a startled look and jumped from the chair. "Erin, what is it? Has something happened?"

"That's what I want to know. We're losing connection with each other, and I'd like to know why."

He exhaled, visibly relieved. "Sorry you feel that way. With work and Grandma Trina—"

"Don't use those excuses. We haven't had any real conversations for months. It's like we live in two different worlds and just happen to occupy the same space once in a while."

"You're right. I'm all yours this afternoon. Do you want to go to a movie or walk the mall?"

"Walk the mall? Do you really think that will make things better?"

He shrugged. Hands stuffed in his pockets, he slouched against the island that separated the kitchen from the rest of the great room.

"See? There's nothing between us, not even communication. It may look like we're living a perfect life, but it's empty. It's pretend."

Cory gave her a long look. "Is that how you see it?"

"That's how it is, and it's been that way for a long time." Something in his voice frightened her, but she forced herself to speak calmly. "We used to have a marriage. Then we had a partnership. I don't know what we have now, but whatever it is, it's not working."

"What do you want from me?"

"I want you to talk to me, to tell me what you're thinking and feeling."

He shook his head. "No, you don't. You want me to say what makes you feel good."

"Is that what you've been doing? Lying to me so I'll feel good? Well, that's not working, either, so you might as well tell me. About the affair."

"You think I'm having an affair?" His laugh was harsh and short.

"If it's not an affair, what is it? Tell me the truth. Right now!"

"You don't know what you're asking for."

"Tell me anyway."

The look on his face was the same as the look she'd seen on the way to Nauvoo in '85 and again after her mother's wedding, only amplified to a degree that frightened her. "You want the truth?" He took a breath as if to speak and then turned away. His back to her, he shook his head, sighed, and walked partway into the dining room. His obvious distress increased Erin's distress.

A look of grim resolution marked his features when he turned back to face her. She held her breath, fearing what he would say. Still he hesitated. Turned away. Turned back. Then spat it out as if it were poison. "I'm gay."

"Wh . . . what did you just say?"

"I'm gay. As in homosexual," he added unnecessarily.

She had been so sure he was having an affair that she couldn't make sense of his words. "You can't be. We've—"

"Had sex?" His laugh was sardonic. "Gay men have sex with women. Gay men get married and have families." When she remained speechless, he added, "There's even a group for married gay Mormons. I heard about it a year ago."

"You've known for a year?"

He shook his head. "Longer than that."

She waited.

"A lot longer." He paused. "Before I went on my mission."

"That can't be true! No bishop or stake president would have let you go—unless you lied in your interviews."

"I didn't lie. Having feelings isn't the same as doing something about them. I was worthy to go. They promised me that if I kept the commandments and followed the plan I'd be . . . not cured but blessed."

Swirling thoughts and nausea made her grip the edge of the counter for support. "I don't understand. If you knew then you were gay, why did you marry me?"

"Because I love you."

"But you knew you were gay! I don't understand."

He hesitated a moment. "I didn't have much . . . trouble when I was on my mission, because I was so close to the Spirit. But when my time was almost up, I started to panic. I was afraid of what would happen when I no longer had something to give myself completely to. When I told my mission president, he said marriage was the only commitment big enough to replace the commitment of being a missionary."

Erin's laugh had an edge of hysteria. "You married me because some mission president said it was the way to save you from yourself?"

"It wasn't that way, Erin. I—"

"Of course it was! You picked me because you thought I was naive enough to believe you when you said you loved me and we could create a Forever Family. You were right. I fell for it. Hook, line, and sinker."

As suddenly as disbelief had given way to realization, realization gave way to fury. Her husband, the man she loved, had deceived her, used her, betrayed her. She grabbed the first thing at hand—a heavy leaded glass saltshaker—and flung it at him. He cried out as it hit a glancing blow across his cheekbone.

"I hate you. I hate you," she shrieked. "Get out of my sight and never come back. Get out. Get out!"

Grimacing with pain, Cory filled a plastic sandwich bag with ice and sat down on the great room couch. She watched him with barely controlled rage as he gently applied the ice to his red, swelling cheek. "When are you going to ask the question?" he said.

*What question?* she wondered. Then headlines about AIDS/HIV burst into her consciousness. "Cory! Are we in danger of that horrible disease?"

"No. You don't have to worry about that. I've had thoughts, yes. I've been tempted. *But I've never done anything.*" His voice rose as he emphasized each word. "You can trust me on that point."

"Really? From my position, I can't trust you on anything." She couldn't believe they were having this conversation, that she was asking such questions. "When did you know?"

He started pacing again, his face white with strain. "I think I knew the year I turned eleven." He described in halting words the sexual uncertainty that had surfaced in the awkward years of puberty, the anguish of feeling different in a way that was unspeakable, and the isolation of having to hide his feelings.

"I felt guilty for no reason other than being who I was. I'd always been taught that I was made in the image of God, and I couldn't understand why he would make me something he abhorred." He flashed her a humorless grin. "The man you see now was created by the boy trying to do everything to hide who he was. Compensation has its value. I always got good grades. I finished my Eagle Scout project before I turned fourteen. I was the star forward on the high school basketball team. I did well at the U of M. I fulfilled an honorable mission."

"Then you married me and fathered children, and it still wasn't enough." *Because I wasn't enough,* she thought, feeling somehow at fault that he was still tortured by dark urges. "If I hadn't asked what was wrong, would you have told me?"

"Eventually." He sat next to her but avoided her gaze. "It hurts like hell when the person you love doesn't know who you are." He struck his chest repeatedly. "Sometime I ache so bad I can't breathe."

"Now that I do know, you should be feeling so much better." She got up and walked as far away from him as she could get and still be in the same room. "What now? Do we tell the kids?"

"No! Why would they need to know?"

"So they understand why we're getting a divorce."

He looked truly horrified. "I don't want a divorce!"

"Isn't that what this is all about? Being gay and free?"

"No. I love you and the kids. If I could have any wish right now, I'd wish to be a happy heterosexual."

"Sorry, but there's no magic spell for that. More's the pity." She filled a glass of water and drained it. Her eyelids were swollen and hot, her ears were buzzing, and her head was pounding. She thought briefly about taking some ibuprofen tablets, but the thought of swallowing them made her want to retch.

"You know what? I think your parents know that you're gay."

Again horror crossed his face. "Why would you think that?"

"I've always wondered why they were nice to me, so eager to make me a part of their family." She paused, remembering what a miracle their generosity and love had seemed to her. Now the sweetness of all they had done for her turned sour. "They courted me as much as you did. I guess they wanted to get you safely married, too."

"That's crazy! They love you, Erin."

"Oh, right. They love me, you love me, everything's right in God's world."

March 15, 1990
My Very Dear Friends,

I found out what was behind the problems Cory and I've been having lately. My handsome, charming husband is gay! He's struggled with these awful feelings since he was young. He swears he hasn't acted on them, but the very thought makes me ill.

I thought he came out to me because he wanted a divorce, but he says that's the last thing on his mind. It might be what I want, though! I feel like our life together has been a lie. He vehemently disagrees. He says it's not a *but* situation. As in, Cory says he loves me, *but* he's gay, so he can't possibly. He says it's an *and* situation. Cory says he loves me *and* he's gay.

I want to believe him, but I feel betrayed and humiliated. And stupid! How could I live with him for so many years and not realize what he was? In retrospect, I can see some signs. We never did get into it hot and heavy before we got married. Or afterward, either. My ideas about sex were so skewed—I grew up thinking it led to trouble and death!—that I didn't realize our sex life wasn't "normal." When I started wanting more action on that front, I thought he wasn't interested because I wasn't good in bed.

The Sunday after he told me, he got dressed and went to church as usual. When I asked him how he could, he said, "I may be gay, but I still know the gospel is true. I have to get straight with the Lord." (Note the Freudian slip!)

He also had an interview with the bishop, who gave him the plain and pure word. He came home deeply frightened by how close he had come to giving in to temptation and doing something that might have led to excommunication from the Church and the destruction of our family. He begged my forgiveness and promised he would be faithful to our marriage vows in both thought and deed.

Juneau, you're probably wondering how I can live with someone I can hardly bear to look at. Well, here's one for a novelist (or a therapist). When I was little and The Women started in on each other, I used to burrow into the back of my bedroom closet where it was warm and dark and safe. When I got older, I discovered I had a closet inside myself, equally dark and warm and safe. I haven't had to use it much since Cory and I got married, but now . . . Isn't that funny! Cory comes out of his closet, and I go into mine.

I'm at Jay's Finishing Touches most Tuesday and Thursday afternoons, so you can send letters to that address or call me there. That way I won't have to worry about little ears or eyes. I've included his business card with info.

Your Erin

P.S. Just so you know, I sent a different letter to Gabby. I told her Cory and I were having trouble, but I didn't tell her he was gay.

P.P.S. Cory's sleeping on the great room couch.

## JUNEAU
March 19, 1990
Dear, dear Erin:

"Beware the Ides of March," the soothsayer told Julius Caesar. Well, I guess the curse still persists.

I'm so sorry you and Cory are facing such a crisis. I include both of you because Cory is suffering, too. It's nearly unforgivable that he didn't tell you about his being gay at the very beginning of your relationship. But to quote your letter, "He's struggled with these awful feelings since he was young." Perhaps he thought he could outdistance them and never have to tell. But I guess it doesn't work that way.

I know your new knowledge colors him a different hue in your eyes, but I'm hoping you don't totally withdraw from him. He can't help the way he is, and he needs some degree of understanding right now. And you must remember that without him you wouldn't have your two beautiful and precious children.

Don't think I'm minimizing your pain. Maybe it's because I write books, but I have to look at both sides of any story. In closing, I'll reprise the Tennyson quotation that Gabby offered to me when I lost Max: "Tho' much is taken, much abides."

> With great love and concern,
> Juneau

P.S. Have you talked with your bishop?

WILLADENE
March 21, 1990
Dear Erin,

Well, heckuba! What a miserable, stinking, terrible, wretched deal! Have you screamed enough? Broken enough things? (Preferably over Cory's head!) Too bad the most appealing ways of venting rage are illegal.

That old fight or flight response can be a @#!!* to deal with. Get lots of physical exercise to keep the adrenaline down. Be sure to take good care of yourself and your kids. Cory will have to take care of himself while you come to grips with what he told you.

Ask for the support you need from the ones you love. Keep asking until you get what you need. Oh, and watch out for chocolate. It starts out seeming like a soothing friend but ends up being the monster in your kitchen cupboard.

If The Griff shows up at your house, smash him flat. Take it from someone who knows what walking the razor's edge is like—you can't afford to let the sorrow, anger, resentment, and self-doubt fill the hole Cory left in your heart. Fight for your right to be happy. Fight for your right to be whole. Fight for your children's welfare.

Cory's saying he loves you *and* he is gay made me think of important *ands* in my life. I've learned that the key to healing is knowing, marrow deep, that our Heavenly Father loves us. We make mistakes *and* our Heavenly Father loves us. We are in trouble *and* our families stand by us. We err *and* we are forgiven. That *and* can be an important word in our search.

So on this beautiful spring morning where everything shouts of new beginnings and hope, I am here to tell you how much you mean to me. You were a stranger and you became my dear sweet sister and I love you. Whatever this new season brings, in growth or change for you or others in your family, remember you are always in my thoughts and prayers and I am only as far away as a phone call.

Love,
Deenie

*Chapter 16*

ERIN

April 25, 1990
Hi, Juneau and Deenie,

I'm writing this letter more for myself than for you, I think. It's a way of sorting out what's whirling around in my poor head.

Since I wrote you last, I've been in a free fall. Everything I thought was solid has been pulled right out from under me. I've been trying to go on as if everything's okay, but I'm not very good at putting on a front. When people ask me what's wrong, I just say Cory and I are working out some difficulties in our marriage.

I told The Jays and Grams pretty much the same thing, but I also admitted I wasn't sure if we'd be successful. I was really nervous about how Grams would react. She and Cory have only recently developed a closer relationship. She just gave me a big hug and said she was sorry for both of us. I don't know what Cory has told his parents.

Cory is doing better than I am. I don't understand how he can go about his life with so much of his perennial good humor intact, but he does. I think it must be the result of hiding the feelings he didn't understand and was ashamed of for so many years. Can you believe he thought we would be continuing with our dance class at the health club as if nothing had happened? I must have given him a look like he was crazy, because he hasn't brought it up since.

I haven't been going to church lately. Cory's been taking the kids, and his mother, Linda, has been helping him with them during sacrament meeting. When I asked him how he was explaining my absence, he said he tells people I'm not doing well. I can just imagine the expressions of sympathy and support he's getting because of "poor Erin" being sick. It makes me furious, but there's no way to change that without exposing his situation.

After I missed yet another Sunday, the bishop asked me to come and see him. I can't say that talking to him gave me much hope for the future, but I know right down to my toes that he understands what we're going through. I was afraid he would tell me that Cory and I wouldn't be having this problem if we were sufficiently humble and prayerful. I think I would have wigged out if he'd said that. Instead, he said we were in a heart-breaking situation, the outcome of which will rest on the choices Cory makes. And he said that what I was feeling—anger, grief, fear, betrayal—was perfectly understandable.

Well, I lost it. I cried and cried. This struggle may be Cory's, but what he does will have a huge impact on me and the kids for the rest of our lives. When I asked Bishop Harding what I should do, he said I should hold to the things that are most important to me—without thinking that by doing so I could create the outcome I wanted. I understood what he was saying. I thought I was doing everything I was supposed to do before, and it didn't keep Cory from having those feelings.

When I asked the bishop if he believed Cory could change, he avoided answering by saying that LDS Social Services offers counseling designed to help gays alter their behavior. When I asked him if it was successful, he said he'd heard from other bishops that it had promise, whatever that means. He wouldn't tell me if Cory had said he would give it a try. He said I should ask Cory about it.

I felt so hopeless, but Bishop Harding said I had to pull myself together and choose how I'm going to go on, just as Cory has to choose for himself. Then he said something that knocked me for a loop. He asked me to prayerfully consider where I had been withholding myself from Cory, my children, and even God. He wasn't suggesting that any action (or inaction) of mine was responsible for Cory's behavior. He was suggesting a way to look at the situation that could lead to a deeper understanding of my purpose in life and my relationship with God.

I don't know about before, but there's no doubt I'm withholding myself from Cory now. Most of the time, I'm either too sad or too furious to talk to him or even look at him. I've been nastily clear I don't want the slightest physical contact with him, which is why he's sleeping on the couch downstairs. He gets up very early in the morning and puts away the bedding, but I'm sure the kids know what's going on. They've been a handful lately.

I don't know what to do, dear friends. I can't see any solution to our situation—unless there's some magical way to make someone not gay. I feel like my skin has been stripped off—vulnerable and tender, needing to have space and quiet. Put our names in your temples, please. We need all the prayers we can get.

Erin

JUNEAU
    April 29, 1990
    Dear Friends,

Erin, my heart breaks for you. Your bishop sounds like a very wise man who has given you good counsel. I wish you well.

You can all wish *me* well. I've decided Misty and I are going to set off for Idaho this month to visit Letitia's empty grave. I'm still trying to coax my mother to come with us. I'm a bit nervous—I have no idea what I'll find there.

During spring break Nicole and Beto went with Marisol's family to the reunion at their ancestral village in the mountains of Mexico (I mentioned it late last summer). They came home all a-shine with a new set of plans. They've decided that when they become doctors, they won't go to Africa (à la Audrey Hepburn in *The Nun's Story*), after all. Instead, they want to go back to that little Mexican village. They say they're needed there, because although there's a resident midwife, the people have to go about fifteen miles to find other medical help. They're only seventeen now, so who knows if they'll actually end up following that dream. It could go the way of digging mummies in Egypt.

Love,<br>Juneau

Despite a lot of coaxing on Juneau's part, her mother found endless excuses why she couldn't, wouldn't, shouldn't accompany her daughter and granddaughter to Idaho to visit Letitia's empty grave. When May came and still no plans, Juneau called yet again.

"Go if you must, but leave me out of it," Pamela said. "And I won't take responsibility for anything you find out. There are reasons why we haven't talked about what went on there. You may learn things you'd be better off not knowing."

On the next class night, Juneau told Clyde she and Misty were finally going to see what they could dig up about Letitia. Without Pamela.

"Maybe you can find where you can dig up the old girl herself," he said, and they laughed together.

Juneau and Misty started out for Idaho on a bright day in May. They talked and laughed about small things as they drove north to Cedar City, where they spent the night. The next day they stopped briefly in Wellsville to say hello to Deenie's family and then hurried on north to Preston, an attractive little town in a broad valley. Juneau's dad, Paul, had given her instructions about proceeding from there. "You go off into the mountains as far as you can," he'd said, "then you go a little farther, and that's where you'll find Mink Creek."

Juneau turned onto a road that wound up through low hills and then swooped down to the floor of a pretty valley with a river. The winding road climbed steadily back into the hills—and beyond, as Juneau's dad had said. When they topped a rise and saw the small sign announcing "Mink Creek, 1 mile," Juneau had an odd feeling that she'd come home. *This is where I should have grown up,* she thought. All of her great-grandparents had come here from Denmark—the Paulsens and the Ostergaards, the Lunds and the Tofts. They'd lived here, raised their families here, and died here. Now they seemed to be welcoming her home.

Juneau drove up a hill to where there were two buildings: a well-kept, U-shaped red-brick church and across from it a red-brick schoolhouse with raised letters over the front door identifying it as "Mink Creek School." Her dad had said it was no longer used as a school. "Apartments now. They bus the kids to Preston these days."

"Dad said the cemetery is behind the church and the school," she told Misty.

"Probably up there." Misty pointed to an unpaved road, which lay alongside a brook lined with trees. "I can see gravestones. Let's go meet the family!"

Juneau laughed as she drove up the hill, praying that this trip to seek out their roots might provide the thread that would sew her daughter back into the whole cloth of her present family.

The cemetery was not large, but it stretched several rows up the hill and down along the slope that eventually fell away to a narrow valley. Up at the top of the cemetery a jeans-clad person with a billed cap rode a mower, cutting neat swaths through the grass.

They left the car on the grass verge, and Misty started up the hill toward the grass-cutting person. Juneau began reading inscriptions on the gravestones nearby and then just wandered. There were monuments of all sizes and shapes. Just beyond a small obelisk on the left side of the road, she saw the large granite stone she was looking for. "Ostergaard" was chiseled across the top of it and underneath that, on the right side, "Orville Adam," with the dates July 7, 1870–September 21, 1945. On the other side was "Letitia Lund" and April 14, 1887–, with the death date blank. Here it was. The empty grave.

She stood contemplating the stone until Misty came back down the hill with the mower person in tow, a slender girl with wheat-colored hair that had been covered up by her billed cap when they first saw her.

"We might be related," Misty called when they were within hearing distance. "Her last name is Ostergaard."

"Cath. Short for Catherine." The girl put out a hand, which Juneau took. "Misty tells me you're looking for Letitia."

Juneau grinned. "Sounds like the name of a book. *Looking for Letitia.* You know her?"

"Don't *know* her," Cath said cheerfully. "Just *about* her. Every college kid who grew up here has written an essay in soph comp about Letitia. You know, The Empty Grave, The Missing Coffin, Where Is My Bride? The story gets more lurid with each generation."

"Can we talk?" Juneau asked.

"You bet," Cath said. "Let's go to my house. Orville, here," she gestured at the gravestone, "built it for Letitia. If you're related to her, then you'd probably like to see it."

Juneau and Misty exchanged glances. "We would indeed."

"My mother is the family historian," Cath said. "She'll be delighted to connect you up on her family charts. Who all are you related to?"

"My mother is Pamela Ostergaard," Juneau said.

"Pamela!" Cath exclaimed. "I guess she's told you Letitia's story."

"As a matter of fact, no."

"Oh, wow," Cath said. "My mom's going to absolutely love meeting you."

As they got into their cars and Juneau followed Cath, Juneau could only wonder if Pamela had been right when she said her daughter might learn things she was better off not knowing.

# *Chapter 17*

JUNEAU

The house was old but well kept, an attractive two-story, pinkish brick structure with an inviting wide-railed porch running along the front and one side. There was a round turret on one corner and a small balcony in the center, cozied up to a jutting south wing. It was big. Actually, to someone brought up in trailers and motor homes, it was a palace. Again Juneau felt a sense of familiarity. Her mother must have had a photo of it somewhere that she'd seen when she was very young.

"What a great house," Misty said enthusiastically as Juneau parked and they got out of the car. "I always wanted to live in one like this."

"Me, too," Juneau said.

Cath motioned for them to come to a door that opened off the side porch. "My mom's going to have a cow! She loves it when parts of the family jigsaw show up. Mom!" she hollered. "We've found Pamela!"

Cath, Juneau, and Misty arrived at the door simultaneously with a pretty, dark-haired woman who wiped her hands on her jeans as she opened the screen door. "Pamela?" she repeated.

"Mom, meet Pamela's daughter." Stepping back, Cath threw out both arms in a grand gesture toward Juneau. "Ta DA!"

"Juneau Caldwell," Juneau said by way of introduction. "And my daughter, Misty."

"Well, welcome home." The woman moved forward to envelop Juneau and Misty in a big hug. "I'm Adrienne. I was just setting the table for dinner. Come on in and eat."

It seemed perfectly natural to sit there in the big kitchen, enjoying the savory chicken stew Adrienne had made. As they ate, Adrienne explained that the house had been inherited by her husband, Clay, who was the oldest son of the oldest son of the oldest son of Orville Ostergaard and his first wife, Abby. "Clay's away on business," she said. "Too bad. I'm sure he'd love to hear the story of your family."

"I'd rather hear the story of Letitia," Misty said.

"It all fits together," Cath replied.

A little later, when they were seated in the cozy parlor with the early 1900s red plush settee and deep, flowered carpet, Adrienne explained her interest in Pamela. "I'm an Ostergaard only by marriage," she said, "but I love doing family history." She held up a thick binder. "So I've collected everything that's been done on Clay's family. I've got everyone in here, except for Pamela. Well, actually, she's here as a teenager, and I recorded her marriage to Paul Jorgensen, but that's all I have."

"Jorgensen?" Juneau said. "My dad's last name is Paulsen."

Adrienne looked puzzled. "Paulsen? I don't know of any Paulsens who've ever lived here in Mink Creek."

Juneau felt as if she'd been dropped down a well. Was even her name a lie? She'd grown up a Paulsen. Daughter of the Peripatetic Paulsens, mystery writers. She turned to Adrienne. "Have you ever read any of the Pillar to Post mysteries?"

"Yes," Adrienne said. "Why?"

Juneau cleared her throat. "The authors—Paul and Pamela Paulsen. They're my parents."

Adrienne stared at her for a moment and then fell back against the back of her chair. "Well, great honk, no wonder I could never find them! They changed their last name!"

Cath was laughing. "That solves your mystery, Mom. What about theirs? The empty grave?"

"I can help you with that." Adrienne looked from Misty to Juneau. "My Grandma Petersen knew Letitia. Was a friend of her younger sister, Hattie." She patted the thick binder. "She told me all about what happened, and I wrote it all down, word for word."

## WILLADENE

April 9, 1990
Dear COBs,

Well, Carl's finally come clean. He says he's not ready to go on a mission. Instead, he is preparing applications for college. We are disappointed—and we love him. I remind myself daily to focus on the second part of that statement.

I wonder how much of his choice has to do with his girlfriend, Ashley. Carl is already complaining about how hard it will be for them to be apart. He must consider the possibility of being separated for two years intolerable.

You can imagine how I felt when the bishop announced that Reece and Ryan have received their calls, Reece to Brazil and Ryan to New York. That's the secret they have been keeping. Carl looked poleaxed by the news. Pat says they've been talking about becoming elders since Stan died. They want to do his work and be sealed to her and Dave.

Will and NeVae are home sorting through their things to decide what to take to California and what to dispose of. Utah has become the place they only visit. They are also spiffing up the old place before Bert arrives with her fiancé, Hal, and his two girls.

Erin, NeVae says to thank you again for your timely advice. She has lightened up on knowing all things Ghanaian and is focusing on what the girls share with her and sharing back honestly. I think Will's relieved that he can go back to being Grandpa Will without added expectations on NeVae's part.

Poor Hal. Bert's brothers, Roger included, are geared up to thoroughly vet him. If he lives through that—and lives up to a quarter of what NeVae says about him—he may be the first canonized LDS saint.

Sophie surprised Sunny this week with an unscheduled visit, a fiancé named Dennis Kerry, and a diamond ring on her left hand. Plans are in the works for a Christmas wedding. The sweethearts took Sunny out to dinner. Sophie asked her to help choose colors for the reception. They settled on gold lamé and red velvet. Sunny was so excited to be part of the planning, especially since it is unlikely she will be able to attend in the winter weather.

Sophie brought us up to date on all the family news. She had some encouraging things to say about how her parents and

Kenny are doing. And it sounds like her fiancé gets along well with both Kenny and Bryan. I bet that's a relief to you, Gabby.

My dad is going around looking too satisfied for words. He has something up his sleeve for my birthday next month. Can't imagine what could be giving him such a charge.

Love,
Deenie

JUNEAU

May 24, 1990
Dear COBs,

Well, girls, I found out the secret of the empty grave. And why my mom has never been back to Mink Creek! The story was told to Misty and me by a lovely woman named Adrienne, who's the keeper of Ostergaard family genealogy.

Seems Great-Grandmother Letitia, who was quite a looker, dreamed of leaving Mink Creek and going out to see the world. But then she accepted a marriage proposal from Orville, an older (he was thirty-five, she eighteen), very well-off man whose first wife had run away with a linoleum salesman, leaving him with two little boys. After Letitia married Orville, she found that the first wife had good reason to leave: he was as stingy as Scrooge. Doled out the money penny by penny and made her account for each one. Instead of seeing the world, Letitia ended up stuck where she was, mothering those two boys and keeping the pink brick mansion Orville was so proud of spotless and shining.

She was a good mother, but as she raised the boys and her daughter, Rosie, the light of her life, she still dreamed about all the places she wanted to see. When the kids were married, she had the idea she and Orville would travel, but then Rosie and her husband were killed in a car accident, leaving my mother, Pamela, an orphan. Letitia willingly took over the job of raising her.

Well, when Mom grew up and was about to strike off on her own, Letitia got fidgety and decided it was high time to make a move herself. That's when old Orville got the idea of wooing her with a gift. Imagine her surprise when he proudly showed her a tombstone for two with their names inscribed on it. Imagine his surprise when she picked up the shovel he'd brought along to the cemetery to plant flowers on their last resting place and whacked him in the neck with it!

Yes, dear COBs, he died three days later of a massive infection (penicillin hadn't yet come into use). My Great-Grandmother Letitia ended up in the penitentiary. Poor dear didn't even make it to Peoria!

At the time, Pamela (my mom) was in love with Paul (my dad) even though he was engaged to marry her cousin Annabelle in just a few days. Paul and Annabelle had been sweethearts before he went away to World War II, and Annabelle made plans for when he returned, not knowing that Pamela had also been writing to him all the time he was away. He didn't have the courage to tell Annabelle he loved Pamela. But then he took Pamela to see Letitia in the lockup. She knew they loved each other, and she told them if they wanted to save themselves, they should run away and get married. Right then!

That's exactly what they did, leaving poor Annabelle with her piles of doilies and embroidered pillowcases! She still lives in Mink Creek. And still itches to get her hands around my mother's neck! No wonder Mom and Dad have never been back. Oh, and they changed their name, too. I should have grown up as Juneau Jorgensen rather than Paulsen. It has a certain ring to it, don't you think?

How's that for a soap opera? No one in Mink Creek knows the rest of Letitia's story. I'll have to wheedle it out of Mom, somehow. Misty and I are processing what we've learned, wondering what insight there is to glean from Letitia and her thwarted wanderlust. Can we blame her for our restlessness? If so, maybe we ought to look at her story as a cautionary tale!

Love,
Juneau Jorgensen Caldwell!

P.S. The night before we headed home we were having a little sing-along at Adrienne's when Misty spied a framed photo on the piano top and picked it up. It was of Adrienne's daughter Cath (short for Catherine) and Rhiannan! Would you believe they were really good friends at BYU? Cath says Rhiannan talked about Trace a lot in the letters she sent from London. Small world, eh?

# Chapter 18

WILLADENE
> May 28, 1990
> Dear COBs,

Thank you for the interesting birthday cards, but thirty-eight isn't over the hill yet! I have the proof in my dad's birthday present—everything I need to qualify for my CCWP (concealed-carry weapons permit). Dad said that since I have the truck, the boots, the dog, and the attitude, I might as well qualify to carry. I wasn't sure about it at first, but I'm taking it on as a challenge.

When Dave the Sheriff heard about it, he said I should go straight to the police academy and take the beastly Bear along with me instead of fooling around with SAR training. He wasn't kidding. The county has been trying to come up with the funds for a police dog and handler. But it ain't gonna be this chickie!

With Roger's input, Dad bought me a Smith and Wesson .380 automatic handgun, a gift certificate for ten lessons with a professional trainer, and a membership to the gun club. He packed the gun in a duffel bag, along with a black leather shoulder holster, hearing protection earmuffs, and emergency supplies for the truck. Mom gave me a box of targets—human outlines with a bull's-eye right in the middle (shudder!). Will and NeVae gave me one of those newfangled cell phones with prepaid minutes to use in case of an emergency.

Roger came with me for my first CCWP lesson and liked it so well, he signed up for the training, too. In this style of shooting you aim at the point of largest mass and shoot with the intent to stop an aggressor. Blasting the middle of a human-shaped target gives me the willies. I can't imagine ever turning a weapon on a real person.

Dave says to get over it or get out of it. He says that unless I am committed to using a gun in self-defense, it becomes more of a liability than an asset and I should leave it at home. I still don't think I would ever point a gun at a living being, even if threatened, but I'm keeping on with my lessons. By the end of the year I can legally be a pistol-packing mama.

Who'd a thunk?

Deenie

P.S. Is there some cosmic message in getting a .380 pistol for my thirty-eighth birthday?

ERIN

June 1, 1990
Dear Juneau and Deenie,

Your last letters were the best reading I've had in ages! Deenie, I can't wrap my mind around your Deenie-to-the-Rescue purse also containing a gun. My mental image doesn't change fast enough to keep up.

And Juneau, I couldn't believe it when I read that dear Letitia had thwacked that clod of a husband with a shovel. Shades of Lizzy Borden! I don't know what struck me so funny (no pun intended), but I can be driving somewhere or working on a room design and all of a sudden find myself laughing about it all over again. Maybe I'm into black humor these days, because it was a terrible thing for her to do. Although he did deserve a thwack, but not a fatal one.

I've been wondering what this means to you, Misty, and the rest of your family. Are you better off knowing? Does knowing answer the questions you had? Do you think of yourselves differently because of it?

I have some good news to share, for a change. At least, I think it's good news. Kayla's love of skating and her steady progress has been noticed by coaches at the rink, and she's been invited to join the Braemar City of Lakes Figure Skating Club!

I wasn't sure we could make the commitment required in both time and money, but Cory said it wasn't fair to let our problems get in Kayla's way. We talked to his parents and The Jays and then decided to go for it. Now Kayla attends the Wednesday night group lesson and has a private lesson with a coach and a practice session. That's a lot for a seven-year-old, but her focus and enthusiasm are amazing.

When you add Mark's Tot Class and Termite Hockey to that schedule, you'd think we'd have enough of skating rinks, right? No!

Cory and I have been meeting the Browns every so often at the Roller Garden in St. Louis Park or Cheep Skate in Minnetonka. I don't know why, but we're all happy then, almost like a normal family. Maybe it's the combination of the music, lights, and almost-hypnotic motion of skating around and around. For some reason, it's easy for me to take Cory's hands while we're skating. For that time, at least, we're in synch and in touch.

Your Erin

WILLADENE
June 17, 1990
Dear COBs,

Juneau, your life is like a novel! I can't wait until the next installment. And Erin, I am so touched by the way you and Cory are putting your children first in a difficult time. That says a lot about both of you.

Speaking of children, Carl graduated from high school in a lovely ceremony in which he was honored as an athlete scholar. As soon as all the senior festivities were over, his girlfriend, Ashley, said she didn't want to be stuck with a scrub who wasn't planning to go on a mission and returned his letter jacket. Brat!

That didn't change Carl's plans to put off his mission. He says going has to be his choice or it won't mean anything. So he'll be attending the University of Utah in Salt Lake City this fall. He made a point of telling us he'll take an institute class so we won't worry about him. But we do and will. Isn't that our job?

During all the hullabaloo Paul quietly turned sixteen. No party, though. He asked his dad to put whatever money we would have spent on a birthday party in his mission fund. I am so amazed at how focused he is on his personal goals. But I worry that he is trying to make up for our disappointment in Carl's choice. That wouldn't be good for either of them.

He'll be a sophomore this fall and plans to go out for track. We are running together daily with the Beast. There's a Who'da for you! Roger thinks Paul has the stamina to be a good long-distance runner. Wicked awesome, as Beth would say.

Beth wants to have a boy-girl party this summer. I told her we would host an activity for the Beehives and the deacons on the condition she limit her use of *like* to one per sentence. That way we would both get something we wanted. We might live in a valley but Valley Girl chat is, ah, like, so totally not my thing.

Roger and I have become part of a social group! We, the Donovans (Lark and Shawn are Danny's parents), and Pat and Dave Fenton have started going out together at least once a month. The men get along great, and I enjoy being a part of another threesome of women. They aren't the COBs, but I love the company.

Will invited Shawn to join the crew on the farm for the summer. He teaches at Utah State, too, and he'd told Roger he wanted to do something really different this summer. It's quite an adventure for a city boy! Lark is spending time there, too, working on illustrations for a book about Milton, a mouse who doesn't believe in the lesson of the three little pigs and builds his house of straw. The Donovans are becoming more like family than just good friends.

Love,
Deenie

P.S. We've received a letter from each of the twins with their written testimony included—a wonderful surprise. Carl gets mail from them, too. I wonder what the three write about.

## ERIN

As summer deepened that year, the difficulties between Cory and Erin deepened, too. She'd been touched at first by his petitions for forgiveness for his not being honest with her prior to their wedding. But lately, she'd rejected them as being false because he couldn't promise, *cross my heart and hope to die,* that he would never, ever act on his desires.

"I don't understand," she said. They were upstairs in their bedroom with the door closed while the kids watched TV downstairs. "If you love the kids and me, why can't you promise?"

"I told you. I don't want to make a promise I'm not sure I can keep."

"Sometimes, the making of the promise gives the strength to keep it. You have to choose us, Cory, every moment of every day, no matter what."

"That's what I'm trying to do. But so help me, Erin, if you want me to succeed in this, you have to give me something to hold on to."

She knew what he was asking for, but she couldn't bring herself to offer a soft word or encouraging touch. "I didn't kick you out. That ought to be enough. Whatever you're going through right now, it's not my fault."

He snapped right back, "It's not my fault, either. I didn't ask for this."

She didn't respond. There was no point in rehashing an argument that always ended with his saying he didn't have a choice about being gay and her saying that either way, he could choose how he was going to act.

"Can't we get by this?" He walked toward her, hands held out in supplication. When she turned away, he said, "I get it. You're going to make it as ugly as possible. Well, let me know when you've got your pound of flesh, okay?" He slammed the bedroom door behind him as he left.

*I hope the kids didn't hear us,* she thought, but when Kayla approached her warily the next day, holding Mark's hand in hers, she knew they had.

"We're not a Forever Family anymore, are we?" Kayla asked.

"Of course we are!"

"How can we be? You and Daddy yell all the time. You don't go to church with us."

Erin felt a sharp pain under her ribcage. "Love is what makes a Forever Family, Kayla. I love you and Mark more than anything in the world, and I'll love you forever."

"Do you love Daddy?"

Erin hesitated only slightly before saying, "Yes, dear. I love your dad." It had to be the truth, didn't it? Why else would she be hurting so much?

They didn't believe her. Even if she hadn't seen the worry in their eyes, their behavior through the next weeks spoke volumes. Half the time, they picked fights with each other and mouthed back to Erin and Cory in a new and disturbing way. The other half, they made heartbreaking attempts to get Erin and Cory to smile at each other. Erin thought her heart would break when Mark took one of Cory's hands and put it in one of hers, patting and squeezing them as if he could make them stick.

August 4, 1990
Dear Friends,

I had two visitors yesterday while Cory and the children were at church: Bishop Harding and my mother-in-law.

Poor Bishop Harding. He came right when I had worked myself into a fine fury, and I took it out on him. I told him I was furious that a mission president would tell Cory everything would work out if he got married and had a family! I asked him if he had any idea how it felt to be used that way, to have my whole life ruined.

You know what he said? That I was right! That Cory should have told the truth about himself. By not telling me, he took away my freedom to choose. He said the mission president shouldn't have encouraged Cory to get married because marriage isn't therapy for those with same-sex attraction!

His compassion and quiet manner calmed me down, but he didn't let me off the hook. Before he left, he asked me to read President Ezra Taft Benson's conference talk on pride every Sunday, because pride is my stumbling block. He said if I'm not willing to do it for myself, I should do it for Mark and Kayla.

He'd been gone only a few minutes when Linda showed up! She was polished and coiffed as usual, but she looked worn down and distressed. When I confronted her about knowing that Cory was gay, she said she'd had a suspicion that he might be, but when he and I got married and gave her two beautiful grandchildren, she thought she'd been mistaken. Or that the Lord had blessed Cory with a miracle. Then she started to cry, poor dear. She begged me to stay with Cory, if not for his sake, for the children's sake.

So I got a double whammy that morning. Both Linda and the bishop know that the one soft spot left in my heart is for Kayla and Mark. I would do anything if it would allow them to grow up feeling safe and happy.

Well, almost anything. But what they said has got me wondering. And yes, I got out the May 1989 *Ensign* and read the talk.

Your Erin

# Chapter 19

WILLADENE
August 1, 1990
Dear COBs,

We're going to theme park heaven in the fall! I'm as excited as the kids are. Since we'll be in Los Angeles for Bert's wedding to Hal Udall, we've decided to make a vacation trip of it.

Evvy goes on and on about seeing Mickey Mouse in his barn. I think she is confusing Mickey with the Milton Mouse that Lark is drawing.

We liked the Udalls. Hal and the girls fit right into the family this summer. No matter what Roger and his brothers threw at Hal, he handled it with calmness and humor. Beth took to Ami and Atsu on sight. It was a delight to see how well they got along together.

NeVae asked Beth how she felt about the girls being *different*. Beth said, "Oh, you mean because their mother was from Ghana?" When NeVae answered yes, Beth said, "Danny's mom is from New Jersey, and I like her," as if that were the same thing. We all took Lucky's advice to heart and hope to keep at it. The Udalls' only real reference to Ghana was to present the women and girls in the family with individual lengths of kente cloth selected and sent by Ami and Atsu's grandparents, the Kufuors, from Accra, Ghana.

Hal explained that the Kufuors, recent converts themselves, won't be here for his and Bert's wedding because they are saving up for their own temple endowments, which they plan to receive in the Los Angeles temple next year. The Kufuors have asked Hal if he thinks Bert would stand proxy for their daughter when they are sealed in the temple in 1991. Mighty open-hearted of them.

Carl will be moving on campus in Salt Lake City after the

wedding. Our nest will be shy its oldest chick and that makes me sad. Roger says to buck up—Evvy has so much energy and mischief in her that she should have been twins. Guess I can count her twice!

Love,
Deenie

ERIN

August 8, 1990
Dear Gabby, Juneau, and Deenie,

Guess what? Kayla passed her pre-preliminary moves test today! It's the first test kids take on their way up the levels in figure skating, so she was totally thrilled. She's already talking about what she needs to do to get ready for her pre-preliminary free skate. There's no hurry to do it, though.

She looked great on the ice. I may be imagining it, but I think her posture and hand positions have improved since she started to take ballet. And with her hair slicked back in a bun and makeup on, she had that look figure skaters strive for, elegant and sophisticated.

We had a family celebration afterward, of course. It was such a normal get-together, I could almost convince myself Cory and I have a future together. Mom says that either way, I should be grateful we still can have such moments, so I am.

Gabby, congratulate Bryan for being the top insurance salesman of the month. I can't understand why he's not married yet— there can't be that much difference between getting a prospect to sign on the line and getting a girl to say yes!

I'm glad Kenny likes his job as a motorcycle mechanic. I worry about him, though. Life isn't easy for newly released convicts, if what I've read in detective novels can be believed. (Yes, they're my new favorites.) It would be a blessing if he and Bryan could become friends.

Deenie, I still can't believe you're getting your concealed-carry permit. You've turned into a totally different woman since we first met. In honor of that and the detective novels, here's a Regina just for you:

*Regina checked her answering machine, expecting to hear a message from Reginald, who had been on a stakeout for the past three days. Instead, she heard a raspy voice say, "I have the information you've been looking for. Meet me on the corner of Smith and Wesson. Leave your husband and your squalling brats behind."*

*Who could that be? Regina wondered. What did he know about the missing heiress? She picked up her purse, its weight indicating that her little derringer was where it was supposed to be. Then she looked into the nursery, where the twins, the triplets, and the quadruplets swarmed over the hapless nannies. "I must be off to save the day," she said. "The kiddies can be rambunctious, I know, but remember, chloroform is the last resort!"*

Love,
Erin

## JUNEAU

August 12, 1990
Dear Gabby, Deenie, and Erin,

Deenie, how great that your family is coming to my neck of the woods for Bert's wedding and your vacation. I'm glad you're going to visit everybody's favorite theme park while you're here. Everyone should go at least once!

Erin, give Kayla a high five for me. I love the way your family celebrates occasions big and small. Your kids will have many lovely memories to look back on.

I've been in a slump following the high of our *Music Man* performances. I may be an actor at heart, because I loved every moment on stage! My whole crew attended both nights to cheer for me, and even a few members of my writing class came on opening night. Now that it's over, life seems a little flat. But Giddy and Philip Atwater are making heroic efforts to perk me up.

Love,
Juneau

As time went by and Juneau was able to reflect at length on the trip to Idaho—and Erin's question about what good knowing the truth did—

she wondered if her mother had been right when she said she shouldn't go. After all, what had been accomplished, really?

She wanted to talk with her mother about it, but Pamela and Paul were gone all through June and most of July on a research trip for their new mystery set in Bar Harbor, Maine. During that time Juneau got two postcards but never an address or phone number where they could be reached. She suspected her mother was purposely avoiding talking about what Juneau had uncovered. But Juneau had been busy, too, with the *Music Man* production. So she hadn't pressed the issue.

She'd loved playing Eulalie and the release from her own problems it gave her. She'd taken Gideon with her to rehearsals. He could sing "Theventy thix tromboneth led the big parade" and "The Wellth Fargo wagon ith a-comin' down the thtreet" almost as well as those who played the parts.

So it had been a good summer, and because Misty had been heavily involved in the choreography of the show, Juneau allowed herself a break from worrying about her daughter following the restless wind or her wandering star or whatever it was that pulled her away from where she should be. But it wasn't so easy to ignore Letitia. Too often, Juneau pulled Letitia from her ragbag of worries and fretted over what she'd learned and what she didn't yet know.

Pamela called in September. "We're home," she said cheerfully.

Her mother's carefree voice set Juneau's teeth on edge. She drew a deep breath before answering. "Hi, Mom. How are you? How's Dad?"

"Terrific. Being on the road again was good for him. But we're both happy to be back to our little stationary home in the woods. And how's everyone there?"

"We're fine." Juneau paused. "Misty and I went to Idaho."

The phone line hummed, and then Pamela said, "So now you know."

"About the empty grave, yes. It explains a lot of things," Juneau said, "but it brings up questions, too. Like, did you stay in touch with Letitia while she was in the penitentiary? Did she ever get out? When did she die? Where is she buried? Do you even care?"

"Of course I care, Juney. She was the only mother I ever knew."

"Then tell me, Mom!"

"You know I'm a lot better at writing than I am at talking. How about I write it all up from my perspective? But for now, I'll tell you this much: It was Letitia's choice to cut herself off from everyone. She said if anybody except me wrote to her, she'd send the letters back. So neither she nor I had any more contact with the family."

"The past is past, Mom. It's time to reconnect with the family again. Why don't you go back to Mink Creek for a visit? The people I met, they were absolutely terrific. All of our family roots are there."

"I can't go back, Juney. I'm sure you found out about Annabelle?"

"Yes. She's still there. Never married. Runs a bed and breakfast place." She hesitated. "Couldn't you go back and make some kind of peace, Mom? After all these years?"

"With Annabelle? She'd shoot me. I ran off with her almost-husband, just days before the wedding."

"That *was* pretty awful, Mom. But you've made progress. You recognize it was a dreadful thing to do."

"I knew it at the time, Juney. But I loved Paul. Still do, more than ever."

"No regrets?"

"Only that I hurt Annabelle. But enough of that. Tell me how Misty and Gideon and the rest of the family are doing."

Juneau knew it would be pointless to try prying further information from her mother, so she did as Pamela had requested, beginning with a funny story about Gideon and his pal, Philip Atwater. Five minutes later, Pamela hung up with a breezy, "Bye now," leaving Juneau with the familiar frustration she always felt after talking to her mother. And a new unanswered question: When, if ever, would Pamela write the promised letter?

*Wait until Clyde hears this,* she thought.

She told him all about her trip and the conversation with her mother as they sat across from each other in their usual spot at Bob's Big Boy, including her doubts about whether she'd accomplished anything.

"That remains to be seen," Clyde said. "Consequences of actions sometimes don't show up for years."

Juneau saw some immediate effects of the trip, however. As the days passed, Juneau noticed that Misty frequently referred to Mink Creek. She spoke of its beauty, how much she liked Cath and her mother, and how at home she felt there. She wasn't just reminiscing, Juneau knew. She was targeting her next place to wander.

Then a letter came from Cath, enclosing a copy of the snapshot of her and Rhiannan. Trace was visiting Juneau on the day it arrived, so Juneau showed it to him.

"Oh!" he said as he took it, rubbing a thumb over the image of Rhiannan. His face twisted, and for a moment Juneau thought he might cry. But then he looked up from the photo and said, "Rhiannan told me about someone named Cath. Said how she was her best college friend. I wonder if they realized they were related."

It was then that the idea came to Juneau, as clear as if it, too, had been printed on photo paper. A picture of the future. Trace's and Cath's future.

"You may have the snapshot, Trace," she said. "Why don't you write to Cath and thank her?"

# Chapter 20

ERIN

Weeks went by, and Erin still rode the pendulum from fragile hope to fury and judgment. In the middle of the arc was numbness, which frightened her even more than the extremes, because she remembered Deenie describing it as an early sign of her breakdown. A crisis was coming, and Erin both feared it and longed for it. Anything to get them out of the bog they were in.

Things came to a head the week after the October Big Barn Sale. That Friday evening everyone was short-tempered and tired, and Kayla was nursing a bruised knee from a fall on the ice. When Erin told her and Mark to wash up for supper, they immediately starting fighting over who got to use the downstairs bathroom. Erin waded into flying fists and feet, separated them, and sent a fuming Kayla to the bathroom upstairs.

"These kids are driving me crazy. Do something about them," she snapped at Cory when she went back into the kitchen. "And don't tell me you need a break because it was a hard day at work."

He turned off the TV. "Cut them some slack. They're scared."

"So, who isn't?" She took a deep breath and willed herself to relax, but the back of her neck radiated prickly energy, making her want to strike out.

As she finished making the salad that would accompany an uninspired hot dish, she could hear Cory talking to the kids, his voice low and intense. However, they were still touchy when she called them to the table, sniping and poking each other.

When Mark pulled Kayla's hair and she jabbed him with her elbow, Erin exploded. "Stop it right now! I mean it. Both of you shut up and sit down." She squeezed her eyes shut, grabbed two handfuls of her hair, and said through gritted teeth, "This whole family drives me crazy."

"Erin!"

Cory's voice brought her to her senses. Seeing the look on her children's faces, she wished with all her heart she could take back her words. "I didn't mean that! I'm so sorry. Please forgive me." She reached out to them, but they sat in silence, staring at their plates.

After a supper eaten in unpleasant silence, Erin sent the kids to their rooms and began clearing the table.

"Pretty ugly, isn't it?" said Cory. "What we're turning into, I mean." He paused. "Our kids are in trouble, Erin, and we're the cause of it."

Erin reached for a sharp retort, but the anger and righteous indignation that had powered her for so many weeks betrayed her by its absence. She felt only a deep, wrenching guilt and sadness.

"Poor Mark. Poor Kayla." She bit her lower lip to keep it from trembling. "I love them, but I don't know how to help them. I don't even know how to help myself."

"I have an idea that might help." Cory looked at her and then busied himself rearranging the jade Oven King salt and pepper shakers. "I'm the cause of your problems with the kids. Me being in the house upsets you, and you end up taking your frustration out on them. Maybe it would be easier if I moved out."

"What?!" She'd wanted him gone for so long, how was it that his words struck fear into her heart?

"With me gone, the kids might not be so much trouble."

"You can't go! You saw how I just treated them. If you're not here, things would be a thousand times worse."

"Maybe, but maybe not. One thing's for sure, you and I can't live like this any more. I've been doing everything I can to be the husband and father you and the children deserve, but it hasn't made any difference, because you won't meet me halfway." He caught her gaze and held it. "You won't forgive me."

She said what she'd thought a hundred times. "I don't want to forgive you. You haven't suffered enough."

"Is making me suffer more important to you than everything else? Think about it, Erin. Because either you forgive me and we give our marriage a real chance—or we call it quits."

Erin gulped. "I don't want to call it quits. I want us to be a family. But I also want a husband who can love all of me. You can't do that."

"Maybe not the way you want, but I have loved you, and we got two beautiful children out of it. It's up to you, Erin. You choose."

A great weariness came over Erin, and she sat down across from him. She had to choose, for herself and her children. And once she'd chosen, she had to give her whole heart to making it work. Her shoulders sagged as she gave up resisting. It was a great relief to say, "I forgive you."

He clasped both her hands in his. The kiss he bestowed upon them was almost like a sacrament. "Thank you, from the bottom of my heart. I feel like I can breathe again."

"Maybe we all can."

"Remember that promise you asked for? I couldn't make it back then, but I will now. I promise you, Erin, I'll never let those feelings get the upper hand, never let them rule my actions. I'm choosing you and the family—and you can count on it."

She blinked back tears of relief and hope. "Thank you, Cory. Only . . . I'm willing to do everything I can to create a happy family. As far as our relationship as husband and wife, I don't know."

"Fair enough."

"One more thing. If there ever comes a time when you can't keep your promise, tell me. Don't make a fool of me again."

WILLADENE
November 4, 1990
Dear Erin, Juneau, and Gabby,

Juneau, you can skip this first part, because it's about Bert's wedding, which you know all about already!

Bert and Hal Udall got married in the Los Angeles temple. A day of festivities followed that were fun, touching, and exhausting. The bride was beautiful in a tailored white suit, the groom was storybook handsome, and Ami and Atsu glowed with joy. From Carl on down, our kids were on their best behavior— they'd been promised an extra day at a nearby theme park if they were! Evvy kept asking when she was going to see Milton Mouse in his barn.

NeVae nearly outshone the bride with her delight, and Will played proud papa to the hilt. He was almost as excited to show off his newly purchased condo not far from where Hal, Bert, and the girls will be living. It's clear he is getting ready to turn the farm completely over to his sons Gordon and Keith.

Juneau, let me tell you again how thrilled I was to meet your family. Giddy is so delicious. He and Evvy made quite a pair at the reception. Beth was sorry Ira wasn't there. She's interested in more stories about Uncle Schlomo and his jokes.

When we got home we had a rush to get Carl settled in his digs at the University of Utah. He's not going to have any problem making the transition to college man. As we left the dorm, he was already eyeing a likely group of young coeds. Yay for him and a raspberry for Ashley.

Beth is thriving in middle school. Why not? There are older "men" for her to moon over. Ninth graders! Paul is continuing to run with me and Bear. The track coach says he has real promise (Paul, not the dog) and agreed with Roger on his long-distance potential. Paul's happy about that.

Even though I have my CCWP (concealed-carry weapons permit), the Smith and Wesson stays locked in Roger's gun safe unless we are planning a date at the gun club.

Love,
Deenie

P.S. Gabby, I thought Sophie's getting married in December was romantic, but on Friday the 13th? I guess you take the date that's free. Juneau and Erin, want to go in together on a present for Sophie?

## JUNEAU

Not long after she attended the sealing of Roberta and Hal, Juneau gave a bridal shower for Isobel, Marisol's daughter, who was getting married in December. Marisol was bright and smiley-faced all during the silly shower games and the happy opening of the gifts. But after the guests left and Vincent and Beto came over to help Isobel cart the loot home, Marisol's face seemed to collapse.

"Why, whatever's the matter?" Juneau asked.

Marisol tried on a smile. "What makes you think anything's the matter?" She didn't quite look at Juneau.

"Marisol." Juneau put her hands on the other woman's shoulders and turned her so they were face to face. "How many years have we been neighbors? How many things have we been through together? How many secrets have we shared?"

Silently Marisol stepped forward and laid her head on Juneau's shoulder. Tears came, as if they'd been dammed up for a long time. Finally she straightened. "Manny's leaving me."

She might as well have said the mighty San Gabriels were leaving, packing up their peaks and valleys, and going somewhere else. Manny leaving Marisol? He whose voice wobbled with emotion when he spoke of his love for Marisol and their kids?

Juneau guided Marisol to the sofa, where she pushed aside assorted torn gift wrappings and ribbons. "Okay, pal," she said. "Shoot."

Marisol drew in a deep breath. "She's younger, blonde."

"Out of a bottle, I'll bet," Juneau said indignantly.

Marisol looked at her, and for a moment they gazed into each other's eyes. Then with a "Pffft," they both broke into giggles, just as they'd always done when confronted with something ridiculous at a PTA meeting or someplace else where they should be dignified.

"What's funny?" Marisol asked when she could stop. "My husband's leaving me!"

"For a scrawny, washed-out, ditzy, dizzy . . ."

"Frizzy," Marisol put in.

Juneau nodded. "Ditzy, dizzy, frizzy, adolescent, dumb blonde," she finished. They collapsed into giggles again. "Have you seen her?"

"No. But I'm sure she's all that." Marisol sat up and wiped her face.

"How long have you known?"

"I suspected as long ago as a couple of years."

Juneau remembered that she'd noticed a sadness about Marisol for a long time. Why hadn't she asked her about it? "So where is the situation at the moment?" she asked. "I mean, has he taken his clothes? Has he moved out his exercise machine? Has he kidnapped the TV remote?"

Marisol tried on a grin. "Nothing that final yet. He's been in Mexico on another buying trip for two months, you know. He told me all about Bambi over the phone. He says we'll talk about it when he comes up for Isobel's wedding."

"*Bambi?*"

"Actually, her name is Barbara. But that's the way I think of her."

"Bambi, Barbie, it all adds up to Bimbo," Juneau said. "Pffft." And they were off again.

"Well," Juneau said eventually, "remember what that great philosopher Yogi Berra said: 'It ain't over till it's over.' Do you want to keep Manny?"

At first Marisol said, "I don't know." But then she changed it to, "Yes, I do. I love him."

"Then we'll figure out something," Juneau said. "I'm good at plotting. Miss Ditzy Dizzy Frizzy Bambi won't know what hit her."

"Yeah, we'll take care of her," Marisol said, slitting her eyes and putting on a villainous face. "Thanks for helping me rediscover my worst side, pal."

Juneau gave her a hug. "What are friends for?"

## ERIN

December 26, 1990
Dear Gabby, Juneau, and Deenie,

*'Tis the day after Christmas, and all through the house, just two creatures are stirring, me—and a mouse.*

It's dark and cold outside, and I'm snuggled up in front of my computer with a throw and a cup of Postum. For the first time in months, I feel content. I figured I should write you right away, in case it doesn't last!

We had a quiet Christmas. Neither Cory nor I had the energy to make a big production. Harold and Cory's parents were feeling sad at the anniversary of Trina's death, and we were all missing The Jays, who went to Connecticut to visit Jake's son and his family.

Isn't it odd that while my marriage is in trouble, my mother's is flourishing? I was so proud of myself when Cory and I were married in the temple. Blame it on the pride of youth, but I thought I was doing way better than my mom had done. Now I'm beginning to see what a remarkable woman she is, and I have a new appreciation for the loving way she raised me under difficult circumstances. I'm so happy that she's happy. She's earned every bit of the joy her life with Jake has to offer.

You can probably tell that I'm in a different place than I've been since Cory outed himself. Chalk that up to one smart (or inspired) bishop who asked me to read President Benson's talk on pride every Sunday. For a long time, I zipped through the words without thinking about them. But a funny thing happened. They got into my head anyway, and they've gradually made their way down into my heart.

I really got the lesson the day I heard Cory talking to Kayla about what it would be like when he baptizes her after her eighth birthday, which is coming up in January. When I questioned him about it later, he got really upset. He said if the bishop believed he hadn't done anything to necessitate disciplinary action and thought he was worthy to take the sacrament and baptize his daughter, how come I didn't?

I realized right then that President Benson was talking to me in the part where he says the proud withhold forgiveness to keep others in their debt and justify their injured feelings. Also in the line about the proud wanting God to agree with them, instead of changing their opinions to agree with God's. I saw that I'd been unwilling to forgive Cory so I could feel justified and punish him for being who he is. I've also been completely uninterested in knowing God's will for us.

Not a pretty picture, is it? I've been truly humbled. The odd thing is, I'm grateful for it, because I can feel my heart softening. So, my dear friends, I can't say I'm optimistic, but I am hopeful.

Best wishes to you and your families.

Your Erin

P.S. I just had to add one more thing—Caitlin called. She invited us to come to the "family manse" (as Cory calls it) for lunch the Sunday after Christmas. I told her we were "watch-ing" Grams while The Jays were in Connecticut, and she said, "Bring her along." When I asked Grams, she said, "Of course I'll go. I want to see where That Catholic Boy lives."

P.P.S. Juneau, what's happened with Marisol and her husband?

# *Chapter 21*

## 1991

ERIN

On New Year's Day, Kayla sat at the last desk in the row of three antique school desks in the great room, working on a list of the people she wanted at her baptism. Looking over her shoulder, Erin saw that the first two names on the list were skaters who shared Kayla's excitement about the upcoming McCandless Competition, which would be held in March. It would be Kayla's first.

Erin knelt down beside her daughter and automatically began to massage the pinkish scar that ran from Kayla's hairline down to her right cheek. Was she imagining it or was it a little thicker and bumpier? "This isn't a party, dear," she said. "It's a family occasion."

"My Primary teacher said inviting people was a way to be a good missionary."

"That's true if you invite people we've already talked to about the gospel. But it might not be the best way to introduce people to the Church."

"I told Smith about it when he wanted to know why we didn't go skating on Sundays. So I could invite him, right?"

Erin couldn't imagine Smith and his parents coming, but she said, "Sure, and his mom and dad, too."

Kayla wrote on the paper and then looked up at Erin. "Mom, did your friend Angie get baptized?"

"I think she wants to, but she hasn't yet."

"I'm going to invite her," Kayla said firmly. "And Grandpa Andrew and Lottie and Caitlin and Shakeela . . ."

Erin smiled as she watched her daughter bend over her list. This was going to be quite the event, if Kayla had her way. Well, why not? It could be a celebration not only of Kayla's baptism but also of the renewal of Erin and Cory's marriage.

In the last month they had gone back to being friends, partners, and

bedmates, though not lovers. She still felt keenly their lack of physical intimacy, but she was incredibly grateful that the year was beginning with
promise instead of despair—it could have so easily gone the other direction.

As Erin started loading the dishwasher, she was thinking about Angie
and Norm, whom she hadn't seen since the Big Barn Sale the past fall.
Her fault, not theirs. After Cory outed himself, she'd found it shockingly
easy to pull inward, pretending that being busy was the same as being
alive.

She'd been thrilled when Angie had announced at the Fourth of July
party that she wanted to have the discussions. She and Colleen had
gladly accompanied their husbands on those evenings, which had been
full of sweetness, serious conversation, and prayer. Not even Norm's
upfront declaration that he had no intention of joining any church had
dampened the Spirit.

Erin was sure that Angie would be baptized, but when the missionaries invited her to do so, she surprised them all by saying she wasn't quite
ready. That had been months ago, and although Angie regularly attended
"her ward," she still had not been baptized.

Kayla interrupted Erin's introspection. "Mom? We get baptized when
we're eight because we're old enough to know things and choose the
right."

"Yes." Erin wondered where Kayla was heading.

"Will Ricky know enough to be baptized when he turns eight?"

"Why do you ask?"

"It takes a long time for him to learn things. If he doesn't understand,
how can he choose?"

"Aunt Colleen and Uncle Steve will probably put off his baptism until
he's older and understands more." Erin laid down her dishcloth and
perched on the top of the desk in front of Kayla. "One more thing. There
are two ways of knowing, Kayla. One is with the head, and the other is
with the heart." Erin lightly touched Kayla's chest. "It's what you know
in your heart that's most important, and there's nothing wrong with
Ricky's heart."

The third Saturday of January, Kayla Marie Johnson was baptized by her father and confirmed a member of the Church by her ninety-year-old great-grandfather, Harold. Then family and guests gathered at the house for a celebration.

While Erin and Joanna put the food on the table, Kayla got into a lively discussion about baptism with Shakeela and Smith. She wanted to know how they could be baptized when they were babies and didn't know anything. Smith told her that Lutherans had godparents, and Shakeela said Methodists did, too. Kayla wanted to know what godparents did. Between them, Lucky and Joanna explained that godparents helped teach the child about Christ. Kayla said she had a whole ward full of god-parents to do that, to which Lucky gave a hearty amen.

Thus encouraged, Kayla went around the circle, identifying the guests who were Mormons. She went on to say, "Grams and Grandma Joanna are Lutherans like Smith and his parents. Shakeela and her parents are Methodists, which I think is kind of the same. My Grandpa Andrew, Grandma Lottie, and Caitlin are Catholic. And Jake was Quaker when he was little." She turned to Angie and Norm. "What are you? Almost Mormons?"

When the laughter died down, Angie said, "That's right." But Norm countered, "I'm nothing."

"Hmmm." Kayla gave Norm a speculative gaze. "I don't think you can be nothing. You have to be something."

"You may be right," he said with a smile.

*What an odd but wonderful bunch,* Erin thought, looking at Kayla's guests. *Like Juneau's collected family.*

After they'd eaten, Cory stood and offered a toast to Kayla, who basked in the attention. Then she stood and said, "I have something I want to read. About why I'm glad I'm a real Mormon girl."

She began with "I got baptized to obey the Lord like Jesus did when he got baptized." She ended with "I got baptized so I can be part of a For-ever Family, because I love my mommy and daddy and my brother, Mark."

Erin grasped Cory's hand tightly, hoping that he understood what she was telling him. *We'll make it, Cory. We will. For them.*

As the evening drew to a close, Angie joined Erin at the kitchen sink. "Thanks for inviting Norm and me," she said. "It's been way too long since we've spent time together."

"I know," Erin said. "Sorry about that—we were stuck in some problems for a while. But on a day like today, it's easy to see what's most important in life."

"True, true." Angie picked up a pot and began absently to wipe it. "I suppose you've been wondering why I never got baptized. I'm in a . . . situation that I haven't been able to work out. And I can't get baptized until I do." Her hands stilled, and she looked at Erin. "Norm and I aren't married."

Erin gaped. She had imagined countless reasons but never that.

"Hard to believe, isn't it?" Angie managed a grin. "We've been together thirty-five years, through some pretty big ups and downs. We love each other dearly. But we don't have that piece of paper." She paused. "I guess that means I'm living in sin."

## JUNEAU

January 7, 1991
Dear COB and COBettes (some days I feel more like an "ette" than a full-fledged),

Gabby, thank you so much for the photos of Sophie's wedding. She and Dennis are a handsome couple. I especially liked the pictures showing the whole family. I'm guessing Kenny is the young man with the shaven head who looks like a rougher, tougher version of Junior.

Once again, I have to apologize for being a poor correspondent. I've kept you somewhat up to date via phone and Christmas card, but as Erin reminded me, I've left you in the dark about Marisol and Manny.

Before I get to that, I'll say that Trace did get an answer back from Cath after he sent the thank-you letter for the picture of Rhiannan. Maybe nothing will come of it, but at least they're in touch. Just call me Cupid, or maybe Yente. "Matchmaker, Matchmaker . . ." Trace needs a girlfriend to replace the image of Rhiannan. No, I don't mean *replace*, because nobody could ever do that for any of us. But he needs somebody here on this side of the veil.

Now to Marisol and Manny. Marisol and I did a lot of conniving and plotting before Manny came home from Mexico for Isobel's wedding, as I mentioned on the phone. We'll give little Miss Blonde Barbie-Bambi-Bimbo a run for her money.

I asked Marisol what it was that first attracted Manny to her, Marisol, besides her obvious beauty. She said he often commented that he loved the way she was so understanding and good-natured. So we decided to build our strategy on that.

Manny arrived home from Mexico just four days before Isobel's wedding, and everything was so hectic they had no time to talk. The wedding, by the way, was lovely. It was at the old San Gabriel Mission, the wedding Mass with all the trimmings. Isobel was so beautiful that I cried all the way through it. At the end of the ceremony, she walked over to lay her bouquet at the feet of a statue of Mary. Sob, sob, sob . . .

But I digress. It wasn't until the day after that Manny told Marisol they needed to talk.

"Yes, we do," she told me she said. "I've been wondering if you plan to take the desk in your office when you go."

"When I go?" Manny repeated.

"Yes," Marisol said. "When you set up housekeeping with Barbara. Since I'll have to go back to work then, I plan to move all my teaching stuff into the office, and I could use that desk. I've always liked it."

Marisol said that Manny looked as if he'd been hit by an asteroid. He stared at her for about two minutes and then said, "Marisol, are you having an affair or something?"

"Good heavens, Manny," she said, sweetly. "How can you say such a thing?"

"You can hardly wait to get me out of the house, that's why." His eyes became slits. "Is it that math teacher you were hanging onto when we went to Beto's open house at school last fall? Lamar something or other?"

"He's nice," Marisol said. "But of course I'm not having an affair with him. He's married, three kids."

"You're married, too," Manny said. "Three kids. Have you thought about that?"

Marisol told me she didn't say a thing. Just smiled. Sweetly. She said she could almost hear the whir of his thinking apparatus. He began turning brick red, and she wondered if he'd blow a fuse. Then he sputtered something about her forgetting about taking over his desk or his room because he wasn't going anywhere. Then he stomped into his room and slammed the door. She heard him talking on the phone.

When he came out, he said he'd cancelled an appointment and would she like to go out to dinner that night?

Marisol says she knows this may be a temporary truce, and that Barbie is still lurking around out there somewhere like a predatory spider. For now, Manny is back at home. But Marisol really is going to see about getting her old teaching job back. Insurance, just in case. Pray for her, please.

Juneau

## WILLADENE

In late January, Deenie hosted a Just Because party for the Donovans and Fentons—just because she and Roger enjoyed their company. As dinner got underway, Shawn Donovan unfolded his tall, lanky form from the chair at the head of the dining room table and raised his mug toward Deenie and Roger, who sat side by side at the other end. "To Deenie and Bear and their level-two certification in search-and-rescue training." Everyone shouted, "Hear, hear!" and clinked their mugs together.

As Shawn sat down, Deenie took the floor. "And here's to our illustrious illustrator, Lark, for her remarkable work on the soon-to-be-released children's book *Milton Mouse Learns a Lesson*." The group cheered Lark.

"Good job, babe." Shawn gave her a resounding kiss. She pushed him away with a laugh and got to her feet. "Let us not forget our beloved Pat and her beloved pastries, pies, cookies, rolls, bread, and tortes. To Pat and

Crafton Catering, now open at its brand-new location in Logan. Long may you bake!" They all toasted that with added enthusiasm.

"Hey, what about us guys?" Dave protested.

"We're feeding you, aren't we?" Deenie said with a grin.

"And you get to go home with the girl of your choice," Pat said, giving Dave a meaningful grin.

"Yeah," agreed Lark. "What more could you ask for?" She passed around a platter of her now-famous Good Philly Cheese Steak sandwiches.

"A refill on the chocolate?" Roger quipped.

Deenie leaped to her feet and gave a flamboyant bow. "Your wish is my command, O Great One." Then laughing along with the rest of them, she refilled Roger's mug from the carafe on the sideboard. As she handed it back, the doorbell rang.

"I'll get it." Deenie opened the door to see a young officer in police blues. "Mrs. Rasmussen?" he asked.

"Yes. What can I do for you, Officer . . . ?"

"Brad Donaldson, ma'am," the policeman said, whipping off his hat. "I'm sorry to disturb you, but I was in the area and thought I'd chance it to see if you could give me a moment of your time."

"Of course. Come in out of the cold before you freeze."

"Thank you, ma'am." Officer Donaldson scraped the snow from his shoes and brushed it from his coat before he entered the house.

"How can I help you?" Deenie prompted, ushering him toward the fireplace.

"Well, ma'am," he said with an exquisite politeness that made Deenie feel ninety years old, "it's about that dog there of yours." He nodded in the direction of Bear, who was watching him alertly. "You see, I'm part of the K-9 unit of the Salt Lake City police department. My partner, Ruger, was killed in a drug bust this past year."

"I'm so sorry," Deenie said. Comments of sympathy came from the rest of the party.

"Thank you. The thing is, I've been looking for a new dog for a while now without finding the right one. I heard about Bear from some friends in search and rescue. He sounded perfect. And I wanted to ask—"

"No," Deenie interrupted.

"—if you would consider turning him over for police training," Donaldson plowed on.

"Officer Donaldson." Deenie spoke in a soft but intense voice. "You're welcome to share my food, my friends, and even my faith, if it suits you. But nobody, nohow, lays claim to Bear except me."

"Yes, ma'am. I just thought . . ."

"Come now," Deenie said kindly, trying to make up for her brusqueness. "Have dessert with us. It's a fresh cream torte with ripe strawberries and peaches in it. If you clean your plate," she added with a grin, "we can go out back afterward and put the Beast through his paces."


"I like that young man," Roger told Deenie later in the evening as they prepared for bed. "You were a little short with him, don't you think?"

"Maybe just a little, but I'll make it up to him." Deenie turned back the covers and fluffed the pillows. "I invited him to visit anytime he's in the area. He'll be back." Deenie knelt by the bed. Roger knelt down next to her.

"Your turn," he said.

Deenie prayed, remembering all the special family needs, gratitudes, and wishes. She even took time to ask for a special blessing on Officer Donaldson "that he might be successful in finding a new K-9 partner."

After the amens they snuggled close together under the blankets piled on the bed against the winter cold.

"Why does Beth need a prayer for special help to feel better about herself?" Roger asked.

"Trouble with an older man," Deenie answered. "Jason Whitmore."

Roger burst out laughing. "Jason Whitmore? He's only in ninth grade."

"Like I said, an older man. Beth thought that because they were friends at church they could be friends at school."

"And?"

"And seventh-grade girls don't walk up to ninth-grade studmuffins when they're with their crowd and start up a conversation. It just isn't done. Don't you remember?"

"Yes, but I wouldn't have been mean about it."

"Well, Beth did, and Jason was, and now she's spitting mad and embarrassed to boot."

Roger harrumphed. "He'll be sorry in a couple of years when he's lining up at the door with the other boys. I hope she gives him his traveling papers."

"It may be sooner than you think," Deenie said, spooning behind Roger and wrapping her icy feet around his ankles.

"Over my dead body," Roger muttered. "Deenie! Your. Feet. Are. Made. Of. Ice."

"I know. But you love it." She nibbled on his ear and whispered in her most sultry voice, "Aren't you going to kiss me good-night?"

## ERIN

February 19, 1991

Dear Gabby, Juneau, and Deenie,

Juneau, it sounds like you and Marisol cooked up quite a plot to pull Manny back from Barbara's arms and charms. I hope it works—long term!

I wish I could tell you my friend Angie's story like you told Marisol's, because it's just as good. Angie's the one who asked Cory and Steve to give her the discussions. She never did get baptized, though, and she never told me why until the party after Kayla's baptism. She and Norm have been together thirty-five years, have three boys and five grandchildren—but they aren't married! I'd imagined lots of reasons, but "living in sin" wasn't one of them.

When she told Steve, he said she should give Norm an ultimatum: marry her or move out. "Right is right, and wrong is wrong, and you have to choose." Poor Angie worked herself into a fine dither before finally talking to Norm about it—he was the one who initially didn't want to "institutionalize" their union.

But when she finally opened her heart to him, he couldn't have been sweeter about it. He called her his "Old Girl" and said if she was committed to "getting dunked," he could see his way to "getting hitched"—as long as it was in front of a justice of the peace, not in a church! So we've attended a wedding and a baptism, followed by a party at the Dunmeyers'.

After we all had dessert, Angie recounted Kayla's talk after her baptism about being a Real Mormon. She said she was now a Real Mormon, too. I had to smile at that, remembering how I'd hoped that attending Education Week at BYU in 1980 would give me the key to being a good Mormon woman. Silly me. There's no single, simple answer to that.

I wonder what Angie, newly baptized and shiny with belief and faith, would think if she knew Cory is gay? Would we be better off if the truth were out in the open? Or worse off? Are some secrets best left buried, like dear departed Letitia?

You don't actually have to answer those questions, unless you really want to! I'm just thinking about the unspoken agreements we sometimes make about the most important happenings in our lives and the consequences that follow. Remember what Gabby said? Put truth on the table. It's only poison when you hold it back until it stinks.

Love,
Erin

P.S. Anything you guys have to tell? Hee, hee!

## JUNEAU

It was a good thing Juneau didn't hold her breath waiting for her mother's promised letter about Letitia, because it didn't come. "Mom!" Juneau prompted in a phone call. "Will you please just write that darn letter and get it over with? It's maddening to get a glimpse of a few bones in the closet but not to see the whole skeleton."

"Oh, I'll get to it, Juney," Pamela said breezily. "But you know how it is when you're pursuing a hot plot. How's your new book coming?"

Juneau had to give her mother points for how good she was at diverting attention away from what she didn't want examined. "Slowly. There's been a lot of family stuff going on."

That was true. This was Nicole's and Beto's senior year. There were college applications to send out. Misty, who'd been aiming toward a computer major, was trying to decide if she should switch to history (another consequence of the trip to Idaho?). Ira would be getting his associate's degree in English literature at Pasadena City College, a junior college, at the end of the next semester. He'd recently gotten a job that he hoped would pay for him to finish his degree at UCLA—he was to be a pickle in a TV commercial. If it went over well, he was promised at least four more commercials, which would help out considerably on his and Misty's college expenses.

"A pickle!" Juneau had howled when he told her.

"Don't laugh," he said. "It'll pay some bills."

Juneau and Greg and their family, as well as Marisol and her troop, gathered together on the night the commercial was to air for the first time. They had pizza, which Greg and Trace made, and then Ira and Misty arranged the chairs in the family room in rows, like a theater. They ushered everyone to a seat and served popcorn. Then they tensely watched the sitcom during which the pickle company had purchased a commercial slot.

All of a sudden, there Ira was, in a warty green pickle costume, cavorting across the screen, saying his lines in a dialect he frequently used when passing on his Uncle Schlomo's jokes. Gideon, perched on Trace's lap, spoke first. His eyes huge, he pointed a finger and chortled, "Iwa!"

It lasted only a few seconds, and then it was over. Everybody hooted, stomped, screamed, laughed, and snorted. Philip Atwater barked and ran back and forth, his tail whirling with excitement. Ira stood up, pantomimed leaning over to speak in a microphone, and said in a deep, fake-sincere voice, "I want to thank you for honoring me with this Academy Award." He held up a teddy bear Gideon had left on the floor. Grinning, he said, "Can't you imagine my mother bragging about 'my son, the pickle'?"

Everybody howled again. Juneau watched them all with delight. She loved it when they had fun together and enjoyed one another's company. This was what the celestial kingdom was about, wasn't it, this finding joy in being with your family? She regarded them all as her family and couldn't bear the thought of ever being separated from any of them, even Philip Atwater, who was getting a bit long in the tooth.


A week later when Misty and Ira dropped by, Ira handed a letter to Juneau. "From my parents," he said.

There were actually two items, Solomon's business card with "Way to go, son" written on the back in thick black ink and a handwritten letter, which Juneau assumed was from Ira's mother. She unfolded it.

"All I told them was that I would be on TV," Ira said, "and when to watch. I didn't say what I'd be doing. Go ahead and read it."

The neatly written note said:

Dear Son,

We had everyone come to the house for your TV debut. We all speculated on what you were going to do—be a contestant on *Wheel of Fortune*, perhaps? A new character in *Baywatch*? Aunt Selma was sure you were replacing Adam Arkin on *Chicago Hope*. None of us even came close to the truth. We were delighted with your stellar performance and happy that the pickle you portray is kosher! Uncle Schlomo laughed so hard the neighbors came over to enjoy the fun. Fortunately, we'd taped it, so we did reruns for them. Your dad went out and bought a jar of the pickles, and we had a celebration! We'll be watching every program on TV from now on to see your next performance! We love you.

Mother

Juneau looked up. "This is lovely, Ira."

He nodded. "I know. I thought they would be flat-out annoyed and embarrassed."

"You were wrong. Ira, they love you," Juneau said.

Ira nodded again. "Yeah, isn't that weird?" He rubbed a hand across his eyes.

*You just never know about relationships*, Juneau thought, *or what might be the agent of change. It could be a pickle!*

# Chapter 22

WILLADENE
> February 4, 1991
> Dear COBs,
>
> Remember that young police officer I told you was interested in
> Bear? Well, he came to dinner, and now he's interested in
> Sunny. He even sent her flowers. When I asked Dad if Officer
> Brad Donaldson understood about her, he said the boy did.
> Roger said the same thing. Paul and Carl, too. Looks like all
> four of them had a talk with our guest after dinner. Mom says
> to stay out of it—they've given Brad permission to call on
> Sunny.
>
> He's young, good looking, world-traveled, well-educated, and
> personable. If he understands the huge limitations of her health
> and the lesser limitations of her intellect, what does he want
> with our girl?
>
> > Wondering in the West,
> > Deenie

ERIN
> March 24, 1991
> Dear Juneau and Deenie,
>
> It's nearly a year from the time Cory told me he is gay. They say
> what doesn't kill you makes you stronger. We're not dead, so I
> guess we must be Robin and Bat Girl—without the capes. Only,
> a year of trying to keep a secret has made me paranoid. I keep
> having this feeling that everyone knows about Cory. I think I'll
> send out a notice: *Dear Friends, we want you to know that Cory is
> gay, Erin is straight, and the kids are confused. You have our per-
> mission to talk to us about it, if you dare!*
>
> I couldn't have made it through this year without the support
> of The Jays and Grams. I wish Cory had the same from his par-
> ents. Skipp and Linda can't bear the thought that their only son

is gay. They fast every Monday in hopes of a miracle, and Skipp has long talks with Cory, quoting scriptures and the writings of the general authorities, as if the very weight of the words could press the gayness out of his son.

On the positive side, I've started going back to church. (Putting my back to the bench, as Gabby says.) At first, I was worried about being a hypocrite, thinking that members would assume by my attendance that things were better between Cory and me and that I believed the same things and felt the same Spirit that they did. Right now, I'm not sure what I feel or believe.

When I said that to Jake, he just laughed at me. He said people who attend church may look as if they're cut out of the same cloth (his words), but they aren't. All of them put their own slant on doctrine, withhold parts of themselves, and resist certain commandments. Getting beyond that is the whole purpose of going to church. He said, "Go. Be with your family. Accept the love of your community, and love them back. That's what it's all about."

Jake's so smart and so kind. Isn't it funny? The father-daughter relationship I wanted with Andrew, I have with Jake. I haven't given up on Andrew and me, though. We're still finding our way. When I was little, I so wanted to have a father. Now, I have two!

> A year older and wiser,
> Your Erin

March 29, 1991
Dear COBs,

Kayla won a silver medal on the limited beginner level at the McCandless Competition! She hasn't come down from the stratosphere yet. In fact, she's been talking nonstop about what she wants to do next. I'm absolutely flat—the tension and excitement of the day has wiped me out. I can't imagine how parents of high-level skaters handle it.

It was a good thing I made a checklist of what we needed to take. Without it, we would have left something at home, guaranteed. (I hear some kids have even left their skates behind!) We went down the list before getting in the car.

Skates, blade covers (soft and hard), warm-up suit, gloves, performance dress, matching hair accessories, and beige tights. Music tape and backup, makeup, water bottle, high-energy snack. Camera. See why we need a list?

We left for the arena early—Cory was as nervous as Kayla was eager. The arena was a hive of activity when we got there. Cory and Mark bought some flowers, one bouquet to give Kayla after she skated and one for an advanced skater she admires. Then they found seats to save for all the relatives. Kayla and I checked in and got the skating order. Because she's in the lowest level, she was one of the first skaters. Before I handed her over to her coach, Allyson Trapp, she insisted I redo her hair twice and kept looking in the mirror to make sure I'd covered her scar with concealer.

My hands were sweaty and my heart pounding by the time it was her turn. Good thing she talked to her coach right before going on the ice and not me. My nervousness might have rubbed off on her. She skated to a Looney Tunes medley her coach put together for her. It was perfect for her strengths— speed, footwork, and jumps. (She has her half loop and half flip.) I suppose every mom thinks the same watching her kid skate, but I can see her going a long way with this.

> Your Erin,
> FSM (Figure-Skating Mom)

P.S. The new dress Mom made for her, a vibrant red with a yellow and blue design on the bodice, complemented her program and music perfectly.

## JUNEAU

April 27, 1991

Dear Threesome,

I'm just back from a week in Oregon with my parents, Paul and Pamela Paulsen. I went to finally pry out the last of the secrets. Yes, Erin, Gabby says secrets kept too long stink. I say, secrets kept too long get too painful to come out all at once. They have to be coughed up, one little hunk at a time. Too bad there's not a Heimlich maneuver for secrets caught in the throat.

Here's what I found out. Letitia was sent to the Idaho State Penitentiary in Boise for voluntary manslaughter. She died in 1959 at the age of seventy-two. In all that time she never had any visitors (if anyone did come, she refused to see them), and the only person she corresponded with was my mom. She was deeply sorry for having besmirched the family name but unrepentant for what she'd done to Orville.

Poor Letitia. Living with Orville made her a little twisted. She wrote a letter to Mom after my birth. All it said was "Poor little woman," no doubt because she felt that her unhappiness came from being a woman with no control over her life. Mom says that day in the cemetery was the only time she ever let it rip and did things her way.

When I asked Mom where Letitia was actually buried, she said, "Nowhere." Letitia had requested that her body be cremated and her ashes scattered on the top of Angel's Roost back in Mink Creek, where they could be carried freely on the wind.

Since Mom and Dad haven't been back to Mink Creek, Letitia's ashes languish in a safe deposit box in Boise. Along with her diaries! So now, dear ladies, I have a new quest: to carry out Letitia's wishes. I want to do that for my great-grandma. And I want those diaries.

One other thing. Mom said Letitia told her right at the end that the best thing she ever did was to tell Mom and Dad to run away and live their lives as they wanted. Mom agrees. She says their marriage had a very precarious start with a lot of stuff hanging over it but that it's been good. Every marriage has its own story, doesn't it?

Every relationship, for that matter. Beto and Nicole are sending off college applications, Beto to Loyola-Marymount and University of California at Irvine (UCI) and Nicole to UCI and BYU. I asked her what her first choice was, fully expecting her to say, "UCI, if Beto is accepted there." Instead, she said, "BYU!"

Makes me wonder if there's a rift between Nicole and her

lifelong buddy. It would be sad if there is. They've meant so much to each other.

Love,
Juneau

P.S. Erin, it's good to hear you sounding so much better. Congrats to Kayla on her skating triumph.

P.P.S. Deenie, I can understand your concern about Brad's interest in Sunny. The question is, how does Sunny feel about Brad?

## WILLADENE

On a cool morning in late April, Deenie and Bear faced a tough search-and-rescue field exam. The first part required Deenie to get herself and Bear to the off-road test site using only a hand-drawn map and her compass. Finding where X marked the spot turned out to be a lot harder than she'd imagined. By the time she pulled up next to Terry's truck in a cloud of dust, she was twenty minutes late and gnashing her teeth with frustration.

"You're late," said her SAR trainer, Terry. Without waiting for a response, he began explaining the next part of the exam. "We've laid track over a 400-meter by 400-meter area with seven misdirections. There are three scent-related articles out there for you and Bear to bring back. Let's get started."

"Hold on a minute!" Deenie said. "'400 meters by 400 meters' doesn't mean a thing to me. Give me a visual."

"Imagine a football field starting right here. Now times the length and width by four, including that slope, the creek, bushes, and grassland. That gives you a rough idea. Did you remember your gloves?"

"No." Deenie wished there were words other than profanity that could describe how she felt at the moment. She took the pair of disposable gloves Terry offered and the scent material he'd prepared for Bear to sniff. The workout was long and grueling. *And disappointing, if Terry's face is any indication,* Deenie thought as she trudged back to the truck.

As if he'd heard her thoughts, Terry said, "That didn't turn out as well as I hoped it might, but it was better than I expected at this point."

"So what should I work on with Bear? I thought he was way ahead of the game with his training." Deenie filled a bowl of water for Bear and then got a drink for herself.

"He is," Terry said. "It's you I'm concerned about. Your commands aren't clear, and your hand signals need to be more precise. If you're in this for the long haul, Deenie, you're going to need more upper body strength, too."

"Great. Just great." Deenie dropped the tailgate of the truck with a bang. "Kennel!" she ordered. Bear obeyed immediately, and Deenie locked up his crate and the back of the truck. "Was that clear enough for you?"

"Better." Terry grinned as Deenie got into her truck and slammed the door shut. "See you next week, same time, same place." he said.

Deenie muttered all the way home. She was still muttering when Paul arrived after school and found her standing over the weight bench in the garage. "Mom, what are you doing?" he asked.

"I need more upper body strength," she said, as though it were all Paul's fault. "How do you use these things, anyway?"

"First of all, you don't start with all the weights on the bar at once," Paul said, obviously trying not to laugh. "And you put your hands this way," he added, repositioning her grip.

Fifteen minutes later Deenie lay gasping and sweating on the floor of the garage. "That's just nasty," she huffed. "Why would anyone want to do that to themselves?"

"You should have started with something lighter, like soup cans," Paul teased.

"Give me a hand. Can't you see I'm dying here?"

When Margaret arrived with Evvy, Deenie was sitting at the kitchen table directing Beth and Paul in dinner preparations.

"Mom hurt herself," Beth explained with a grin. "Trying to lift weights in the garage with Paul."

"Deenie, what in the world?"

"I told her she should have used soup cans," Paul said, and Margaret burst out laughing. She put Evvy down on the floor at Deenie's feet. The little girl immediately put her arms up for her mother to lift her. Deenie could bend only enough to kiss her daughter on the forehead and told her to go play with Bear.

"You really did hurt yourself, didn't you, dear?" Margaret's laughter faded.

"Don't worry, Mom. I've taken an anti-inflammatory, and I'm just about ready to lie down with an ice pack."

"Well, if you're feeling better by next Friday, why don't you and Roger join us for dinner? That nice young officer you introduced us to is coming for a visit, and we're all going out together."

"Sunny, too?" Deenie asked in surprise.

"Of course. You don't think Brad is coming all this way to see your father and me, do you?"

## ERIN
May 23, 1991
Dear Friends,

It's no secret to you two that I've been caught up in my drama this past year. I badly needed something to shift my focus and offer a new perspective. When the bishop asked me to teach the Beehive class—twelve-year-old girls!—I said yes, because I couldn't think of a good enough reason to say no. It turned out to be just what I needed, because I met Melina Frank.

My heart went out to her the minute I saw her. She had such a look of neglect—shapeless hair, rumpled clothes, thick glasses, an outbreak of pimples. She was sitting in a corner of the classroom with a buffer of empty chairs all around her, poor thing.

Dar Polanski, the Young Women's president, told me later that Melina's mother, Althea, is an agoraphobic and a hoarder. Her dad, Gerald, works two jobs to keep the household afloat, so he's home only to eat and sleep. Melina's basically on her own, living in a house that would probably be condemned if a public health official saw it.

I think Dar could tell I was ready to make a list, marshal the troops, and make things better. She said, "What Althea needs is a lot more complex than a good housecleaning. What Melina needs is simple human kindness."

I couldn't resist asking, "How about a haircut?" But I knew what she was saying. I decided that every time I'm with Melina, I'll make sure she knows that she's been seen and heard and that she is loved. I think I'm getting through to her, because lately I've noticed that she smiles more.

How amazing! I can make a difference by slowing down, being available, and allowing another person to grow and bloom in my presence. No *doing* involved. Although . . . I *did* take my scissors to a Young Women's activity, and I gave her a cute haircut afterward!

Seriously, I've stopped trying to cram so much into every day. I've started sitting down on the couch in the evenings, even when tasks are calling my name, and it's interesting how often Cory or one of the kids will sit down with me. Even if we don't talk long, it's a moment of connection that can be quite sweet.

Mom and I had an especially sweet time with Grams when we surprised her with a trip to Holland, Michigan, during the tulip festival. She's been talking more about her childhood these days, and when she started reminiscing about going to that festival with her mother every year, we decided to make a pilgrimage. First we spent a day in Holland, enjoying the fields of brilliant colors, the picturesque windmills, and the klompen dancers in their wooden shoes. Then we went to a family reunion at the home of a niece of Grams whom I'd tracked down. I was worried that it would make Grams sad, especially since all of her brothers have passed, but she quite enjoyed meeting nieces and nephews and reminiscing about the past. She seems to be at peace with her life, which is a miracle to me.

Love to you all,
Erin

## JUNEAU

In the summer of 1991, Gideon was three and a half and very capable of getting around on his own. Philip Atwater followed him everywhere, displaying the remnants of a herding instinct somewhere in his muttiness because he often nudged Giddy away from something that he, in his doggy mind, had decided was not appropriate for his small charge. As for Giddy, of all his playmates he loved Philip Atwater the best.

He expressed that feeling one day when he and the dog and Juneau were intertwined in a large easy chair while Juneau read aloud. She had just finished Gideon's favorite A. A. Milne poem about "James James Morrison Morrison Weatherby George Dupree," the three-year-old boy who took good care of his mother. Gideon stared thoughtfully at the book. "Philip Atwater takes good care of me," he said.

Juneau nodded. "Yes, he does."

Gideon squirmed around so he could hug his furry friend. "I love Philip Atwater," he said. "He thinks I'm somebody."

Juneau couldn't stop the sudden welling of tears. The simple statement held profound truth. Gideon knew she loved him, as did so many other people in his world. But to them all, he was just a little kid, powerless and dependent. To the dog, he was a *someone* who could dispense food and wield a grooming brush, who could open doors and reach toys and turn lights on and off. He was significant.

*Isn't that what we all need?* Juneau asked herself. *Significance?* It was a good theme for a young adult novel. Or a book for any age, actually. Or for a life. Mentally filing the thought in her "to bring out later" folder, she kissed Gideon on the head. "I think you're somebody, too, pal," she told him. "What should we read next?"

He straightened up. "The da DUM-DUM-da-DUM-DUM-da-DUM-DUM-da-DA. I really like that one."

Juneau knew the one. Gideon liked poems with a decided rhythm, and Juneau read him everything from the childlike poems of A. A. Milne to Gilbert and Sullivan lyrics (he liked "I am the very model of a modern Major-General") to what he was talking about now: Byron's *The Destruction of Sennacherib*. The da-DUM-DUM-da-DUM-DUM one.

"The Assyrian came down like the wolf on the fold," she said, knowing it by heart:

> And his cohorts were gleaming in purple and gold;
> And the sheen of their spears was like stars on the sea,
> When the blue wave rolls nightly—

"—on deep Galilee," Gideon chanted. He snuggled against Juneau, sighing with deep contentment. "Galilee was where Jesus lived, wasn't it, Mama?"

She marveled endlessly at how much could be absorbed by a three year old. Gideon was a small miracle, as all children were miracles. She hadn't fully realized that when Misty and Nicole were small. She hadn't taken the time to just simply sit with them in her lap, as she was doing now with Gideon. And Philip Atwater. She hadn't savored them like this. Life went by so fast.

She was reminded of that a few days later when Beto came to talk to her. He'd been accepted at both universities he'd applied to and had enrolled at Loyola-Marymount in Los Angeles. Nicole had decided on BYU.

Beto was obviously troubled when he knocked at the door of the little workroom in the garage. "Got time to talk, Mrs. Caldwell?" he asked politely.

"Sure, Beto," Juneau said. "Gideon is napping, and I'll be glad to take a break from my computer." She gestured for him to sit on the sturdy office armchair she'd bought at a garage sale.

He sat. "My mom took that job she was offered."

"Great!" Marisol had come over a couple of days before to say that she had a chance for a position teaching French at Monrovia High School for the coming year. "Congratulate her for me, will you?"

Beto fidgeted. "Mom and Dad are busting up. Did you know?"

"I didn't know for sure," Juneau said. "But I knew they might."

Beto traced a circle in the rug with the toe of his shoe. "Mrs. Caldwell, that's why I have to go to Loyola. I need to stay here. I mean, with Isobel married and gone, and Vincent in the Marines, and Dad . . ." His voice trailed off.

Juneau looked at his serious face. How had he so suddenly become this tall, earnest young man, ready to take on heavy responsibilities? Shouldn't he still be in the backyard with Nicole, digging for mummies? Why couldn't you put time on hold for a while and enjoy the lovely parts of life?

"I admire you for your decision," she said. "You'll get a good education at Loyola."

"Is it going to be all right, do you think?"

"You mean you and Nicole going to different institutions?"

He nodded. "What if she meets somebody there?" He peered closely at Juneau. "Would you like that better, if she meets a good Mormon guy that she'd like to marry?"

That was a question she'd often asked herself. Would she prefer that Nicole married a Mormon, a returned missionary kind of guy who would take her to the temple? That was important. But Beto was important, too. He'd been an adjunct member of their family for his whole life. How could she ever give up this gentle, soft-eyed young man?

"Beto," she said, "it's not for me to say who Nicole marries. But I'll tell you this: You are a person of great significance to me. To all of us."

He smiled and then said, "But do you think things will work out okay?"

He was asking her? Where was that Delphic Oracle when you needed her?

"Life doesn't come packaged up with guarantees," Juneau said. "But you know what your mother is always saying: '*Que sera, sera.*'"

"'Whatever will be, will be.'"

"Yes. But it never hurts to help things along a little."

"Like letters and stuff." Beto nodded slowly. After a few moments he said, "I couldn't go to BYU, Mrs. Caldwell. I'm a Catholic. I mean, I loved going to Primary and the rest of it with Nicole. But deep down, I have to be what I am." With that, he stood up, gave Juneau a heart-melting smile, and left.

She watched him go, thinking that Nicole had come to much the same decision as he had—that she had to be what she was. She had enjoyed the catechism classes and said they had really added to her knowledge of religion in general. She'd mentioned her hope that Beto possibly might convert. Now Juneau knew that he was not headed for baptism.

Trace was. He told Juneau one day when he came to play with Gideon. "I've decided," he said. "I go to church all the time. I've been working with the Scouts, along with Greg. I'd like to join." He looked down at his hands. "Rhiannan would be happy."

"I guess the two of you talked about it," Juneau said.

Trace nodded. "She said I'd make a good Mormon. Cath says that, too." He grinned. "I don't know what they see in me."

"I do," Juneau said. "Trace, you are a person of significance."

She wrote to the COBs a few days later. After recounting all that had been going on, she continued:

> You have no idea how much I'd like to tap into your combined wisdom when these young people come to talk to me. They think I know something. I don't. What I do is race around in my mind to figure out what Gabby might say. Dear friends, all of you, you can't even imagine how much I've benefited from knowing you, especially now when things are changing so fast. Even so, I wonder how I'll ever be able to keep up.
>
> I know what you'd say, Gabby: "Think of that hymn we sing, Juneau. The one that goes, 'Change and decay in all around I see; / O thou who changest not, abide with me!'"
>
> I'll keep that in mind and also what I learned from Gideon—that everybody needs to feel like they're somebody. Including me.
>
> Love,
> Juneau

# Chapter 23

ERIN

June 17, 1991

Dear Deenie,

I have a new appreciation of the work you and Roger have done the last three years. I didn't realize how tough joint counseling sessions could be until I started going to them with Cory.

I knew our relationship wasn't the best in the months before Cory told me, but I had no idea we were as bad off as our counselor thinks we are. She says we're good at "crisis conversations" but lousy at everyday communications. We make assumptions, give incomplete information, and just plain don't listen. Worst of all, we withhold. If there's a rap song out there with nothing but that word repeated over and over, it's our theme song.

According to our counselor, Noreen, the reason Cory and I lasted as long as we did was that our marriage served our needs in a strange way—deep emotional and physical intimacy would have scared the socks off both of us. Our belief in the Church and our need to create a Forever Family held us together. I needed a Forever Family so I could feel like I belonged; Cory, so he could prove he was acceptable to God. Having two energetic kids who like to be on the go helped us pretend—we could focus on being good parents and keeping them busy and happy.

Today's session was the worst yet—Noreen asked Cory to honestly describe what it was like living with me. Listening to him was the hardest thing I've ever done in my life. He said I'm a master at freezing him out with a look and a tone of voice. I blame others, hold grudges, feel sorry for myself, and don't accept (or trust) the love that others have for me. Just like Grams!

I'm feeling pretty beaten up right now. If you asked me to write down something positive about myself, I don't think I could do it. All I heard in that session was that I'm unloving and unlovable, which has always been my deepest fear.

Deenie, did you and Roger go through anything like this? I remember how great you looked when I saw you at Park City: energetic, strong, and full of self-confidence. How did you get that way? If you have a lifeline, throw it to me fast, because I need something to hold on to.

Your Erin

WILLADENE
   June 26, 1991
   Dear Erin,

Seeing ourselves as others see us can be downright miserable. Roger and I went through a session just like the one you described, and I came away pretty shredded myself.

The next time I saw Dr. Greenwood she asked me how much of what Roger said about me I would accept as true, and she had me write it down. What a list! Fearful, demanding, picky, single-minded in a negative way, etc. After we talked about that list, she had me make a list of words that described who I thought I was and another of words related to who I wanted to be.

She cut up all the lists, mixed the pieces in a bowl, and gave it to me along with an outline of the human form with blank puzzle pieces drawn inside. Then she said, "After you fall apart, sometimes it's a puzzle to figure out what parts of you to keep and what you want to throw away. Pick one word to go in each of the blank spaces until you've put yourself back together again." The whole point was to remind me that at the end of the day, I choose who I am going to be.

I took the puzzle with me when I went to pick up Evvy at Mom's. Mom said I hadn't made any room for who God wanted me to be. I wrote that all around the outline of the puzzle, as if that stitched it all together. I still look at it to remind me of all the good things I am and will be, by the grace of God.

So be easy with yourself, Erin dear. Be gentle. You have all the time there is to pick and choose and make those puzzle pieces fit. You can do it. I know you can.

Love,
Deenie

## WILLADENE

July 26, 1991
Dear COBs,

Everything is changing around here. Bert is pregnant! We're getting ready for visitors from Africa. The Kufuors, Bert's in-laws, are coming here after their sealing in the Los Angeles temple. And Beth has become a guy magnet. Boys stop by on a regular basis to see her on the flimsiest of excuses. Even Jason Whitmore, though he claims to come to talk to Paul about track.

Carl is home for the summer, a handsome, responsible, studious young man. My Carl? I'm baffled. Roger says to trust him. Paul gets that wise old man look of his and says, "Hey, Mom. Have some faith."

Mom, Dad, and Aunt Stella are spending the summer playing. No kidding. Sunny often stays with me here when the senior citizens are on the loose, and I love it. Sometimes Brad shows up, and we all visit and play games.

Although Sunny blossoms under Brad's attention, she is always quiet and contemplative, and she holds Evvy especially tight after he leaves. She is troubled by something but won't say what. I'm troubled, too. By this whole relationship.

Survival training is grueling—climbing mountainsides, scrambling through the brush. I'm either going to be dead or so fit it will be scary. Maybe I should enter one of those women's muscle-builder competitions. Can you see me striking a pose?

Gabby dear, I'm glad your roses are excessively beautiful this year, but what's up with Sophie? Jonas says she's not feeling the best. What's going on with Bryan? Give!

Missing you all and hoping for a visit soon.

Deenie

# Chapter 24

ERIN
>August 10, 1991
>Dear Friends,
>
>Remember that postcard I sent you in July, the one from Split Rock Lighthouse on Lake Superior? Cory and the kids and I had spent a week in the cabin belonging to Pete, his boss. It's between Gooseberry Falls and the lighthouse, with a big deck looking out on the lake and two flights of stairs down to a beach of little rocks. We had a fabulous time, the best vacation ever.
>
>Well, Cory told Pete that I said I'd love to spend a week there with my friends, and he offered us the cabin for the second week in September! That's quite the deal, because Pete doesn't pass out weeks like candy. Also because September is the prettiest time of year on the North Shore except for high color in October.
>
>So, dear COBs! Are you up for it? Can you leave kith and kin to come for an adventure on the North Shore? Check your dates. I promise you'll have a wonderful time.
>
>>Erin

JUNEAU
>August 15, 1991
>Dear Erin,
>
>Kith and kin are dumped. There's nothing that would tempt me to spend a single day away from darling Giddy except a coven of COBs meeting on the North Shore! I'll be there.
>
>>Juneau

WILLADENE
>August 17, 1991
>Dear Erin,
>
>Yes, thank you, I would love a trip to the North Shore. The visit

from all the family went well but was tiring beyond belief. Richard Kufuor is outgoing, and I liked him. His wife, Flora, is charming, too, but more reserved. I couldn't always tell if she was enjoying herself. Bert is pregnant and due in December. NeVae drove us all bonkers by hovering over her every single second.

Yes, I am coming to the North Shore.

Bear and I take our certifications tests for level-three SAR handler and dog in November. He has developed an interesting sound to alert me when he finds a scent. Roger calls it his pig grunt. It does sound exactly like a big pig wallowing in his trough. But it's beginning to sound like music to me.

And if I haven't already told you—yes, I would like a break at the North Shore!

See you soon,
Deenie

P.S. I tried talking Gabby into joining our party, but she says cavorting among the rocks along the North Shore sounds like too much work to her. But she asks that we send a postcard from every place we visit. I'm bringing plenty of stamps, so don't let me forget.

## WILLADENE

Deenie and Juneau stood in front of the Lindbergh Terminal of the Minneapolis–St. Paul International Airport watching eagerly for Erin to arrive in her van. Deenie saw it first and waved Erin into an open space at the curb.

"I'm so glad to see you guys," Erin said, hugging one after the other. "This is so exciting!"

"I can't wait to see what it's like 'Up North,'" Juneau said.

"Me, too." Deenie hefted her bag easily into the back of Erin's van and did the same with Juneau's, sliding them into the space Erin made by shifting the boxes of groceries she'd purchased for the trip. Then they set out for Duluth, three and a half hours north.

They stopped midway at Tobie's in Hinckley for gas and sticky buns.

"It's a tradition," Erin said, leading them into the restaurant part of the complex.

"What is?" asked Juneau, grinning. "Stopping here on the way to Duluth, or us eating our way through our vacations?"

"Us eating," Deenie laughed.

Her first sight of the harbor at Duluth and the sparkling expanse of Lake Superior beyond made Deenie catch her breath. She listened avidly as Erin recounted the history of the area while negotiating the narrow streets of downtown. Food was the last thing on her mind when Erin stopped in front of a café and said, "Figured it was time for lunch." But she did enjoy her Reuben sandwich and sauerkraut and felt like a kid out of school as they ducked into several antiques stores before setting off on the last leg of their journey to the cabin.

As they headed north out of Duluth, Deenie found she couldn't take in the view fast enough to see all she wanted to see. Her eyes feasted on the endless blue of the lake and the early dashes of color in the mixed forest of pine, maple, and birch. She wanted to stop at the town of Two Harbors and Gooseberry Falls State Park, but Erin drove on by, assuring her she'd see both of them the next day.

Finally, they reached the turn-off marked Voyageur's Haven, the fanciful name Pete had given his North Shore cabin, an A-frame with a wall of windows overlooking the deck and the lake.

"This is a cabin?" Deenie's voice was incredulous. "Fantastic."

That's what the next three days were—fantastic. This was the first vacation Deenie had had since Evvy was born, the first she'd ever had when she felt so strong and competent. When they went to the state park the next day, she hit the trail up to Gooseberry Falls eagerly, leaving Erin and Juneau in her wake. Without a bit of chagrin, she climbed to the top of the falls and negotiated the crossing to the other side of the river over wet, mossy rocks, grinning when she turned to see the expressions on her friends' faces. "Piece o' cake!" she called.

"Better be careful," Erin called back. "If you needed help, we couldn't rescue you!"

Deenie chortled. "Don't worry about me! What do you think the last three years have been about? I've been learning to rescue myself." She struck a double-arm pose. She loved her new physical strength, and she reveled in it.

When she returned to the other side, she said, "Ladies, if you wanna be COBs, you've got to keep up with me!"

"Deenie, what about your heart murmur?" Juneau asked.

"Well, it's still there, but the rest of me is so much stronger that at the moment, it's not a problem."

Later, when she led the way down the steep path back to the parking lot, she set a pace that left the other two trailing behind.

When Juneau reached the van, she leaned against it, puffing. "I've had all the physical activity I can take for one day. Let's celebrate our new resolve to get fit by eating a piece of that huckleberry pie advertised at Betty's Pie Shop."

## ERIN

When they got back to the cabin, they all took naps, ate supper, then took s'mores ingredients down to the beach. They built a fire of driftwood and sat in lawn chairs pulled up in a semicircle while holding marshmallows over the flame. Juneau and Deenie laughed when Erin let hers catch fire and burn black before blowing it out. "Carbon is good for you, didn't you know that?" she asked.

As it grew darker, they saw the lights of passing freighters heading to or away from the harbor at Duluth. Watching them, Erin started singing Gordon Lightfoot's "Wreck of the *Edmund Fitzgerald*," the tale of the ore ship that went down in Lake Superior in 1975. She didn't get very far before trailing off for lack of words. They sat quietly for a while, and then Juneau said, "Just seeing the lights on the freighters makes me want to know where they are going."

"Could be anywhere in the world after they get through the Great Lakes and out into the Atlantic," Erin said.

Deenie made a sound. "That's farther than I'll ever go. Do you know this is farther from Wellsville than I've ever been before? Imagine me, east of the Mississippi! I have made it west and south to Pasadena, Juneau, but that will probably be it. I love Wellsville. As small as it is, it's the center of my life."

"Who knows where we'll end up, any of us? Sometimes life takes us where we never intended to go." Erin's voice was pensive. She glanced briefly at Juneau. "It's the Peoria Syndrome."

Juneau nodded. She and Deenie turned solemn. Then Juneau said, "Peoria isn't all bad, you know. Sometimes there are compensations."

"You're thinking of Max. And Gideon," Erin said.

"Yes. One lost, one an unexpected blessing. I love my Giddy so much. He can be a handful, especially when he wants what he wants. And when he gets stuck in an endless loop of *whys* and *how comes*. But I can't imagine life without him." Juneau's eyes glittered in the firelight. "I love watching Greg with Giddy. He's softer, more patient. We're all better because of him."

"I can't imagine life without my kids, either." Erin's voice was thoughtful. "It's like what you told me in that letter a while ago, Juneau. A lot of good has come from my marriage to Cory, and not just Mark and Kayla. That's true, no matter how things turn out."

"I thought you two were working things out," Deenie said.

"We are, and some days we're actually happy. But The Great What If pops up every now and then, reminding me that Cory is what he is. He has times of . . . freedom, I guess. Or grace. Other times, I can see in his eyes the pressure of constantly having to choose one path when one's whole self wants to go a different direction . . ."

In the silence that followed, Erin heard Juneau struggle to stifle a giggle. "I'm so sorry, Erin. I don't mean to make light of his situation, but what you said sounds just like I feel when I'm off chocolate. My whole self wants something, anything, chocolate in the worst way. I'm sorry to say that I always give in. Eventually."

Erin smiled a little, choosing to ignore the grief and fear creeping into her heart. She turned to Deenie. "What compensations do you see?"

"Getting my mother back," Deenie answered without hesitation. "For years, I'd lived with the pain of thinking she didn't love me." Her smile was brilliant. "Now, we have the sweetest relationship. I wouldn't want to go through 5 West and the rest of it over again, but I wouldn't trade where I am now for anything."

"Sometimes, though, it's got to be harder to see the compensations," Erin said. "Like when Rhiannan died, Juneau."

"Yes. I was thinking I needed to say something about her death, because it was the hardest for me. But some good things have come out of it. Flint and I have learned how much we mean to each other, especially now that we're closer geographically. I don't think he would have transferred to Camp Pendleton if Rhiannan hadn't died."

"I hope we're not saying that we learn through suffering." Erin added driftwood to the ebbing fire and stirred it back to life. "There's got to be an easier way."

"I'd sure like to think there is." Deenie's voice was thoughtful. "Unfortunately, we sometimes get so caught up in daily life, we need something to catch our attention. Something to wake us up, change our perspective."

Juneau, who was toasting another marshmallow, nodded. "It's like the play *Our Town*. The main character, Emily, comes back after her death—against the advice of those on the other side—to live one day of her life over. She sees how people breeze through important moments without recognizing them. Without seeing what's going on with their loved ones or hearing what they're trying to say." She paused. "I think that's why we need the wakeup calls once in a while. To make us stop and see our lives from a higher perspective."

Erin stirred the fire again, sending sparks flying skyward. "If you ask me, we've all had enough wake-up calls to last us a lifetime."

September 17, 1991
Dear Gabby,

This postcard shows the view of the Split Rock Lighthouse that people come from all over the world to photograph. Every place we've been on this vacation, we talk and think of you. We've had tons of fun with our Gabbyisms list and creating *The COBs' Little Book of Wisdom* (or as we laughingly call it, *The COBs' Book of Little Wisdom*) was a blast. It almost seems like you're with us.

Love,
Juneau, Deenie, and Erin

# *Chapter 25*

WILLADENE

"What do you and the Beast have on the docket for today?" Roger asked from the breakfast table.

"After lunch and a nap, Evvy has an early Halloween party at Sister Evans's house with her Sunbeam class. I'll have an hour free, so Lark and I are going to take Bear for a run along the canal road. Then we'll do some outdoor shooting at the rifle range on the farm and check out the homestead."

Roger shook his head. "Dave stopped by last night to tell me about some high-stakes vandalism he's discovered recently around the valley. Stay close to home today, will you?"

Deenie handed him a plate of cheesy scrambled eggs. "What kind of vandalism?"

"Worse than the usual names sprayed on barns. Someone broke into the Harrises' summer cabin and smeared the interior with softened rat poison. The winter feed in the Harlands' silo was drenched in gasoline."

"That's terrible, Dad," Beth said.

"Exactly."

After breakfast and family prayer, Deenie wiped lipstick off Beth's mouth, buttoned her shirt one button higher, gave her a quick kiss, and pushed her out the door before she could complain. Paul ducked her kiss and gave one to Evvy. Grabbing his coat, he hollered, "See ya later," and loped down the walk toward the bus stop.

When Roger was ready to go, he didn't hurry off as usual. He stood by the door until Deenie gave him her full attention. "Deenie, I don't want you going out to the homestead alone until this is all cleared up, okay?"

She gave Roger a speculative gaze. "You're not having a premonition or anything like that, are you?"

He shook his head. "I'm asking you to use common sense and caution."

Deenie and Bear were ready and waiting when Lark showed up at three that afternoon. "Let's get out of here," Deenie said. "This day is too gorgeous to waste."

"Not too far out," Lark replied.

"Did Shawn give you the same talk Roger gave me?"

"The 'Don't Go Anywhere Alone' talk? Um-hmm." Lark shivered. "It's creepy, isn't it?"

"It's more than creepy. How about doing loops around the Tabernacle block instead of running country roads?"

During the next few days, they kept to roads in or near town as the vandalism continued and the level of violence of the hit-and-run attacks escalated. In her darkest What Ifs, Deenie had never come up with What If a Vandal Terrorized Wellsville? In November someone shot the watchdog on a farm near the Rasmussens' place and slit the udder of a milking goat in Mantua. The peace of the bucolic valley was replaced by caution and fear.

When an elderly fellow—a retired sheriff—was robbed, assaulted, and left bound in his own house (most likely by the shadowy vandal, according to Dave Fenton), Deenie started wearing her gun beneath her jacket whenever she was on the road by herself.

ERIN

December 17, 1991

Dear Gabby, Juneau, and Deenie,

I just had to write, because I'm reveling in all the sights, sounds, and smells of the holiday this year, which was definitely not the case twelve months ago!

We had a nice afternoon of cookie baking at our house today. Grams and The Jays came, of course, but they didn't stay long. Grams has been really tired lately and is having trouble breathing. Her doctor suspects congestive heart failure and has scheduled tests. We'll know the results soon.

The cookie baking crew was rounded out with the Harringtons

and Melina, the girl from my Young Women's class. Ricky and Mark spent the afternoon snitching dough and otherwise harassing the girls, who got along quite well. At least they were united in ignoring little pests!

Yes, I'm still trying to be Little Miss Fix-It when it comes to Melina. But I found out that she's been playing piano since she was seven, so she's not as deprived as I imagined. Actually, she thought *we* were deprived because we didn't have a piano so she could play carols for us.

I would like to be friends with Melina's mom, Althea, but it's difficult when she can't leave her house and wouldn't think of inviting anyone in. She has more problems than you can shake a stick at, but I've learned lately that you can't write people off. Wherever they are, at any given time, it's not the end of the story.

Happy Christmas to you all!

Love,
Erin

P.S. Juneau, do writers really come to the end of a story, or do they just find a good place to stop?

## JUNEAU

December 23, 1991
Dear Erin,

I had to get right back to you with the answer to your burning question!

Unlike life, which often leaves threads dangling, stories generally come to some kind of conclusion. The question posed at the beginning is answered, and the writer wraps up the story. Except in art stories, where the ending is more like real life. And in . . .

Erin, I could list exceptions from here to Sunday, so I'll just say Merry Christmas—and bring this to an end!

Love,
Juneau

WILLADENE

When Deenie sat down early one December morning to write her Christmas letter, she found herself staring at the typing paper with its border of smiling forest creatures peering out of an evergreen hedge, and she wondered what on earth she could write that would live up to the cheerful pattern. For weeks the entire community had centered its energy on keeping safe from the unidentified danger that lurked in the hills. That awareness of potential harm waiting outside the door or around the corner tainted every holiday festivity and left everyone edgy. *I certainly don't want to write about that!* she thought. *No, I want to write about good news of the season.*

Within the hour, Deenie was inundated with good news. Hal called to announce the birth of his and Bert's baby, a healthy, hefty, nine-pound baby boy they named Timothy Wilford Udall.

Elders Reece and Ryan Crafton, newly returned from the mission field, stopped by to offer a personal invitation to Deenie and Roger. "We're being sealed to Mom and Dave Friday after the ten o'clock endowment session," Reece announced.

"Where I'm doing the work for Stan," Ryan added. "Then Reece will stand proxy for our big brother so he can be sealed to Mom and Dave as well. We'd like you and Roger to be there."

"Absolutely!" Deenie hugged them both. As they left, she remembered the two rebellious and troubled young men who had first come to Grandma Streeter's in 1982, chins up and visors pulled down low, trying to be strong. Now they carried a quiet air of true strength of the Spirit. Deenie was eager for Carl to see the amazing transformation.

The mailman arrived as the twins left, bringing a bundle of letters that filled Deenie's good-news cup to overflowing. First, she received notice that she and Bear had passed their SAR level-three certification and were now part of the team. Included was a picture of them both in their full regalia with the words Certified and Search Ready scrolled in gold across the bottom.

Next was a particularly loving note from Carl saying he would be coming home early for the holidays and staying late into the New Year. Then Deenie opened a flowery invitation from Sunny asking her and

Roger over to spend a special evening with Brad, Margaret, and John. Deenie wrote her acceptance with a pensive smile; each additional day with Sunny was a gift and a blessing.

The morning of good cheer was topped off by an unexpected call from Lark asking if the Donovans could attend Christmas services with the Rasmussens. "We've attended almost every other church in the valley," Lark said, "and decided it was time to try yours." Deenie was overjoyed.

"Ask and ye shall receive," she said as she finished entering all the good news of the day on the computer and printed out multiple copies of the family Christmas letter. She picked up Evvy, who was playing with crumpled paper beneath the desk, and swung her in the air. "Christmas is on its way!" she declared, giving Evvy a happy kiss. "Let's go see your Aunt Sunny."

# Chapter 26

## 1992

WILLADENE

"Brad and Sunny are beginning to look like sweethearts," Aunt Stella whispered to Deenie while nodding toward the couple at the other side of the room where the whole family gathered on New Year's Day. Brad sat in front of the couch where Sunny reclined on a pile of pillows fluffed up by Beth and Evvy to ease her breathing and her tired heart. One of his hands rested on the hand Sunny had draped over his shoulder. "Ain't love grand!" Aunt Stella added.

"Is that what it is?" Deenie sat back and put her feet up on the hearth of the crackling fire, content to watch Paul and Carl take on Roger and John in a wicked game of Battleship. Every so often, she pitched a treat to Bear, who caught it with lazy ease.

*This is what I call a perfect day,* she thought. *A perfect moment, when everyone I love seems to have everything they need, right here and right now. Even Sunny. When Brad is present, Sunny seems whole in a way I never would have foreseen.*

"Wahoooo!" Roger yelled when he and John soundly trounced Carl and Paul. "Who's the man now?"

"Forfeit, we get a forfeit," Margaret called. "What will it be? Song? Dance? A secret? Or poetry?"

"Make them sing," Sunny said. "Make them sing Primary songs like 'Once There Was a Snowman.'"

"'Head, Shoulders, Knees, and Toes,'" Beth challenged.

"Sing Sunny's sunshine song," Evvy insisted.

Carl and Paul sang the first two songs with good humor, hamming it up all the way.

"Now I have a secret to share," Carl said when they finished. He pulled a well-handled envelope out of his pocket and handed it to Deenie. "It's your New Year's Day present," he said, beaming with excitement. "Open it."

Deenie felt her heartbeat speed up. There was only one thing young men Carl's age presented to parents with such excitement. "Mission papers?" she gasped as she unfolded the contents. "These are mission papers with your name on them! I thought . . ."

"I never said I *wouldn't* go on a mission, Mom. I said I wasn't *ready* to go. Now I am." Deenie gave Carl a huge hug and a noisy kiss on his cheek. The rest of the family crowded around him for hugs and hand-shakes of congratulations. "Who's the man now?" Carl challenged when Roger pulled him into a bear hug. Even Brad left Sunny long enough to shake Carl's hand, and Carl took the time to collect a sweet kiss from Sunny.

"Do I still get my song?" she asked.

"You bet," Carl said.

After the excitement over Carl's mission papers died down, he and Paul took center stage again. When they started to sing "You Are My Sunshine," everyone joined in. Even Deenie had to admit she was touched by the way Brad lifted Sunny's hand and held it to his cheek.

ERIN
January 13, 1992
Dear Friends,

Another Christmas, another New Year's Day, another birthday—Kayla's ninth. If there's anything I've learned the last few years, it's that Life Goes On—If You Keep Breathing! How's that for an addition to *The COBs' Little Book of Wisdom*?

I loved the photo card you sent, Juneau. It's easy to see how much Greg loves his Giddy. They have the same big smile, those two. I don't think our new photo looks that much differ-ent from last year's—except for new pjs and nighties, this time in red with white reindeer and snowflakes.

I don't know when Mom found time to sew them. Grams has been diagnosed with congestive heart failure. Don't panic, it's not as horrible as it sounds. With her meds, she's feeling well enough to go to the senior center with Marcella again. Even so, Mom is concerned about leaving her alone so much. She's thinking about doing some of her work at home, which Jake says is no problem.

Jake and Mom are still disgustingly lovey-dovey. I wish Cory and I felt that way about each other. We're getting along much better as partners, but I want to have a lover, too! When I told our counselor I just keep stumbling over the fact that he will never really want me like I want him, she said, "So, what's unique about that?" She said that even if couples have basically compatible levels of libido, they don't always have the same interest at a given time due to stress and other issues. Her advice? Tell your partner what you like and make it work! Hah.

We're on the road a lot these days taking the kids to their activities, especially now that we've added piano lessons to the schedule! For months, Mark has been plunking out tunes on the Primary room piano, so we decided to buy a nice Yamaha console. He's now taking lessons from a Suzuki piano teacher at the MacPhail Center downtown, and he's going through the first repertoire book like gangbusters. This method (learning by listening) requires a lot of parental involvement. Add Suzuki piano coach to my resumé! We play the repertoire CD mornings and evenings, so we all know the songs by heart.

As you can tell, the kids and all their activities keep Cory and me so busy we don't have much time to think about our life as a couple. I don't know if that's good or bad. I'm just glad they aren't old enough to leave home!

Happy New Year and blessings on you all.

Love,<br>Erin

WILLADENE
February 15, 1992
Dear COBs,

Carl has received his mission call to the Alaska Anchorage Mission. We are floored, flabbergasted, taken aback.

I've always thought of Alaska more in terms of calving glaciers and killer whales than a mission field. I can't imagine Carl so far away, but he is pleased with his call and eager to go. He's due at the Missionary Training Center (MTC) on March 10 and will speak on the preceding Sunday, along with Roger and Paul. Carl says he doesn't want any hoopla afterward, just a family dinner. The Donovans, who have been joining us occasionally for sacrament meeting, have made a point of saying they're coming to hear Carl's talk. He feels as if his mission has already started.

I had my first official SAR call for a missing skier near Powder Ridge up Ogden Canyon. The whole thing was over before I got there, but now I know how it feels to do the checklist under pressure and hit the road as quickly as possible. Talk about adrenaline rush.

Here's news, not ours, but ours to share if you haven't heard. Miss Heather Hughes is sporting Bryan's diamond, and Sophie is due the first part of April. It's a girl, whom they plan on naming Ella, using part of Gabby's full name, Gabrielle.

Thinking of you all when I can think at all,

Deenie

P.S. The vandalism and animal killing in Cache Valley have stopped for the present. We are all relieved, but Dave says it's too soon to let up on security. The neighborhood watch is still on alert round the clock for anything out of place, and everyone is still traveling in pairs. I keep my Smith and Wesson handy. Creepy, huh?

## JUNEAU

By the time Gideon turned four on February 1, 1992, his most used word in the entire language was *why*. "Why is the grass green, Mama?" "Why does Philip Atwater bark instead of talk?" "Why does Sister Kittridge wear a beep-beep around her neck?" "Why do we sing about warts in church?"

The last one was a puzzlement to Juneau. "Do we sing about warts?"

"Yuh." Gideon nodded emphatically. "That song about the kind wart."

Juneau mentally ran through all the hymns she could remember.

Kind wart? Aha! The one that said, "To those who fall how kind thou art." Or, to the unschooled ear, "How kind the wart."

Gideon knew about warts. He'd had one on the inside of his right ring finger, a rough, grainy thing that had scraped on his clothing and brought on extensive conversations about where he'd got it (Tanner Melton in his Primary class told him he'd got it from a toad) and how he could get rid of it (Tanner said he'd have to have his finger sawed off). The wart had shriveled and dropped off after a few applications of a medication Dr. Tim Hart had recommended to Juneau at church one day. Ever since then Gideon had called Dr. Tim "the wart doctor."

"Sweetie," Juneau told Gideon, "I think the song says 'how kind thou'"—she paused to separate the words—"'art.'"

"OOOooooh." Gideon drew the word out to indicate he was trying to comprehend. "Why?"

Juneau wasn't totally sure what this why was about, so she just said, "You must be a writer, pal."

"Why?"

"Because you ask so many questions. That's what writers do." Before he could add another why, she said, "Let's get Philip Atwater's leash and go for a walk."


When Misty insisted on giving the family birthday party for Gideon, Juneau thought of a *why* of her own. Misty must have sensed it, because she added, "After all, I am his mother."

"So where do you want to have it?"

"Our place," Misty said. "Mine and Ira's. There's room for all of us."

"Sounds good." Juneau never opposed Misty's infrequent forays into the realms of parenthood. Gideon had been told as soon as he could possibly understand that Misty was his mother, the one who had carried him under her heart. He also knew that Trace was his father, although he hadn't yet questioned how that came about. All involved agreed that they would dole out further information as he asked for it. In the meantime, he called Juneau and Greg Mama and Daddy, and no one tried to change that.

Juneau gave a "friends" party for him with the seven other members of his Primary class plus the neighborhood kids and Philip Atwater. They had games in the backyard on a warm and golden February day and ate hot dogs and brownies, Gideon's choices. It had been a successful party, except that Gideon told Juneau and Greg later that Tanner Melton had put the stink eye on him.

"Okay, I'll bite," Greg said. "What's the stink eye?"

"I don't know." Gideon tossed a ball he'd gotten as a gift. "But Tanner says it's bad. He says it will make me have bad luck."

"Forget it, buddy," Greg told him. "You don't have to pay any attention to what he said. He doesn't have any power over you. Do you know who has the most power over you?"

Gideon nodded. "You!"

"Nope." Greg tapped the boy's chest with a finger. "You," he said. "You're the most powerful person in your life. If Tanner says it again, you just say, 'Nobody can put the stink eye on me.'"

Gideon repeated it, adding, "Not even Tanner Melton."

When Misty told him she was giving him another party, he asked if Tanner would be there.

"No," Misty said. "Just you and me and Ira and Mama and Daddy and Trace."

"Okay. But that's only . . ." he counted on his fingers, something he'd recently mastered, " . . . five people. Can you have a party with just five people?"

"Six, counting you," Misty said. "You can have a really cool party with six people."

"Okay," Gideon agreed.

Juneau had to admit Misty handled the boy well, even though she didn't play the part of mother very often. Juneau left the details of the party to her daughter.

Misty and Ira lived in an apartment that had been carved out of the upstairs rooms of what had originally been a one-family home in Alhambra. It was the first time Juneau and Greg had been invited into it, and Juneau was glad to see they'd created a comfortable home for themselves with interesting and eclectic choices, including a fifties chrome-and-yellow Formica kitchen table that reminded her of Erin and a brick-and-board bookcase reminiscent of Juneau and Greg's first furniture.

They all pitched in to make spaghetti, assemble a salad, and set the table. Juneau felt herself relax as they enjoyed dinner, followed by the birthday cake, which Misty had decorated with colorful frosting and candles. The party was a success, even though Misty was somewhat curt and abrupt. But for moody Misty, it wasn't that unusual.

The only thing Juneau disapproved of was the entertainment Misty had planned. It was too active for Gideon, given that it was almost his bedtime. They all played a raucous game of musical chairs, and then the Guy's Club played "keep away" with a Nerf ball in the small living room while Juneau and Misty cleaned up the kitchen. Listening to the thumps mixed with laughter, Juneau commented that maybe they could do something a little less lively.

"Stuff it, Mom," Misty said. "You've been bubbling over with disapproval all evening. This is my house. I'll call the shots."

Juneau gasped. "Misty!" she said. "What are you talking about?"

"You know well enough what I'm talking about," Misty said, scrubbing vigorously at the spaghetti pot. "The first thing you did when you got here was straighten up the books in the bookcase and dust the top shelf with a Kleenex. Then you scoured the sink before you washed the lettuce for the salad, and I can imagine you did the same for the bathroom sink when you went in there. Probably Cloroxed the toilet, too."

"No, honey, I didn't." Juneau attempted some humor. "Not the toilet, anyway. I'm sorry. I thought I was being helpful."

"You were telling me I'm a slob of a housekeeper." Misty turned to glare at Juneau. "You probably think it isn't clean enough to have Gideon here."

"I had no such thought," Juneau protested. But she had noticed the carpet needed vacuuming and had made a mental note to bring over her good Hoover some time. "I'm sorry, sweetie," she said, meaning it.

"Yeah," Misty said, "as if you've ever been sorry. You've never approved of anything I've ever done."

Something in Juneau snapped, the way it had done the time Misty ran away to her grandparents' Airstream when she was thirteen. "Well, some of the things you've done have been pretty far out of line, Misty. What kind of parent would I be if I hadn't disapproved?"

Juneau expected a sharp answer back, but instead Misty's scowl faded, and she smiled. "It hasn't all worked out bad, has it, Mom?"

Juneau rearranged her own face to smile back. "No, honey. It hasn't."

The tension lessened, and Juneau was glad when Misty said, "Let's go join in the fun and games." But her disapproval returned when she saw how flushed and excited Gideon was with the game of keep away that was still going on. She was grateful to Ira, who said, "Hey, Giddy, how about playing something a little more low key now that the Cinderella brigade has joined us?"

"No," Gideon said. "I want to play keep away with Mama."

Misty must have taken that to mean her because she crouched down and said, "Way to go, Giddy. Ship it to me." She held up her hands, and Giddy threw the Nerf ball in her direction. Trace intercepted, tossing it to Greg, but Misty reached out and nabbed it. "Over there," she yelled to Gideon, who raced toward the dormer alcove where he tripped and fell, striking his forehead on the edge of one of the bookcases. Blood spurted. Gideon wailed.

Juneau leaped forward to go to him, but Trace got there first. Pressing two fingers over the wound, he picked Gideon up with the other arm. "Easy does it," he said. "Somebody get a towel."

Greg rushed to wet a kitchen towel under the cold water tap and handed it to Trace, who swabbed at the split in Gideon's forehead. Blood drenched the towel.

"Head wounds bleed a lot," Trace said tersely. "We'll need to get him to an emergency room."

"I'll drive," Ira said.

*This shouldn't have happened,* Juneau fretted. *I should have stopped that roughhousing, no matter if Misty objected. I should have protected my boy.*

My boy. For the first time, she realized she'd crossed that line. She no longer thought of Gideon as Misty's. She thought of him as hers.

And Gideon? Who did he think his mama was? When his forehead had been stitched up at the hospital, he reached out his arms, saying, "I want Mama." No one disputed it when Juneau took him.

He was subdued and a little limp on the ride home but curious. "Why did the doctor sew my forehead?" he asked.

"So the skin will grow back together and you won't have a scar," Juneau told him.

He was silent for a moment and then said, "Why didn't the wart doctor do it? Doesn't he know how to sew?"

"Yes," she said, "but he works in a different part of the hospital."

Again Gideon thought about it. Then, "I wish I hadn't've fell, Mama. It was fun at Misty's."

"Yes," Juneau agreed. "You just had a bit of bad luck."

"Yuh." Gideon nodded. "It was Tanner's stink eye that did it."

When Juneau sat down to write Gabby and Willadene and Erin that night, her thoughts were in turmoil. Misty had been right. Juneau didn't think Gideon was safe in Misty's apartment. Or in Misty's care. But her heart hurt too much to write about that, so she began with "I found out why sometimes things go wrong just when you think life is good. It's the stink eye that does it."

*Chapter 27*

ERIN

That spring Erin so wanted to believe that the improvement in her grandmother's health was real that she didn't acknowledge what was right before her. When Grams asked her a question about something with an obvious answer, Erin thought, *Old age is a bummer.* When Kayla said it wasn't fun to play cards with Grams anymore, Erin shrugged it off. Kayla didn't like playing games with her, either—she didn't make her moves fast enough.

She couldn't avoid reality when Joanna sat her down and said bluntly, "Grams is in trouble. You must have noticed."

"She's forgetful now and then, but—"

"It's more than that, Erin. She dials a number and then forgets who she's calling or why. She doesn't remember how to bid in pinochle and often forgets what trump is."

"Not Grams! She loves pinochle."

"Marcella told me that it's getting so bad that some people don't want to play with her anymore." Joanna paused. "This morning I saw her standing in front of her coffeemaker. She couldn't remember where to put the filter."

"But she's made coffee every morning her whole life!"

"That's what worries me. Forgetting names and dates is one thing. Forgetting how to do something as basic as making coffee is a whole other animal. I'm taking her in for some tests tomorrow."

"Are we talking Alzheimer's?" Erin asked.

"That, or some other type of dementia."

"What are we going to do?"

"Take it a step at a time."

Erin made a strangled sound. "I'm so sick of hearing that!"

"Sorry, dear, but it's the truth, however much it irritates you. We'll get her started on whatever meds the doctor prescribes. Then Jake and I will talk to her about her situation and find out how she'd like to handle things as time goes on."

"I hate this!"

Joanna gave her a soothing pat. "Her life won't change that much for a while, dear. The folks at the senior center are going to keep an eye on her. They'll try to interest her in activities that she can do, even as the forgetfulness get worse."

"Is it safe for Grams to be home alone when you're at work?"

"I don't think so. On Saturday, Jake and I are going to set things up so I can work full time from home. Marcella's already agreed to come over and stay with Grams if I need to make a run to Finishing Touches."

"You're going to ask someone who's almost ninety to baby-sit someone who's eighty-two?"

Joanna grinned. "Why not? Marcella's doing amazingly well for her age, thanks to good Scandinavian genes. Besides, two little old ladies aren't likely to get into much trouble. Mom's forgetful, but she's willing and pliable. She'll do what Marcella tells her."

"I can't believe you're taking this so well," Erin said, feeling resentment rise. "It's not fair, when Grams finally has some peace and joy in her life! And you and Jake—you're still practically newlyweds."

"So? Like the bumper sticker says, Life is what happens while you're making other plans."

April 9, 1992
Dear Friends,

Grams has been diagnosed with Alzheimer's. Life is just not fair! Right when she's learned to love life, she gets robbed of her capacity to enjoy it. I'm not asking What If? I'm asking Why? Why? Why?

Your Erin

WILLADENE
April 19, 1992
Dear Juneau, Erin, and Gabby,

Erin, I was so sad to hear about Grams's situation. Dealing with Alzheimer's disease is tough for the whole family. As far as your Whys go, sorry, friend. With disease there's often no answer. My advice is to buy some pretty flowers to brighten her deck and spend as much time with her as you can.

With the coming of spring, all kinds of things are blossoming here, including a romance between Sunny and her police officer! He takes her (and Mom and Dad) on such adventures: a trip to the Golden Spike Monument, bird watching in the salt marshes, the movies, and, this summer, the opera.

I still had my doubts about his intentions, so I ignored Mom's orders to mind my own business and had a confrontation with him. He told me, nicely, that I wasn't doing Sunny any favors by ignoring what an attractive and interesting and remarkable woman she is. He thought if it weren't for her health problems, she'd probably be married with a family of her own by now.

That stopped me cold. Have we kept Sunny more dependent than necessary by expecting less of her because of her health? Could our well-thought-out plans based on love and good intentions have gone awry? The idea makes me sick to my stomach. Especially since Mom says he's right.

As if that wasn't shock enough, Sunny heard what I said to Mom. She told me in no uncertain terms that her relationship with Brad was none of my business! She's not talking to me at the moment, so I'm in need of a triple whammy of advice from the three of you—COB and COBettes all.

Love,
Deenie

P.S. Gabby, tell Bryan congratulations on the new house and on his engagement.

P.P.S. The police in St. George have picked up someone they think may have been causing the mayhem in our area. We're waiting for confirmation.

## JUNEAU

When Juneau turned the calendar to April, she noticed that Passover began the day before Easter. She'd planned on the traditional Easter dinner, always a simple matter in the Caldwell household, with family gathered around the table. But after all the years of knowing him, she wondered how Ira felt about that, especially in the absence of any Passover observance.

The next time Ira and Misty came over, she asked him about it. He spoke wistfully of his family tradition of getting together for a Seder, marking the beginning of the Passover season. He missed the lighting of the candles and the rituals that went along with this special dinner, to say nothing of just being together with his family and laughing over Uncle Schlomo's jokes and devouring Aunt Sarah's special poppy seed cake.

"Couldn't we do a Seder?" she asked. "You could tell us what we'd need to do."

Ira's face brightened. "Would you really do that? A Seder?"

"Just tell me how." It touched her to see how pleased he was. Even Misty looked at her with some degree of approval. Juneau hoped that it would ease the strained relationship she'd had with her daughter since the blowup at Gideon's birthday party.

On the first night of Passover, Juneau set the table for herself and Greg, Gideon, Misty and Ira, Trace, Marisol, and Beto, who commuted to Loyola University in Los Angeles each day but was home at night. She thought of the missing family as she worked—Nicole in Provo; Marisol's oldest son, Vincent, in the Marines; and Isobel and her husband in Colorado where they were attending school.

As per Ira's instructions, Juneau set an extra plate for the prophet Elijah, the unseen guest, who was said to visit the Passover Seder in the guise of a poor or oppressed person. By the treatment he received, he would know whether the people were drawing close to God.

Gideon, who knew about Elijah from Primary, was somewhat perturbed by this. "Is he really going to come?" he asked. "The Bible guy?"

"He won't really be here," Juneau told him. "Only in spirit."

"You mean he's a ghost?" he whispered.

Juneau squatted down so she could look him in the eye. "No, not a ghost. We set a plate for him to show that he's welcome to come in."

"Why?"

Juneau wished she'd read up on Elijah and his role in Jewish tradition. "Because we want him to tell us how to be better people and follow God's commandments."

Gideon frowned. "How can he tell us if he's not here?"

"You know what, Gideon," Juneau said, "maybe Ira can answer all those questions."

Juneau put the roasting chickens for the meal into the oven well ahead of time, and Ira came to help in whatever way he could. Together they assembled everything needed for the ceremony—unleavened bread or matzoh, a boiled egg for each person, a lamb shankbone (Juneau had wheedled one from a friendly butcher at Safeway), apples, walnuts, cinnamon, parsley, horseradish, salted water, and fruit of the vine.

"You can make the haroseth," Ira said. "Chop up apples and walnuts with a pinch of cinnamon and a little wine."

"Grape juice," Juneau amended. "This is a Mormon Seder."

Ira grinned. "Grape juice it is. Put a small grape juice glass at each place. Put the rest of the stuff on a plate in the middle of the table."

When everything was ready, Ira called them all and bade them sit. After passing out copies of the Haggadah, a booklet telling the story of the Exodus, he said, "The Passover begins as the mother of the household kindles the festival lights and recites the traditional blessing . . ." He paused, looking at Juneau, and then said, "in Hebrew."

Juneau choked. "In what?"

Everybody laughed.

"Read it from the Haggadah," Ira said, handing her a match.

She struck it and then carefully lit the two little white candles Ira had told her would be needed. She was reminded of the sweet scene in *Fiddler on the Roof* when Golde lights the Shabbat candles, and her throat closed so that she could barely say the unfamiliar words. "*Baruch Atah Adonai Elohenu Melech Ha-olam* . . ." Following the Hebrew words was the translation: "Blessed art Thou O Lord our God, King of the universe, who has sanctified us by your commandments and has commanded us to kindle the Festival lights."

The ceremony went on, with Ira reading the Leader's parts and everybody at the table responding at the appropriate times. There was the washing of the hands and the dipping of the parsley into the salted water, with Ira reading, "The parsley reminds us of the hyssop brush with which the children of Israel applied the blood of the Passover lamb to the doorposts of their houses. The salt water represents the tears shed by the Israelites in slavery in Egypt. So, too, it represents the tears we shed when we remember our slavery to sin."

When Ira got to the part where he asked Gideon to open the door for Elijah, the little boy hesitated. "Do we have to let him in?" he whispered.

"Yes," Ira whispered back. "But it's all right. He's a little like Santa Claus that way. He comes and he goes and nobody sees him."

Santa Claus was someone Gideon was familiar with. He wasn't afraid of Santa Claus. "Okay," he said, running to the front door and opening it.

The ceremony ended with everybody reading together, "Lord, we thank You and we all exclaim . . . 'Lashanah haba'ah bi Yerushalayim!' Next year in Jerusalem!"

There was silence for a moment. Juneau felt a little teary, and she saw Marisol dab at her eyes with a corner of her napkin.

"Thank you for doing this," Ira said softly. He sounded a bit choked up himself. "It's probably a little . . ." He seemed to hunt for a word, " . . . a little exotic to you."

Greg reached out to touch his hand. "It was a pleasure, and it's not exotic at all. It's the foundation of our own religions, Marisol's and Beto's and ours. We should do it every year."

Misty reached over to hug Ira, and Juneau was grateful for the effect it seemed to have had on her.

Just then the door slammed. Philip Atwater leaped to his feet and barked.

"Must have been a breeze," Trace said.

Gideon shook his head. "Elijah."

JUNEAU
May 1, 1992
Dear Ladies,

I have fabulous news! Actually, *two* fabulous newses. First, Trace was baptized last week. He said he goes to church all the time, so he might as well enjoy all the benefits. Greg has snagged him as an assistant Scoutmaster.

The second news is that I've been invited to speak at a state conference of teachers of English in August. This is a big step forward, a recognition that my writing is of value to young readers.

The book that brought about the invitation was my third novel, *Beyond,* the one I wrote after Rhiannan's death. One of the reviews called it a "significant" book.

I took the experience of losing a beautiful and promising young person and fashioned around it the story of a girl who loses her best friend to death. It's about how she learns to concentrate not on the loss but on life itself. Writing it helped me do that for myself.

The conference is in northern California. I'm thinking that would be a good time for Greg and me to enjoy a weekend away.

> Still on cloud nine,
> Juneau

## WILLADENE
May 17, 1992
Dear Juneau and Erin,

Awesome, Juneau! I bought the book the day after I got your letter. Good thing I had a box of tissues handy while I read. You deserve the recognition, my dear.

I thought you needed an update on Gabby and family. We made it to Provo for the blessing of Sophie's baby. Sophie and Dennis are thrilled to be parents, and little Ella is a doll. Gabby looked well and happy, though still thinner than I think is healthy.

Cecelia and Junior put on a good front, but from their rather formal interactions with Gabby, it's clear they're still estranged from her. It was nice to see their children getting along better, though. Sophie's husband seemed to be on friendly terms with both Bryan and Kenny. Maybe he will be a bridge between the brothers.

Bryan introduced us to his sweetheart, Heather. They're planning a fall wedding.

Love,
Deenie

## ERIN

May 21, 1992
Dear Juneau, Gabby, and Deenie,

I've been thinking about all of you since we talked on Mother's Day, especially you, Gabby dear. One of the speakers in sacrament meeting said we all have many mothers. We have our birth mothers, who love, care for, and protect us the best they can. Then we have the women who nurture us in ways that our own mothers can't or didn't, for whatever reason.

As an individual, I'm grateful for my own sweet mother, who has become my hero, and for you, dear COBS. As a mother, I'm grateful to every person who steps up for Mark and Kayla when what I have to give isn't enough or isn't wanted. There are so many of them! And you, Juneau, your book will fill a space for many who read it. A Grab-the-Tissues book!

I recently had the opportunity to step up for Melina, the girl in my YW class. Kayla, Mark and I went to her piano recital. Her agoraphobic mom, Althea, can't leave the house, and her dad, Gerald, can't get time off his weekend job, so Mark and Kayla and I were stand-ins.

I was more nervous that night than I've ever been before one of Kayla's tests or competitions. I guess that was because I didn't have a hand in it. But I didn't have to worry. Melina looked very cute, though her dress was a little wrinkled, and she played a Beethoven sonatina beautifully. When she was taking her bows, Mark dashed up to the stage with the bouquet Kayla suggested we bring to give her. Melina's smile was one for the picture books.

Mark, who loves to play for anyone who will listen, said we should have a home recital starring him and Melina. I knew Melina's dad was feeling bad at having to miss her recital and realized that would give him the chance to hear her. So we invited over one and all for a family home recital evening!

Mark performed like a seasoned pro. He's had lots of experience playing in Ms. Northrop's group lessons and monthly studio recitals. (She's a brilliant teacher. She makes learning the repertoire a fun challenge for both Mark and me—I'm his home coach, remember? She also has a way of making Mark feel confident and able.) After Mark, Melina played the Beethoven she'd learned for her recital and Scott Joplin's "Maple Leaf Rag," which Ricky got up and danced to.

Then Ricky asked for his favorite Primary songs, "The Ox Cart" and "I Want to Be a Missionary Now." Insisted on them, I should say. Mark picked them out by ear, and Ricky danced while he sang, flapping his arms. He's got an oddly rough voice for a little guy, but he was very enthusiastic.

I think the evening meant the most to Gerald, who was very proud of his daughter, and to Grams. She loves listening to Mark play and has her favorites from the repertoire. They soothe her when she's feeling agitated.

The day afterward, I got a call from Althea to thank me for doing something so special for Melina and Gerald. We talked for almost an hour. She's sharp, witty, and enormously well-read. And she loves Melina dearly. That must make up for a lot.

Love and hugs to you,
Erin

P.S. Deenie, how sweet that Sunny has love in her life.

WILLADENE
June 16, 1992
Dear COBs,

Erin, how COBish you are sounding these days! Finding mothering when we need it is a gift.

Juneau, we loved having Nicole with us as the end of the BYU semester. Has she mentioned to you about meeting Reece and Ryan? The sparks still fly between the twins whenever she's mentioned. Even Paul was looking a little glassy-eyed in her company. The twins are headed to the Y in the fall. Is Beto out of the picture, in case they start competing for her attention?

I can't imagine having Beth as far away from me as Nicole is from you. I still want all my chicks under my wing. It helps that Carl is so faithful in writing home. He loves Alaska and the people he works with. Roger and I are already thinking of visiting when he's finished.

Dad and Mom have more free time by themselves, and they're making the most of it. You'd think they were courting all over again. They regularly attend the temple, too. I wouldn't be surprised if they are called to be workers one of these days. When I go I put all your names in the temple. Sometimes twice when I get troubling news. I hope God doesn't think I'm a pest.

Love,
Deenie

P.S. I guess the suspect in St. George wasn't our man, since another barn burned to the ground in May. Someone asked in church the other day, "Is the Lord trying to get our attention?" I said I thought the Lord didn't have anything to do with it.

JUNEAU
June 20, 1992
Dear COBs,

They say pride goeth before a fall. I guess that must be true. The pride part was me feeling great about my invitation to speak at the writer's conference. The fall part? Me standing on a rickety old chair to get something off a high shelf in the garage. Overreaching, losing my balance, and falling. Landing on my right leg—on the lawnmower. Which doesn't give. If you're thinking "Ouch," think it in all caps.

Trace had taught Giddy all about 911, and he made the call while I was out of my head with pain. I ended up in surgery with a compound fracture of my right femur. Now I'm home, but with an ankle-to-hip cast, I'm pretty well out of commission.

If anything good has come out it, it's the way Misty reacted seeing me out flat with that cumbersome cast. She said, "I'll

take care of you," and she has, in a most unexpected and wonderful way. I'm so grateful for the closeness we feel, at least for
now. Her wanderlust seems to have momentarily cooled a bit.
Maybe the answer is to make her feel more needed. I wonder.

It's a lot more fun to be on the giving side than the receiving
side, though. I about rose up and walked when Sister Kittridge,
my little octogenarian friend, brought over a casserole! She
gave me a talking to, saying, "You've always been the one to do
things for others. Now lie down and be done for. Give the rest
of us a chance to do."

I'm trying, but it's not easy. I think of Milton, who said, "They
also serve who only stand and wait." Except in my case it's
"who only sits with her leg propped up and is waited on."

> Thinking of you,
> Juneau

P.S. My doctor says the conference in August is out. So much
for fame.

# Chapter 28

ERIN

July 9, 1992
Dear COBs,

How are you doing, dear Juneau? I have to say sitting and being waited on sounds pretty good from where I am!

I just got back from a support group for wives of gay men. Noreen, the counselor Cory and I see, said I needed to go at least once. I'm pretty sure once was enough.

It was really painful to listen to wives who know their husbands are gay . . . and their husbands know they know . . . but nobody's talking. It's The Dead Horse in the Middle of the Dining Room Table. I told them our Gabbyism: Truth kept secret stinks. I don't think they appreciated it.

It was even harder to listen to the women (non-Mormon except for me, by the way) who have come to some "accommodation" with their husbands regarding "outside relationships." It's like they were willing to put up with almost anything because they still loved their husbands and wanted to be with them. Or they were scared of life without them. I thought my situation was tough until I heard what those women had to say.

At the end of the session, the facilitator started talking about the stages couples in our situation go through. They're a lot like those stages of grief people go through when they know they're going to die, which makes sense. I felt like something had died when Cory told me.

Cory and I are at the stage where we have to figure out who we are, individually and together. Supposedly, that leads to having a sense of personal power and feeling comfortable about setting boundaries. Then partners can make choices and move on with their lives, whether together or alone. Alone is a scary thought.

When I told Noreen I'd learned a lot from the group, she

suggested that I should consider going to a seminar about the parenting issues facing gay fathers. I said I needed some time to think before I took that one on! Did you ever see that lovely movie called *Educating Rita*? Well, if I were in the movie, it would be entitled *Educating Erin!*

Love,
Erin

JUNEAU
July 15, 1992
Dear Girlfriends,

You can't imagine how much I appreciate all your cards and phone calls since I had my Big Break. They've helped to keep me cheerful while I've been glued to my Chair of Pain, which is what I now call Greg's big recliner. It's the only place I could get my leg comfortable the first couple of weeks, and I practically lived there day and night.

I'm getting around pretty well now with my pizzazz-y bright purple walker, which Misty picked out. She said if I have to hobble around for a while, I should do it with flair.

Nicole, who's working in Provo for the summer, keeps asking if I wouldn't like her to come home and take care of me, since she plans to be a doctor and says it would be good practice for her. But I tell her I have Nurse Misty, who does a wonderful job.

Beto, also a future doctor, is here a lot, and he and Misty "consult" on my treatment plan. He talks a lot about Nicole and what she's doing, so apparently they exchange letters and phone calls. I'm glad.

Her relationship with Beto (whatever that is at the moment) didn't stop her from forming a very positive impression of the Crafton twins when she visited you, Deenie. She talks about them often when she calls.

She especially liked hearing them tell about their missions. She's mentioned she would like to go on a mission herself in a couple of years. What with competition between the twins and the possibility of her serving a mission, who knows what lies ahead for her and Beto.

Ira is taking summer classes at UCLA so he can continue on toward his bachelor's degree there. Misty is not attending school at present because she's taking care of me and Gideon. But Greg is spending a lot of time teaching her computer stuff, which is as good as taking a class. Gideon has grown closer to her now that she's here more, and he even calls her Mama sometimes. I should be happy that they are getting to know each other better. But The Great What If rears up: What If she decides she wants to take him back?

Trace and Ira are often here helping me, and Greg has been wonderful since my accident. He makes a real effort to figure out little things that will please me—like he brings me juicy strawberries he's picked up at the farmers' market on Saturdays or a crossword puzzle page he's torn from the *New York Times,* which he has charmed from the periodicals librarian at Cal State.

He told me last night that he's getting a super fast new computer. He's upgraded the one I bought him, several times, but even so, it doesn't have the power to handle the projects he's working on. I'll inherit the old computer, which does word processing just fine. The new machine will be expensive but worth it, I think. Greg has been doing interesting stuff in his field, and he's hoping to get his promotion to full professor soon. If it doesn't come, I get the impression he might start checking out what's available in the private sector. How do I feel about that? Don't ask.

Speaking of computers—Ladies! You must sign up for e-mail. Greg got me all fixed up with AOL, and instead of calling when he's at the university, he now sends me e-mails. It's so cool!

So who's left to report on? Philip Atwater, of course. He stayed at my side all the time I was in the Chair of Pain. He's getting old, poor fella, and I can really sympathize now when I see how painful it is for him to get around.

That's about it, except that I've been reading a lot of romances since I've had my activities curtailed. They made me wonder what has happened with Regina and Reginald since they've been loaded up with responsibilities.

*Reginald gazed fondly at Regina as she struggled with the cookpots while trying to keep the triplets, Hazel, Filbert, and Wally, and the quads, Daisie, Maizie, Margie, and George from burning their sweet little mitts on the hot stove.*

*"Let's go away for the weekend, darling," he whispered. "Let's take a leisurely drive up to the lake and sit on the porch overlooking the whispering pines while we sip sparkling grape juice from long-stemmed goblets."*

*Regina glanced briefly at him and then her eyes shifted to the far corner of the family room, where the twins were climbing the drapes. "Denzel!" she hollered. "Daphne! Down!" Hastily stirring the scorching gravy, she turned to Reginald. "What was it you said? Something about going away for the weekend? Are you out of your tree?"*

*Reginald sighed. "Regina," he said, his voice heavy with longing. "What's happened to us? You just aren't the fun person you used to be."*

Well, that's all for now. Keep those cards and calls coming!

Love,
Juneau

Juneau left out one important piece of news. The man named Clyde had come to see her. She'd been reluctant to mention him to the COBs ever since Gabby and Willadene had expressed their disapproval of her relationship with him. He came on a Thursday night before Mrs. Jarvis's class. Juneau hadn't been to the class since the accident because the stairs up to the classroom were too difficult to navigate.

She was alone when Clyde came, except for Philip Atwater. Greg had late student office hours, and Misty had taken Gideon for an outing.

When Juneau saw Clyde standing there on her porch, it took her a moment to recognize him in a different context. Not that she didn't know who he was. It was just that he looked out of place there in her doorway.

"Hi," he said. "We've missed you in class."

His eyes said *I've* missed you in class. Juneau was flustered. "Come in," she said, fluttering one hand in a gesture of invitation.

Clyde reached down to pat Philip Atwater as he came in. The dog had heaved himself painfully to his feet and was there, wagging his tail, giving his stamp of approval. "Can't stay," Clyde said. "I brought you a gift." He handed her a small package.

"How nice of you!" Juneau leaned on her walker with one hand while she took the package with the other.

"It's just a tape," Clyde said. "Thought you might enjoy a little Gilbert and Sullivan while you recuperate. You know—'When you're lying awake with a dismal headache, and repose is taboo'd by anxiety . . . '"

She smiled. "Very appropriate. I'll enjoy it. Thank you, Clyde." She couldn't think of what else to say and was somewhat relieved when he turned to go. Her Guilty Secret department was glad no one had seen him there.

But someone did see. Beto came over from next door just as Clyde said good-bye and started to walk away. Courtesy told her that she must introduce them.

"Clyde," she said, "this is Beto, Nicole's friend. Beto, this is Mr. Foster, from my writing class." She had in mind an explanation of why he was there but decided to drop it right where it was.

The two guys shook hands, and then Clyde said, "Don't want to be late for class." He gave Philip Atwater another pat on the head and hurried away.

Beto turned to Juneau with a quizzical look, and Juneau realized to her horror that she was blushing. She held up the tape. "He just brought something to entertain me while I'm laid up."

She was going to have to mention Clyde's visit to the rest of the family, now that Beto had seen him, and she did, that night. But she realized that if Beto hadn't come over, she would have filed the visit away with all her other secrets.

Greg's reaction was mild. "Are you good friends with this guy?" he asked.

Juneau showed him the tape Clyde had brought. "We both like Gilbert and Sullivan."

Greg grinned. "Glad you have *somebody* to discuss them with." He'd frequently expressed his dislike of Sullivan's "jumpy" music and "rattling" lyrics.

Marisol didn't let her off that easy. Apparently Beto had told her about Clyde's visit because the next time she saw Juneau she said, "How come you're having gentlemen callers, my friend?"

Juneau could feel her face flushing. "He's just a guy from my writing class," she said lamely. "He's harmless."

Marisol's eyes narrowed. "That's probably what Manny said when he first started seeing Miss Barbie-Bambi-Bimbo."

Juneau was silent for a moment. It was the first time she'd really considered her friendship with Clyde in that light.

"Message received, friend," she said. "Thanks." Privately she assured herself that Marisol was like Willadene. They both tended to take things to the extreme.

## WILLADENE

Friday morning was the perfect time for Deenie and Lark to run the canal road on the farm with Bear. Evvy and Beth were occupied helping Grandma Margaret put up tomatoes. Lark's daughter, Danny, was spending the week with her grandmother in New Jersey. And with all the Rasmussen men and Lark's husband, Shawn, working on the farm, they would be perfectly safe.

"If we have time, can we try out the pistol on the rifle range?" Lark asked as she filled an extra water bottle for Bear from the kitchen sink.

"Sure. Just let me get it out of the gun safe." When Deenie returned to the kitchen, she was wearing her shoulder holster loaded with her Smith and Wesson. She picked up her cell phone and said, "All set and ready to go."

They ran the canal road two miles up and back, throwing Bear's ball for him until it was soaked with slobber. "Wasn't that more than we usually do?" Lark bent at the waist and gasped for breath.

"Yes!" Deenie grinned as she panted. "Bear and I were showing off." She offered Lark a bottle of water, filled a dish for Bear, and took a bottle for herself.

"Still up for the rifle range?" Deenie asked. Lark puffed and nodded. "Then let's get this mutt in the back and go."

When Deenie pulled into the farmyard and parked the truck, Lark commented on how quiet the place seemed. "Roger said something about problems with the irrigation on the other side of the south pasture. I bet the guys are all working on it," Deenie said.

Bear started to whine and scratch at his kennel. "What's the matter with your dog?" Lark asked.

Deenie frowned as the whines turned into furious barking. "Something's bothering him."

She climbed out of the cab and ran to the back of the truck to release Bear, who was by now in a frenzy. She'd thought to grab his collar as he left the kennel, but he charged out with a howl of rage and hit the ground at a dead run. Just as she started after him, she caught the flash of sunlight against metal, heard the crack of a shot, and then the sound of shattering glass where the truck was behind her.

"Get down!" She screamed the order to Lark without taking her eyes from Bear, who was lunging toward an armed man. The man knocked Bear to the side with the butt of his gun and then shouldered it to take a second shot.

Things happened so fast, Deenie was barely aware of her training taking over, doing for her what she wouldn't consciously have done: She drew her gun, flipped off the safety, pointed at the center of mass and double tapped, firing twice in rapid succession.

The man staggered but continued toward her. Deenie fired again, and then Bear was on him, driving him to the ground and burying his teeth in his arm. "Call 911! Now!" Deenie screamed at Lark, who was still behind the truck. Then she dashed forward to kick the rifle out of the man's reach.

"Git 'im off! Git 'im off me!" the man howled, pounding at Bear with his free hand in an attempt to free himself. "You shot me, you crazy _____. I'm bleeding!" He followed up with a string of profanities.

Keeping her distance, Deenie steadied her stance and tightened her grip. "Lie still," she ordered. "I won't call him off until you do."

When the man stopped struggling, Deenie gave Bear a release command but kept her weapon trained on the intruder. He was filthy and stank. His eyes glittered above a wild beard, and he was bare-chested under an old-fashioned frock coat. Deenie swallowed hard as she noticed blood from his shoulder wound soaking the sleeve.

"They're coming," Lark said from behind her.

Deenie felt her focus waver. She couldn't afford to be distracted by her friend's presence. "The keys are in the truck. Get out of here. Now!"

"But—"

"Do it!" Deenie said harshly. When she heard the truck roar onto the road, she relaxed enough to pull a kerchief from her pocket, wad it in a ball, and toss it within the man's reach. "Press it to your shoulder," she said. "It'll slow the bleeding until the ambulance arrives."

She was still standing in that position when two police cars barreled into the yard, the ambulance close behind. After a brief struggle with the officers, the unknown assailant was cuffed to a gurney, loaded into the ambulance, and driven away. Then Dave Fenton quietly approached her. "It's safe now, Deenie," he said. He put his hands over hers in a calming gesture. But Deenie didn't feel safe. Her fingers were frozen in the grip she'd been taught, and she couldn't let go. She started to shake and was on the verge of bursting into tears when she felt Bear rubbing against her thigh.

"Good dog," she said in a trembling voice and slowly lowered her weapon. She slipped on the safety and handed the gun butt-first to Dave.

After that, everything was a blur until Dave gently guided her and Bear into his office at the police station. Deenie kept her fingers twined in Bear's ruff as she made her official statement. She'd just finished when she saw Roger come through the door. She flung herself into his arms, and they held each other in a fierce embrace. She only pulled slightly away when she had to sign her statement.

"That's it," Dave said as she finished. "Barring testifying against the assailant in court, the worst is over."


*Dave didn't factor in what Beth's reaction might be,* Deenie thought, watching her daughter stomp across the family room.

"You're joking, right?" Beth said in horror at the news. "You didn't actually shoot someone with a gun, did you? Like, going crazy wasn't enough? And driving a red truck with Bear in the back? You had to go and shoot somebody! I'll never live this down." Wailing, she ran from the room.

"That kid could use a serious smack," Paul said, sitting close to his mother and father on the couch. "She doesn't get it! Just think," he added in a tone of voice Deenie knew was designed to lighten the moment. "All of this because Carl shot a chicken when he was twelve."

"What?" Deenie asked, not following.

"Think about it. If Carl hadn't shot the chicken, you wouldn't have decided to go to the shooting range with Grandpa John. If you hadn't practiced target shooting with him—and gotten good at it—he never would have given you that gun and suggested you get your permit." He paused, and his expression turned serious. "If you hadn't done that, you wouldn't have had a way to protect yourself today. But you did. And you're safe. All because Carl shot Grandma NeVae's chicken when he was twelve. He'll be so proud."

Deenie sputtered. Then she laughed. She had to. It was so awful, so grotesque, so bizarre, and so real. She knew there were flaws in Paul's stream of logic, but at the moment it made as much sense as anything else. She felt her laughter slipping out control when Paul added, "I'm proud of you, Mom. And I'm glad you're home and you're safe." He leaned over and gave her a voluntary kiss on the cheek. "See you in the morning. And don't worry about that dope, Beth. She'll come around."

That night Deenie cried out her exhaustion and fear in Roger's arms. In the wee hours of the morning, when she felt as if she could finally sleep, she said, "You can let go now. I'm all right. I know you sleep better when you can sprawl."

"Well, I'm not all right, Deenie." Roger tightened an arm around her, running one hand up and down her back as though to reassure himself that she was safe. "I keep seeing it in my head the way the officer who picked me up described it. Blown-out window in the back of the truck, the blood on the ground, all of it. And I think, what if Bear hadn't been strong enough? What if you hadn't been quick enough? It could be you in the hospital instead of that criminal. It could be you, dead. And it could be me, without you. I don't know how to get over this, Deenie, so just let me hold you, okay?"

*Chapter 29*

WILLADENE
September 10, 1992
Dear Juneau, Erin, and Gabby,

Roger and I are spending the next two weeks by ourselves at Jonas's condo in St. George. Evvy and Beth will stay at Mom's. Not even Bear is coming.

I wish I could say it's all in the name of relaxation and fun, but it's more in the way of a prescription from our good friend Dr. Greenwood, along with the admonition to crack the therapy notebooks and start using them again.

I have been having nightmares, my dear friends. Ugly visits from ghouls and ghosties and men with rifles and maybe even a little of The Griff. They are scary and have lots of blood in them and sometimes my children are in them, calling for help.

Shooting someone is a bigger deal than TV and movies make it seem. I never took the time to face that after the incident at the farm. I just jumped back into the swim of things with the family and SAR. When I told Lark and Pat that I needed some recoup time, Lark said, "Like big duh!" Pat said she'd known it for weeks and had wondered if she was going to have to tell me or if I would figure it out myself. I should have caught on when I wanted to hit someone every time I had to explain yet again that it wasn't an accident—I meant to shoot the guy.

The other part is dealing with the fact that Lark and I were in mortal danger. If I hadn't had Bear and my gun, there might have been widowers and orphans that night. The near miss (I mean it literally) makes me ill.

Anyway, we are off for Rest and Recuperation. Roger says he intends to see I get them all and a little necking in the moonlight if I'm a good girl.

Love,
Deenie

P.S. The man's name is Rodney Tulley, a felon on parole. When they arrested him, he had a list of area people he thought had treated him and his dad badly when they were hiring out in the sixties. All the Rasmussens—us included—were on it, because they'd worked for a while at the family farm! Will liked the boy well enough, he said, but the father was a thief, so Will had to let them go. Gives me the shivers. One good thing: Tulley has accepted a plea bargain, so I won't have to testify.

ERIN

September 12, 1992
Dear Deenie,

I am so glad that you are safe and well. Lark and Bear, too. If you hadn't been doing target practice ever since the Year of the Dead Chicken and Almost Dead Dog and hadn't had the courage to act when it was necessary, I might at this very moment be packing a black dress to go to your funeral. The thought makes me ill.

Until I read your letter, I thought it was funny in a black sort of way that Letitia did in what's-his-face with a shovel. Now it seems horrible. What am I saying? It *was* horrible! She went to prison and the lives of many people changed because of it.

I'm not surprised that you feel out of synch with yourself. I mean, Deenie the Rescuer has morphed into Deenie the Defender. You are going to have to figure out how they can coexist in the same person. Roger, the children, your ward, and your community will have to work on that one, too.

I don't know what else to say, except that I love you and I am so incredibly thankful that you, Lark, and Bear are safe!

> Your Erin

JUNEAU

September 12, 1992
Deenie, I'm so impressed by you!

> In awe,
> Juneau

ERIN

>November 14, 1992
>Dear Friends,
>
>Do you ever wonder what you're doing and why?
>
>I realized the other day that I don't have any connection with women in my daily Minnesota life except for relatives, other skating moms, and business acquaintances. It's been ages since I've been to lunch or the movies with Lucky or Angie, and I don't have any "best friends" from our ward to hang out with. I know I'm busy, but it frosts my cookie when a well-meaning sister says, "We had a great time picking apples at the Honey Bee apple orchard. We would have asked you, but we know how busy you are!" Aarrgh!
>
>Sorry, Deenie, it was either your favorite word or a cuss word. I hate it when people say no for me. Maybe I would have declined the invitation, but I sure would have liked the chance to choose for myself!
>
>But when I see how the kids are learning and growing, I know it's worth whatever little sacrifice I make. Just this Saturday, we drove up to St. Cloud so Kayla could skate in the St. Cloud Competition. She did well enough on her level to win a trophy! I could tell by the look in her eyes that she's imagining our sofa table sporting a collection of trophies and medals.
>
>She loves the freedom of skating and thrives on the challenge of learning a new move. Landing a new jump for the first time lights her up! Sometimes, she's so at one with her blades and the ice that she disappears into the skating. There is something miraculous about those moments.
>
>At those times it's hard for me to remember that she's still a little girl. She's not even ten yet! But let me tell you, it's plenty obvious when she's tired, has a melt-down over not finding the shirt she wants, or fights with Mark over the computer. Or when she snuggles up next to me or Cory for a bedtime story and kisses us goodnight.
>
>It's easy to think Mark is older than his age, too, but for a different reason. He thinks about things. He wants to know how

things work and why they are the way they are. Listening to him and Jake talk while they play checkers is quite the education.

Mark doesn't mind being dragged along to Kayla's events, the sweet boy, especially now that I give him my full attention during piano practice and lessons. Jake goes with him to his group lesson, sweet man! And there's always a bunch of us at his teacher's studio recitals. His hockey practice, too. He loves getting the same kind of support that Kayla gets with her skating.

I don't think I had the faintest idea of the responsibility that comes with having children. I sure didn't know how much I would love them. Right now, they're the bright stars in my heaven.

Love,
Erin

P.S. Kayla had laser surgery on her scar, and she feels much better about pulling her hair back in the "skater look."

## WILLADENE

December 10, 1992
Dear Family and Friends,

Among the Christmas messages we have received this year was a wonderful letter from our son, Carl, who is currently serving in Seward, Alaska. It was filled with his humor, love for the work he is doing, and a new understanding of the word *cold*.

Paul, who graduates this spring and turns nineteen on June 2, is already preparing his mission papers. The letters fly fast and furiously between the two brothers, who soon may be serving in the mission field at the same time.

Mom and Dad are doing their own kind of missionary work by attending the temple several times a week.

Even Beth has caught the missionary spirit and is doing everything she can to get Danny to attend church with her on Sunday. She hasn't given up on getting her to register for seminary next year so they can have all their classes together. And, glory be, Lark has asked to talk to the missionaries. Roger says it's time for him to get serious with Shawn.

What better gift could anyone receive for Christmas than the good news of the gospel? We want to do our part, too, so instead of sending goodies this year we are sending each of you copies of the Book of Mormon with our testimonies inside. Instead of sending gifts to us, we ask that you pass the scriptures on to someone new.

We wish you all Joy this Christmas Season.

Deenie and Family

ERIN

December 27, 1992
Dear Gabby, Deenie, and Juneau,

I just had to write you to say what a fabulous holiday we're having. And all because Jake was asked by a local organization to be Santa Claus for their Christmas program for disadvantaged children.

Mom decided to get involved, too, putting together gift boxes. She was so enthusiastic about it that Cory and the kids and I helped out one evening. We also attended the Christmas party, where Jake was the star, of course. He looked fantastic in his costume—no padding necessary! The white wig and beard were a little cheesy, but his warm, deep voice, twinkly eyes, and loving manner made him a real Claus.

The night before Christmas we picked up the Jays and filled the back of the van with gift baskets to deliver to people on Jake's list. The kids thought it was the most fun to dash up to a house, put the baskets in front of the door, ring the doorbell, and dash back to the car. They almost got caught once, which thrilled them no end.

I can't tell you how much that involvement did for all of us. Not one of us was thinking about what we needed, or wanted, or didn't want, or were disappointed about. We were thinking about someone else, for a change. What a relief that is!

Deenie, I gave that Book of Mormon you sent to a client

who's always asking about the Church. I think she was more interested in learning about you and Juneau, how we got together, and The Pact than in the book. I'll let you know if it leads to anything.

Blessings on you and yours,
Erin

## Chapter 30

### 1993

WILLADENE

When the phone rang at 5:00 A.M. the Sunday after New Year's Day, Deenie knew someone was missing. When she answered, Dave said without preamble, "Fred Randall wandered away from Pioneer House Rest Home some time early this morning. Terry's on his way with Grizwald. Will you come?"

"I'm on my way," Deenie said instantly.

"We don't have much time. It's started snowing again."

"What's going on out there?" a sleepy Beth called from her bedroom.

"Search and rescue," Roger said as Deenie started pulling on her thermals.

"Can I help?"

"Make some toast and juice for Mom. Paul?" Roger called down the hall. "Warm up your mom's truck."

Deenie dressed rapidly, glad she'd gotten into the habit of having proper clothing always at the ready. She pulled a ski hat down over her uncombed hair as she clattered down the stairs and then yanked on her boots over a double pair of socks, grabbed her down gloves and jacket, and checked her utility pack. Roger waited at the door with Bear, who was quivering with excitement. Deenie bent to fasten on his gear. The bell on his harness rang with the movement.

"Got your radio?" Roger asked as he helped her into her jacket and walked out to the truck with her. "Baggies? Scissors? First aid? Tennis ball?"

"Yes and yes. Kennel!" she commanded, and Bear leaped into the truck bed, where Paul locked him in his travel crate. Beth waited by the hood with toast and juice in a travel cup. "Thanks, guys. Say a prayer for us."

All the way through Logan and north toward Smithfield, Deenie said her own prayers for Brother Randall and his family. She prayed for Dave

Fenton and the other SAR teams. Lastly, she prayed for the snow to stop, for herself, and for Bear and his remarkable nose.

Sheriff Fenton was waiting with his crew when she pulled to a stop in the nursing home parking lot and got out. "Wanna work? Wanna work?" she chanted to Bear as she released him from his crate. Terry Madsen pulled up, parked, and had Grizwald leashed and on the ground before she could say hello to the sheriff. Bear settled down immediately in the presence of the more experienced dog.

Nodding a terse greeting to Dave and the two deputies on their team, Terry asked, "How bad and how long?"

"Don't know how long for certain," Dave said. "Best guess is between three o'clock bed check and when the parking lot was plowed before five. At least we know he got dressed before he went out."

Dave led them to the window the old man had climbed through and handed them a bag containing his pajamas. Terry and Deenie each snipped a piece from the pajama collar and put it in a plastic bag. The snow began to thicken on the ground as they defined the search area, perimeter, and grid, and then broke into teams.

Deenie offered Bear the small piece of cloth from the pajamas. "Check it out. Check it out," she instructed as the big dog sniffed. Then she tucked the sample back in its bag. "Search," she commanded, and Bear stepped forward.

They worked the ground beneath the window and then moved across the sidewalk and through the snowbank. Bear moved back and forth, sniffing the ground with agonizing slowness. Keeping the officer working to the left of her within her line of sight, Deenie moved forward. The wind picked up. The snow began to blow stinging shards against her cheeks and chin. She could hear the bell on Grizwald's harness ring in discordant harmony with Bear's as the dogs moved apart into the darkness.

Passing the beam of her flashlight back and forth, Deenie scanned for any clue. "Fred," she called as loudly as she could and then strained to hear even the faintest sound as she counted down on her fingers before calling again. Time lost importance except for those twenty-second intervals. "Brother Randall! Fred!"

In the distance the faint sound of other bells and other commands told Deenie more SAR teams had joined in. The wind shifted, and the sky began to lighten in the east. An hour passed, and then two. Deenie could now see Bear in profile ahead of her. He was standing still as a statue, his massive muzzle lifted into that freshening wind. Then he made the sound she had been praying for—his pig grunt. He had found the scent! "Go on," she called. Quickly radioing her position, she scrambled after him, filled with hope.

Less than ten minutes later she heard him woof out his alert. In the dim light ahead she could see him digging happily into the side of an abandoned straw stack. Deenie waded in with both arms, flinging the moldy, wet straw away. The sounds of help coming rang out over the field as she dug harder, deeper into the straw and found Fred alive, though floating in and out of consciousness.

Deenie let out a yell of pure triumph, cleared away the remnants of wet straw clinging to Fred's face, checked his vital signs, and chafed his hands and arms until Dave and Terry arrived, paramedics in tow.

"What should I do now?" Deenie asked.

"Play with your dog," Dave said, smiling. "Play with that wonderful, marvelous, monstrous Bear of a dog."

Deenie pulled Bear's favorite green tennis ball out of her pocket and tossed it, yelling, "Fetch!"

Though it felt like she had been gone for days, Deenie made it home in time for lunch. "I'm glad you found Brother Randall, Mom," Beth said as she helped Deenie take off her coat. Since she was now nearly as tall as her mother, she managed it with ease.

"So am I." As she tried to pull her sweaty and dirt-streaked shirt over her head, a sharp pain from shoulder to wrist made Deenie suck in her breath.

"Are you hurt, Mom? Do you need help taking the shirt off?"

"Please." Deenie rubbed the offending limb. "I got a little enthusiastic trying to move half a straw stack by myself."

Chuckling, Beth helped Deenie wriggle out of the dirty shirt. "You're not going to do your sprained ankle trick again, are you? When you didn't tell anyone for days and tried to do too much?"

"Not likely. Wait until I get out of the shower, and I'll let you wait on me hand and foot."

As Deenie dressed, Beth told her what the family had done while she was gone. She suddenly realized that her daughter had taken on a new, mature look overnight. She even looked taller than she had the day before, if that were possible. "Did you grow an inch while I was in the shower?"

"Maybe. Dad asked me the same thing when he got home from work last night." Beth helped Deenie finish towel-drying her hair. "Uh, I saw Jason Whitmore at church this morning. He said he might stop by later."

"I thought Paul was going to the Donovans' with the missionaries."

"He knows that, Mom."

"Oh." Deenie grinned as the light dawned. "Beth, honey."

"I know. I won't be fifteen until November," Beth said in a singsong voice. "And fifteen is still a whole year away from being sixteen. We're not going on a date, Mom. We're just talking."

"The old we're-just-talking routine, hmm? Well, stay in sight."

Beth blushed. "Can I go with you to your next SAR meeting?" she asked.

"Sure," Deenie said, "if you rub my feet. But why?"

"I have to write a big-deal essay on what I want to be when I grow up and then do a research paper on the job. Everybody in class seems to have an idea but me, and I thought maybe going with you would give me some inspiration." Then she pronounced with a dramatic flourish: "What am I going to be when I grow up?"

"You'll be an older version of who you are right now. A well-loved daughter of your Father in Heaven."

"Oh, Mom, you know what I mean. Everybody wants to grow up to be someone important."

"I know what you mean. I want to make sure you know what I mean. You were born important. A child of God deserving to be loved and cared for. That's who you are. The rest is what you do."

"I know that, Mom!"

"Well, I didn't. And it took me landing in the loony bin to get it straight. I had to start all over, and understanding that right down in the core of me was the rock solid foundation that made it possible."

"Oh," Beth said in a small voice.

*Maybe I've laid too much on her all at once,* Deenie thought, seeing Beth's hesitant look. She put her arm around her daughter and said, "I think I need hot buttered milk. How about you?"

February 11, 1993
Dear COBs,

Our Evvy has turned five! How time flies. She will start kindergarten in the fall and is already talking about going to *her* school. She's more than ready.

Carl has passed the one-year mark on his mission. We're counting down the days until we will see him, and he tells us he's looking forward to every hour of daylight he can get in the field. At home our missionary efforts go forward. Lark has asked to be baptized. Danny is taking seminary, and Shawn is taking his time.

Roger's old mentor and advisor from the University of Utah has joined the staff at the University of Florida. He's been writing to Roger extolling the virtues of the campus. I'm very glad the job inquiries Roger is now sending out are for K–12 school administration, not another university job. Otherwise I'd be worried about his sending feelers to Gainesville. Alligators in the backyard? No way!

Bear made his first find in January, rescuing an Alzheimer's patient who had wandered away from his facility. We are all proud!

Love,
Deenie

P.S. I finally have a new Church job. Nursery leader. Does that deserve an arrrgh or what!

## JUNEAU

February 20, 1993
Dear Aspiring COBs,

Deenie, hang a medal on Bear. What a dog! Maybe he'll be able to do something about those alligators in the backyard, if you do move to Florida!! Sounds like an adventure.

I'm kind of pensive today, realizing my shortcomings. My latest realization that I may never make it to COBhood, i.e. wisdom, is that for all the years of my life, I've blamed my parents for a disjointed youth of never having a permanent home. So what am I drawing on in writing my books? The wonderful privilege of living all over the country (even Florida)—and having a "permanent home" in the hearts of my parents. No matter what their faults, they always loved Flint and me.

Have I loved them back? I wonder. I've always grumbled that they don't stay in touch very well. Okay, so why haven't I figured out that it's up to me to make the effort to stay in touch? Flint called last week to say that Daddy is quite unwell. I resented being the last to know until I thought, "Well, whose fault is that?" Flint called *them.* I called nobody. Now I call them every day, and next week I'm flying up to see what's going on.

Keep working on those Donovans, and please don't hold my confessions against me!

Love,
Juneau

## ERIN

April 7, 1993
Dear Gabby, Juneau, and Deenie,

Deenie, why did you put the part about Bear at the bottom of your letter? And why didn't you give yourself some credit for the rescue, too? Come on, girl! That story deserved a headline.

And Juneau, what's this business about never making it to COBhood? So you have faults. Big deal. All that's required for COBhood is that we recognize our shortcomings (which you have) and do something about them (which you are). Isn't that right, Gabby?

Thanks for the card for my thirty-fifth birthday. For some reason, it feels like a bigger deal than thirty was or forty will be. But Caitlin made sure I didn't get down in the dumps by throwing a party for me at the family manse. What a fun group was there! Lottie and Caitlin, of course, The Women, Paula, Colleen, Lucky, and Angie. You could tell how different these ladies were by the range of outfits, from Lucky's black polyester and kente cloth to Grams's White Stag knit outfit with little embroidered flowers.

Halfway through, another guest arrived—a surprise guest, even to Caitlin. A woman with very blonde hair and very blue eye shadow burst into the room, breasts first. She said, "A party! How nice!" Then she opened her arms and said, "Caitlin! Give Mama a kiss."

It was Caitlin's mother, Brenda! She'd flown in just to meet "the other one" (me) and Mom. She had boxes of leis, and she gave one to each of us. From that point on, the whole evening revolved around her. She's not nearly as ditzy as she'd like you to think, though her recitation of how she met, married, and divorced her last three husbands was absolutely hilarious.

All the women were still laughing when I went downstairs to Andrew's office to say good-bye. He must have been fuming since Brenda arrived, because he was in a right foul mood. Before I could say boo, he asked if I was happy now that I'd heard all his secrets. He didn't believe me when I said Brenda hadn't talked about him at all.

I've never seen him look so uncomfortable. He was in a confessional mode—comes from being a Catholic, maybe. He said he'd made a lot of mistakes when he was young because he had his priorities mixed up. And because it took him a long time to figure out that his mother wouldn't die if he didn't do everything her way. He ended up by saying, "I guess you're disappointed in me."

You should have seen his face when I told him I couldn't be disappointed in him—he was my father, and I loved him. I think he wanted to say it back to me, but he didn't. I'll have to wait for it some other time.

Still hoping,
Erin

JUNEAU

April 7, 1993
Dear Erin,

Loved the part about the blonde woman bursting into the room breasts first. I thought for sure it was Dolly Parton! Brenda sounds a lot like the mother of that girl Starette I've told you about. They lived in one of the trailer parks up in Washington where we were when I was ten. Except Starette's mother was dark haired rather than blonde. But she had a string of husbands and could keep us entertained for hours telling about them. I liked her a lot.

Love,
Juneau

# *Chapter 31*

WILLADENE

Ever since the confrontation with Rodney Tulley, Deenie toured the house after everyone had gone to bed to double-check the locks on the doors. On the way back to her room one night, she noticed a thin strip of light coming from under Beth's door. She knocked gently and then went in. Beth was sitting up in the middle of her bed, arms around her legs, chin on her knees.

"Can't sleep?" Deenie asked, sitting down beside her.

Beth shook her head. "I've been thinking about what you said the other day about being born deserving love because you're a child of God. Do you think that's true for everyone?"

"Yes."

"But does it stay true?" Beth asked. "When you're born, you're innocent. When you grow up, you're not."

"That's why we have baptism and repentance," Deenie said, ready to launch into a teaching moment on gospel principles.

"I mean people in the world who are really evil, Mom. Murderers. Robbers. Rapists."

Deenie put her arm around Beth's shoulders. "That's a hard one," she said. "Heavenly Father isn't asking us to tolerate sin. He doesn't. But he does ask us to love all his children despite their actions."

"Love the sinner, hate the sin?" Beth asked.

"Something like that," Deenie said.

"Even that horrible Tulley?"

Deenie felt an inner shudder. She could tell by Beth's expression that this was the crux of the conversation. "Even him."

"But, Mom! Do you love him as a child of God? Do you forgive him for trying to kill you?"

"No," Deenie said honestly. "But I want to be able to forgive him, sweetheart."

"I won't ever forgive him, and I don't want to. He's a terrible, wicked man. What did he do, anyway? Just wake up one morning and say, 'I think I'll kill me some people today?'"

"That's pretty close to the truth," Deenie said. "From what the sheriff's report said."

"And God wants me to love him?" Beth's voice was shaking.

"Maybe not all at once. And maybe not tonight. But when you're ready." Deenie paused. "When I'm ready." They sat side by side in silence. Beth's breathing gradually slowed to a calmer pace. So did Deenie's. "Do you want me to say prayers?" she finally asked.

Beth shook her head. "I think we should get Dad. I think we both need a blessing."

Roger came willingly. After listening to a reprise of their conversation, he gave Beth the father's blessing she'd asked for.

"Me next," Deenie said when he finished. Roger blessed her, too. Then together they tucked Beth back in bed.

When Deenie turned off the light Beth asked, "Is Bear in his kennel, or is he roaming the house?"

"Roaming," Deenie said, understanding exactly what Beth was asking. *Are we safe tonight? Is Bear guarding us?*

"I'm sorry I was such a pill about it, when it first happened," Beth said. "I didn't understand."

"I know, sweetheart." Deenie closed Beth's door, thinking, *I still don't.*

## ERIN

April 12, 1993
Dear Friends,

My heart is in my throat, and I can hardly breathe. I am married to a crazy man! Pete had the whole company take training on team building, and as part of it, they all bungee-jumped off a bridge! Not once but twice. Cory said the jump was part of a segment on taking reasonable risks, once you're sure that you've done your homework (checked out the company doing the jump) and that you're prepared (your equipment properly set up). I guess that means making sure the bungee rope is tied to the bridge before you fling yourself off it!

Cory came home totally pumped. He said it was the biggest rush he's had in a long time, and he can't wait to do it again. All I have to say is, he's lucky he didn't hurt himself, because if he had, I would have killed him! Really, what business does a grown man with a family have flinging himself off a bridge with a rubber band tied to his ankles?

But Cory's exhilaration made me wonder if I shouldn't do something that's a little outside my comfort zone—but doesn't risk life and limb. There was an article in the paper last summer about a couple of women outfitters who lead ladies-only canoe trips in the Boundary Waters Canoe Wilderness Area between Minnesota and Canada. I think I could go for that. In the fall, maybe.

Your Erin

JUNEAU

May 1, 1993
Dear Erin and Deenie,

Sorry I've been skimpy with the e-mails. Giddy and I spent a couple of weeks in Oregon with my parents, so I've kind of gotten behind in everything.

Speaking of flinging oneself off a bridge attached only to a bungee cord, I'll say that's kind of how I feel right now. Greg has decided to switch jobs, something I've been half-expecting for some time. He's been going through some kind of mid-life crisis where he feels inadequate for not making more money than a professor's salary, especially when he has the potential to make a bundle in the computer business.

He's investigated a couple of jobs, one in Seattle and another in Michigan. I said, "Whither thou goest, I will go," etc., but he decided they weren't right. Now he's "plunging off the bridge" by investing in a computer business with another professor here, which isn't without its risks. He'll teach fall quarter, and then he'll leave Cal State, except for teaching one graduate seminar a quarter. How do I feel about it? Nervous. We're investing a lot, and . . . but I'll think positively. This is something Greg needs to do. He says he wants to have enough money so we can travel and also build on a second-story writing room for me. I could do without either (except I'd love to see Egypt, where Nicole and Beto used to plan on digging up mummies). But I can't do without Greg being happy with himself. So here goes . . .

My dad is doing much better now. While Giddy and I were with my folks, we did a lot of reminiscing, and you know? I've decided I had a fine childhood, wandering or not.

Next event in our lives: Cath Ostergaard is coming to visit. You recall, she's the young woman Misty and I met in the Mink Creek cemetery. I'll let you know how it comes out and if what I hope happens happens. Is that clear?

Love,
Juneau

Juneau was pleased when Trace told her Cath was coming to California in early May. Trace and Cath had corresponded through endless e-mails and phone calls ever since Cath had sent the college photo of herself and Rhiannan, which Juneau had given to Trace.

"She just got her master's degree," he said. "She wants to see what kind of job opportunities there are in California. Says she's tired of Idaho winters."

"Any other reasons?" Juneau teased.

Trace reddened slightly. "Might be."

Juneau had great hopes that things would work out between them. It had been more than four years since Rhiannan's death, and Trace still seemed tangled in some kind of web from the past. He'd met girls at the singles ward he attended, had even brought a couple of them home to dinner and to meet Gideon. But he'd assured Juneau they were *friends*, not girlfriends. It was as if he were determined to go through life lonely and alone. Juneau hoped Cath would change that.

"What kind of job is she looking for?" Juneau asked

Trace shook his head. "Don't know, exactly. She's been studying some kind of therapy through music and art and drama."

"Interesting," Juneau commented.

Trace nodded. He was majoring in the computer field at Cal State, but he didn't have the passion for it that Greg did. His real love, Juneau knew, was his music. He'd made the practical choice when going into computers, however. He knew he couldn't make a living picking up occasional music gigs.

"I'll e-mail her that our hotel is open," Juneau said. "Good thing Nicole decided to stay some extra time in Provo, so the room is available."

Cath arrived just in time for dinner on a rainy evening, after driving for the better part of two days, all the way from Idaho.

"Hey," she said as Juneau met her at the door, "I thought 'it never rains in Southern California.'"

"Rain?" Juneau said. "That's just heavy dew! Come on in, Cath, you cute thing. You're just in time to feed your face."

She'd invited Trace to dinner with her and Greg and Gideon that night, thinking the meeting between the two might be easier without too large an audience. A good decision, since Trace looked awkward as he met Cath, not seeming to know where to wear his long arms when they stood face to face.

Cath took care of that. "Well, give me a hug," she said. "I've driven a long way to see you!'"

Grinning and obviously relieved, Trace closed the gap between them and wrapped his arms around her.

"After all those letters and e-mails, I feel as if I know you well enough for this," Cath murmured into his shoulder.

"Yes, *ma'am*," he said, lifting her up and whirling her around. When Gideon pushed in between them, he picked him up, too, including him in a group hug, with Philip Atwater barking and whipping his tail in approval.

Watching them, Juneau remembered that lovely day at the theme park in the summer of 1988 when Trace and Rhiannan had walked hand in hand. They had been a study in contrasts, her hair and eyes dark and his light. Trace and Cath looked like a matched set, both with blue eyes and wheat-colored hair. They looked like they belonged together. Juneau e-mailed Deenie and Erin later that night.

Maybe I should get my Yente license. I think I've made a perfect match.

*"Reginald, darling," Regina whispered, "after all these years together, we're still the perfect combination, like salt and pepper, chips and salsa, cookies and milk, bacon and eggs . . ."*

*"Like cats and dogs," Reginald declared, "night and day, thunder and lightning, oil and water . . ."*

*Regina's heart sank as she listened to him go on. What was he trying to tell her?"*

If you haven't guessed already, I was really hoping that Trace and Cath would like each other. Watch your e-mail for the next thrilling episode.

The next day was Saturday, and Trace and Cath, with Gideon in tow, set off for the beach. That night, when Juneau put Gideon to bed, he whispered, "They kissed, Mama. Trace and Cath."

Juneau wondered where the wedding would be, in Idaho or California. Oh, Idaho, of course. That's where Cath's family was.

"It's just like writing a book," she e-mailed to Erin and Deenie that night. "You just set up your characters right, and they'll get together."

They'd all go to Idaho for the wedding, she thought happily. Then they'd zip over to Boise and take Letitia's ashes and diaries out of the safe deposit box where they'd been for so long. Everything was working out so well!

Cath had some job interviews, including one she was really interested in out in Thousand Oaks. She wouldn't hear the results of the job interviews for a couple of weeks, so before she returned to Idaho, she relaxed for a few days, sometimes playing for long periods with Gideon. Juneau noticed that occasionally she practiced her therapy theories on him, drawing him out with songs and little dramas she made up starring him and Philip Atwater. They were both willing guinea pigs, loving the attention. In one of the little "plays," Cath got Giddy to act out his anger at Tanner Melton, who was still plaguing him with his stink eye. Cath made up a little song about how nobody needs to fear the "silly stupefying stink eye." Giddy loved it and practiced until he could sing the song perfectly. It helped him to cope with Tanner Melton.

Juneau hoped that when Trace and Cath got married they would live nearby so that Cath would be another tile in the family mosaic. The two hadn't spoken of future plans, but Juneau knew they were right for each other, and she fully expected some kind of announcement before Cath's departure. When they said good-bye with just another big hug and a "swing-around," as Giddy called it, Juneau couldn't believe it.

"That was it," she e-mailed to Deenie and Erin that night. "Trace said he really likes her, that she's just about the best friend he's ever had, but that was all. Sigh. . . . Next time I make noises about matchmaking, remind me, please, that I'm just a lowly writer and should keep my fingers on the keyboard and out of other people's business."

# Chapter 32

WILLADENE

The last Thursday of May, Deenie got a phone call from Sophie, telling her that Gabby had broken her hip in a fall and that she was resting well after surgery. "She was up on a chair, trying to get a mug down from the top shelf. It belonged to Caleb, Dad's younger brother." Sophie paused. "He went missing this time of year, you know."

"Gabby told us about Caleb when we met in Park City," Deenie said.

"She lost her balance, fell, and hit her head on the table." Deenie gasped as Sophie continued. "She's been on blood thinners for a clot in her leg. Dad said she could have bled to death if Kenny hadn't found her."

"I didn't realize he'd reconnected with Gabby since his release."

"He hadn't. He drove by her house really late that night on his way to deliver a pizza—it's his second job—and he saw all her lights on. He knew she wouldn't be up that late, so he stopped to check on her. Thank heavens."

"Does Gabby know he found her?" Deenie asked, knowing Gabby's negative feelings for her troubled grandson.

Sophie made an unladylike sound. "We told her, but she's sure it must have been Bryan."

"Shall we come?"

"I'll let you know when we have an idea how long she'll be in rehab."

When Sophie gave Deenie a tentative date for Gabby's return home, Deenie made arrangements to pick up Juneau and Erin at the Salt Lake City airport on the way to Provo. They had been calling and sending e-mails about all the things that would make Gabby comfortable, and they were eager to get to Gabby's and start work on their list. But instead of an empty house, they were greeted with sounds of activity and the scrumptious smell of something baking.

Erin sniffed the air. "Cowboy cookies? Who do you think's making them?"

"Sophie?" Deenie guessed. "And Bryan must be the one taking care of the outside. He took a job in Orem so he could be close to Gabby."

Deenie was wrong. She was floored to discover that Cecelia was doing the baking while preparing a casserole for their supper. Cecelia welcomed them warmly and made a point of showing them the freezer full of single-serving, marked casseroles. "I thought, 'What would Deenie do?'" she said, which made Deenie blush.

She was even more chagrined to find that Junior and Kenny—not Bryan—were mainly responsible for the fine shape Gabby's house was in. Father and son moved with the same alpha male swagger and smiled the same broad smiles as they excitedly showed Deenie, Juneau, and Erin the changes they'd made to ensure that the house was safe for Gabby. They were especially proud of the escalator chair they'd had installed on the staircase wall. Junior cajoled Juneau into giving it a try, and everyone applauded as she glided up to the second floor.

"We've found a former nurse tough enough to stand up to Gabby," Cecelia added. "After you girls leave, she'll come to be her live-in companion."

"You've done a great job," Erin said, and Deenie noticed how the compliment pleased Cecelia.

*Why did Gabby lead us to believe they were contentious and indifferent?* Deenie wondered. She had reason to wonder about Gabby's behavior again when Junior and Cecelia brought her home late that afternoon.

The woman Junior helped out of the van and steadied in front of a walker looked so fragile that Deenie had to bite her lip to keep back tears. She, Juneau, and Erin embraced their friend carefully. Then they carried in her things while Junior helped her up the front stairs.

The first thing Gabby said when she stepped into her living room was, "What smells so good? You must have been busy, Deenie! And however did you girls get that chair installed so quickly?"

"We didn't," Erin said quietly. "Cecelia took care of the food, and Junior and Kenny got the chair installed. They're the ones who put necessary items within reach and cleared pathways for your walker."

"Really?" Gabby turned to Junior. "I can't imagine you and Kenny doing that." Her indifferent tone pained Deenie, as did Junior's response. "Well, Mother, this time you weren't here to stop us when we wanted to help."

ERIN

Erin slept poorly that night, kept awake by her distress over Gabby's attitude toward Junior, Cecelia, and Kenny. It had been painfully cool in contrast to her response when Bryan, Sophie, and their families arrived later in the evening. Even Bryan's assertion that he hadn't been the one to find her hadn't warmed her attitude toward Kenny.

The next morning Jonas joined them in the living room after breakfast. He had shrunk with age, but his carriage was still erect and his manners elegant as always. His deep affection for Gabby was obvious as he fussed over her and then took her hand when he sat down next to her. "It's so good to have you home."

"I came back to quite a welcome, Jonas. My COBs were waiting for me."

"And the delicious supper Cecelia made," Deenie added.

"And that cool elevator chair Junior and Kenny put in," Juneau said. "That took some doing."

Jonas gave Gabby's hand a squeeze. "See, Gabrielle. You can't pretend that Junior and Cecelia and Kenny don't love you. They care about your welfare." He paused. "And they don't want anything from you except that you love them back."

"Don't start that again."

Gabby tried to pull her hand away from his, but he held on. Leaning so he could look directly at her, he said, "Do you really want to meet your Maker without having straightened things out?"

Startled, Erin looked from Jonas to Gabby. She couldn't believe he would so bluntly bring up what she, Juneau, and Deenie had talked about until late in the night.

Gabby harrumphed—a sound very like the one Grams used to make in her crotchety days. It flipped a switch inside Erin, and she spoke without thinking. "Why, Gabby! You're acting just like Grams used to, when she made Mom and me suffer because of something eating away at her insides. You're making Kenny and his parents suffer for the same reason."

"There's not a thing wrong with my insides," Gabby snapped.

"But you push away people who love you. Why? Grams did it because she hated herself for not being with Gramps when he died—" Erin stopped at a sudden insight. "Do you blame yourself for Caleb?"

Gabby's face turned white, and a raw sound escaped her throat.

*What have I started,* Erin asked herself in a panic. *Why didn't I keep my mouth shut?* She rushed to kneel at Gabby's side as her old friend gave way to grief. "I'm sorry I said that. I'm so sorry."

Jonas touched Erin's shoulder. "Let her cry. She needs to."

So they clustered around Gabby as she wept, Erin patting her knee, Deenie handing her tissues, Juneau stroking her back. Erin's relief was profound when, after endless moments, Gabby shuddered and wiped her eyes and cheeks. "Don't fuss over me," she said, with a touch of her old asperity, swatting them back to their seats.

She turned to Erin. "You're right. Something has been gnawing away at me. Something I've avoided dealing with for years. As you three have so often written in your letters, I'm the one who said truth kept secret stinks. Guess it's time I told you the truth about what happened the day Caleb disappeared."

Erin reached for Deenie's hand as Gabby began her story.

"The week before we went up the canyon with the boys, I found out H. G. had ousted his long-time partner in the car dealership. What he did was legal and probably necessary for the business, but to my mind it was immoral because the man had been struggling with a critical illness for months, and now he was jobless, too. I was at H. G. night and day, trying to get him to admit he'd done something wrong. When Junior got into a fight at school with the partner's son and H. G. backed him up, I accused him of turning Junior into an angry boy who didn't care about morals or ethics—just like himself.

"I was in a fine fury the weekend we took the camper up to our favorite place in the mountains, and after lunch the first day, I started in on H. G. again." She hesitated slightly; her voice wavered as she went on.

"Junior said later it was the sound of my shrill voice that drove Caleb away. Away from me—and to his death. It was my fault that Caleb died."

She didn't allow them to protest that statement, continuing as if needing to get it all out at once. "I've lived with that guilt ever since that day. I hated H. G. for not being the man I thought he should be. I hated Junior because he knew why Caleb left camp. I hated myself because of the condemnation in his eyes every time he looked at me."

She paused and glanced at Erin "When Kenny was born and he looked just like Junior, I imagined I saw the same condemnation in his eyes. I couldn't bear to be around them, so I found reasons to push them away. I've been making them pay for my guilt."

"I'm so sorry," Erin said again.

Gabby's eyes welled, but her tone was crusty as she said, "For making an old woman face the truth before she meets her Maker? Jonas has been trying to get me to do it for years. For my spiritual welfare," she added archly, but her eyes were warm when she smiled at him. "If I live long enough, I may thank both of you for it."

Deenie leaned forward earnestly. "I learned something really important when I was in 5 West after Evvy's birth. The purpose of guilt is not to make us suffer but to give us the opportunity to choose again."

"You're saying I have time to clean up my mess, right?"

"I wouldn't put it that way, but you can make a difference, not only for yourself but for Junior and Cecelia and their children."

Gabby shuddered as though ridding herself of something odious. "You said something in Park City about God being the source of our love. I hope that's true. My old heart needs a mighty infusion to make up for what I've withheld all these years."

She stood, balancing herself on her walker. "Jonas, help me into the kitchen. Girls, you come, too. I want one of you to get something for me."

"The mug you were looking for when you fell?" Erin asked.

Gabby nodded. "Caleb's mug. I bought one to commemorate the birth of each of my boys and had their names engraved on them. Junior's mug should have gone to Kenny as his firstborn son, but I couldn't bring myself to give it to him. He looked so much like Junior and H. G." She shook her head sadly. "I'm ashamed to say that I gave it to Bryan instead."

She drew herself taller. "It's time that Kenny got the other mug. Caleb's mug. I kept it up there."

When she pointed to the upper shelf of a kitchen cabinet, Juneau shook her head. "Don't ask me." She touched the leg she'd broken in '92. "I've sworn off climbing on chairs to look for something."

Gabby chuckled. "We make a pair, don't we?"

"I'll do it," Erin said, "if Deenie will hold the chair steady." She got onto the chair, stood on tiptoes, and ran her hand along the back of the shelf, finally bringing down a beautifully shaped mug with engraved designs.

"That's it," Gabby said. "Caleb's mug. A reminder of all that I've loved and lost."

"But . . ." Erin looked at Gabby, confused. "This isn't Caleb's mug. It's Junior's."

Gabby took the mug and turned it around so she could see the engraved name. "Hyrum Golden Junior," she read. "The other boy I lost that day. Maybe . . ." She held the mug to her breast, her eyes shining. "Maybe the lost can be found."

WILLADENE
   June 10, 1993
   Dear COBs,

If my heart wasn't tenderized enough by our visit in Provo, Brad finished up the job nicely at an evening picnic he hosted for Mom, Dad, Roger, and me at the mouth of Logan Canyon. First, he thanked us for accepting him into our family. He said that in his job he saw people at their worst, and being with us reminded him that people could be kind, decent, and good. He said if more people had someone like Sunny in their lives the world would be a better place. Then he kissed her hand and said how much he loved her! A three-hanky evening at least.

Later Sunny and I took a walk along the water. She took my hand as though to reassure me and said, "I haven't been a little girl for a long time, Deenie."

When I asked her if that was how we'd treated her, she said yes. For a long time it hadn't mattered, but now that she had Brad, it did.

We all thought we knew what was best for her, and we never asked her what she wanted. Whoever said the beginning of wisdom is realizing you don't know nothin' was right!

Still learning,
Deenie

ERIN
June 27, 1993
Dear Friends,

Remember back when I mentioned maybe taking a trip to the Boundary Waters—to do something different, maybe get that adrenaline rush Cory talks about? Well, I did it! And it was some trip, let me tell you.

Seven women had signed up for the ladies-only canoe trip in the gorgeous chain of lakes between Minnesota and Canada. When I asked our guides if they were going to give us a "paddle test," Willow laughed and Betty said, "Nature will do that." (You would love those two. They're in their sixties and COBs for sure.)

The first three days were glorious. The minute we shoved off, we were in another world, silent except for the sound of paddles dipping into the glassy water. Forest-covered islands sat low in the water, the dark of the trees broken here and there by brilliant reds and yellows of leaves just starting to turn.

We canoed from one peaceful inlet to another, portaging when necessary. (Ugh! I could have used your muscles, Deenie!) After supper we had campfires on the beach and listened to the call of the loons. One night the moon rose huge and round, making a path of light across the bay. I think if I'd had enough faith, I could have walked on it.

The third day out, the plan was to cross a very wide stretch of open water, a real test of what we'd learned so far. We hadn't been on the lake long when a storm whipped up. We were soaked and freezing within minutes. No matter how hard we paddled, the wind kept pushing us back. It took five hours of desperate paddling and praying to reach shore. I honestly thought it was going to be the end for me.

That night the tension and fear broke something loose. Everything I'd dammed up these last three years came out in a great gush. Lucky held me while I bawled my eyes out. When I finally got hold of myself, she reminded me of the work she and Doug do in the after-fire cleanup business, dealing with people who are grieving their losses. She said, "You know what I think? I think your house has burned down around you, and you haven't gone through the rubble yet. You don't really know what's salvageable, what isn't, and what's not worth the effort to try to save."

At that I started crying again, because she was right. I've known ever since Cory started skydiving that we aren't going to make it. I just didn't want to admit it. I spent the rest of the night doing battle with The Griff. Finally, I blew him away by declaring that the What Ifs I was dealing with were the ones I had to look at to go ahead with my life.

No, I didn't confront Cory the minute I got home. I decided to give us a little time, just in case I'm out in left field. But I swear, when I drove up to our house I could smell a whiff of smoke.

Erin

## WILLADENE

Deenie loved cuddling with Evvy on her bed during her daughter's nap time. On an afternoon in early July, Deenie was dozing, Evvy in the crook of her arm, when Paul came quietly into the room.

"It's here, Mom." Paul poked Deenie awake as he whispered.

"Mmmm. What? What's here? "

He waved an official-looking envelope in front of her face. "My mission call!"

Deenie slipped off the bed without waking Evvy and followed her son into the hall, where she gave him a big hug. "Let's call everyone and plan a family gathering. They've been waiting to hear the news."

"Do you mind if we don't?" Paul asked hesitantly. "I want a chance to think about it some and talk to you and Dad before we announce it to the rest of the family."

"Then that's what we'll do." Deenie stroked his cheek affectionately. What a fine young man he was! Then she grinned. "How about if I take just a tiny peek first?"

She grabbed for the letter, but Paul held it easily out of her reach, a big smile on his face. "Wait until tonight. We'll all find out together where I'm going."

July 21, 1993
Dear COBs,

Paul has received his mission call to the Texas South Houston Mission. Our armchair travel now stretches from the coldest inhabited places in the Union to one of the hottest, from ice storms to hurricanes, from the tundra to the Gulf Coast. Shawn Donovan lived in San Antonio when he was younger and told Paul to keep in mind that most Texans consider themselves Americans by birth and Texans by the grace of God.

Paul reports to the Missionary Training Center at the end of the month. He has asked that we go to Provo a day early so that he can have a visit with Gabby and Jonas. He doesn't want to leave anything unsaid to the people he loves.

Following his example, I love you both and am thinking of you and keeping you in my prayers.

Love,
Deenie

P.S. Roger was offered a job as a supervisor for a boys' reform school in the middle of New Mexico that has its own police force. I was so relieved when he told them, "Thanks, but no, thanks." Teaching gun safety is as close as I want to get to needing protection like that again.

JUNEAU
July 28, 1993
Dear Deenie and Erin,

Boy howdy, Deenie, give my best to Paul as he sets off to his Texas mission. I'm sure ya'll will reap big blessings from having two young men in the mission field!

Erin, at first the description of your trip made me think I ought to get off my duff and do something. But then I got to the part where you said, "No matter how hard we paddled, the wind kept pushing us back." I thought that sounded too much like real life! I decided I'd rather get my adventure vicariously, sitting in front of my computer!

Speaking of computers, Greg is getting things set up with his new partner in the computer business—consulting and that kind of stuff. He's so sure things will work out that he went out and bought a new stereo system, with speakers that rattle the walls. Now we'll need that upstairs writing room just so our little house can absorb all the SOOOOUND.

Cath got the job she wanted in Thousand Oaks. She'll be coming down from Idaho in about six weeks to get started. Am I thinking she and Trace might still get together? Not! I'll do all my matchmaking in my books from now on, which isn't all that easy because even my characters get obstinate now and then.

Love,
Juneau

*Chapter 33*

ERIN

The first day of the Big Barn Sale was perfectly glorious—cool, crisp air and warm sun that turned yellow leaves into liquid sunshine. It was the kind of day that brought out customers, and Erin was delighted as she watched the throng of shoppers wandering in and out of the barn and lingering in front of booths.

The whole family was there to help, even Grams, who was very much at home among the antique items that reminded her of her childhood. At times Erin had the suspicion that she was lost in the past, but her lively descriptions of how to use certain items entranced customers.

In the early afternoon Cory and Erin took their breaks so they could join the family at a picnic table for lunch. Cory's parents were there, as well as Andrew and Lottie. At Erin's suggestion Kayla ran into the Harringtons' house to invite EJ and Ricky to join them for bratwurst and chips. They were all chatting and enjoying their food when suddenly Steve appeared. "Hey, guys," he said to EJ and Ricky, "your grandmother wants you in the house."

"No, she doesn't," EJ said, reaching for the potato chips. Ricky shook his head vehemently. "I'm eating with Markie and Kayla."

Steve hesitated, frowning, and then joined them. His presence brought an awkward feeling to the previously boisterous group, and Erin wondered what in the world was caught in his craw. Then she noticed that whenever he looked at Cory, his face was closed down and frosty. She was about to ask him if something was wrong when Caitlin called to her from the barn, saying a customer needed help.

As the sun dipped low in the autumn sky, Jake made the rounds, politely letting the lingerers know they were shutting down for the night. Erin and Colleen checked out the last customers and then sat down with the cash boxes. Once they'd balanced revenues with receipts, they carried the boxes to the basement of the Harrington house and put them in the safe.

Erin sighed with relief as Colleen shut the heavy door. "Time for all of us to get some rest. Cory and I'll be here at seven, okay?"

"Sure." Colleen smiled, but it wasn't her usual easy expression, which made Erin wonder if whatever was bothering Steve was bothering her, too.

"Colleen, is everything all right?"

Colleen coughed, clearly embarrassed. "Why do you ask?"

"I got this funny feeling when I was around Steve today, and now I'm picking up on the same thing with you. It's not very pleasant."

"I don't know why that should be."

"We've been friends for . . . what? Fourteen years? We've been business partners almost as long. If you have something to say, you should say it."

Colleen shifted uncomfortably. "It's just . . . you know. The trouble with Cory. I hate to say it, but it makes me and Steve quite uncomfortable."

The movie *The Trouble with Harry* immediately popped into Erin's mind. The trouble with Harry was that he was dead. Cory was only gay. "What trouble might that be?"

"Oh, Erin. You know." When Erin didn't respond, she said, "Somebody told Steve that he'd heard that Cory is . . . *homosexual.* That person heard it from someone in your bishopric, so it must be true."

In the past few years, Erin had had times of flaming, volcanic fury. The fury that gripped her now was cold. She pointed a finger at Colleen and told her to stay put where she was. She rushed out into the yard, scanning the crowd until she saw Cory. "Go into the basement right now and wait for me and Steve," she ordered. She headed for Steve without waiting for Cory's response. When she strode up to him she could tell by the look on his face that he knew why she demanded he come with her.

As Steve descended the stairs, he gave Colleen an accusing look. "She asked!" Colleen cried. "What was I supposed to do, lie?"

Cory looked from Steve to Colleen. "What's going on?"

Steve blustered and paced, sending angry glances Colleen's way.

Finally he turned to Cory. "First, I want to say that someone has broken a confidence, or I would never have heard about your situation. That should never have happened."

"What did you hear and who did you hear it from?"

"The second counselor in your bishopric told a counselor in my ward that you're gay. He thought I should know because our families spend so much time together. He didn't think it was a good idea to have our kids exposed to . . ." He finished his sentence with a gesture.

"Say it."

"Homosexuality."

Cory's cheeks were tight with strain. "Did you tell him he was out of bounds? That in all the years we've been friends—and our families, too— you've never seen anything to concern you?"

Steve was silent.

"You're my friend. Why didn't you defend me?"

"Why did I have to hear it from somebody else?" Steve shot back.

"Because I was afraid you'd act just like you're acting now! I know what a straight arrow you are. How judgmental. You would have thought the worst of me and started shutting me out of your life, just like you're doing now. What I want to know is why."

Steve held up his hands. "It's something I don't want to deal with, okay? It makes me uncomfortable."

"Why?" Cory sneered. "Does it threaten your own sexuality?"

Steve turned florid and launched toward Cory. "Stop!" Erin cried, flinging herself between them. Her heart hammered in her chest as the two men stared at each other.

Finally, Cory made a rough gesture of dismissal. "I'm leaving. I can't stand to be in the same room with you."

"Steve, please. Go after him," Colleen cried. "Tell him you didn't mean what you said."

"Have some compassion." Erin's voice wavered.

Steve shook his head. "What he is, that's wrong."

"And you're perfect? You don't have any secret struggles you'd just as soon nobody knew about?'"

Steve opened his mouth, closed it, and went up the stairs after Cory.

## JUNEAU

October 17, 1993

Dear Erin and Willadene,

With just six weeks of full-time employment left, Greg is finding new ways to spend money. I can't blame it all on him. I guess we just got tempted (the devil made us do it). Anyway, we bought two weeks of a timeshare at a resort on the beach in Carlsbad. We figured it's the only way we'll ever get away each year on some kind of vacation. Greg says if one week a year is enough for him (he's such a workaholic!) I can invite the two of you dear souls to come for the second week and enjoy the beautiful condo, the swimming pool, and hot tubs in the lovely enclosed courtyard, the ocean just outside the lobby. Maybe soon?

Cath will arrive next week to stay a few days with us until her accommodations are ready in Thousand Oaks. She's signed up to start some further classes that will help get her an official therapist's license, so she'll be pretty busy with working full time, too. Gideon is excited. He says, "I like that stink eye song lady."

I don't know how Trace feels about his "best friend" coming. I don't ask. I definitely don't make plans.

Stay in touch,
Juneau

## WILLADENE

When Deenie got home from running with Bear the afternoon of October 19, she found a frightening message from Paul's mission president on her answering machine. "Elder Rasmussen insisted that we contact you with this urgent message. Check on Sunny. He said you'd know what he meant."

The minute Deenie heard the message, she called her mother and then Aunt Stella. No one picked up. Filled with dread, she called the hospital. A nurse confirmed that Sonya Stowell had been admitted. Deenie could scarcely breathe as she asked Grandma Streeter to meet Evvy at the bus stop and stay with her and Beth until she or Roger got home.

Then she called Roger's office and left a message for him to meet her at the hospital.

She arrived to find Sunny lying pale and still in her bed, attached to the usual monitors, oxygen feeding through a nose tube. Deenie walked quietly into the room and touched her mother on the shoulder. When Margaret glanced up, Deenie was frightened by the sad resignation on her face.

"Pneumonia?" she asked. Margaret shook her head. "Oh, Mom." Deenie knew that meant Sunny's heart was failing and her body was shutting down. She pulled up a chair next to her mother's side, took her hand, and waited.

Sunny woke up when Roger arrived. She acknowledged him with a slight smile and then motioned for Deenie to come closer. "Do you believe in heaven?" she whispered.

Deenie took her sister's hand in both of hers. "You bet I do, Sunshine."

"So do I," Sunny said and drifted back to sleep.

"How did you know we were here?" Margaret asked Deenie softly. "Everything happened so fast, we didn't have time to call."

"Paul. He had his mission president leave us a message to check on Sunny."

Margaret began to weep softly. "I guess the Stowell Sight was there for Sunny when she needed it after all."

As the word spread, Aunt Stell, Nathan, and other family members began a vigil at Sunny's bedside. Brad joined them, stricken with grief. As the days passed, it had become harder and harder for Sunny to breathe. When it was clear that all that kept her among the living was her tortured breathing, her father, John, blessed her through the power of the priesthood that she would be freed from pain and welcomed home. As they said amen together, Brad lifted Sunny's hand and kissed it. A soft sigh later she was gone. On a prayer and a kiss, she had left them.

Deenie had been stoic up until that moment, but when she felt Sunny go, felt her sweet spirit caress her cheek in passing, she broke down.

The next day John invited Brad to join the family when they

gathered to decide how best to honor Sunny's life. It turned out to be an
inspired idea, because it was soon clear that Brad was the only one who
knew what Sunny wanted. He was the one she had shared all her
thoughts with, the thoughts she had worried would be too hard for her
mother and father and even Deenie to hear. So it was with an awkward
gratitude that John and Margaret asked him to tell them what to do, and
Brad read from a letter Sunny had written to him. "I want white daisies
like the kind you gave me and sunshine songs like 'There Is Sunshine in
My Soul Today' and 'You Are My Sunshine.' Have everybody sing them."

"She wants it short," he added, "because funerals always made her
tired. And no 'she did this and that' stuff in the beginning, just her
favorite scripture read by Beth, if you will? A song in the middle, and a
talk by you, Nathan, on God's love."

Deenie's brother Nathan nodded his head, like the rest of the family,
too touched and grieved to speak.

"She asked that you have the family dinner at the Bluebird because it
was her favorite restaurant and because she didn't want Deenie and her
mother to have to cook—except for a batch of your coconut oatmeal
cookies, Margaret. She wanted you to bring them for dessert."

That request was so completely Sunny that it brought a watery
chuckle from them all.

The funeral was exactly as Sunny had requested. The daisies Sunny
had asked for came in an airy casket display with a banner saying, "My
Sunshine Girl" draped across the top. Deenie didn't have to ask who had
sent them.

After the dedication at the gravesite, Deenie saw her father put an
arm around Brad's shoulder and pull him into the family circle.

"She knew she didn't have much time left when she got sick in the
spring," Brad said. "She told me there were things that only God could
fix." It was a statement that sounded like a question to Deenie.

"Yes," John said kindly.

"And she's all right now?" Brad asked.

"Yes," John said again, with a conviction that gave way to a few tears.

"You'll see that she gets that endowment thing she wanted done for
her?" the young man asked, turning to Margaret.

"We will," she said, stroking his cheek.

"That's good, then." Brad turned to walk away.

"Won't you stay?" John asked.

"Thank you, no. I'm going to have to work through this one on my own."

"But, Mom . . . ," Beth said, expressing the sadness they all felt as he left.

"I know, honey," Deenie said, thinking, *I wonder if we'll ever see him again.*

## ERIN

October 26, 1993
Dear Deenie,

My heart goes out to you and your family. Sunny's nickname was a perfect reflection of the light and love she brought to you all. I know you'll miss her terribly. She was lucky to have such a wonderful big sister.

Your Erin

## JUNEAU

October 26, 1993
Dear Deenie,

I feel it a privilege to have met your Sunny, and I mourn her passing.

With great sympathy and love,
Juneau

## WILLADENE

Deenie found the exact thank-you cards she wanted in a dusty corner of the neighborhood pharmacy. They were quaint and covered with spring flowers—just the kind of thing Sunny would have appreciated. Deenie bought them on the spot.

The message she included in each one was basically the same but nonetheless sincere. *Thank you for your thoughts and prayers,* she wrote. *And for* (here she filled in food or flowers or whatever way Sunny had been honored or the family helped). *The extended family of Sonya Marie Stowell—Sunny.* Underneath she signed, *Willadene Stowell Rasmussen.*

She wrote one longer and deeply personal note to Brad Donaldson. A week after she mailed it, it came back stamped "Not at This Address."

# Chapter 34

JUNEAU

November 1, 1993

Dear Friends,

Cath came over for dinner and Trunk-or-Treat night at the ward, where parents park in the church lot and hand out treats from their car trunks. She and Trace and Gideon dressed up as hobos. Cute. They look like a family. I won't say anything more.

> Keeping the lip zipped,
> Juneau

ERIN

November arrived with gray skies and flurries of small, dry flakes that blew along the streets and sidewalks and accumulated at the base of trees and in entryways. Erin watched them through her kitchen window as she assembled the ingredients for her first batch of stew since the previous spring.

They were enjoying a rare Saturday afternoon at home. Mark and Kayla were on the area rug engrossed in a game of Sorry. Cory was in his recliner, watching a football game. She looked his way, glad that there would be no more skydiving or bungee jumping for a while.

A movement caught her eye, and she saw that Cory's right leg was bouncing up and down, a nervous tick she'd only recently noticed. His lips were pressed in a tight line and his forehead was furrowed. As she watched, his leg went faster and faster, until it seemed to propel him of the chair. "I'm going for a run," he said abruptly. "I'll be back in an hour."

"In this weather?"

"It's not that bad. You just have to dress right."

Mark jumped up. "I'll go with you, Dad. I don't mind the cold."

"Not this time, son. I'll being going too far and too fast."

"You always say that." Mark pulled on Cory's arm. "Let me go with you. Please?"

Cory jerked away. "I said no!"

Erin confronted him as he was pulling on layers to protect against the cold. "What's gotten into you? Why not run around a couple of blocks with Mark? Then you can drop him off and run your heart out, if you want to."

"I'm not going on a kiddy jog around the block, okay?" Then he was gone.

When she went back into the great room, Kayla was explaining something to Mark in her big-sister voice.

"Don't be scared about being baptized. Daddy knows how to do it. He puts you down and brings you up real quick."

Mark drew a card and made his move. "I think I want Uncle Steve to baptize me."

"Dads baptize their kids," Kayla said. "Steve's not your dad."

"Sometimes I wish he was."

The plaintive tone in Mark's voice made Erin's eyes sting. What was Cory thinking, to treat Mark that way! He'd done it all too often lately, leaving his son to do things with Smith and his dad, or Steve and Ricky. Today, when Cory could have had that elusive 'quality time' with his son, he'd wanted nothing more than to get out of the house.

The stew was simmering on low and the biscuits were just about ready to come out of the oven when Cory returned. She caught him as he was taking off his coat. "I hope you've had time to think about what you did to Mark," she hissed. "He's so upset, he said he's not sure he even wants you to baptize him!"

She saw with satisfaction how her words hit home. "Change clothes and get back down here. We'll eat, and then you"—she jabbed her index finger at him—"you spend some time with your son."

Later, after they'd had story time with the kids and put them to bed, Erin asked Cory if he'd talked to Mark. "Did you tell him you'd be honored to baptize him?"

"Yes." Cory paused. "But I also told him it's okay if he wants Steve to baptize him. We haven't been getting along very well lately."

It took a moment before realization dawned. "That's not the reason," she said flatly.

"It's one reason."

She asked the question she didn't want to ask. "Cory, are you worthy of baptizing Mark?"

"If you go by the letter of the law."

"What are you trying to tell me?"

Anger flashed in his eyes. "I don't jump out of airplanes or off bridges for fun, Erin. I do it because the moment of terror when I jump wipes out everything else I'm feeling. For that moment, I forget the pressure that's building up inside. I forget the struggle."

"It's back, then." She said it with certainty. And sorrow.

"I don't think *it* ever went away. The more I try to ignore my feelings, the more they clamor for attention. It's getting harder and harder not to do something about it."

"Are you giving in? After all this time?"

Anguish etched his face. "I guess you could see it that way. To me, it's more like deciding to stop fighting what and who I am. Just once, I'd like to wake up glad to be me instead of hating myself." He looked down and twisted his ring. When he spoke his voice was so low she had to strain to hear him. "I can't keep going like this, Erin. I've had some bad thoughts. About another way out."

For a second she wasn't sure what he was saying. When she grabbed him by the shoulder and made him face her, the look in his eyes told her everything. "Cory, listen to me! Don't even think that. We love you and want you to be part of our lives. I can see you're in pain, but we can work something out."

"There's nothing *to* work out. Don't you understand that yet?" He looked up and held her gaze. "I have to stop playing this charade."

"And start living as a gay man."

He nodded.

When he'd first outed himself, Erin had been caught up in a whirlwind of emotions, but now she felt nothing. She took a step back, her gaze sober. "I understand what you're saying—I just hope you do. Have you really thought about the consequences?"

"Yes. The kids will be devastated. My parents will probably disown me. Dad at least. I'll be starting over . . ." His eyes pleaded for understanding. "What scares me the most is that I have no idea what I'll be walking into. I just know that I can't do this anymore."

She caught on the first thing he'd said. "You can't mean to tell the kids!"

"The counselor leading the gay fathers' group said he thinks they're old enough—ten and eight—to hear the truth. As long as I don't go into details."

"I don't agree! Cory—"

He held her back with raised hands. "I know. They could end up hating me. Especially if you make me out to be a monster."

"If you tell them the truth, they may come to that conclusion on their own." She saw him wince, but she continued. "You're going to pay a steep price, and not just with family. The path you're going on will cut you off from the Church, and that will feel like having your heart cut out."

The look he gave her made her catch her breath. "I feel that way every day. It's devastating to be told you're a son of a loving God but that there is something intrinsically bad—evil, actually—about who He created you to be. You feel so shamed and flawed, it does something to you inside. What you want more than anything is to know that God loves you as you are—a gay man."

"He does. Bishop Harding has said that over and over again."

"No. He says God loves an *abstinent gay man*."

"Cory, think of the unmarried heterosexuals in the Church. They choose to be abstinent. What's the difference between their situation and yours?"

"Easy. If they find someone they can love both body and soul, they can get married and make a life for themselves. Gays can't. I want to be free to see if maybe there's a chance for love."

Erin made a disdainful sound. "I find that ironic. When you asked me to stay with you back in 1990, you were essentially asking me to give up the hope of having that kind of love."

"I know. And I'm sorry."

When Erin and Cory told Bishop Harding they had decided to divorce, he didn't try to dissuade them. Instead, he asked them to explain what had happened to bring them to that point. He apologized for the indiscretion of his counselor and assured them it would be addressed. He expressed his love for both of them and reminded them that God's grace was sufficient for all. In the presence of such compassion, Erin gave way to tears, grieving losses that were now becoming real.

"When are you going to tell your families?" he asked when she had regained control.

"Soon. I don't want the kids to accuse us of tricking them into thinking things were fine over the holidays, just to drop the bomb after New Year's." She attempted a smile. "I don't know why, but I sure have lousy Christmas karma."

They told Cory's parents first. Linda accused Erin of giving up on Cory. Skipp said if Cory left his family, he would be lost. Breaking the news to The Jays and Grams was a little easier but not much.

"I don't understand," Grams said in a querulous tone. "You love Erin and your children. Why would you get a divorce?" They gave her the briefest of explanations, knowing that any understanding she might have would soon disappear into the fog she now inhabited. The Jays offered to support them in every way possible, and then Jake put his arm around Cory and said, "Be careful, okay? There are hazards out there."

Unpleasant as those conversations were, they paled in comparison to the raw emotion that erupted when they told their children.

"You can't divorce us!" Kayla's eyes were full of fear. "We're your kids. You love us!"

"Of course we do," Cory said. "Getting a divorce doesn't change that. What will change is that we won't be living in the same house anymore."

"We have to move?" Kayla's voice was tremulous.

Erin nodded. "You and Mark and I will need to find a smaller house."

"And I'll be living in an apartment somewhere downtown," Cory added.

"I won't move. You can't make me," Kayla screeched.

The outburst almost masked Mark's solemn declaration: "I'll go with you, Daddy. So you won't be lonesome."

"Sorry, buddy," Cory said, patting his shoulder. "An apartment isn't the best place for kids. But I'll fix a room for you, so you and Kayla can visit on weekends."

"See! They don't care what we want," Kayla cried. "They're ruining everything."

That's the way it went for the next hour—Kayla out of control, Mark retreating inward. When Erin thought there was finally nothing more to say, Mark asked solemnly, "If Kayla and I stop fighting, can we stay together?"

"Oh, sweetie." Erin tried to hug him. "You kids have done nothing wrong."

"Then who has?" Kayla demanded.

*Leave it to her to ask that question*, Erin thought. "Nobody."

"See?" Kayla shook Mark's arm. "She's lying again."

Cory cleared his throat. Frantically, Erin shook her head, thinking, *No, don't say it! They're too young to understand!* If Cory saw the gesture, he gave no indication. "Do know what it means to be gay?" he asked.

Mark's answer, succinct and accurate, made Erin's jaw drop. "Where did you hear that?"

"From a kid in my class." Mark looked at Cory. "So what?"

"That's what I am."

Kayla's pale complexion turned slightly green. Mark's eyes went wide. "That kid told me gays were bad. His brother's Scout leader had to quit because he's gay."

Cory's face blanched. "Look at me, son. Being gay doesn't mean a person is bad."

Mark regarded his father solemnly and then stood. "I don't think I like you anymore." He started up the stairs, Kayla following.

Halfway up she stopped, turned to look over the railing at both of them. Her freckles stood out on her paper-white cheeks. "What about my skating?"

"Don't worry," Cory said, his voice firm with resolve. "Some things will change, but not your skating."

When Kayla was gone, Erin shook her head. "You shouldn't say that, Cory. Everything will change."

December 28, 1993
Dear Friends,

I hate to send you this news by e-mail, but it seemed at least somewhat better than scribbling it on the family Christmas card. Cory and I have decided to divorce. We gave it our best, but the situation has been incredibly difficult. Cory's gone through a terrific struggle. I don't understand it, but I've seen what it's done to him—the light went out of his eyes and the joy out of his smile. Whether or not he'll ever find them again remains to be seen.

We are committed to the process being amicable, although I think "amicable divorce" is an oxymoron. The next few months are going to be hard, no matter how well he and I handle the legalities and the logistics of splitting up a household.

For now, we're still living together. Sort of. Cory has set himself up a sleeping corner and workspace in the basement. I use our bedroom upstairs. We meet on the main floor, where we have supper with the kids most nights, help them with their homework, and coordinate who is going to drive to the rink, piano lessons, and Cub Scouts. We'll keep that arrangement until we put the house up for sale in the spring, when the market is more active.

Yes, we're going to sell the house. It is too big for Cory alone, too much for me to handle on my own. Besides, the divorce will change our financial situation significantly. We're going to have to save every way we can so that we can afford to keep up with Kayla's skating and Mark's piano lessons. I'm not sure that's possible, but we'll cross that bridge when we come to it.

I'm okay. I think. On a certain level, I've been preparing for this moment ever since Cory first told me he is attracted to men. Does that mean I didn't do everything I could have to make our marriage work? If so, there'll be plenty of time later for me to deal with my G&G (our shorthand for Grief and Guilt, remember?) and do battle with The Great What If.

My counselor says I'll feel like a victim of Cory's choice unless I make some choices for myself, but I think it will be a long time before I'll be able to consider what I want personally. As a single mother, I have to choose what will create a safe and happy home for my children. I hope that one day they'll understand the decision Cory and I have made. I hope they'll know that we love them—and that we loved each other—despite our personal difficulties.

Please don't let this news make you sad for too long. There is so much to celebrate this time of year.

Your Erin

## WILLADENE

December 29, 1993
Dear Erin,

I was sorry to hear your news about the divorce. You have worked so hard to keep your sweet family together. I appreciate your keeping in touch during such a difficult time. If there is anything I can do to help smooth the way for this transition in your life, just ask.

Best blessings always,
Deenie

## JUNEAU

December 29, 1993
Erin dear,

My prayers are with you.

Love,
Juneau

# Chapter 35
## 1994

WILLADENE

January 2, 1994
Dear COBs,

I'm in a reflective mood today. I should be looking forward. It's the beginning of the New Year, after all. But I keep looking back, thinking about Sunny. I miss her terribly but often feel as though she is nearby, keeping a watch over us all. Paul says to tell it like it is, "She is nearby, watching over the family."

We're all dealing with Sunny's death in our own way. Sometimes I'm sure Evvy, who's almost six, understands that Sunny is gone, but other times she says she's been talking to her. Mom is lost without her to care for. She can't bring herself to put away any of her things and spends a lot of time in her room. I'm hoping she's not making it into a shrine!

I guess I'm not the one to talk. The room Sunny used at our house has been left as it was when she was last there, except that Beth has taken a few things into her own room—a doll dressed in pioneer clothes, the blue sweater Bert gave Sunny to wear in the hospital years ago, and the set of scriptures Sunny kept here.

For my part, the daily training to keep myself and Bear search-ready has helped. Lark still runs with me and lets me talk about Sunny all I want. The other day she asked if I'd heard from Brad since the funeral. Unfortunately, the answer is no.

Keeping on keeping on,
Deenie

ERIN

The first week of January, Erin and Cory met with the mediator they had chosen from the list Skipp had given them. Daniel Nordstrom, a small, neat man with impeccable manners, had extensive experience helping couples work out all the issues pertaining to divorce without going to court.

They agreed that Erin would file the petition for divorce, listing as grounds the irretrievable breakdown of the marriage relationship. She signed the papers with Nordstrom's warning echoing in her head: "I know you're trying to go through this in an adult and friendly manner, but it's going to get ugly. You can't avoid it."

It got ugly when Erin said she wanted Cory to promise he would never have any of his new friends visit the apartment when the kids were there. "The divorce is hard enough on them. They don't need to deal with the realities of having a gay father on top of it. Maybe when they're older, but not now."

Cory was hurt and deeply disappointed, but when Daniel said it was a reasonable request, he acquiesced.

It got ugly again when Erin had to reveal the existence of her secret savings account—and Cory admitted that he'd been buying stocks through an investment club for the past five years without telling her.

"I see you both have secrets." Daniel put his fingertips together in a tent and leaned back in his chair. "If there's anything else you've been hiding, either one of you, 'fess up now. I don't want to have to run the numbers more than once."

They sat in silence as Daniel added the new numbers to his worksheet. Erin looked at Cory's bowed head, wondering if he felt the same deep sadness as she did. They'd both been hedging their bets.

With so much stress in her life, Erin wasn't surprised when she began waking up with a headache every day. She often started her morning by swallowing some ibuprofen with a diet cola. When she began feeling queasy as well as headachy, Colleen said she probably was having "sick headaches." Erin's doctor, whom she finally saw after a miserable month, had another diagnosis.

"You're pregnant."

Erin let out a strangled sound somewhere between hysteria and hilarity. After so many years of sporadic intimacy between her and Cory, followed by months of none at all, they had come together in December, expressing their grief, loss, and love. How ironic that a child should result.

Cory was struck dumb when she told him. He couldn't have looked any more shocked, dismayed, and then terrified had a volcano erupted in the backyard.

"Don't worry," she said. "It doesn't change anything. With luck, the kids and I could be well settled in a new place by the due date in August."

"What do you mean, it doesn't change anything! It changes everything." Grim determination showed in the line of his jaw. "Forget the divorce, forget house hunting. I'll just have to—"

"What? Pretend that you're not really gay, that you were just going through a phase? Buck up and sacrifice yourself for your family?" She stood with arms akimbo, challenging him. "The only thing worse than finalizing the divorce would be pulling back because of the baby and then going through with it after all."

"The idea of us getting a divorce when you're pregnant is ridiculous."

Her lips twitched. "My being pregnant at all is what's ridiculous. God's sense of humor is a bit off, if you ask me."

He rewarded her attempt at humor with a slight grin. "How are you feeling?"

"Pretty well. Just a little queasy."

"Let me stay with you, Erin. We'll go through with the divorce, if that's what you want, but we could continue as we are now—me in the basement and you upstairs—at least until after the baby's born."

It was so tempting. She'd felt anxious, with little spikes of terrified, ever since learning she was pregnant. Still, she shook her head. "It will give the kids false hope. Besides, I need to get used to being on my own."

"I don't want to miss out on our child growing up."

He looked so sad, she reached out to him. "You won't. I expect you to be my birth coach, like you were for the others. Once we're home from the hospital, you can visit us any time."

"It won't be the same." He sighed deeply. "When do you think we should tell the kids?"

"Might as well tell them now. They can't hate us any more than they already do."

JUNEAU

January 17, 1994
Dear Erin and Willadene,

I'm lucky to still have electricity to fire up my computer. Our new year here in Southern California started with rumbles and rattles this morning when a major earthquake (6.7 on the Richter scale) hit at 4:38 A.M. We all leaped out of bed, and Gideon climbed right up Greg's frame, bellowing, "Take care of me!" To tell the truth, I wanted to do the same thing! Philip Atwater was terrified out of his mind, barking and whining and trying to crawl up anybody's frame! Gideon had another opportunity to be a person of significance as he comforted and soothed the old dog. Taking care of the weakest among us helped us all manage our own fear.

We didn't have much damage in Pasadena, but around the mountains in the Northridge vicinity houses slid down hills and buildings collapsed, killing several people. The call has gone out for help, and I'm going to volunteer with the Red Cross for a couple of days to supply food to those affected. I'm so grateful my own family is safe.

Gideon, who's been looking forward to his sixth birthday on February 1, was worried. "Can you still have birthdays if there are earthquakes?" he asked. "Oh, yes," I said. "Your birthday is coming no matter what." To take his mind off what was being reported on TV, I asked him who he wanted to invite to his party. He named me, Greg, Misty, Ira, Trace, Cath, Marisol, Beto, and Philip Atwater. (Nicole is, of course, up at BYU.) I'd thought he'd want to invite his entire kindergarten class because he loves school so much, so I asked, "That's all?"

He nodded solemnly and said, "Yes. If I invited my class, Tanner Melton would come and put another stink eye on me." The word for Tanner is *bully*. He's convinced Giddy again that his stink eye can cause him grief if he doesn't do what Tanner says. Any advice gratefully accepted.

Love and happy New Year!
Juneau

ERIN

January 30, 1994
Dear Gabby, Deenie, and Juneau,

I don't know how to tell you my news except to blurt it out. I'm pregnant.

Yes, Cory's the father. I can see you asking, "How on earth did that happen?" Easy enough, when one thing follows another. So I'm seeing both a gynecologist and divorce lawyer these days. I should probably make an appointment with a shrink!

Kayla said, "I hope you take better care of this one than you did me." I thought she'd forgotten that her doctor said I didn't take good care of her after her scar got sunburned. Obviously not. (By the way, her scar is virtually invisible now.) Mark is threatening to move in with the Harringtons, because he needs a "real dad." He couldn't have come up with a meaner thing to say.

Cory is very tender to the coming baby and me. The other night as we sat on the couch, he put his hand on my tummy and talked to our new little one, just like he did to Kayla and Mark before they were born. What he said to our child—we're both sure she's a girl—was a beautiful father's blessing.

At that moment, I saw her right before me, a tall, grave child with the same high forehead and blue eyes as Grams and Mom. She let me know that she understands the circumstances she's going to be born into, that she loves Cory and me, and that I shouldn't worry, because everything is going to be okay. Then she smiled and said something I'll never forget: "You don't have to try so hard. What you need is already given."

Her name is Hannah.

> Love,
> Erin

JUNEAU

January 30, 1994
Dear Little Mother!

I'm so delighted to hear your news that I have to e-mail you right back. Sometimes babies show up unexpectedly, but I'm sure Hannah will be, as Gideon is, an absolute blessing. She's coming for a reason.

Love from doting Aunt Juneau

## WILLADENE
February 1, 1994
Dear Erin,

Pregnant? Wow!

Love,<br>Deenie

## JUNEAU

Gideon's sixth birthday party was just for family members. The menu was ordered-in pizza plus homemade ice cream created by Trace in his recently purchased machine. "My grandma always made ice cream for special occasions," he said, and Juneau wished he would tell them more of his background. All she knew of it was what she'd gleaned from just such offhand remarks.

Trace brought Gideon a special gift—a smaller version of his own guitar. By the end of the evening Gideon had learned the three basic chords.

Juneau would remember the party as her last worry-free occasion for some time. After February, the year seemed to shatter. Misty announced that she was taking off for Idaho, with or without Ira. Since Ira had just signed a contract for another pickle commercial, he couldn't leave. He asked Misty to wait at least until the end of the school year when he'd get his bachelor's degree from UCLA, but she said she couldn't hang around that long. Why? No reason. It was just time to move along.

She went. Ira stayed. He kept the apartment in Alhambra and invited his "family" over every week for a meal he prepared himself.

Trace and Cath were doing what they did best—being "just friends."

Nicole, in her junior year at BYU, was enjoying the popularity that came from being a beautiful blonde California girl. In the old days, the Beto days, she'd never seemed even to notice she was good-looking. Now it appeared that she was capitalizing on it. Juneau worried. She didn't want to lose Beto, but when he brought a lovely dark-haired girl named Carlina home to meet his mother, she feared he probably would never be part of her family. Both she and Marisol mourned, but what could they do?

One day little Sister Kittridge called. "Juneau, dear," she said, "I want you to come over and say good-bye. Bring Gideon, too. I always love to see him."

"We'll be over," Juneau said. "Where is it you're going?"

"I'm going to die," Sister Kittridge said. "I want to say good-bye to all of my favorite people."

Juneau was stunned. She'd gone to Sister Kittridge's house two weeks before to visit teach, and the little lady had seemed the same as usual, frail at age ninety-two but still ambulatory and independent. "Are you sick?" Juneau asked.

"No, dear," Sister Kittridge said. "Just dying. It's time, Juneau. When can you come?"

"Right now."

Gideon was pleased to go visit Sister Kittridge. "I'll take my guitar," he said. "I'll sing for her." Trace had taught him to play and sing "Home on the Range" a few days before.

Sister Kittridge answered the door when they got there. Juneau checked her out visually for signs of impending death. Other than being a little pale, the old lady looked the same as usual. "Sit down," she said cheerfully. "Would you like some lemonade?"

"Yes," Gideon said.

Sister K tottered a bit as she headed for the kitchen. "I picked the lemons this morning. I'm going to make a batch of lemon pies for when my kids come."

"They're coming?" Juneau asked. "All of them?"

"Yes. They'll all want to be here for the funeral."

Juneau couldn't believe her ears. Sister K was speaking as if her death were totally within her control.

After they drank the lemonade she brought, Gideon played and sang "Home on the Range."

298 Se WomenCOMPANY OF GOOD WOMEN

"That's lovely, Giddy," Sister K said when he finished. "Did you know that's one of my favorite songs?"

Gideon glowed. "Mine, too," he said. He looked around a little shyly. "May I go look at your stuff?"

"Surely," Sister K said. "Go ahead."

Gideon loved Sister K's old-fashioned "stuff," like the gold faucets on her ancient claw-footed bathtub and the small chest in her bedroom with eighteen little drawers that held buttons and old letters and marbles.

As soon he was gone, Juneau turned to Sister K. "Now what's this about dying and funerals?"

"It's going to happen," Sister K said. "Soon."

"You're not going to do something, are you?"

"Suicide?" Sister Kittridge laughed heartily. "No, dear. I would never do that. I'm not anxious to go. There's so very much to leave." She took a moment to look around her little house and out the window at the pleasant street lined with majestic magnolia trees. "But my heart's worn out," she went on, "and I want a hand in planning for the end."

Juneau couldn't speak.

"I've made out my funeral program," Sister K continued. "I want my scorched family history records displayed." She smiled at Juneau. "You did me a real favor when you turned on my oven that day and charred my journals and pedigree charts. It's the only bit of fame I've ever had. They've been a real hit at family history exhibits." Juneau started to say something, but Sister K held up a hand to indicate she wasn't finished. "I want each of my kids to speak," she said. "And I want Gideon to sing that lovely song."

Juneau took a deep breath to get her voice under control. "Maybe he and Trace could do a duet."

Sister K clasped her hands. "Oh, how lovely that will be. I wish I could be there!"


That's how Gideon made his singing debut. As Sister Kittridge had suspected, her heart gave out just a week after she invited Juneau to visit.

All of her children were present when she went peacefully during a nap. Her funeral was just as she'd planned.

Gideon was fascinated by the whole proceeding. "Where did she go, Mom?" he whispered during the service in the chapel.

"To heaven, to be with Heavenly Father."

"How are we going to visit teach her there?"

"We won't," Juneau said. "We'll let the angels do it."

That satisfied him. He listened to Sister K's children tell stories of their life with her, and he stared at the shiny walnut coffin in front of the crowd who had come to say good-bye. He and Trace sang "Home on the Range" so beautifully that all of Sister K's children hugged them afterward. Then there was the trip to the cemetery and the luncheon in the Relief Society room, to which Juneau and her family were invited. Gideon took it all in.

Later, he looked up at Juneau and said, "I liked that. When can we do it again?"

"I hope not for a long time," Juneau said.

But it wasn't a long time. A month after Sister Kittridge's funeral, Philip Atwater reached the end of the road. It had been coming for some time. His hips didn't work well anymore. He was nearly deaf and half blind. He still wagged his tail enthusiastically when anyone picked up his leash, but he gave out fast on walks, panting and wheezing after just a few blocks.

Greg made the decision because Juneau couldn't. "We have to let him go, Juney," he said. "His life is a burden to him now." And then he cried. He wasn't a crying man, so Juneau knew how much the old dog meant to him. She hugged him, letting him cry it all out with just her there so he could be strong in front of the Guy's Club.

They explained it to Gideon as best they could, saying Philip Atwater was going to heaven and maybe could be Sister Kittridge's dog there. Now it was Gideon's time to cry. He'd never known life without his faithful Philip Atwater.

Greg and Juneau took care of it on a day when Trace whisked Gideon off to the park for a few hours. They tenderly loaded the dog into the car and drove to Dr. Smith's veterinary clinic. They stayed with him, patting his grizzled old head and talking softly to him until he was gone. They had decided beforehand they would have him cremated so they could bury him at home. It was against the law to bury an animal as large as he was on a city lot.

Gideon insisted on a funeral. Trace and Ira came, as well as Beto and Marisol, and they all sat on the chairs Gideon set up under the pomegranate tree in the backyard. He asked all of them to speak about their life with the dog. He and Trace played their guitars and sang "Home on the Range." Then they buried the metal box containing Philip Atwater's ashes in a deep hole Greg had dug next to the resting places of Max's little Christmas stocking and Rhiannan's scarf.

At bedtime that night Gideon was thoughtful. "I loved Philip Atwater," he said.

"We all did," Juneau and Greg said together.

"He took care of me, and then I took care of him."

"That's the grand cycle with families," Juneau e-mailed to Erin and Deenie, "and it goes on despite earthquakes, or tornadoes, or floods, or old age, or 'change and decay,' as the hymn says. It all works out if we take care of one another."

# Chapter 36

## WILLADENE

"It's cold," Beth said. She wedged up next to Deenie on the couch.

"It's March," Deenie said, pulling her close.

"Light the fire," Evvy demanded from her place on her mother's lap.

"Mint tea sounds good," Margaret suggested, but no one moved. They were suffering from the same slump in energy that had hit the whole family after Sunny's death. When the doorbell rang, no one answered it. It rang again. Then pounding started. Over the racket Deenie could hear Aunt Stella yelling.

"Willadene Rasmussen, if you don't get off your keister and open this door right now, I'm going to haul over the closest neighbor to break it down."

With a sigh, Deenie opened the door. Aunt Stella walked in, grabbed her by the hand, and dragged her into the family room. She took one look at Margaret and the girls and snorted loudly.

"What's wrong, Aunt Stell?" Beth asked.

"I'll tell you what's wrong. There are people outside this house who are in desperate need of assistance, and I can't recruit so much as an ailing cat to help me out. And here you sit, four able-bodied females wallowing in what? Self-pity. Now wouldn't that make Sunny proud."

"We're trying to work through our grief, Stella!" Margaret retorted.

"No you're not. You're indulging in it," Stella shot back.

Deenie felt a niggling bit of guilt. She could imagine Sunny wagging her finger and saying, "Some things only God can fix. He has. I'm fine. What's the matter with *you*?"

"You're right, Aunt Stell," Deenie said. "What do you have in mind?"

"You could start by making me a sandwich, and then we'll talk."

Thus began the Stowell women's bimonthly Saturday lunches, which were followed by brainstorming sessions in which they planned projects designed to bring attention to Stella's elder-care program and gain support for it.

"I'd like to learn more about how this all works together," Margaret said one Saturday at the Bluebird.

"The best way to do that is to spend a couple of days with me on my rounds," Stella answered.

"I'll do that," Margaret said.

"You will?" Deenie looked at her mother. "Then I will, too."

"Bring your dog," Stella said as the waiter served the salads. "The folks at Pioneer House Rest Home consider him a hero."

A week later Deenie, Bear, and the girls were the first to arrive at Pioneer House Rest Home outside Smithfield. The place was bustling with activity. It looked cheerful. Lively. That wasn't a word she would normally associate with nursing or rest homes, which she thought of as warehouses for the unwanted, a place the elderly went to die.

"Shall we go in?" Beth asked.

"Might as well," Deenie said. Hand in hand, the three Rasmussens crossed the parking lot and entered the rest home.

Evvy stopped just inside the door. "It smells funny in here," she said in a small voice.

"It does, doesn't it," the lady behind the reception desk said. She stood and came around, offering her hand first to Evvy and then to Beth and Deenie. "I'm Susan Banks, the charge nurse," she said. She knelt down next to Evvy. "We use a soap that kills germs when we clean around here," she explained. "It stinks something awful. And three times a day we have to cook the kinds of food that our patients can eat. Sometimes all those smells get together, and the result is pretty funky."

Evvy looked up at Deenie for reassurance and then nodded.

"This must be Bear, the famous rescue dog," Susan said. "I was here when Fred Randall wandered away and Bear found him. May I pet him?"

"He'd be insulted if you didn't. It's all about gratification and attention for this mutt," Beth said.

Stell and Margaret arrived shortly thereafter. Stell introduced Margaret to Susan, who then took them on a tour of the facility. Margaret had questions at every stop. Surprisingly, so did Beth. As they finished up, Susan said, "There'll be a group gathering in the recreation room in a few minutes to see your dog, Deenie. Then you can meet our residents."

Everyone there loved Bear, although they were somewhat intimidated by his size. They petted him and had him put his big paw on their knees and shake hands. Deenie had him fetch, lie down, roll over, heel, and everything else she could think of asking him to do.

As Bear worked the room, Beth arranged the flowers she had brought in simple glass vases provided by Susan and placed them where they would be most enjoyed. Evvy slipped quietly away from Deenie's side and took a chair next to an elderly gentleman who hadn't responded to anyone. Deenie's heart swelled with pride as Evvy showed him the book she'd brought. "This is my favorite book," she said. "I can tell you about it if you want. It's called *Wind in the Willows*."

Later, Susan introduced them to another volunteer, Addie Spencer. Addie was a small, elegant woman in her sixties with dignified speech and a twinkle in her eye. "I do a read-aloud program here and at the senior centers. Beth and Evvy should join me sometime. We could produce a delightful show for the patrons."

Evvy giggled, and Beth looked intrigued.

"I'm going to come back next week," Margaret said as they left the building.

Deenie noticed how she was standing taller, her shoulders squared. *Maybe it would be good for all of us*, she thought. "Bear, Evvy, and I will join you."

"Me, too," said Beth.

"Call first, hmm?" Stella suggested. They walked to their cars, laughing.

## ERIN

In March of 1994, the year that Erin and Cory began divorce proceedings, Erin found the perfect house. It was a 1930s Sears Roebuck "Beaumont" bungalow on Upton Avenue, a few blocks from Lake Harriet and the cluster of little shops in Linden Hills. It was in need of a horrifying amount of work, but she fell in love with it at first sight.

Cory was upset when he saw the house from the outside. "English cottage flair, my foot! It's a wreck." But Erin loved the steeply pitched roofline of the entryway and the bank of triple windows with flower boxes underneath. Never mind that they were rotting.

"It's a classic layout," Erin explained as they walked through the front door. "Living room, dining room, kitchen, breakfast nook, and bathroom downstairs; three bedrooms and a second bath upstairs." With glee, she showed him the 1950s Roper gas stove the previous owners had left behind. He countered by pointing out the rust-stained porcelain sink and the cracked linoleum darkened with waxy buildup.

"I know it will take some work, but it's structurally sound, and the basement is dry. When I get it in shape, I'll have a unique place with real value."

"When will that be? Two years from now?"

She got much the same reaction from Skipp and Linda, Caitlin, and The Jays.

"But it's my house," she stubbornly asserted.

"It does have promise, but you're in no condition to take it on," Jake said. Joanna agreed.

Erin took their comments into consideration—and bought the house. She was proud that she could do it on her own, using her share of the combined secret funds for the down payment and her self-employment record to qualify for a mortgage. She was even able to get several thousand dollars extra to do the most urgent work. But the moment after she signed the papers, she wondered what in the world she had done. That's when she called Andrew.

Andrew didn't hide his disapproval of her choice. He started taking notes as he walked through the main floor, muttering as he went. He'd scribbled two full pages by the time he went down into the basement. When he saw the antiquated furnace, he spouted a string of colorful invectives.

Erin sat down on an old paint-spattered stool and began to cry.

"Aw, don't do that," he said.

"I can't help it," she sniffed. "I always get emotional when I'm pregnant."

He smacked his clipboard against the huge metal monster that took up a large portion of the basement. "What in the world were you thinking!" he shouted, which made her cry harder.

A day later Caitlin called to say that Andrew wanted to meet with her and the whole clan. "What for?" Erin asked.

"That's for me to know, and you to find out."

When everyone was assembled for the meeting, Andrew put it to them very bluntly: He was unwilling to have his new grandchild come home to a house that had peeling paint, drafty windows, a furnace that was on its way out, and no air conditioning. He had made arrangements for contractors he knew to do the big repairs and painting at a significant price break, and Erin would get materials and appliances at his cost.

Ignoring Erin's sniffles, he explained the schedule he'd worked out with the contractors, noting the jobs he expected the family to take on. Then he thrust a sheet with a breakdown of costs at Erin. "Do you think you can handle this?"

She was so dazed, she had no idea what she was looking at, but she said, "Yes."

"Okay. Here's the next part."

He spread a plan out on the table. It was a rendering of an addition with a family room, mudroom, and laundry across the back of the first floor, and a master suite and office on the second floor. "The renovations I talked about earlier are just the basics—this is what Erin and her children really need to make the house livable for an active, growing family."

Erin took one look at the plan and blurted out, "I can't afford that!"

"I know." Andrew glanced at Lottie and Caitlin, who smiled back at him. A conspiratorial smile, Erin thought.

"I sent one daughter"—Andrew motioned to Caitlin—"to a private college in St. Paul. I've come to regret that I didn't offer my other daughter the same opportunity." He cleared his throat and pointed at the plan. "Erin, this will set me back about the same amount as a BA at a liberal arts college. It's my gift to you. Unless you would rather apply to Macalester or St. Kate's."

Erin burst out, "In my condition? Yeah, right!"

The sounds of excited voices filled the room as, laughing and crying at the same time, Erin flung herself into his arms. "Thank you, Dad. Thank you, thank you."

"Hey. What else are dads for?"

WILLADENE
>  March 25, 1994
>  Dear Erin,
>
>  Congratulations on the successful house hunting. The new place sounds like it's just you. Style with a lot of character and a lot of promise to boot. How terrific to have the whole family helping. Andrew's gift blew me away! Just think, you got your house up and running with a completed new addition in just three months. It took me twelve years!
>
>  >  Love,
>  >  Deenie
>
>  P.S. How is Cory doing? I don't suppose the family has rallied around him as he steps into his new life?

JUNEAU
>  March 26, 1994
>  Dear Erin,
>
>  The details of your house sound wonderful. It makes me think I may indeed want to do something with mine if Greg's new business works out as he hopes. I've decided I really would like a second-story workroom with a great view of the mountains. But I'll need you to come decorate it for me. Not one of my talents!
>
>  >  Love,
>  >  Juneau

ERIN
>  May 25, 1994
>  Hello, Dear Friends,
>
>  Well, it's over. I am now a divorced woman and single mother. I thought I would feel relieved, but I don't. Probably because we haven't even thought of temple implications. So we're still connected.

Moving day was horrible! When the movers started on Kayla's bedroom furniture, she sat down smack in the middle of the stairs, shouting accusations and sobbing. Mark simply disappeared. I've never been so frightened in my life! Skipp and I finally found him sitting in a dark corner of the garage, his dusty cheeks marked by tears.

After that fiasco we sent the kids off with Skipp and Linda while Cory and I went to the new house to tell the movers where to put the furniture. Linda called a while later to say that the kids were eating supper with them, so Cory and I got LeAnn Chin carryout. It's kind of ironic that my first meal in the new house—where I will be raising my children as a single mother—was with Cory.

When Skipp showed up with the kids, he gave us all a talking to. He said things were going to be difficult, and we needed to remember that we loved each other. Then he said a prayer, calling down blessings on all of us. The good Lord knows that we need all we can get.

The kids and I were a little spooked about being in a strange house, despite having an alarm system. It's been several days now, and the unfamiliar noises of this house still give me the creeps. Maybe I need a big shaggy dog to keep me company.

Love,<br>
Erin

P.S. Mom missed out on all the excitement of moving day, because Grams has been ill with pneumonia—the second time this year.

*Chapter 37*

JUNEAU

Gideon seemed to mope a lot that summer, and Juneau figured it was because he missed the companionship of Philip Atwater. But when she asked him if he'd like to go to the Humane Society and pick out a puppy, he shook his head. "I just wish I still had Philip Atwater."

Then one June day when Juneau and Gideon went grocery shopping, they saw something disturbing in the Albertson's parking lot. Two mid-teen boys were tossing what looked like a ball. But as Juneau parked, Gideon cried out, "Mom! They're throwing a kitten!"

Quickly Juneau got out of the car, telling Gideon to stay inside. Sure enough, the "ball" the boys were tossing had legs, and it gave a terrified yowl each time it was passed back and forth.

"Boys!" she said sharply, hurrying toward them. "What are you doing?"

The boys both turned to look at her. "Just having fun," one of them said. "What's it to you?" He held the small gray kitten upside down in his hand, ignoring its mews and struggles.

"That's a living creature," Juneau said, hoping her voice sounded authoritative. "You mustn't treat it that way. Please give it to me." She walked closer, holding out her hand.

The boy holding the kitten grinned at his companion. "Here," he said. "Catch." He tossed the kitten in a high arc. The other boy caught it.

"Give it to me," Juneau demanded.

"We haven't finished with it yet," the boy with the kitten said. He tossed it back to his friend, who asked, "How much will you give us for it?"

Juneau considered her options. If she left now to call the Humane Society or the police, they would simply run off. With the kitten. "Ten dollars." She knew they'd never go for five.

The boys looked at each other.

"Now!" Juneau said. She fished in her purse and pulled out a bill, waving it in front of the larger of the boys.

The kid grinned. "I can already smell those french fries." He reached for the money.

"The kitten first." Juneau held out her other hand, palm up. The second boy dumped the little cat onto it, grabbing the bill as he did so. The two delinquents ran, laughing, around the corner of the store.

The terrified kitten climbed up her arm, its sharp little claws leaving marks in her flesh. It went on up her body and clung to her shoulder, trembling violently.

Gideon got out of the car, his eyes big. "I was afraid those big guys would hit you," he said, hugging Juneau's leg. Then he reached out for the kitten, which buried its claws in Juneau's shirt and clung. "Come to me, honey kitty," Gideon crooned. "I'll take care of you."

Juneau helped him transfer the traumatized animal to his shoulder, where it hitched itself up into a small ball and buried its head just under his ear.

"Mama?" Gideon said, "Can we keep him? He needs me."

She gazed down at his pleading face. "We have to go check with the store manager, first, Giddy. Just to see if anybody has reported a missing kitten."

Nobody had. "People dump unwanted pets in the parking lot all the time," the manager said. "Take it home. It's one of the lucky ones."


That's how they got the successor to Philip Atwater. Not what they'd planned for at all. But it showed up when it was needed, and so it must have been meant to be.

The kitten was handsome, with solid gray, shiny fur. A male, Greg declared after checking it over, with a Russian blue progenitor somewhere in its ancestry. Its only flaw was an angled tail, probably from an early injury. The inch or so that "listed toward two o'clock," as Greg said, seemed to be numb, and that brought about his name: Numbtail.

The change in Gideon was remarkable. No more moping. Once again he was significant, a Very Important Person. And, Juneau found, she herself was a VIP, too. She heard Gideon telling the story over and over again about how his mama went up against two "great big, mean guys" to rescue the kitten. The guys got bigger with each telling until you'd think she was Wonder Woman.

She told Clyde about it on a Thursday night at Bob's Big Boy. "Isn't it interesting what being looked up to will do for a person?" she said.

"A basic need," Clyde said. "For all of us."

ERIN
June 3, 1994
Dear COBettes,

Cory just picked up the kids for their weekend with him. They were excited, because they'll be picking out furniture for their room in his apartment, but I'm a mess. I can't stand knowing that someone else is taking care of them, kissing an owie when they get hurt, answering their questions, and joining in their laughter. Even if that someone is their own father or one of their Johnson grandparents. (They're often at Skipp and Linda's on those weekends.)

Just before they left, I had the sweetest moment with Kayla. I don't know if one of her grands has been talking to her, or if it's because she's eleven, but she's just realized in a new way how much time and money Cory and I are putting toward her skating. She gave me a big hug and thanked me. Then she made a whole list of unnecessary promises, including getting a medal at regionals next fall.

Her dedication has brought her a long way, but at regionals she'll be up against skaters who practice two hours or more every day. I worry about her being disappointed, so I told her what her coach, Allyson, always says. "Skate for yourself, because you love it."

Oh, dear. I'm blubbering onto my keyboard. That can't be good.

Your Erin

JUNEAU

June 7, 1994
Dear Erin,

Have faith in Cory and his parents. They'll take care of your dear ones. You take care of yourself.

Love,
Juneau

WILLADENE

June 19, 1994
Dear COBs,

Isn't it funny how one moment—or one morning—can change everything? Ever since we went to Pioneer House Rest Home with Aunt Stell, we've made a commitment to be available on Saturday mornings for whatever Aunt Stell has scheduled for us at various nursing homes or at the Logan senior center.

You wouldn't recognize Mom! She's a new woman since she teamed up with an old friend named Merinda Davis. Merinda has been an elder advocate for fifteen years. She and Mom attend hearings that affect elder law and help older folks who want to stay in their own homes find ways to do it. Mom's even set up to provide a meal in a hurry if those on wheels mess up.

Dad says she's so busy, she needs a full-time secretary, so—get this!—he has put the family furniture store up for sale. He's been headed in that direction for the last few years, so it wasn't too big a surprise. What is surprising is the new lease on life this focus has given them both.

Beth and Evvy continue to come with us on our visits to the nursing home and senior center. They "perform" their Dr. Seuss books, dramatizing the lines. The two put on quite a show. Beth has made friends with another volunteer named Addie Spencer, an elegant widow in her sixties with a worldwide education and outlook. She was delighted when Addie invited the Stowell Women (that's how she refers to Stell, Mom, Beth, Evvy, and me) to her home for tea. She lives in the historic part of the west side of Logan in a perfectly restored Victorian house that would send you, Erin, into paroxysms of joy. (Yes, I still read romance novels—one every year.) It was all quite grand.

It's wonderful to have Carl home. He and Roger will be working on the farm for the summer, although Carl has been looking for a job that would give him training in another field. Ha ha.

Roger has received two more job offers, one for an inner city school in Cincinnati and one for an alternative school in Denver. Both had more to do with disciplining students than anything else. So far nothing has appealed to Roger enough to make him want to move. Thank heaven.

Speaking of moving, I was glad to hear you're in your new home, Erin, and loving it. That's wonderful news. But are you taking care of yourself and that bambino inside?

Love,<br>Deenie

## ERIN

July 11, 1994
Dear Friends,

Guess what?! I am now the owner of a one-year-old yellow Lab named Rascal. Cory thinks I'm crazy (what's new about that?), but even with the alarm system, I get nervous in this house, especially when I'm alone.

You're partly to blame, you know. When I was still weighing the pros and cons of dog ownership, your charming stories about Philip Atwater, Rauf, and Bear put a lot of weight in the pro column.

Rascal stole my heart the minute I saw him at the Humane Society, probably because he came right up to me and started giving me loves. He is such a charmer, with an eager smile, intelligent eyes, and gorgeous coat the color of ripe wheat. He's been to obedience school, so he's well mannered. We'll go again, this time for my benefit.

I wish you'd been here when I brought Rascal home. It was absolutely hilarious watching Kayla and Mark try to ignore that golden charmer. They lasted about seven seconds! I don't think any of us have smiled or laughed that much in years. I think

God must have been in a good mood when he created dogs!
(Not to say that Numbtail isn't a wonder, too.)

Love,
Erin

P.S. Mark and Kayla insist on going to their old schools next
year. There's open enrollment in Minnesota, so they can, but
someone (guess who!) will have to drive them each way. What
with trips to the arena for figure skating and hockey, the
MacPhail Center for Mark's piano lessons, Cub Scouts, Young
Women, and who knows what else, I might as well get a van
and outfit it with a traveling office and nursery! At least we're
in the same ward as before.

## JUNEAU

July 18, 1994
Dear Deenie and Erin,

Aren't animals wonderful? Numbtail can't measure up to Bear
and Rascal in size, but he's worked his magic just as they have.
He's an appendage to Gideon these days, and if Giddy isn't
available, he occupies my lap while I work at the computer.
Nicole says she'd like to take him with her when she goes back
to BYU next month. He's such a people cat! Greg, who always
said cats are far inferior to dogs, cuddles and pets him and
remarks about his rumbly purr. Poor Greg isn't home a lot these
days. The computer consulting business he and his friend Arnie
started is faltering a little, like a baby learning to walk. But it
will soon be up and running, Greg says. Let's hope.

Love,
Juneau

## WILLADENE

July 21, 1994
Dear Erin,

Bear says good job! Congrats on the new canine member of the
family. Go, Rascal. Watch for coupons for dog food coming in
the mail.

Love,
Deenie and Bear

ERIN

August 22, 1994
Dear Friends,

Baby Hannah says thank you for the cards and gifts. Deenie and Gabby, the braided rag rug is perfect in front of the rocking chair. And Juneau, the nine-month-size Oshkosh B'Gosh outfit is so darling!

Yes, Hannah's birth was early, and she came really fast! Thank goodness Cory was with me in the delivery room. I came close to breaking every bone in his hand the moment she crowned. When they laid her on my stomach, she looked right at me as if she knew who I was. I had no doubt who she was—I'd seen her the night Cory gave her that sweet blessing.

The kids absolutely melted when they first saw her. They call her Hannah Banana. Unavoidable, I guess. They've never spent much time with a newborn before, so they were astonished at how perfect she is, especially her little fingernails. Now that they're comfortable holding her, they jump to her side the moment she makes the slightest sound. I hardly get a chance to hold her except when she's nursing or needs changing!

Rascal is handling this change in the family quite well. He loves sitting on the couch with us while I nurse Hannah, his snout on my knee. To make sure that he gets enough attention, I've added a new chore to the kids' lists: Play with Rascal! They're more than happy to do that.

We've had a stream of company. When Colleen came to visit, she said she didn't understand the choices I've made and how I can let Cory be such a big part of my life, considering. Then she said she loved us both and wished us God's blessings. Very odd.

I don't know what I would do without Cory's continued support. I was watching him rock Hannah when he was here the other night. He looked up at me, and we both smiled. It reminded me of the smile Andrew and Mom give each other when they're around Kayla. Whatever went before, we created this lovely little creature, and we're proud to be her parents.

That sweet moment was followed by a bittersweet one the Sunday Skipp blessed Hannah. It was hard for Cory to sit next to me when he should have been in the circle. He still struggles with warring parts of himself. He was moved by his father's words and touched by the genuine warmth with which ward members greeted him. But he left directly after sacrament meeting. So sad.

On another front, I wish things could stay as uncomplicated as they are right now, but no such luck. School will be starting soon, and Cory and I are working out how we'll get Kayla to her morning practices and both the kids to their old schools and then to after-school activities.

This sort of problem isn't unusual, according to moms I've talked to at the rink. Skaters and their siblings tend to be very active, and most families rely on grandparents to help out. Lucky for us, Cory's parents and Jake are picking up shifts. (Mom isn't, because she doesn't leave Grams alone these days.) It's asking a lot from them, but they have made it clear they'll help in any way they can.

Chalk it up to the baby blues, but I just burst into tears! I don't understand how grief and gratitude can exist in the same heart, but they do in mine.

I'll send you photos soon.

Love,<br>Erin

## JUNEAU

August 27, 1994
Dear Friends,

Bad news. Misty is talking about divorcing Ira. Both Greg and I tried to talk her out of it, but she says she doesn't want to come back here and it's not fair to Ira to keep him tied to her when he doesn't want to leave California. I can't believe that's the entire reason. I think she's found herself a cowboy there in Idaho. She's mentioned spending quite a bit of time on a ranch over near Bear Lake. She's twenty-three now and her own boss, so I guess we'll just have to let her careen on through her life, leaving wreckage wherever she goes. At least she calls to speak with Gideon almost every week.

Ira is depressed about it all, of course. His career as a pickle is going well, with a third commercial in the pipeline. Misty says her friends in Idaho and our relatives, too, are impressed that she's married to Mr. Pickle. But that doesn't seem to have any effect on her plan to undo her vows.

Once again, Greg asked Misty if she would be willing to sign adoption papers so we could legally be Gideon's parents and have him sealed to us. Once again, she said she wasn't ready to. It's particularly frustrating because Trace has agreed to sign them. So we're still waiting for her to realize that it would be the best thing for Gideon.

There's better news, about Nicole this time. She's decided to go on a mission. Even so, the Crafton twins and Beto are still in the picture. Nicole's confused about the twins and whether she likes one better than the other. They've both been writing to her while she's been home for the summer. She's also been hanging out with Beto, almost like in the old days. What I don't know is whether it's a case of "just friends" now, like Trace and Cath. So perhaps a mission is the best solution. She's submitting her papers this week and not returning to BYU for her final year.

As for me—what do I know about anything?

Love,
Juneau

P.S. Erin, the photo of Hannah is so sweet. I can just imagine how it would feel to snuggle her up on my shoulder.

WILLADENE
September 5, 1994
Dear COBs,

Erin, cherish every day with that little sweetheart of yours. The years will go by way too fast! I'm feeling it myself, because Evvy started first grade this year. Her teacher already called to say that she's going to be a problem—in a good way. She's far ahead of her classmates in her reading. Not surprising, considering all the reading she's done with Beth this last year.

Beth's a junior in high school this year. If they tested for emotional maturity, she would already be earning college credit. I attribute the great strides she has been making to her relationship with the remarkable Addie Spencer. Due to her influence, Beth is more committed to whatever she undertakes, more introspective and more refined in her behavior. Mom and I are both a little jealous, but then I think of your letter, Erin. The one you wrote about all of us being mothered by many women at different times of our lives. Then I feel grateful for whatever it is that Addie provides for Beth.

Beth has also sent off the first young man on a mission who has asked her to write to and wait for him. Jason Whitmore! Can you believe it? Beth didn't. She told him not to be silly.

Here's real news. Dad has sold the furniture business but not the building. The store will continue to occupy the first floor. The second is being used for a new enterprise: The Cache Valley Elder Advocacy Center and Reading Room. That's the name of a nonprofit created by Dad, Mom, Aunt Stell, and Merinda Davis to help seniors who want to remain in their homes. Dad's installed benches in the big service elevator, so old folks can get upstairs easily. The Center has a roster of volunteers, including Beth, who stops by when she has time.

You wouldn't recognize my parents compared to who they were after Sunny's death. Helping others has given them something to focus on. They're so energized, Dad is even talking about finding a space for a badly needed adult day care center. Amazing!

Carl has started school at Utah State to finish up general requirements, and he's joined the Air Force ROTC program. He hasn't found a sweetheart yet. He insists he's not looking. Beth says, "As if!"

I am still in the nursery at church and have decided I would be happy to stay there. Maybe I am getting close to grandma age and developing a natural hunger for little ones. Who knows?

Gabby, I was thrilled to get your note about joining us for the Harvest Festival. We found places for your whole family. With NeVae's permission, Sophie and her family and Bryan and Heather will be at the homestead. (Congratulations to Heather on expecting the next member of the family.) Junior and Cecelia have a place at my folks' house, and Kenny and his girlfriend can stay here. (What's her name?) Everyone in the neighborhood is looking forward to meeting the clan. Can't wait to see you all myself.

Love,
Deenie

# Chapter 38

ERIN

September 27, 1994
Dear Juneau and Deenie,

That note we all got from Gabby was pretty enigmatic, wasn't it? *Expect something to come by delivery truck. Don't get in a dither or make assumptions. I'm just making sure that the people I love get something special from me before my old bones lie down. I want to be around to get the thank-yous!*

I can't wait to see what she sent me. Call me the minute your surprises arrive!

Your Erin

WILLADENE

October 4, 1994
Dear COBs and especially Gabby!

Guess what came to our house, courtesy of FedEx? One of the pioneer paintings done by Gabby's grandmother! I am touched beyond words by the beauty and generosity of the gift. I can't wait to find a permanent place for it in our home. The scene of the young girl walking alongside the ox cart could have come from my own family history. No matter where I hang it, it will make the room.

Gabby, you'll never know how much that means to me. Thank you from the bottom of my heart.

Love,
Deenie

ERIN

October 7, 1994
Dear Juneau and Deenie,

I was on pins and needles, waiting for my gift to come, especially after you called to say what she'd sent you. Juneau, I can just see you writing at that handsome oak secretary. And Deenie! How perfect that she sent you one of the oils her grandmother painted of pioneers crossing the plains. Every time you look at it, I'll bet you think of your ancestors.

Can you guess what she sent me? That wonderful painted pioneer dresser that stood in the large guest room upstairs. I put it in my bedroom where I see it the first thing in the morning. I've arranged photos of the family and you two and Gabby on top of it.

That sweet Gabby. I don't know how long we'll have her with us. I sent her a thank-you right away, and I've been making sure to call her every Sunday evening.

Your Erin

## JUNEAU
October 8, 1994
Dear Erin and Deenie,

Erin, I know exactly the dresser you're talking about. Gabby sent each of us the perfect gift, the one that would mean the most to us. The oak secretary isn't right for a computer desk, so I'm using it as a place to organize my bills and all that kind of thing. I called her as soon as it came, and I guess I've sent her at least three thank-you notes. I love it! I love her! I love you guys!

Love,<br>Love,<br>Love,<br>Juneau

## ERIN
October 16, 1994
Dear Friends,

Today Cory invited me to come see what he's done with his apartment. He's furnished his living room with masculine, modern pieces—a leather couch and loveseat and a classic Eames lounge chair, all in cognac and dark brown. He let the kids go all out in their room, including a media wall with TV, VCR, CD player, video game player, the whole works.

I think the real reason he invited me over was that he's lonesome. When I asked him what he missed most about our life together, I was surprised by what he said. A house with people in it to come home to. (I understand that!) Hearing Mark practice the piano. Our dance lessons. And church.

He's tried going to some other churches, but he hasn't found one he's comfortable in. The music may be beautiful, the speakers great, and the people friendly, but he says it doesn't feel the same to him.

Before I left, I cranked up the courage to ask if he's found someone he's interested in. He says no. He's not interested in the gay scene, to tell the truth. He wants a relationship, and that's not easy to come by.

I could have reminded him that he had one, but I didn't. I still love him, after everything we've been through. I so want him to be happy.

Feeling sad and lonesome,<br>Erin

## WILLADENE

October 7, 1994
Dear Erin,

Hang in there, friend. You're in our hearts and prayers, always.

Love,<br>Deenie

October 24, 1994
Dear Juneau,

Thank you for being mother to Bert when she miscarried. With Will and NeVae here for a visit at that time, she felt so alone. The whole family wants me to let you know how much we appreciate the way you stepped right in and helped her cope. I know Bert's told you so herself.

I had that talk with Reece and Ryan you requested. They were both very gentlemanly about it and understand that Nicole has other priorities in her life. Has she turned in her mission papers yet? When do you expect her to receive her call? How is Beto handling it all?

Say, have you heard that Kenny's getting married this coming Valentine's Day? He has made an amazing turnaround, which is a credit not only to him but to Gabby and the rest of the family. Jonas, too. Roger and I are looking forward to celebrating this occasion with them.

Isn't this e-mail stuff great? No more snail mail for me, if I can help it.

Love,
Deenie

JUNEAU

November 14, 1994
Dear COBs:

Sorry I didn't let you know sooner, but Nicole received her mission call to Mexico City last month. We had her farewell testimonial yesterday. There was a big crowd at the meeting, including Beto, who resembled a lost puppy. I don't know what happened with Carlina, the girl he brought home a while ago to meet Marisol, but it's obvious he carries a big torch for Nicole. He'll finish up at Loyola-Marymount next spring, and he hopes to gain admittance to the UCLA medical school so he can stay close to home for Marisol.

Anyway, Nicky is thrilled about going to Mexico. Think it might revive her old dreams of going with Beto to his ancestral village as a doctor? Since she had such success as a Golden California Girl at BYU, I'm not sure she still has all those altruistic dreams. I'm hoping the mission will ground her again and that she'll see where her life should go.

*Hermana* Caldwell will enter the Missionary Training Center next week. She already speaks almost fluent Spanish, from being so close to the Sanchez family all her life and also from four years of Spanish in high school.

Love,
Juneau

P.S. Deenie, I was honored to be a stand-in mother for Bert. I think it helped her know I've been through the same thing.

## WILLADENE

November 17, 1994
Dear COBs,

Sunny will be receiving her endowment this Saturday, with me as proxy. I was surprised when Mom gave me that honor, because I'd thought she'd want to do it herself. But she said that with me sitting beside her as proxy for Sunny, it would be like having both her daughters with her all the way through the ceremony. Sunny will be with us, I'm certain of that. Dad, other family members, friends, and neighbors will be going through the temple with us. We'll all have to have extra tissues, but what better way to start our Thanksgiving celebration!

Love,
Deenie

## ERIN

November 28, 1994
Dear Juneau, Gabby, and Deenie,

I really feel like this is my house now—we've had a party! Mark invited five kids over for his ninth birthday: Smith from the old neighborhood, a couple of kids from school, and a couple from his hockey team. Amazing the amount of noise six nine-year-olds can make!

You'll notice that Ricky wasn't among the guests. When I asked Mark why he didn't invite Ricky, he said the other boys wouldn't understand what was wrong with Ricky, and he didn't want to have to explain. I was really surprised, because they've spent quite a lot of time together lately. When we discovered that the games Grams can still play—Uno, Old Maid, and Go Fish—are ones Ricky likes, we started inviting him and EJ to an afternoon of games at Grams's place every so often. It's been great because Ricky doesn't care if Grams makes a mistake. He giggles in that raspy voice of his, which makes everyone laugh.

Mark's also been helping Ricky with the requirements for his

Wolf badges. Colleen and Steve decided right from the first that Ricky would meet all the markers other boys do—he goes to regular classes (with extra tutoring, of course), he was on a soccer team this summer, and he started Cub Scouts when he turned eight. (There's no talk of baptism yet. Colleen says they want to wait until they are sure he understands its significance. She says they'll know when the time's right.)

Anyway, I think Mark felt bad about not inviting Ricky, because he invited the Harringtons to come to the family party on Sunday night. He played all the games that Ricky likes. When Ricky said, "I want to sing!" he sat at the piano and played every song Ricky requested. Grams wanted some songs, too, only . . . it's so sad. She couldn't think of the names. So Mark played everything he knew she liked until she was satisfied.

I think the relationship between Steve and Cory has changed forever. They try really hard to act like they've always acted, but it comes off wrong, somehow. Like they're playing a part called "friends" instead of being friends. I was trying to find a word that describes the invisible barrier between them. I think it's fear. Now, why is that? It's not like being gay can rub off on Steve.

With Thanksgiving and Mark's birthday crossed off on the calendar, Christmas looms on the horizon. It's going to be different this year, and not just because Cory and I are divorced. We're managing, but there's not a lot of shekels left over once the bills are paid. I've talked to the kids about it, and they reacted better than I'd expected. They know a good chunk of the money pays for their activities.

The grandparents are doing what they can to help maintain a sense of normalcy. The Jays have already invited the whole crew over for Christmas Eve, and Cory's parents are doing dinner for us all on Christmas Day. We'll rely on traditions to carry us through.

Hope you have a lovely holiday season, dear friends. Give your men an extra squeeze! You're lucky to have them.

Love,
Erin

## WILLADENE

December 4, 1994

Dear Juneau, Erin, and Gabby,

Erin, I can sympathize, as far as the shekels go. It's time to retrench in the Rasmussen house, too. We're in the red, and the biggest reason for that is . . . me! Lately, I've been buying whatever I wanted without discussing it with Roger first. Instead of cooking nutritious, delicious meals for my family, I've gotten in the habit of swinging by the deli on busy days. Bear's vet bills have taken quite the chunk, too. Teeth cleaning alone set us back $300!

The upshot of it all is I am back to homemaking instead of just housekeeping. The kids are thrilled, and Roger is relieved. What could be a better time to get back to home cooking than the holidays?

On a brighter note, we loved having the entire Farnsworth crowd here for the fall festival. The weather was perfect, and it was perfectly delightful to see all of Gabby's dear family together. We had a chance to get to know Ariane, Kenny's fiancée. It's easy to see why you like her so much, Gabby. She is kind and loving, with that quirky sense of humor that all COBs appreciate. We're looking forward to joining you for the wedding on Valentine's Day.

Love,
Deenie

P.S. Roger has received an invitation to interview for the job of assistant principal at The Academy America—Excellence in Education. It's an upscale, superconservative boys' school in Gainesville, Florida. He was recommended by his former University of Utah advisor, who now works for the University of Florida in Gainesville. Roger is thrilled about it. It offers everything he's been looking for. I may end up with those alligators in the backyard after all.

JUNEAU

January 5, 1995
Dear Gabby and other COBs,

Gabby, I'm so glad you ventured into the world of computers and e-mail when we all decided to go that route. I love staying in touch with your dear self, and it's so much easier to dash off an e-mail than to send something via snail mail. I haven't licked a stamp for quite a while now, except for bills and Christmas cards.

I was excited by all your news—Kenny's unpcoming wedding, Sophie's expected baby, and all. Family celebrations are such wonderful events. So hopeful.

Things are going along for my family. Some good, some bad. Nicole will soon be finished at the MTC and will head for Mexico City. She rejoices. Beto mourns. I wonder what will happen with the two of them. I can come up with numerous scenarios—I *am* a writer—but children are even more recalci-trant than characters. They do what they will do.

Misty is still in Idaho and hasn't yet gone through with the divorce idea. She says she's very busy. With what, I'd like to know. She has a job involving computers. Ira is busy, too, with another pickle commercial, which offers some distraction. Trace and Cath still hang out a lot together. She has a job where she provides therapy through music and the arts. Trace helps her out now and then, playing the guitar and leading troubled kids in fun songs, like "Farmer Potter's Pig" and other songs The Caldwez (Caldwells plus Sanchezes) Family Players sang when Rhiannan was with us. I wouldn't be surprised if he decides to go into the arts therapy field.

Greg is worried about the shaky condition of the new company he and his friend Arnie started. We both try to think positively. Gideon is Mr. Terrific. He and Numbtail are such a delightful partnership! As for me, hey, good news. I've been told I'm getting the Notable Book Award at the spring luncheon of the Children's Librarians and Authors group on April 15! It's for *Beyond,* the book I wrote after Rhiannan's death.

In the meantime, I'm following the advice you gave us a long time ago, Gabby—Pull up your socks and keep going!

Love,
Juneau

ERIN

January 9, 1995
Dear Gabby, Juneau, and Deenie,

I agree—e-mails are great, Juneau. But I can't tell you all how much it meant to me to hear your voices when I called on New Year's Day.

Yes, I know. Our Christmas card photo of the family—Cory included—on the staircase of the new house was kind of déjà vu. It's a hint of the strange Christmas we had. Some things have changed, yet most have remained the same. The whole family was together on Christmas Eve at The Jays' house and for dinner the next day at the Johnsons'. Cory wasn't with us New Year's Eve or Day, though. His absence made it clear that he has a life we know nothing about.

On New Year's Day, the kids and I had brunch at Lottie and Andrew's. Theresa came in just long enough to help Caitlin get the food on the sideboard in the dining room and wish us *Prospero año neuvo.* She has come up with a nickname for Caitlin and me: *Las dos Pelirrojas.* The Two Redheads. Juneau, your *Hermana* Caldwell can pronounce that better than I can, no doubt! She's probably rattling on in Spanish by now. You might want to take a class in it yourself. Otherwise, when she gets back, she'll be carrying on long conversations with Beto and his family that you won't be able to understand!

After we ate, we watched the videotape of Kayla's skating programs. We've got footage starting with her at five dressed in a little tutu for the spring show on up to her most recent competition, in which she won a silver medal on the junior level.

After that, Mark got to play on the beautiful Steinway, which he loves. He says it has a much better tone than our piano. Well, *duuuh!* It cost ten times as much. Hannah didn't need to do anything to entertain but be herself. Lottie held her most of the afternoon. I think she's grandbaby hungry.

Later, I took some time to think about the year before me. What an odd experience. All my life I've been looking ahead to the next thing to do. Keeping my eyes on the horizon, so to speak. But the only way I can see into the future now is when I'm thinking about what's next for the kids. I have no idea where I'm going or even where I want to go.

I finally wrote down things like Lose fifteen pounds. Read scriptures every night. Do something social once a week. Get a regular manicure and pedicure. But that's just holding ground, with a little gilding on the lily. What about the rest of my life?

One thing's for sure, I'm not looking for romance! I've been invited to some singles' events at church, but I'm not interested in being part of a group distinguished by being unchosen or divorced. Not much of a recommendation. Bishop Harding says I'm way off base with that assessment, and he may be right. But I much prefer spending time with my kiddies, especially Hannah Banana, who at five months is quite the charmer!

> Much love,
> Erin

P.S. Gabby, thanks for your latest contribution to *The COBs' Book of Little Wisdom:* "Getting your knickers in a knot just makes you walk funny." You're going to have to stay with us a long time so that we can keep collecting your wise sayings.

## WILLADENE

"What on earth are you doing, Mother?" Beth asked Saturday morning as she came into the living room where Deenie stood on tiptoe on the hearth leaning toward the over-the-mantel mirror. February light brightened her reflection.

"Naming wrinkles," Deenie said.

"Oh really?" Beth's tone mimicked Addie's exactly.

"Yes, really!" Deenie pointed to an odd crescent moon of a wrinkle underneath her lower lip. "I got this one the day you nearly crashed Grandpa Will's tractor mower. It's the Almost Dead Daughter wrinkle."

Beth smiled. "Addie could probably help you with those. She has a cream she found in Sweden she says almost makes them disappear overnight."

"These wrinkles tell as much about me as my journal, and I intend to keep them. I don't need Addie's help, thank you very much!"

"Mom! You're not jealous of her, are you?" Beth asked in surprise.

"Sometimes. I bet Danny is, too."

"No way. The only time we're not together is after school when she works on the school paper and I go to the senior center." She paused. "I noticed the dining room table's set. Guess that means the Stowell Women are lunching here today?"

Deenie nodded. "Evvy has such a bad cold I thought we'd meet here. I didn't want to cancel the planning session for the volunteer appreciation lunch at the senior center." But that wasn't the only thing that was on the agenda. She had decided this was the time to tell Aunt Stell and her mother about the invitation Roger had received to interview for the prestigious job in Florida. She wasn't sure how they were going to take the news.

When the women arrived, right on time, Aunt Stella walked into the room, talking. "We found flowers on Sunny's grave this morning when we stopped at the cemetery."

"White daisies in a bright yellow basket with all kinds of pastel ribbons," Margaret added, shaking the snow from her coat and draping it over a chair. "I guess that means Brad's back in the area."

"I hope so," Beth said. "I'd like to see him again. He's a nice man. I was impressed by how sweet he was with Aunt Sunny."

Margaret raised her eyebrows at Deenie, who read the unspoken question, *When did she go from being sixteen to thirty?* Deenie shrugged.

All through the lunch, Deenie felt her nervousness about the Florida announcement rise. She had to tell them, and soon.

"What do we hear from our missionary boy?" Aunt Stell asked.

"His last letter was all about hot weather and hurricanes," Beth said. "He's been transferred to Galveston."

Sensing an opening, Deenie said, "We could be in for some hot weather ourselves." She made it sound as though she were divulging a grand secret. She didn't want them to see how unsettled she was by it. "Roger's going to Gainesville, Florida, to interview for a position in administration with a private boys' school. His advisor from the University of Utah set it up for him."

The gasps of surprise and horror were precisely what Deenie expected.

"Are you going with him?" Margaret asked.

Deenie shook her head. "He's taking Carl this time, and they'll do some sight-seeing afterward. If he makes the cut for the round of interviews that includes wives—that's in June—I'll make the trip."

"Florida in June," Stella said with a shudder. "Can you imagine that?"

ERIN

February 8, 1995
Dear Juneau, Deenie, and Gabby,

Have you ever heard of a Baby Welcome? Well, that's what we just had for Hannah, thanks to Lucky.

When Lucky first called with the idea, she said it was a family tradition also called the Gathering of Mothers. All the women who will be important in a child's life gather to give her the gift of one of their positive attributes. I asked Lucky if that was an African tradition, and she laughed. "No, it's a family tradition!"

Lucky started out using that southern preacher cadence she can assume when she wants to. "We're all here to surround this baby girl with Motherlove. Motherlove is magic. Ain't nothing that can harm Miz Hannah with Motherlove around her."

She paused, waiting for a response. When no one said anything, she put her hands on her hips and said, "Guess I'm not going to get any, 'Yes, Lord! Amen, Lord,' outta you white women!" Her laughter was so infectious, we all doubled over, too. The next time she paused, Angie yelled out, "Amen!"

Oh, the gifts Hannah got! I gave her love. Mom, hope. Angie, laughter. Caitlin, curiosity and enthusiasm. Colleen, yearning for the Spirit. Linda, commitment to family. Lottie, compassion. Paula, confidence and tenacity.

Grams didn't understand what she was supposed to do, so she took Hannah's hands and played patty cake. "Fun!" she said. That from a woman who didn't learn to have fun until late in her life.

EJ gave Hannah "smarts." Shakeela, *at-ti-tude*. Kayla said, "I give you me." As the last giver of gifts, Lucky picked Hannah up and gave her a big smooch. "I give you lusciousness."

I thought that the ceremony was over then, but Lucky had Shakeela, EJ, and Kayla stand in the middle of the circle, because they needed Motherlove, too. You should have seen their eyes shine as we gave them our gifts—it meant so much to them to be acknowledged. Wonder what the Young Women's president would think about having a circle for all the girls in our ward. I'd like all of them—Melina, especially—to experience it.

> Missing you, dear friends,
> Erin

## JUNEAU

February 11, 1995
Dear Erin,

What a lovely ceremony! Makes me want another baby so I could do a Gathering of Mothers, too! That's not likely to happen—another baby, I mean, since I'll turn forty-nine this year. That means I'll reach the big five-oh next year. Where is the wisdom I hoped to have by the half-century mark? Where is my COBhood?

> Still striving,
> Juneau

## WILLADENE

February 16, 1995
Dear Erin,

I'm going to have a Gathering of Mothers for every new baby who comes into our family! And I also like the idea of giving gifts to our young women, too.

I think the mothers probably give a gift they value and hope to have more of themselves. So when a woman says, "I give you hope," or "I give you courage," she's opening herself to receive it back in her own life as well, so she can give it again. I like the sense of increasing measure in the perpetuation of the gift. More hope, more courage, more lusciousness.

The big event here lately was Kenny's wedding to Ariane at a reception center in Provo. The ceremony was touching, but what meant the most to me was seeing the love and kindness shared by Gabby, Junior, Cecelia, and their children. When Junior escorted Gabby to her seat on the groom's side of the aisle, the look on their faces had me fishing for a tissue, the first of many I used that day. Miracles never cease!

Love,
Deenie

*Chapter 40*

ERIN

March 4, 1995
Dear COBs,

I'm on my way to the hospital. Grams was admitted with pneumonia again, and her doctor doesn't think she'll be with us long. He's advised against heroic measures, given her overall physical decline. It's sad that she's leaving us, but to be honest, we said good-bye to the Grams we knew and loved a long time ago. Alzheimer's is such a wretched disease. Thank heaven there came a point when Grams didn't realize what she'd lost, because she didn't remember what she'd had.

Say a prayer for us, please.

Love,
Erin

March 13, 1995
My Dear, Dear Friends,

Thank you for the sweet cards and phone calls after Grams's death. We had a service at the funeral home, which Jake led in a Quaker-style meeting. Mark expressed his feelings by playing a selection of her favorite songs. Great-Grandpa Harold, a little gnome of a man at ninety-four, said she had been "a friend in his old age." We ended by singing a hymn she loved, "Children of the Heavenly Father." I cried through the middle verses:

> Neither life nor death shall ever
> From the Lord His children sever;
> Unto them His grace He showeth,
> And their sorrows all He knoweth.

> Though He giveth or He taketh,
> God His children ne'er forsaketh;
> His the loving purpose solely
> To preserve them pure and holy.

Kayla is taking her great-grandmother's passing hard. Her way of handling it is to say she's going to bring home a medal from regionals this fall in her honor. As for Mark, he's gotten very quiet. I often hear him playing Grams's favorite songs. He has a lovely touch, and he puts such heart into his playing, I have to grab a tissue. (We're blubberpusses for sure, Deenie!)

I'm glad Grams got to meet Hannah before she passed. Some of the sweetest moments in her last months were when she crooned to Hannah in Swedish, songs neither Mom nor I had ever heard her sing before. We think she learned them at her mother's knee when she was very young. Mark picked them up by ear, and he plays them when he's missing her.

I'm feeling very tender. Wish I could hug someone right now, but the kids are in bed. Guess I'll go pet the dog.

Love,
Erin

## WILLADENE
March 15, 1995
Dear Erin,

Thank you for telling us about Grams's funeral. The tribute Harold gave her made me sniff. Those two getting along is definitely a Who'da! We put your family's names on the temple prayer list.

Love to you all,
Deenie and family

## JUNEAU
March 18, 1995

Erin, dear, here are hugs via e-mail. I've been thinking about your Grams a lot lately. I feel there's something missing from my own life with her gone. Isn't it interesting how your family and Deenie's and mine all seem like part of OUR family after all this time?

I think you can take comfort in the magnificent progress Grams made from the time we first met each other until now. She went on with high marks on her report card.

Love and BIG HUGS,
Juneau

WILLADENE

April 1, 1995
Dear COBs,

Seven things not to be confused with April Fool's jokes:

1. Roger likes Florida. He has been called back for the second interview—with wife—at The Academy of America–Excellence in Education in June. Arrrgh!

2. Addie Spencer says she hopes Beth can take a trip to Europe with her some day. Over my dead body! She's teaching French to Beth, who now wants to be called Liz. Hey! I speak more than one language, too. Baby. Toddler. Teenager . . .

3. Paul's thinking of marine biology as a career when he gets home. Makes me wonder what he's doing in Galveston on his preparation days?

4. The flowers that have been appearing on Sunny's grave are being sent from out of state, says the florist. So we still don't know where Brad is. I am relieved. Roger says I'm imagining the faraway look Beth gets in her eyes whenever he's mentioned, but I'm a mother, and we mothers see things fathers don't. Like you, Juneau, and that look in Misty's eyes.

5. Terry Madsen says I'm ready to starting training to certify as an SAR trainer. But do I want to?

6. Carl has taken on a load of history classes and is poking around in the social sciences along with his tech classes. He says if you're going to make the military your life, you'd better understand how the world got to where it is. *Hoo-hah!*

7. I gave away all my maternity and baby things. If that's tempting fate, maybe I'm the April fool!

Deenie

## JUNEAU

Juneau had belonged to the Southern California Children's Librarians and Authors group, or SCCLA, for several years and had always been impressed at their annual luncheon when they gave out various awards for outstanding books. She couldn't believe she was actually going to receive an award this year. It would involve giving a seven- to ten-minute speech, the thought of which made her heart pound. She'd given numerous talks in church, and they'd never bothered her a whole lot. But this would be before an audience of her peers and critics. Scary.

The event was to be at a large hotel near LAX on a Saturday in April. Her family was invited. Another reason to be nervous. She didn't want to embarrass those she loved best.

Mrs. Jarvis announced the coming award in her class. Several of the class members belonged to the organization and said they'd be there, which made Juneau even more nervous. For a reason she couldn't explain, she was glad Clyde was out of town for an extended period.

She tried out several speeches, finally deciding just to talk about how the award-winning book came about. She'd tell the story of Rhiannan and then how she'd used the basic idea Clyde had given her—that when someone passes, it helps to concentrate on what the person's life meant. She'd expand on that, saying that Rhiannan's life went on through her book. She'd use the quotation Erin said her bishop had told her: "The story's not over yet."

The story of a life was never over, really.

The luncheon was pleasant, with a large crowd in attendance. Juneau accepted the award, an impressive wall plaque with her name and the title of her book, *Beyond*, on it, and posed for a photograph. Then she walked to the podium and looked out over all those people seated at the tables. Her throat closed. Her speech left her mind. She sought her family; when she found them, Gideon waved, and Trace and Cath smiled encouragement. Greg was looking down, scribbling something on the edge of his program. What was it she'd planned to say? Her gaze skidded around the room until she locked eyes with . . . Clyde. He smiled. Nodded slowly. Blew a kiss.

Juneau cleared her throat, and the words of her speech flowed into her mind. She looked at everyone in the audience as she began, but it was Clyde to whom she spoke. Afterward, her family crowded around her, along with a lot of other people. She accepted their congratulations graciously. Then Clyde was there. He wrapped his arms around her and planted a big smack on her cheek. "I'm glad I got back to town in time," he whispered in her ear. "You're magnificent!"

As they drove home, Greg asked, "Who was that man who gave you the bear hug?"

"He's in Mrs. Jarvis's class," Juneau said in an offhand manner. "He gets a little enthusiastic, doesn't he?"

She felt a twinge of guilt because she hadn't identified him as the classmate with whom she talked until late after her Thursday night class. And another, bigger, twinge when Greg seemed to accept her brief explanation without question. But she also felt, deep inside her, a warm glow when she remembered Clyde's words.

ERIN
May 20, 1995
Dear COBs,

I've made it through a year of being a divorcée and a single mother, and I'm still alive and well. Imagine that! I've put on about fifteen pounds, though. Guess it was the buttered popcorn and chocolate I indulged in last winter. Caitlin and I look even more alike now that my cheeks are round like hers.

The kids have weathered their first year of toggling between parents pretty well, although sometimes they don't want to go when it's their weekend with Cory. They're tired of the artificial togetherness. (Poor Cory tries too hard. Skipp and Linda, too.) We talked about what might improve the situation for Kayla and Mark, and Cory's decided to move to a homier three-bedroom apartment west of Calhoun Lake Club. I think that Mark and Kayla will be a lot more comfortable there.

The move won't make much difference for Hannah, who is

thriving. That little miracle doesn't seem to care where she is, as long as she's with the people who love her. I'm sure she'll ask questions when she gets older and realizes that this isn't the usual arrangement, but for now, she smiles and giggles her way into everyone's hearts.

I can't say I've adjusted to my new state. I keep asking myself what we are—a Forever Family minus the father? That doesn't make sense. I still feel out of place going to church with people who knew me and Cory as a couple. When the kids and I sit with his parents, his absence is painfully obvious. I'm beginning to think there are some hurts that don't heal.

I'm learning to live with it, though. There are days when I actually wake up happy to be me.

Love,
Erin

Erin wasn't shocked when Cecelia called to say that Gabby had died on May 22d with her family around her. "The funeral is on the 26th," Cecelia said. "I've called the other girls, and we'd love it if you all came."

Erin immediately called her mother to see if The Jays would be willing to move into the house while she was gone, which seemed the least disruptive way to make sure the kids were taken care of. Then she got the ladies on a conference call, and they started making their plans.

A few days later, Deenie picked up Erin and Juneau at the Salt Lake airport and headed south on I-15. On the drive down to Provo, they reminisced about their years with Gabby. Sometimes Erin found it hard to tell if they were laughing or crying, they did so much of both, sometimes at the same time. Each told her favorite stories, and they listed as many Gabbyisms as they could think of.

"Don't plow the same field twice," Erin said.

"Everyone has their own bag of rocks to carry," Deenie added.

Juneau finished up with, "Wisdom isn't just laid on you; you have to earn it." She sniffled and then added, "Such good memories."

"You know, we're at the top of the ladder now," Deenie mused. "Gabby was always ahead of us, but now that she's gone, we're it."

Erin shivered. "I hope that doesn't mean that there are COB wannabes looking up to us."

"Of course there are," Juneau grinned. "I can name a few. Nicole, Misty, Beth, Evvy, Kayla, Sophie, and a whole lot more. Some we don't even know about."

"That's a scary thought," Deenie said.

After a moment of silence, Juneau said, "What's scary is how many people we've buried since St. George."

"People *and* beloved pets," Deenie amended.

"Right." Juneau began counting. "Max was before, and then Rhiannan, Grams, Philip Atwater, Rauf, Sunny, Sister K, and now Gabby."

"Don't forget three of Cory's grandparents," Erin reminded them.

"That's quite a list," Deenie said. "I think it comes with the territory when you get to be our age."

"I read something once, I can't remember where," Erin bit her lip to keep her emotions in check, "'We all come and we all go, the best of us and the worst of us.'"


Jonas met them at Gabby's with a key. They let themselves in, dragged their suitcases upstairs, and got dressed to go to the viewing. "No black!" Cecelia had instructed. "Gabby said we're to have a celebration." So Juneau dressed in green, Deenie in blue, and Erin in brown with blue accents. They got to the church early, so they could spend time with the family in the Relief Society room where the viewing was to take place.

All those closest to Gabby were there when they arrived. Junior and Cecelia, their children Brian, Sophie, and Kenny, each holding a spouse's hand, and the diminished but still stately Jonas. Entering the room, Erin felt as if she were walking into a wave of love. She fumbled in her bag for a tissue, not because she was sad but because the feeling that filled the room was such a tribute to dear Gabby.

Junior guided them gently to Gabby's casket. They stood quietly, looking at the dear face that in the repose of death looked lovely. *But,*

Erin thought, *not like Gabby herself.* After a few moments, they gave a collective sigh and turned away.

Jonas cleared his throat. "There's something Gabby wanted me to give you girls, and Junior and I decided this was the right time." He held a handwritten note at an angle and read:

*Dear Juneau, Deenie, and Erin,*

*You sweet things have looked up to me as a Crusty Old Broad ever since we met in 1980. Well, I wasn't one, not then. There was a very important lesson I needed to learn, and some very important tasks I needed to complete before real COBhood.*

*I couldn't have made it without you. Bless you for challenging an old lady to see her mistakes and deal with the consequences. Without that, I wouldn't have reached out to Junior and Kenny and asked for their forgiveness. I wouldn't have healed the breach between Cecelia and me. But you had the courage, and because of that, my dear family gathered around you right now knows that I love them with my whole heart.*

*Jonas has something for you. Gasp if you must, but everything's been set up and you can't refuse it.*

*With deepest love and gratitude,*
*Gabby*

They were all weeping freely by the time Jonas finished reading. Cecelia, who was weepy as well, passed the tissue box. They wiped their eyes and blew their noses and then looked at Jonas.

He handed each of them an envelope with the logo of a tour company on the cover. Erin's fingers trembled as she opened it. Inside was a voucher for a deluxe trip to Hawaii, first class all the way, including side trips, evening sailboat rides, massages, and luaus on the beach.

They all gasped at the same time and then began babbling excitedly. Junior and the rest of family watched with big grins. "Gabby wanted to make sure you had a week of pure luxury where *you* were taken care of for a change," Junior said.

When the excitement turned to protests, Jonas added, "Don't worry, Gabby took good care of her family. You're not depriving them of anything by accepting the trip. Besides, the vouchers are nontransferable and nonrefundable and must be used within six months."

"Then we accept," Deenie said.

Junior stepped up next to Jonas. "There's one more thing Gabby made me promise to do." He pulled a gladiola stalk from a nearby spray. In a stentorian voice he said, "I proclaim you first-rank COBs," touching each of them on the shoulder with the stalk.

Erin gulped down her tears. The words were like a blessing from their dear friend, a last gift of love. At the same time, she couldn't help wondering what it would take to be COBs with no qualifiers attached.

# *Chapter 41*

JUNEAU

June 1, 1995
Dear Deenie and Erin,

I'm trying to get used to that "top of the ladder" position we find ourselves in, now that Gabby's gone. I keep fumbling it. Misty called to say she's doing her divorce from Ira by way of a do-it-yourself site on the Internet because there were no children and property issues to settle. She also confessed she's found someone else she's interested in. I fell apart, telling her she's making a terrible mistake. That, of course, drove her even further away. But what else could I say? It's the truth. I love Ira like a son. He's not handling the news well. His father called me, saying they are flying out to try to comfort him somehow.

The rest of us are as okay as we can be, under the circumstances.

Love,
Juneau

ERIN

June 5, 1995
Dear Juneau,

Sounds like you've got some more of those rocks in the stream, dear. Ira, too. I feel for him. I've never met him, but for some reason I always think of him as the Johnny Depp character, Benny, in that sweet movie from a couple of years ago, *Benny and Joon*. Quirky and dear and vulnerable. 'Course, I think of Trace that way, too. Misty must attract that type. Or pick that type.

I used to get so ticked when someone would tell me, "Remember the Serenity Prayer." I still wanted to believe that hard work and prayer could make everything turn out right. It's hard to watch the people we love make bad choices, but you know, there is that pesky principle of agency. We watch, we grieve, we love, and in the end, we stand at the ready.

I've been learning to find that place of peace, regardless of circumstances. I've had to. I know you can find it, too. But if you need to howl to the moon, call me. I understand howling!

Love,
Erin

## WILLADENE

"It's so hot," Deenie complained, wiping the sweat from her face for the second time in as many minutes.

"There's got to be a better word for it!" Roger peered through the windshield of their rental car into the Florida twilight. The air conditioner was blowing full blast but barely seemed to make a difference.

"Simmering, sweltering, steaming?" Deenie asked as she lifted a bottle of chilled water from the fold-up cooler on the front seat, drank gratefully, and held it out to Roger. He shook his head; he was concentrating too hard to take the offered water. In the next moment, he slammed on the brakes at a fast red light and pounded his hands on the steering wheel. It began to rain.

By Friday, the day of their interview with the directors of The Academy America–Excellence in Education, Deenie had completely lost her appreciation for the absurdities in life. Still being wet after she dried off from a shower and the shocking result of naturally curly hair exposed to Florida humidity had seriously diminished her enthusiasm for the opportunity the Academy offered Roger.

"People have to have perfect skin in this humidity," she grumbled while dressing for the interview. "Makeup melts off your face."

"Are you going to give this any chance at all?" Roger asked. He stood in front of the dresser mirror, holding up one tie and then another.

"Do men even wear ties here?" she asked.

"You're not helping."

The grounds of The Academy America–Excellence in Education were like a set for a movie on Kentucky horse racing—without the horses. Or maybe Tara from *Gone with the Wind*. Deenie gasped as the mansion that was the administration building and central teaching facility of the school came into sight.

"Told you," Roger said with satisfaction.

"Amazing," Deenie breathed.

"Wish us luck then?" There was a slightly wistful edge to his voice.

"I do. Where are we supposed to meet the good old boys?"

"Board of directors," Roger corrected but laughed. "In the mansion."

Deenie was excused after the first part of the interview, in which the board had made it crystal clear that spouses of the staff of The Academy America–Excellence in Education were expected to be actively involved on campus. She spent the rest of the time with the board's secretary, Marsha Warrington, who showed her through the mansion and graciously answered her questions about alligators in the pond out back and what "gator spotting" was.

"If you end up coming to us, we'll see that you feel right at home in no time," Marsha went on. "We have a wonderful wives' association. What kinds of things do you do, Mrs. Rasmussen?"

Deenie was tempted to say, "I've been known to shoot an intruder and track gone-missings with Bear." She stifled the impulse when Roger and the board of directors came down the hall.

"Then I'll expect to hear from you before the end of the month," Roger said, shaking hands with each member in turn.

"Oh, I don't think we need to wait that long," said Ferris Tucker, the man Deenie knew was in charge. "As long as we can agree on no prose-lytizing, the job is yours."

"Thank you, Mr. Tucker. I'd like a chance to talk this over with my family. I guess I'll be the one getting back to you."

"No proselytizing?" Deenie asked as they walked down the steps of the mansion.

"I have to agree not to initiate discussions about Mormonism with students except as a guest lecturer in American history. I don't see a problem with that. Home rules, Deenie. It's their backyard. Did you see the tennis courts?"

As Roger talked on, Deenie was beginning to realize this was less of a look-see trip and more of a done-deal-if-you-agree visit. By this time next year she could be living in a house with alligators in the pond out back and a strip of duct tape across her mouth!

## ERIN

The first day of July, Erin's house was full of activity as Mark and Kayla packed for their month with Cory and his parents. Erin already had Hannah's clothes, toys, and diaper bag packed. They were to spend the first week at Cory's apartment, after which they, Skipp, and Linda would take a trip to the Black Hills. Skipp had already rented a big motor home for the journey. Erin wasn't sure how Hannah would manage a long trip, but Cory had said, "If you and I were the ones taking the kids, she would go." Which was true.

"Mom, where's my favorite shirt?" Mark hollered to Erin, who was in her upstairs office. "I can't find my jeans shorts!" Kayla muttered. Rascal ran from room to room barking, and Hannah, upset by the hectic energy, started to howl.

Erin picked Hannah up and rocked her back and forth. "Don't forget to pack what you'll want on your trip," she called to Mark and Kayla. "Swimming suit, hat, sunscreen, sunglasses, shorts, water bottle . . ."

Kayla rolled her eyes, but she was grinning as she did. Then her expression turned serious. "Mom? Do you think it's all right for me to go? I mean, a whole week without practicing . . ."

Erin put Hannah down on Kayla's bed and gave her a plush animal to play with. "What did your coach say?"

"That it's a good thing to take a break now and then. But I don't see how that could be right."

"Even the best skaters take a break now and then. Doing something different can give you new perspective and energy."

"Hmmmm."

"Mark will be taking a break from practicing, you know. And he's got the Suzuki Institute coming up in August."

"Yeah. But he'll be taking his repertoire tape to listen to while we're gone."

"So, take your music CD and visualize your program every night. You know, see yourself landing every jump perfectly, doing spectacular spirals."

"I could, couldn't I?" Kayla smiled brightly and hugged Erin. "Thanks, Mom."

Cory arrived on the dot, eager to start his month with the children. Erin had to stand back as they took the bags out to the car. She wanted nothing more than to start directing traffic, reminding the kids up until the last minute of what they needed to take. She wanted to tell them to be careful when hiking and swimming. To stay on the path when they went into the cave. She wanted to tell Cory every detail of what Hannah liked and didn't like these days. But she didn't.

When the car was loaded, she put Hannah into her car seat and buckled her in. Then she hugged Mark and Kayla and gave Hannah a final kiss. "Be good for Mama," she said. Hannah made the sound that was her version of "bye-bye" and waved her hand.

Rascal stood by her as she watched the car go down the street, bearing her family away. "Well, feller, I guess it's just you and me." She sat on the front step, the dog at her knee. They were still comforting each other when the phone rang. It was Caitlin. "Have they gone?" she asked.

"A few minutes ago."

"Then you need to get out of the house."

Erin grinned slightly. "What do you have in mind?"

"Going to a locale overlooking the Mississippi River. It's a see and be seen place. The guys mostly are looking for twenty-something blondes, but it's fun anyway."

"Nah. I don't think so."

"Don't be a stick in the mud. You are a single woman, you know."

"Single with children."

"So what? I bought us each a sexy silk tee. Come here first so you can choose which one you want."

An hour and a half later, Erin stood before Lottie and Theresa, modeling a shaped turquoise tee with embroidery edging the V neck. Caitlin had insisted she put turquoise dangles in her ears and tie a colorful woven sash around her waist. It matched the one she wore. "They're from Theresa," she said. She pulled Erin next to her, facing Theresa and Lottie. "How do we look?"

"Dangerous," Lottie laughed.

Theresa nodded. "*Los hombres* better watch out for *las dos pelirrojas* tonight."


The locale Caitlin had chosen was obviously popular. Cars filled the parking lot and lined the street, the outdoor seating was full, and those waiting walked along the balcony and down to the riverbank. The two women checked in with the hostess and then got margaritas (a "virgin" for Erin) and joined the crowd on the balcony.

Erin had known that Caitlin was a flirt. She was always dating, sometimes two guys at a time. But she never stayed with any one of them very long. *Like Misty,* Erin thought. Seeing Caitlin in action was quite the education. She did something with her eyebrows, which, along with a wicked grin, gave clear notice that she was available and interested. Several times guys came over to chat for a while. Caitlin exchanged cards with one.

The whole routine made Erin highly uncomfortable. She was relieved when their table was ready. "Out of practice, aren't you?" Caitlin said.

"I was never *in* practice. I don't know how to make small talk, and I have no idea how to flirt. I'm not sure I know how to have fun, either."

"Guess that's what comes from being Lutheran first and Mormon second," Caitlin said laughing.

Their conversation was interrupted by the waitress, come to take their orders: Erin, a southwestern Cobb salad; Caitlin, a pasta salad with artichokes and sun-dried tomatoes.

"You know he's looking at us," Caitlin said when they were alone again.

"Who?"

Caitlin made a slight motion leftward with her head. "That guy over there. I think he's intrigued by *las dos pelirrojas.*"

Erin looked in the direction indicated—right into the eyes of a rather rugged but interesting looking man with a mop of tawny hair falling over one eyebrow. She flushed and looked away.

"Oh, my. You really are a novice at this."

"Yeah? Well, I never flirted just for the sake of flirting. When I met Cory, I was looking for a real relationship. Real love."

"I know. Your Forever Family."

Erin bristled at Caitlin's slightly sarcastic tone. "I didn't get it, but at least I took the risk. You've never done that—you go on to the next guy before things get serious. Why is that?"

Caitlin took a sip of her margarita before answering. "Maybe because I'd rather love 'em and leave 'em without going to the altar. I'm not interested in being a serial divorcée, like my mother."

"It doesn't have to turn out that way."

"The odds are against true love. Look at you. You try harder than anyone I know to do what's right, and you still ended up alone."

That hurt, but Erin said, "I still believe in love."

Caitlin looked briefly in her direction and then away. "Who's saying I don't?"

When Erin arrived home late that night, she opened the door to a house that was dark and quiet. Then she heard the welcome sound of Rascal's nails on the wood floor. "Oh, you good dog," she cried. She wasn't alone. There was another living being in the house. She put her arms around him and tipped her head so he could lick her cheek.

## WILLADENE

A week after they got home, Roger called a family meeting and presented the possibilities offered by a move to Florida. If he took the job, they would move at the end of the next school year—June of '96. "What do you think?" he asked the assembled family.

"If we do decide to take the job in Gainesville, what will we do about the house?" Deenie asked.

"Paul and I can live here while we go to school, if you aren't planning to sell it," Carl said.

"What about me?" Beth demanded. "I'm not going to Florida. If the boys get to stay in the house, why can't I?"

"Can I stay here with Beth?" Evvy piped up. "Bear could stay, too, so you wouldn't have to worry about him being eaten by alligators." Bear responded to the sound of his name with an excited whoof.

"Enough of that!" Roger shouted over the hubbub. "First, we are not selling the house. I think having you two boys living here would be fine, but you're going to have to talk it over with your mother. Second, Miss Evangeline Rose, where your mother and I go, you go. Elizabeth, we'll talk to you later. Right now, your mom and I are going for a walk."

He took Deenie's hand. As they started for the door, Roger said, "Make yourself useful. Liz and Evvy, start dinner. Carl, get the yard in shape."

Deenie let out a long sigh as they walked silently hand in hand across the Wellsville Tabernacle grounds, stepping over the shallow irrigation water running down the side of the street. "My favorite time of year," she said. "Except for spring and autumn."

"There's no winter in Florida," Roger reminded her.

"I know. They have three seasons. Hot, humid, and hurricane."

They walked down the long block to an open field where children splashed in a shallow creek and climbed up the shinny tree. *I did that same thing when I was little*, Deenie thought. She sat down on the remnants of a pioneer retaining wall made of hand-cut stone, running her hands over the rough, warm surface. Everything around her reminded her of her faith and her family. She remembered a conversation she'd had with Juneau, who'd said, "Your geography is your history."

*How much of me is Cache Valley?* Deenie wondered. *How much of me will be left behind, wedged in the warm crevices of this wall? Tucked in the corners of the garden? Even buried with faithful old Rauf in the freezer in the back yard? With Sunny?*

Roger sat down next to her, tipping his face toward the sun. She leaned against his shoulder.

"Life would be different in Florida," she said. "We wouldn't be near aunts, uncles, or cousins."

"But near the ocean and incredible theme parks," he responded.

"We wouldn't have big family gatherings for the Fourth of July or Pioneer Day."

"We'd have a ward family to invite to celebrations."

"We would be far away from parents who might need us."

"Only a phone call or a flight away, Deenie girl."

"Paul's not even home from his mission yet," she protested.

"But you'll have ten months with him before we move."

Deenie fell silent. Roger had an answer to everything. Would he have an answer to what was really troubling her? "I'd be a fish out of water," she finally said.

"That's the real issue, isn't it?" Roger gave her a reassuring hug. "You're not the only one with those concerns. I used to think that Wellsville was conservative. Hah! It doesn't hold a candle to this school."

"But you've already made a connection with the good old boys. I could tell by how they talked to you before we left. You'll fit in." She shifted so she could look into his eyes. "Which Deenie are you thinking of taking with you to Florida, Roger? Deenie the Defender, Deenie the Search and Rescuer? The woman with a gun and a dog as big as Sasquatch? I can't imagine how that will go over on campus. How about Deenie the Fixer? Deenie the Demure?"

Roger pulled her against his chest, patting her back and stroking her hair. "How about if I take all of them?" he asked with a soft chuckle.

"You really want to go, don't you?"

"I'm pushing forty-nine years old with no practical experience in my field. This may be the only chance I'll have to get the kind of job I want. It's a minor miracle I got it at all, and I wouldn't have, without Dr. Serling's help. I want to tell them yes. But I'll tell them no if you want me to."

"That would make me a poor excuse for an eternal companion, wouldn't it?" Deenie said. She kissed him lightly and then added, "Ready or not, Florida, here we come."

# Chapter 42

JUNEAU

August 15, 1995
Dear COBs,

Ira's folks have come and gone. They were delightful. I keep thinking that if Misty had come down and met them, she'd never have divorced Ira. But that's wishful thinking. They came to dinner twice during the week they were here, and then Solomon hosted all of us for lunch at Cantor's over in Hollywood one day. He said that's the most authentic New York deli in Southern California, and he wanted us to know what we were missing! The hot pastrami sandwiches were heaven, and their french fry potato wedges are a world away from McDonald's. (I've always thought *their* french fries were the best until now!)

We had such a good time with them. Solomon is an older and more mature version of Ira, and Thelma is a whole lot like me: a mother who worries about her children and just wants them to be happy. I think the rift between Ira and his parents is largely healed. He couldn't help but see how much they love him. Besides, his youthful rebellion is over, I think.

It seemed as if we laughed the whole time they were here. Ira has treated us to some of his Uncle Schlomo's jokes, but Solomon could tell them even better: "My brother is so cheap he took his children out of school because they had to pay attention. That was all right because they are so dumb they had to have a tutor to pass recess." I told him he could be a stand-up comic after he retires from his psychiatric practice. They've gone home now, but we feel we've made a couple of wonderful new friends.

Nicole wrote from Mexico City with great excitement that she has taught some converts: a lovely single mother with two teenage children. They are being baptized next Saturday. She is really into missionary work!

Guess what? I've been asked to sign books at a local store for their pre-Christmas sale! Kind of makes up for my having to miss speaking at that teachers' conference in 1992.

Till next time, I send this e-mail with love.

Juneau

ERIN

August 20, 1995
Dear Friends,

Mom and I took Mark to Steven's Point, Wisconsin, for the Suzuki Institute last week. What a time we had! The campus was crowded with young musicians—pianists, string and flute players—some of them very young, like the little violinist who couldn't have been more than four years old. Every single day was full of activity—private and group lessons, theory classes, recitals, lectures for the parents. When he wasn't busy with music, Mark played pickup soccer or board games with the other kids.

Having Hannah there was no problem. She does well traveling, as Cory said after their trip to the Black Hills. And she loved being around all the activity and music. She's heard the repertoire every day of her life (she's one now) and several times started gurgling and clapping along with the kid who was playing. I was embarrassed, but everyone else thought it was charming.

Mark was invited to play in the honors piano recital, which was . . . well, an honor! I couldn't believe it when Cory drove all the way from Minneapolis just to be there for his son. You should have seen how Mark's face lit up when he saw his dad was in the audience.

Your Erin

WILLADENE

The day a fat manila envelope from The Academy America–Excellence in Education arrived in Wellsville, Roger called the traditional family gathering for a reading of the letter. Everyone in the family oohed and aahed over the contents of the package: the generous contract, the glossy promotional folder from the school showing the grounds, the unexpected perks—season tickets to the Gators games and the promise of a roomy kennel to be built in the backyard of Number 137, Teachers' Row, brightly colored pamphlets on every local attraction, and at the bottom of the pile a hand-written note from Marsha Warrington welcoming them onboard. It was clipped to the address of the closest LDS chapel and a Polaroid of the building.

"Are we going on a mission?" Evvy asked in a confused voice, picking the photo out of the stack of information.

"Yes, Pumpkin," Roger said, giving her an exuberant hug. "I believe we are."

"But that means we have to leave home," she wailed in sudden understanding.

Roger nodded. "That means we have to leave home."

JUNEAU

September 22, 1995
Dear Deenie,

You've got an adventure ahead of you, girl! I imagine you're wondering how you'll fit in down there. Like Gabby said once, "A fish out of water either flops or flies!" I'm expecting you to fly. Once you get settled, Erin and I will have to come visit. If we can detour to Peoria, so to speak, we can detour to Gainesville.

> Best of luck,
> Juneau

ERIN

September 23, 1995
Dear Deenie,

I'm still in shock over your phone call! Whenever I think of you, I picture your lovely home in Wellsville, your magical apple orchard, the beautiful valley. I can't picture you in a big city in flat Florida. What a change that's going to be!

In a way, I envy you making such a big leap into a new phase of life. It seems to me that being in such a different place will give you the opportunity to show up as the person you are, not the person everyone expects you to be. I'm a little jealous. I sometimes feel restricted by my life, though I'm not complaining.

The news here is that Andrew and Lottie are going to sell the family manse. They don't entertain much any more, and with her health issues, Lottie would be more comfortable in a smaller place all on one floor. It'll be a big change for them, but they have to look to the future. I wonder if they'll take Theresa with them when they move. She seems more like a part of their family than an employee.

It takes courage to make big changes like that, as I ought to know. But it can be fun when the change is by choice, like you and Roger choosing together to make the move. I wish you all the best. And I'll be expecting updates all along the way!

Blessings,
Erin

WILLADENE
October 1, 1995
Dear COBs,

I still have a hard time writing that, realizing that Gabby, the original, is no longer among us. But since we're working so hard to earn the name for ourselves, I guess we should use it.

When Paul returned home from his mission, we celebrated with the usual Rasmussen fervor. He thinks the move to Gainesville can only be for our good. Does that sound like a newly returned missionary, or what!

He went right on being a missionary and, at her request, baptized Danny last week. We hosted the celebration afterward. When he thinks no one is noticing, Paul gazes at Danny the same way he did at Nicole when she visited.

About the move. Now Evvy says she doesn't care if we leave home as long as she gets to be baptized here next February so she can have a big party like Danny. Beth-Liz-Lizzy, who's taking advanced French as a senior thanks to Addie's coaching, goes about her life as though it won't affect her at all.

So we have begun the great sorting. What we want to take is in constant conflict with what we can fit into one of the small one-floor ramblers on Teacher's Row, a housing strip on campus where new staff are expected to live their first year. Roger says I'm overthinking it. We'll be back for most of the summer in '97. What could be so important that we couldn't manage without it for one school year? My sanity perhaps? The trip to Hawaii in January looks better and better.

> Best blessings to you all,
> Deenie

## ERIN

October 27, 1995
Dear Friends,

Forget the USA hockey team's Miracle on Ice, when they beat the Russian team in a thrilling upset in 1980. Kayla has had her own Miracle on Ice at the Upper Great Lakes Regional Championship in Duluth—she qualified to skate in the final round!

You know from my e-mails that she's been working toward this event for a long time. It never occurred to me that she would get that far, given the other skaters she was up against. But her preliminary program was her personal best. It was absolutely fantastic! She landed all her jumps, her footwork was exciting and clean, her spirals tight and fast. Her artistic quality was several notches higher, too. She was in the zone, for sure.

The magic wasn't there for the final round, but she skated well enough to end up in eleventh place, which pleased her immensely. She hasn't come down from her high yet, and Cory and I are glad we decided to support her dream. We couldn't have managed without the help of Cory's parents and Jake as chauffeurs. And the outfit Mom made her was stunning in scarlet and burgundy. The skirt had great flow when she skated, and the bodice had a beautiful design in colored sparkles. Mom is getting quite the reputation for skating dresses. She could start her own business making them, going by the number of calls she gets. She says no way. What makes Kayla's dresses special is the love she puts in them.

Your Erin

P.S. Juneau, remember when you told us about Giddy and setting the place for Elijah when you did the Seder for Ira? Well, when we had the family celebration after Kayla's Miracle on Ice, she set a place for Grams at the table. She put her medal on the empty plate, saying, "I thought of Grams when I skated. I did it for her."

*Chapter 43*

ERIN

When Mark turned ten and moved up the Cub Scout ladder from Bear to Webelos, Erin sat beside him on the couch as he went through the Webelos handbook, dog-earing the badges he wanted to earn. "Your dad will love helping you with these," Erin said.

Mark shook his head. "Jake is going to help me. And Grandpa Skipp and Uncle Steve."

"Why not your dad?"

"You know why." He got up from the couch. "I'm going upstairs to write down what I want to do."

"Mark? I think you and I need to talk about how you've been treating your father lately."

"I don't want to."

She was about to demand that he sit back down, but why bother? She knew from experience that if he didn't want to talk, he wouldn't talk.

She'd been encouraged when Mark came back from his month with Cory full of tales of the things they'd done. He'd especially enjoyed the trip to the Black Hills and seeing Mount Rushmore. And he'd seemed very pleased when Cory had driven all the way to Stevens Point, Wisconsin, when he'd learned that Mark would be playing in the honors piano recital at the Institute. Despite that, Mark had recently begun saying he didn't want to go when it was Cory's weekend with the children. And he'd stopped inviting his dad to pack meetings. Worse still, he'd begun specifically inviting Steve to come as a stand-in dad, bringing Ricky along.

When she and Cory were first divorced, Erin had been relieved and grateful when Steve had offered to make the long round-trip to pick up Mark for a Saturday with Ricky, or had worked with the boys on badge requirements, or had taken them cross-country skiing at Lake

Independence. It had been good for both boys, but now Erin was beginning to question the advisability of letting it continue.

Steve had apologized to Cory after the blowup at the Big Barn Sale, but their relationship remained strained, mostly due to Steve's poorly concealed attitude about gays. And Erin had the feeling sometimes that Steve got a hidden pleasure out of usurping Cory's place as Mark's father. She wondered if he didn't get *schadenfreude* over Mark's withdrawal from Cory. The word, which she'd learned from Jake, expressed it perfectly—pleasure in someone else's misfortune.

She picked up the phone and punched in Cory's number. It was time they had a talk about their son.

Erin ended up with more than that on her mind, however. The day she dropped into Stefani's on a whim to see if someone was free to cut her hair, she was enveloped in a big hug from Henri, whom she knew from the days when she and Angie had been stylists there. "I can take you, sweetness," he said. Flamboyant, loquacious, and the epitome of a limp-wrist gay, Henri fussed and cooed over her, telling her how good she looked and exclaiming over her descriptions of the house.

In the very next breath, he began talking about his friend Simon, who worked at a salon downtown. "Simon was telling me the other day that his roommate, Brandon—he's an assistant buyer at Target—is interested in a handsome blond Minnesota type named Cory Johnson. I thought to myself, I wonder if that could be Erin's Cory? He's cute and he's blond. And he's gay. By the way, dear, I was so sorry to hear that, for your sake. I can't imagine . . ."

He went on, not noticing that she'd stopped listening. Her ears felt hot and her mouth dry. In a state full of Johnsons, there could be a thousand Cory Johnsons, and, statistically, a number of them would be gay. Still, she knew in her heart that the Cory Johnson he was talking about was the father of her children.

Cory had agreed to come to her place early that Friday evening, so Erin asked Joanna if she and Jake would be willing to have the kids over for a game night. "I know Hannah's getting to be a handful, but it would really help me out." At one year, Hannah moved with astonishing speed and took great delight in her explorations of every drawer, cupboard, or closet she could open. Erin had put child safety locks on the cupboards containing cleaning and first-aid products.

Joanna grinned. "I don't mind, even if she does run me ragged. She's such a happy little soul. I love to hear her sing and jabber."

"You must not have heard her say no yet."

"Oh, I have. But she's so cute when she says it."

Cory arrived as the grandfather clock chimed seven. He came in smelling of cold and a light, citrus-scented cologne. They gave each other a cheek-kiss, and then he followed her into the living room, where snacks and a thermos pitcher of hot spiced cider sat on the coffee table. She filled two mugs and sat down opposite him.

He took a sip of the cider and then leaned back, crossing one leg over the other. "This is nice. Feels like home."

"It does have the same feel as the old house, doesn't it? But I like what you've done with your new place, too. It's much more welcoming than your first apartment."

He nodded. "The kids like it better, because they each have a room. I should have realized they were getting to be an age where privacy matters."

"It's hard to believe they're ten and almost thirteen."

"Kayla's been acting like a teenager for months now. Man, I don't know what to do when she has a meltdown."

Erin held her hands up and out. "Don't look to me for advice. I'm as flummoxed as you." She motioned toward his mug. "Is your cider okay?"

"Tastes great." He took another sip. "You wanted to talk about Mark?"

She nodded. "He's getting more stubborn about not wanting to go with you on your weekends. Do you know why?"

Discouragement replaced the cheer in Cory's eyes. "No. I've done everything I can to make him comfortable at my new place. I ask him what he wants to do after hockey practice, but he says he doesn't care. Then he complains about being bored, even when we're doing things I know he likes. Kayla's quite disgusted with him."

"Have you asked him what's going on?"

"Of course," he snapped. "But he won't tell me. Maybe you should ask him."

"I have, but he's not talking to me, either. He spends a lot of time in his room, and I'm not welcome there. I wish I knew what was going on in his head."

"I can guess." Cory put down his mug with a frustrated mutter. "Remember what he said when we told the kids about me? I can quote it exactly: 'I don't think I like you anymore.'" He held his hand up to stop Erin from speaking. "Don't tell me he didn't mean it, because the way he's acted since then shows he did. I wish to high heaven I'd never told him."

"I do, too. They'd both have to know sometime, but maybe in this case, later would have been better than sooner." She paused. "Uh, Cory, is it possible he's overheard something Skipp or Linda might have said when you guys stayed there overnight on one of your weekends?"

"He might have. Dad really wants to be supportive, but he still can't accept who I am. Every now and then, he tries to argue me out of being gay." Cory sighed. "If Mark overheard us, I can see how he'd think that I'm not worthy to be his father. That would explain his actions."

"Do you think it would help if Skipp talked to him?"

"No way. Anything he'd say would only make it worse. Besides, the only person Mark trusts these days is Steve."

"I know. If you ask me, Steve should leave Mark alone and take care of his own problems."

Cory raised a questioning eyebrow.

"EJ has started hanging out with some tough kids from her school. That sweet little girl we all loved has disappeared behind kohl-rimmed eyes and a nasty attitude."

"EJ? I can't believe it."

"Me neither. She's named after me, remember? Erin Joy. When she was little, I thought of myself as her godmother, responsible for helping her find her way as she grows up. Lately I keep feeling like there's something I should be doing for her. Or with her." She sighed. "But Steve and Colleen would probably react to that the way we're reacting to Steve's attempts to help Mark."

"Not unless you were on a campaign to alienate EJ from Colleen, the way Steve's driving a wedge between me and my son."

Erin nodded. "We do have to talk to Steve. I have no idea how to go about it, though."

"Me neither. I'd probably punch out his lights."

Erin chuckled, unable to imagine Cory getting physical over anything.

"Let's both give it some thought and then make a plan of action." He looked at his watch. "Anything else we need to discuss?"

She smiled slightly at his not-so-subtle hint. "Why? You planning to meet Brandon?" His reaction was priceless. *Man, I wish I had my camera,* she thought. A communication direct from heaven wouldn't have taken him more by surprise.

"How do you know about Brandon?"

"I know someone who knows someone . . . It's that six degrees of separation thing. Word gets around."

Cory's distress was painful to see. "Mark can't find out about Brandon. It would make things a thousand times worse."

"Well, he won't hear it from me."

## JUNEAU

Mrs. Jarvis asked Juneau to stay after class one warm night in November. Juneau hardly expected what Mrs. J had to say, which was, "How would you like to take over my class? I'll be retiring at the end of the semester in January."

Teach the class? Try to walk in Mrs. Jarvis's shoes? Impossible! Greg, with his advanced degrees, was the teacher in the family. "Oh, I can't do that," she said. "I'm not qualified."

"All you need is a junior college credential, which you can apply for," Mrs. J said. "You have a B.A. and you have the expertise, Juneau. Besides, this is an extended learning class, so it's not as if you'll be on the regular faculty."

"But I—I—I . . ." Juneau seemed stuck on one sound. "I've never even considered teaching."

"You'll be good at it," Mrs. J declared. "Think about it and let me know soon. I'll recommend you. Of course, you'll have to be interviewed and all that."

Juneau agreed to think about it.

She found Clyde waiting outside the classroom door. "You can do it," he said.

"Were you eavesdropping, Clyde?" He shook his head. "No. Mrs. Jarvis told me she was going to ask you, so I waited to congratulate you."

"How do you know I'll take the job?" She narrowed her eyes. "And how come she told you?"

He grinned. "She asked several class members for recommendations. As far as I know, everybody named you. And as for your first question, of course you'll take the job. Think how good it will look on your resumé."

"What resumé?" Juneau said. But then she grinned back. "I need to talk about this. How about I treat you to a cuppa at Bob's Big Boy?"

When she got home, she e-mailed Willadene and Erin. "Guess what! I've been asked to teach Mrs. Jarvis's class after the first of the year. All I can say is, 'What? Me teach?'"

Even though she had doubts, she was elated that Mrs. Jarvis and apparently some of the class members thought her capable of taking over the class. That elation carried her through the next couple of weeks, until the signing she'd agree to do at a local bookstore for their pre-Christmas sale. The event was well advertised. Juneau looked forward to it. And it started out very promisingly. She and another local author were at a table near the entryway of the bookstore. The trouble was that the other author had more than a hundred titles and was known all over the country. The people who came into the store lined up in front of her, sometimes glancing over at Juneau, as if wondering who she was. Only two people—her ward friends Sharma and Donnabeth—bought any of her books and asked her to sign.

She put on a brave front for Greg, telling him the signing was okay and that a lot of people waited in line. She didn't tell him whose line, though. "I'm proud of you, Juneau," Greg said, making her ashamed that she'd dissembled. But she waited until she was sitting across from Clyde at Bob's Big Boy before she let her true feelings out. "Do you have any idea how horrible it is to sit at a table for two hours, hoping and praying someone will pick up one of your books? To say nothing of buying one! I've never gone through anything as excruciating in my whole life. And I'll never do it again! And someone else can teach that stupid class, because I'm not going to."

"Hey, calm down," Clyde said, running a hand over her shoulder. "So you had a slow afternoon. So what? Your books sell. They're in libraries across the country. They even get reviewed. That's a big deal."

"But I felt stupid!"

"Ah. Hurt pride." He paused. "Better get a thick skin, Juney. This business isn't for sissies."

His use of her nickname caught her off guard. Only her mother and Greg ever called her that. She muttered something in reply and then said she was sorry but she had to leave early. The next day she said yes to teaching the class and applied for a credential, despite dire misgivings about the whole venture.

WILLADENE
December 4, 1995
Dear COBS,

Last week Addie Spencer dropped a bombshell on Roger and me. She wants to hire Liz (will I ever get used to calling Beth that name?) for a year, starting as soon as she graduates from high school! We are all astounded. Addie explained that she wants to travel slowly through Europe and can't find anyone with the time or inclination to join her. She said she would like to take Liz with her as a "paid companion," à la Jane Austen!

We are all astounded! No wonder Liz wasn't worried about moving to Florida. Addie proposes to pay her expenses, provide pocket money, and see that it's a learning experience. Aunt Stella, who knows Addie well, says it's a great opportunity and Liz couldn't be in better company.

I want to say no—loudly. She's too young to leave the nest. But everyone, including my own better self, says yes. Even Danny is all for it, because she'll be working the whole summer in New Jersey at a newspaper job her Grandfather Donovan has arranged for her.

In spite of all the comings and goings in our lives, we'll have the whole crew here for a holiday celebration. Every Stowell and Rasmussen relative within driving distance will be descending for an open house on the nineteenth. The senior Rasmussens and the Udalls will be flying from California, and even Brad Donaldson, who is back in Utah again, will be here. It will be a celebration of wondrous proportions.

But the plans do little to assuage the loneliness I am already feeling for long talks with my mother and afternoons with my dear daddy—who tells me to snap out of it! He's refusing to spend the next six months listening to a Deenie Dirge. You gotta love a guy like that.

Deenie

# Chapter 44

JUNEAU

Gideon and Numbtail enjoyed a mutual admiration society, and Juneau loved watching them together. She often thought about how much Misty was missing by taking herself out of Gideon's life. Misty did, however, call faithfully each week to speak with him. But she scarcely ever mentioned her life in Idaho and always avoided questions. So Juneau was surprised when Misty called in early December to say that she was coming home for Christmas.

"I'm glad, sweetie," Juneau said. "I'm happy that one of my girls will be here. Nicole seems so far away, missionarying down there in Mexico City."

"How about your 'boys'?" Misty asked, using the tag she'd pinned on Ira and Trace. On her lips it sounded faintly derogatory. "Will they be there?"

"Yes. Trace has nowhere else to go, and Ira says he'd rather visit his folks in New York when it's warm."

"Should be an interesting Christmas. You and Dad and my two exes."

"And Giddy," Juneau said.

"Of course." Misty paused. "I have something for him. A surprise." She paused again and then said, "Okay, I'll let you know when to pick me up at the airport."

Juneau had some misgivings about Misty coming, mainly on Ira's behalf. But then eternal hope arose, and she thought perhaps there might be some way they could be reconciled.

"You never give up, do you, Juney?" Greg said when she told him.


Misty came the week before Christmas, saying she'd leave again the day after. She looked good, somehow more mature, and her hair was its natural color, for a change. She joined Juneau in last-minute shopping, made Christmas cookies including Gabby's cowboy hunks, and helped Gideon decorate the tree. She was so pleasant and funny and upbeat with Ira that Juneau thought her hopes might actually be realized.

Misty also took part in the caroling party Trace and Cath put together just before Cath left to go home to Mink Creek for the holidays. It was after they returned to the house for refreshments that Misty revealed a little of her Idaho life. In answer to a question about what she'd done for Thanksgiving, she said, "I spent the day at Whitford's ranch. You should see how they do Thanksgiving there!"

Cath's eyebrows went up. "Whitford Morgan?"

"Yes. He says he knows you."

"He knows everybody. And everybody knows him. He's Mr. Big Business in that part of Idaho, into ranching and real estate and potatoes and politics and just about everything. Runs it all right from his ranch."

"I know," Misty said with a sly grin. "I've been working for him. Dad's good training on computers has come in handy."

"I understand Whit's available these days," Cath said in a teasing voice, "since his wife left him."

"Oh, that was over a year ago." Misty dismissed the former Mrs. Morgan with an airy wave of her hand. The look on her face gave her away, though: She liked Whitford.

Juneau's worry about that news rose as her hopes for an Ira-Misty reconciliation plummeted. "Well, tell us about him," she said, glad that Ira and Trace were out in the computer room with Greg.

"He's rich," Cath said, rolling her eyes.

"A few years older than I am," Misty added. "Great looking. Owns a really cool house."

Juneau had the uneasy feeling that he sounded like Orville Ostergaard. And she wondered if the look in Misty's eyes was the same look Letitia had had in hers when considering the well-off Orville and his big house.

Christmas Day started out delightfully. Gideon loved the cowboy suit, complete with boots and red bandanna, which Misty gave him. She didn't say that was the surprise, though.

"Hey, Giddy," Trace said when the boy was all dressed up in the outfit. "All you need now is a pony."

"We can take care of that, too," Misty said.

Juneau thought later she should have gotten a clue right then. But they went on to open the stack of gifts around the Christmas tree. Juneau was touched once again by Trace's wonder at being part of it all and by Ira's continuing delight in a tradition he had not grown up with. Later, as they were sitting in the living room after dinner and Giddy was in the family room playing with his new toys and Numbtail, Misty sprang her surprise. "I'm taking Gideon back to Idaho with me."

Juneau froze. There was a moment of total silence. Then Greg said, "You mean for a visit."

Misty shook her head. "For good."

In the shocked silence, Trace stood up. "You can't do that, Misty."

"Yes, I can. I'm his mother."

"And I'm his father! And Juneau and Greg have raised him from the time he was three months old. They have guardianship papers."

Misty's face hardened. "Any judge would reverse the guardianship. I didn't sign anything permanent. And your name isn't on his birth certificate, Trace."

Juneau was so stunned she could neither speak nor move. Even so, she realized how hard it was for Greg to keep his voice even when he broke the silence.

"Misty, please. Think of Gideon. He's in the middle of a school year. He'll be getting baptized in a little over a month. He's excited about that. You can't disrupt his life on a whim."

"Whim!" Misty stood akimbo. "Look, I know I used to be a little flaky. But I've got a good job now. A nice apartment near a good school. And I go to church all the time. Giddy can be baptized in Idaho just as well as here." She jutted out her chin. "Whitford says the law is on my side."

"Whitford!" Ira narrowed his eyes. "What does this Whitford have to do with it?"

"He's an attorney, among other things," Misty said. "He knows about stuff like that. He says I'm within my rights. Gideon is going with me!"

Ira rose and grabbed her arm. "Don't do this, Misty."

She shoved him away. "I'll do what I want!"

That at last broke Juneau out of the shock that had kept her immobile and silent up to now. She leaped to her feet. "What *you* want!" she gritted. "Misty, consider what *Gideon* wants. Have you thought about what it would do to him to be yanked away from the only family he's ever known? Have you thought about what it will do to *us*? You'd be ripping out our very heart."

She saw something flicker in Misty's eyes and went on. "Remember, Misty, how all of us, you included, suffered when we lost Max? Multiply that by ten million, and you'll get an inkling of what it would mean to us to lose Giddy. Think of somebody else for once in your life. Don't destroy us and him, too, by tearing him away from us!"

Misty's face was impassive. "I'm taking him. And I'm willing to get real ugly to do it."

"Then at least do it right," Greg said in his teaching voice, the one that demanded attention. "First, let's set a court date to void the guardianship." He stood, jabbing the air with an index finger. "Second, give us time to prepare him. To prepare ourselves. In a few months . . ."

Misty interrupted. "I've already bought his airline ticket. We're going. Unless you're willing to create a horrible mess to stop me."

"Mama?" Gideon stood in the doorway. He looked from one person to another, his face distressed. "I heard yelling. What's the matter?"

Juneau reached out for him, but Misty pulled him into her arms. "Nothing, honey," she said. "How would you like to come with Mama up to Idaho and have your very own pony?"

Gideon turned to Juneau. "Mama? Are you going to Idaho?"

Misty twisted him around to look at her. "No, with this mama." She tapped her own chest. "Wouldn't you like a pony, Giddy?"

"I don't know," he said.

A horn beeped outside. Juneau knew with a sick certainty what it was. Not today! Certainly Misty wouldn't snatch him away on Christmas

Day! She moved toward Gideon, but Misty steered him away. "We're going on an airplane, Giddy. You'll love that."

Gideon looked bewildered. "Can I take Numbtail? I need him."

"No, sweetheart," Misty said. "We don't have time to get him ready. But there'll be lots of cats and dogs where we're going." She pushed the boy toward the door. "Our suitcases are already outside. Let's go."

*She's planned this all along!* Juneau thought with horror. Misty had known from the beginning that her visit was going to end in a hideous scene.

"I want to take my guitar," Giddy said, tugging on Misty's arm.

"Okay, okay," Misty said impatiently. She held onto Giddy with one hand and grabbed the guitar with the other.

"We could block you." Greg stood in front of the door. Trace and Ira moved up alongside him.

"How much are you willing to put him through?" Misty hissed. "Do you want him to remember you screaming and hollering and yanking him back and forth?"

"No!" Juneau couldn't bear the thought of them fighting over Giddy like a pack of dogs over a bone. "Misty! How are you going to get from the airport in Salt Lake up to Idaho? You're not going to hitchhike like you used to do, are you?"

Misty gave her a scornful look. "*Whitford* is meeting us."

Even though she'd never met him, Juneau hated Whitford Morgan with a virulent, grinding rage that she hadn't known was in her. This had to be his fault! How could Misty, her own daughter and Giddy's mother, be capable of such cruelty? Such selfish disregard of consequences to all of them but especially to Giddy?

She looked at Giddy, and the fear and confusion she saw in his face struck her heart. Making a decision, she motioned Greg, Trace, and Ira away from the door. "For Giddy's sake," she said shakily. She felt as if she were at the epicenter of an earthquake as they took turns murmuring their good-byes and be-goods. All the way down the walk, Juneau kept pulling Gideon to her for one more kiss, one more hug. Then they were at the taxi and there was nothing to do but let Misty load him inside, clutching his guitar case. They stood there watching until the vehicle turned a corner and was gone.

*Chapter 45*

1996

JUNEAU

Juneau dozed to the sounds of the engines humming and Erin and Deenie chatting softly beside her during the long flight from LAX to Honolulu. The combined murmur helped soothe her tired body and ragged nerves. Since Misty had taken Giddy away, there had been little sleep or peace in her life.

"I'm looking forward to meeting the breasts-first Brenda," Deenie whispered with a giggle. "Is she really as over-the-top as you told us?"

"Just wait and see," Erin said. "She's meeting us at the airport."

When Brenda had heard from Caitlin that the COBs were visiting Hawaii, she'd called Erin with the suggestion that they come earlier than the rest of their tour group and stay on the Big Island for a couple of days as her guests. A travel agent and occasional tour guide herself, she was eager to show them her favorite places on the island she loved—places regular tour guides never went. Juneau had felt relieved when Erin told her and Deenie. It sounded like the kind of low-key tour through restful beauty Juneau had hoped for.

She found a more comfortable position in the narrow seat and drifted into a deeper sleep, imagining the bottle-blonde Brenda in a chartreuse mini muumuu standing in the airport strumming the ukulele and singing aloha songs.

The well-proportioned and stylish woman with honey-colored hair and a fresh, glowing face who greeted them in the airport terminal was a surprise to them all, especially Erin.

"It's me!" Brenda laughed and enveloped Erin in a huge hug. She gave them each a sweet-smelling lei, an "Aloha," and a kiss on each cheek.

"What happened to you?" asked Erin, who wore a dazed expression.

"Guess I should have warned you, huh?" Brenda pointed to her hair and then her bosom. "After I divorced my last husband, I decided to go *au naturel.* Do you like it?"

"You look great."

Brenda linked arms with Erin and beckoned to Juneau and Deenie. "Come on, girls. Let's get out of here."

Once out of the airport, Brenda drove them along the coast toward Diamond Head until she turned inland into a neighborhood of older homes on a foothill ridge looking out toward the ocean. She pulled to a stop in the driveway of a charming bungalow of salmon-colored brick with a lanai across the front and around the side.

"Leave your bags for now," Brenda directed. "There are comfy chairs and a great view waiting for you on the lanai."

Erin galloped up the steps, Deenie following her. "Would you take a look at this," she called, waving her arms in an expansive gesture. Juneau followed more slowly, trying to be as cheerful and as excited as her friends—as excited as she had been when they had first received the vouchers for the Hawaiian extravaganza from Jonas. But that was before Misty took Gideon.

The pretense now was exhausting. Instead of standing at the rail looking out at the fantastic view, Juneau collapsed into a deeply cushioned rattan chair and covered her burning eyes with her hand. She felt a light touch on her shoulder.

"Juneau, are you all right?" Deenie asked.

"Just tired."

"Looks like travel fatigue to me," Brenda said kindly. "You girls stay where you are. I've got the perfect remedy for it chilling in the fridge."

Juneau blinked back tears brought on by their concern. Now was not the time to break down. She hadn't broken down when Misty hauled Gideon off in the taxi on Christmas Day. And she'd managed somehow to be strong that night when Greg broke into anguished sobs. She'd even maintained some composure when she'd called her mother, whose response to every problem was to pretend everything was all right. "Put on a brave face, dearie," Pamela had counseled. "It's best for everyone." Only Clyde had called it what it was, in words Juneau couldn't repeat.

"It's Giddy, isn't it?" Erin asked softly.

Juneau held up her hand, forestalling any further comment as Brenda came onto the lanai carrying a tray of frosty glasses filled with an orange-colored drink. "Here you are," she said, handing them each a glass. "Papaya mango orange delight. The best antidote to travel fatigue. Now, Caitlin said to ask you about Gabby Farnsworth and how she came to give you this wonderful vacation."

The mention of Gabby was the last straw for Juneau. The repressed grief over the losses she had suffered in the last year crashed over her, shattering her composure. She tried to hold back the emotions clawing their way out, to no avail. Harsh sobs came in waves that wracked her body. She was only vaguely aware of Deenie's arms around her and Erin holding her hands, trying to comfort her with words and caresses. "Gideon!" she wept. "My boy."

That brought up the image of Gabby saying, "Caleb! My boy." Then Rhiannan floated into view. Everything that hinted of love and loss, even Great-Grandma Letitia and Juneau's odd relationship with her parents, the Peripatetic Paulsens, brought on new waves of grief.

She was embarrassed beyond words when she finally got herself under control again. "I'm so sorry," she apologized to Brenda, who now knelt anxiously by her chair as well. "I didn't mean to lose it like that. It's just . . . I've tried so hard to be strong since Misty took Gideon. I can't do it anymore." She burst into a new round of tears.

When she finally dared to look at the women clustered around her, she saw they were weepy, too, touched not just by her grief but grief of their own. "Oh my," she said.

Deenie smiled wanly. "Oh my, indeed. We tend to get into the big stuff without preamble, don't we?" She shared her fear of the future, of leaving herself behind when she moved to Florida, that strange land with history and customs so different from those of Cache Valley.

"My turn," Erin said as Brenda passed out tissue. "The future is look-ing pretty scary to me right now, too." She told of her uncertainty con-cerning Mark and Kayla as they moved into the teen years and Hannah into the terrible twos, of her longing for love and her fear of making another terrible mistake.

"May I join in?" Brenda asked.

Juneau noticed her eyes were bright with incipient tears. "Feel free." Juneau's embarrassment at having broken down so thoroughly had begun to subside with Deenie and Erin's confessions. Brenda's desire to be part of that sharing left her feeling completely accepted and at home.

"I've made more than my share of such mistakes," Brenda said, and then she spoke of her own regrets, especially regarding Caitlin. "When I married Andrew, I had dreams of a little house with a picket fence and a passel of children. Like any good Catholic woman."

"What happened?" Erin asked.

Brenda shook her head. "It's a long story and too sad for a lovely night like this. Bottom line is, I ended up a long-distance mother and multiple divorcée." She tried on an unconvincing smile. "You never know where life will lead, do you?"

"Seems we've all ended up in Peoria," Deenie said.

"Metaphorically speaking," Juneau said. She told Brenda how she'd described the loss of Max so many years ago as packing for Hawaii and ending up in Peoria instead.

"Ah." Brenda nodded. "I understand completely. But you know what, Peoria isn't a final destination. It's only a stopover. The story isn't over yet. For any of us."

"Isn't there a country song that has the refrain, 'It ain't over yet!'?" Juneau asked with a soggy grin. "You know, the one where everything goes wrong in the verses—the husband leaves, the house burns down, the dog dies—and then comes the refrain . . ." She raised her arms as if to bring a choir in on the beat. They all shouted out, "It ain't over yet!" and collapsed in laughter.

"There's life after Peoria," Deenie affirmed.

Juneau felt her heart lighten. "Maybe there's even life after Giddy." She felt her resolve harden. "That story definitely isn't over yet."

The women pulled their chairs close together then and sat knee to knee, talking until the sun was low in the sky. Then Brenda stood up. "You have to see this," she said, motioning them all to join her at the railing around her lanai. They looked out over lush green vegetation and on to the endless expanse of the Pacific, where the sunset was beginning to turn the blue into shades of pink, magenta, orange, and lavender.

"I feel like I'm on the prow of a ship," Erin said. "Heading . . . I don't know where I'm heading."

"I know where I'm heading," Deenie said. "At least there aren't any icebergs in Florida." She grinned slightly. "Only hurricanes."

Juneau nodded. "I just hope there are plenty of lifeboats aboard my ship."

"Come on. Stop worrying." Brenda gestured to the ocean, now flaming with color. "Remember the old saying? 'Red sky in morning, sailor's warning. Red sky at night, sailor's delight.' There'll be smooth sailing ahead." She looked at them all with a brilliant smile and added, "At least for tomorrow."

# Discovery Questions

1. What is the theme of *Three Tickets to Peoria*? How is the theme developed in the book?

2. All of the women in the book keep important information secret. What secrets do each of the COBS, including Gabby, have? What are the consequences of keeping secrets?

3. Erin asks Juneau if it's better to know the truth. Are there any situations in which you would feel justified to withhold truth from others, perhaps "for their own good?"

4. What do you think of Erin's choice to stay with Cory after he tells her he's gay? How do you feel about her choosing to divorce him later, even though she's pregnant?

5. How did you respond to Deenie's metamorphosis into Dead-Eye Deenie? What choices did she make along the way that led to her shooting Rodney Tulley? What would you do if called upon to protect your family against imminent danger?

6. What was your response to learning that Juneau allowed Nicole to go to catechism with Beto? What do you hope for Nicole and Beto's relationship?

7. When Juneau sounds out the COBs about her relationship with Clyde, Gabby and Deenie warn her that sharing her thoughts with another man can be dangerous. Do you agree with them? Why? Do you think one can have nonthreatening relationships with a member of the opposite sex? How can one know where the line is?

8. Gabby had a blind spot regarding Junior. What blind spots do the other characters have? Have you been made aware of a blind spot of your own?

9. Give examples of situations in which characters grew in response to their challenges. Do you feel you've gained insight or understanding from seeing how they handled difficult situations?

10. What do you think of the husbands in the book—Greg, Roger, and Cory? What are their strengths and failings as husbands and fathers?